FAITH'S FOLLY

THE WILLOWBROOKE CHRONICLES: BOOK 1.

T.D. HOLLAND

SPELLBOUND BOOKS

First Published by in 2024 by SpellBound Books

To Mum, Dad, and Jan Jan, my darling sister.

I miss you.

WILLOWBROOKE VILLAGE

CHAPTER 1

'Faith, have you even heard a word I've been saying?' The voice on the other side of the phone was laced with frustration. Faith's attention had drifted away long ago, her gaze lost in the mesmerising dance of colours outside her window. The sky a canvas of blue hues, bleeding into each other like a watercolour masterpiece. It was still early in the morning, her first cup of coffee sat untouched, cold and unappetising.

'Ben, your excuses have been ringing in my ears for the past hour and a half. The situation remains unchanged. You need to sell our flat and give me my share, Faith's' voice was calm but firm.

'You're being unreasonable Faith. I have clients to entertain, and Eloise and my child to consider. Do you want them homeless?' Ben's voice had an edge of desperation.

Faith took a deep breath, steadying herself before replying, 'I understand your predicament, Ben. Here's a thought - why not use the money from Eloise's house sale and her divorce settlement? Pay me my share and keep the flat.' Ben's retort was swift and biting, '

'You never understood the sacrifices necessary for a successful career. Raising a child requires funds, something you wouldn't understand.'

Faith felt a pang in her heart, 'Yes, Ben, you've made it abundantly clear. I was robbed of the chance to understand when you crashed our car into that tree.' Ben's response was a mix of guilt and resentment, 'Are you going to hold that against me forever, Faith? It's a low blow, even for you.'

Faith could feel the conversation spiralling into a futile argument, 'Ben, this is getting us nowhere. I thought we could sort this out without involving lawyers, but I see that was a mistake. You have two months to settle this or expect a letter from my solicitor. And do give my best to Eloise.' With that, Faith ended the call, her heart heavy with regret and disappointment.

After the final divorce papers hit the table, Faith had gone straight back to being Harrington. It was like she wanted to erase every bit of her ex-husband from her life, sweep away the heartache. She stood there, gazing out the window, toying with the idea of taking her camera for a stroll. The morning was filled with the kind of crisp, inviting light that photographers dreamed about. Plus, she had plenty of time on her hands, why not?

Photography had become Faith's sanctuary. The quaint, old cottage she'd inherited from her late aunt, nestled in the heart of Willowbrooke, was a world away from the city. She placed her half-empty coffee cup in the sink, marvelling at how much her life had changed in the year since she'd moved back. The house was brimming with memories of her childhood summers spent with her sisters, their laughter singing through the hallways and across the sprawling grounds. Her aunt had been her greatest supporter, encouraging her artistic pursuits and recognising her talent.

She moved to the hallway, her fingers gently adjusting a slightly askew painting. It was a beautiful landscape of the Folly near Eglantine Hall, painted by her aunt, Penelope Harrington, a renowned artist whose works were highly sought after. A pang of nostalgia swept over Faith as she admired the painting, her aunt's favourite piece.

Faith reached for her coat; her walking stick ever-present by her side. She paused before the mirror, her reflection revealing a tall woman with an oval face and a playful, upturned nose. Her light copper hair was secured in a loose bun, a few rebellious strands framing her face. She slung her camera around her neck, her fingers brushing against the cool metal with a sense of familiarity.

Stepping out of Cherry Tree Cottage, she found herself on Eglantine Lane, a serene road in Willowbrooke. The town was a picturesque haven, cradled by the verdant countryside and watched over by the grand Eglantine Hall. The hall, a relic from a bygone era, stood majestically atop a hill, its grandeur undiminished despite being unoccupied for centuries.

The quaint cottages, reminiscent of the era when the hall was built, were passed down generations, each holding stories of the town's rich history. Willowbrooke was a charming blend of old-world charm and modern convenience, its inhabitants a colourful mix of characters. As Faith began her walk, she noticed two such characters strolling down the lane, their animated conversation filling the quiet morning air.

Arthur and Minerva Holcombe, twins in their twilight years, were the proud proprietors of the quaint Comfy Bottom cottages and caravan site, nestled just beyond the outskirts of town. The name Comfy Bottom was a playful twist on the original 'Comfrey Bottom', a tribute to the profusion of the medicinal herb that once flourished there.

The Holcombe's, once the crème de la crème of Willowbrooke, had weathered many a storm, including their father's ill-advised ventures that cost them their mother, wealth, and nearly their dignity. Yet, they rose from the ashes, thanks to Minerva's shrewd decision to sell parcels of their lands and the grand hall, transforming their remaining cottages into a charming holiday retreat.

Minerva, who towered over her brother by a good three inches and had the advantage of being born five minutes earlier, assumed the mantle of leadership. Today, she was clad in her father's vintage brown stockman's coat, a relic from his Australian sojourn, and a pair of sturdy brogues. Her silver hair was neatly coiffed into an austere bun, a style she had sworn by for as long as Faith could remember. Minerva's face bore the marks of time and weather, her petite mouth set in a firm line of determination. Her delicate nose and slender neck seemed a misfit with her otherwise robust frame, hinting at a past of grace and beauty. The only remnants of her joyous past were her striking cerulean eyes, which twinkled merrily, adding a dash of warmth to her otherwise stern demeanour.

'Arthur, quit dawdling.' We have those French arriving tomorrow and we have lots to do. Minerva called out in her deep, resonant voice, her gaze periodically darting back towards her brother. Arthur, a charming man with the same captivating blue eyes, was quite the ladies' man in his prime. As he sauntered past Faith, he tipped his hat and winked, 'Going to rain today,' evoking a chuckle from her. 'On my way, Min,' he responded cheerily.

A clatter of hooves behind her announced the arrival of Churchill, the scruffy, black and white goat with an uncanny resemblance to a children's book troll. He had one broken horn, and crooked teeth. Arthur had won the goat in a card game, much to Minerva's chagrin had nurtured the frail creature back to health. Today, Churchill was a robust animal, ambling along at his own pace, nibbling on a clump of dandelions. 'Morning, Churchill,' Faith greeted, her smile widening as the goat bleated in response.

The Front street of Willowbrooke was positively thrumming with life today. The holiday season had ushered in a fresh wave of visitors, drawn to the town's quaint charm and historical allure. The ancient library, hewn from the same stone that gave Willowbrooke its Jane Austen-esque appeal, was a particular magnet. Its existence had been a lifeline to the town's inhabitants, providing much-needed employment and stemming the youth exodus to the bustling metropolis of Cedarby. Faith, a local herself, had returned to Willowbrooke just a year ago. As she took in the familiar sights - the sprawling croquet lawn, which was to the locals misnamed as it was just a large piece of grass, the array of craft shops, the majestic chestnut tree with its tender new buds - it was as if she'd never left.

'Faith, love, would you mind fetching me a coffee?' Her mother's voice broke through her reverie. Rowan Harrington, the fiery-haired proprietress of Heaven Sent, was a force of nature. Her shop, brimming with aromatic candles and magical herbal skin creams, was a tourist favourite. Rowan and her sister Hazel had travelled to Willowbrooke from Scotland in their twenties, their belief in the potency of herbs and flowers initially raising eyebrows among the locals. But with tenacity and hard work, the sisters had earned their place and affection in the community.

Faith felt a pang of inadequacy as she looked at her mother. Despite the challenges of raising three children, Rowan still radiated youthful vitality, her skin smooth and unmarked by age. Men still turned their heads when Rowan and Hazel walked into a room. Faith's sister Charity shared their striking looks, while Hope compensated with her sharp intellect. Faith, however, felt plain in comparison, her only traits being her creativity.

'Give me five minutes, Mum,' Faith replied, setting off towards the town's beloved coffee shop, The Grinder.

Her mother's forgetfulness was legendary - she could conjure up scented potions with ease, but the mundane details of life like coffee, taxes, and appointments often fell by the wayside.

Passing the general store, Faith caught the tantalising aroma of coffee. The Grinder was the jewel in Willowbrooke's crown, its freshly brewed coffee and artistic cakes holding a special place in everyone's heart. It was, as her mother liked to say, the best coffee shop in the world.

As the door creaked open, an intoxicating medley of chocolate and cinnamon wafted through the air, wrapping her in a comforting embrace. Krista Hunter, the proprietor, was busily straightening up the large oak table that dominated the front of the coffee shop. The interior was a charming blend of contemporary chic and rustic charm, with wooden tables, glass jars filled with colourful confections, and slate flooring lending a cosy, inviting atmosphere. But today, it wasn't the sanctuary she needed.

'Fancy bumping into you, Faith,' a familiar voice drawled. 'How's the leg? Still playing the limping damsel?' Nathan Crawford, the husband of her school friend Mirry, was leaning against the counter, a smirk playing on his lips.

Faith shot him a cool look, 'Hello Nathan. How are you today?'

Nathan's chest puffed out slightly, 'Business is booming. Sold two houses this week. Seems everyone wants a piece of the countryside.' He paused, as if waiting for applause.

Faith didn't indulge him. 'A shame really. The influx of city dwellers is driving up the prices and making it difficult for the locals to afford homes.' She retorted.

Nathan simply shrugged, his smirk never leaving his face. 'There are plenty of houses on the estate, just outside Cedarby and in Stanton Brook.'

Frustration bubbled within Faith. 'Nathan, these people were born here. It's their home. I'd rather see them living here than have the houses sit empty all week.' Nathan just smiled, clearly unbothered. He turned his attention to Krista, 'Krista, do you have my special brownies?'

Krista's gaze momentarily drifted upward before she gestured towards the bustling counter. 'The orders are prepped and packaged, just have a word with Liam.' Nathan, his demeanour as brash as ever, made a beeline for the counter, shoving his way to the front with an air of entitlement. 'My order's special, waiting just for me.

I'm sure you can see, I'm a man in a hurry.' A murmur of disgruntled protest rippled through the queue, but Nathan was unmoved.

'You're aware there's a queue, right?' Liam's tone was laced with irritation as he served coffee and sandwiches to the customers Nathan had so rudely dismissed. The tension between the two men, always simmering beneath the surface, was palpable. It was no secret that Nathan had once been romantically involved with Krista, a fact that seemed to forever sour their interactions.

'Krista, love, could you remind your husband that I'm always served promptly when I come in?' Krista, after setting aside the dishes she had been clearing, obliged. Slipping on a pair of disposable gloves, she retrieved a brown paper bag from a refrigerated drawer. After swiftly preparing a coffee, she presented both to Nathan with a polite smile. Nathan, in return, kissed Krista's hand with a charm that bordered on insincere. 'Service from such a beauty, it's a good thing I'm happily wed, or I'd whisk you away.'

As Nathan sauntered back towards Faith, his grin faded. 'If it weren't for their nut-free brownies, I'd take my business to a more reputable establishment.' His comment was a stark reminder of his severe nut allergy, a condition that had nearly claimed his life in school. Faith recalled the incident vividly, the memory of a close call that had left Nathan perpetually cautious about his food choices.

'You still catching up with Mirry later, Faith?' Nathan's tone was casual as he prepared to join a group of his solicitor friends.

'Yes, after helping mum this morning, we're meeting at noon.'

'Enjoy, girls.' With that, Nathan sauntered off, leaving Faith to approach the counter for her coffee.

Krista took over serving and Liam retreated to the kitchen to prepare for the lunch rush. As Krista started Faith's order, she paused, her attention momentarily caught by Nathan's boisterous laughter.

'Nathan can be so...' Faith chimed in,

'Self-assured?' Krista chuckled.

'Something like that. How's Liam?'

'Irritated. Nathan knows just how to rile him.' Krista secured the lids on the coffees. 'He needs to let it go. I love Liam, he should trust that. It's just...'

'Nathan's always been like this.'

'Mirry's been acting quite odd, hasn't she?' Faith mused, leaning against the counter, her eyes clouded with concern. Her fingers traced the edge of the paper cup. 'I'm seeing her later today. I hope she opens up about what's been bothering her.'

'Ah, I heard about a bit of a row at the pub last week,' Krista interjected, her gaze fixed on Faith. 'Liam saw it. Mirry was in tears, accusing Nathan of something. He seemed to be in a hurry to leave, practically yanked her out of the place.'

Faith's heart clenched at the revelation. 'She hasn't said a word. That's what's troubling me.'

Krista shrugged, trying to sound nonchalant. 'Faith, Liam and I argue all the time. It'll sort itself out.'

Faith thanked Krista for the coffee and pastries, then made her way to the door. The weather outside had turned dreary, the sky painted with dull grey clouds that promised rain. It would be a busy morning for her mother's shop, but not the best for her photography business.

Across the road, Arthur and Minerva were approaching. Suddenly, a flash of white caught her eye. Churchill was charging across the road. Faith instinctively jumped to the side, landing awkwardly on her injured leg. She quickly realised she wasn't the target. Nathan, who had just stepped out of the café, was oblivious to the impending disaster. He was still engrossed in his conversation with the solicitor, a bag of brownies in one hand and a cup of steaming coffee in the other. Faith tried to warn him, but it was too late. Churchill lunged at Nathan's bag, missing it by a nose as Nathan held it above his head. The coffee cup wobbled dangerously, splashing its contents onto Nathan's immaculate white shirt.

CHAPTER 2

'Blasted beast!' Nathan's fury was palpable, his cheeks flushed a deep crimson as he hastily shrugged off his jacket and untucked his shirt in a futile attempt to shield his skin from the scalding coffee. His usually polished London accent had slipped, revealing the rougher edges of his working-class dialect. Faith couldn't help but smirk at the spectacle.

Minerva and Arthur had emerged from across the street, the latter grappling with Churchill, who was primed and ready for another round of chaos.

'Control yourself, you brute!' Minerva's foot stamped on the ground with a force that made even Nathan flinch. 'Churchill—Halt.' The command was so authoritative that both the goat and Arthur froze on the spot. Nathan's gaze darted between the trio, his pristine Saville Row suit and silk shirt now stained with coffee. 'This suit is worth a fortune, and this shirt—do you have any idea how much silk costs?'

'Not a clue, and quite frankly, I couldn't care less.' Replied Minerva.

Nathan was clearly outmatched in this encounter and Faith savoured every moment of it. Nathan's face reddened even further,

'You'll care when I send you the bill.' He turned to Faith, 'I'm going to report that beast. It's a public menace. It could seriously injure someone. It could have rabies?'

Arthur began to drag Churchill away, muttering under his breath, 'Churchill, what's gotten into you?' Faith watched them disappear down the street, a puzzled frown on her face. Churchill's behaviour had been unusually aggressive today. He was typically more of a stealthy thief than a confrontational menace.

Minerva's voice brought her back to the present, 'That man hasn't changed a bit since he was a boy.' Faith nodded in agreement, 'He's always had a chip on his shoulder.' Minerva snorted, 'More like two, one on each shoulder to keep him balanced.' She turned on her heel, heading towards the café, 'He won't be getting a penny from me. Serves him right for wearing such fancy clothes in the countryside.' With that, she disappeared into the café, leaving Faith alone with her thoughts.

Carrying the steaming cups of coffee, Faith made her way back to her mother's shop. As she sat sipping the hot beverage, Faith regaled her mother with the morning's antics. 'Mother, you should've seen the look on Nathan's face; it was as if he'd swallowed a bee,' Faith said, her eyes sparkling with mischief. Rowan, her mother, paused from her task of arranging creams on the shelves, her eyebrows raised in surprise.

'Churchill, vicious? That's preposterous! He's the gentlest creature around me, never even snatches a treat. I wonder what got into him today,' she said, a giggle escaping her lips. 'Though I must admit, there are times when I too feel like hurling something at Nathan. His condescending attitude can be quite grating.'

Her mother took a sip from her coffee, her eyes closing in delight. 'This is pure ambrosia, Faith.' She took another sip, her tongue darting out to catch the froth on her upper lip. 'But you must admit, it must have been quite a spectacle for the shoppers, right?' She asked, her eyes now twinkling with mischief too.

Faith let out a soft chuckle, her fingers tracing the rim of her coffee cup. 'Oh, it was a spectacle alright. I thought Nathan was going to have an aneurysm. His shirt was completely ruined and when Minerva turned her back on him...,' she trailed off, her laughter filling the small shop. Her mother joined in, her laughter mingling with Faith's. 'I wish I could've seen it. Imagine Nathan meeting clients in a soiled shirt. The scandal!' She exclaimed, her eyes dancing with mirth.

Faith nodded, her eyes distant. 'I think he must've rushed home immediately. He wouldn't dare tarnish his immaculate image by being seen in public like that. And then, he must've called Mirry, or even Dad, demanding them to 'send the hounds and hunt the evil creature down', she mimicked Nathan's pompous tone, causing both of them to burst into laughter again. 'He even accused Churchill of having rabies, can you believe it?'

Leaving her mother's shop just before noon, Faith crossed the road to the Hung, Drawn and Quartered, one of the oldest pubs in the area. The pub was an old stone building, its exterior adorned in the summer with cascading roses.

As a child, Faith had spent countless afternoons in the pub's beer garden with her parents. Outside the pub stood a life-size model of a man hanging from a gibbet, a sight that Faith had always found macabre. But the holidaymakers seemed to love it, often flocking to take pictures with the grotesque figure in the background.

The pub was owned by Chris and Judy Carpenter, a couple who had moved to the town from Cedarby ten years ago. It had taken a while for the townsfolk to warm up to them, their outsider status a barrier that was hard to overcome. But that didn't stop the pub from being the local favourite, always brimming with people and serving the most delectable meals. Faith made her way to the bar, where Chris was serving a local farmer.

'Just a moment, Faith,' Chris said, topping up the man's pint and turning back to her with a smile. 'What can I get you today, are you here to eat?'

With a sparkle in her eyes and a mischievous grin tugging at the corners of her mouth, Faith retorted, 'Why, who in their right mind would desire to dine elsewhere when the maestro of the kitchen, Chef Massimo, is crafting his gastronomic masterpieces?' Her laughter, light and infectious, filled the room.

'Try convincing my wife of that,' came the rueful response, a hint of exasperation seeping through. 'She's already threatened to toss him into the gibbet twice this morning alone.'

Her gaze then turned towards the entrance, scanning for a familiar face. 'When Mirry makes her entrance, do let her know I'm stationed near the window, won't you?' Her voice had softened, the words spoken more like a request than an instruction.

'Consider it done, Faith,' came the prompt reply, accompanied by a nod of understanding.

As Faith settled into a chair by the window, her gaze fell on the river and the hall on the hill. She took a sip of her wine, her mind wandering to Mirry and the cause of her friend's recent distress. She was pulled out of her thoughts by Chris's voice.

'Do you want another drink, Faith? You've been here for 30 minutes now. Is Mirry running late?' He asked. Faith shook her head, her worry for Mirry growing. 'She hasn't called. I've tried to ring her twice, but her phone is off,' she said.

The sky was a wash of greys and off-whites as Faith stepped out of the pub. The rain had stopped but the gloomy weather and her missed dinner were doing nothing to lift her spirits. She had been looking forward to meeting Mirry and finding out what was bothering her. She was also curious about what Krista had said about the argument and Nathan's heavy-handedness. If Mirry needed help, Faith wanted to be there for her. She may not have been the best person to give relationship advice, but she was a good listener.

The once bustling main street had now surrendered to the whims of the weather, its usual cacophony replaced by the rhythmic patter of rain. The holidaymakers and locals had taken refuge indoors, leaving the street eerily quiet. As Faith walked past her mother's quaint little shop, the familiar chime of the bell and a warm wave from her mum through the rain-speckled window were the only signs of life.

'Stay dry, love!' her mother called out, her voice barely audible over the rain.

A few houses up the road and just slightly down on the other side from hers stood Mirry and Nathan's abode, a once charming stone cottage now stripped of its original charm by Nathan's incessant modernisation. The once lush front garden, a riot of colours and fragrances, had been replaced by a sterile concrete frontage adorned only by two lonely plant pots flanking a garish red UPVC door. The sight of it made Faith's heart ache. 'Nathan, you're turning our beautiful town into a soulless concrete jungle,' she muttered under her breath.

As she walked around the side of the cottage, she noticed the absence of Mirry's car. Nathan's green Jag, his prized possession, sat unused in the garage. The sight of the garage door left ajar made Faith frown. 'That's odd. Nathan would never leave his car exposed to the elements,' she thought, her curiosity piqued.

Faith continued towards the back door, her heart pounding as she found it open as well. The interior was a mess, the stone floor littered with wet puddles and papers strewn about.

'Nathan are you home?' she called out. Her heart skipped a beat as a loud bang reverberated through the house. She froze in her tracks, gripping her stick and a tennis racquet she found near the door.

She pushed open the living room door and stupidly stumbled over her own walking stick. As she tried to regain her balance, her eyes fell on a leg protruding from behind Nathan's enormous leather chair. She gasped, her heart pounding in her chest.

'Nathan?' she murmured. She moved closer, her hands trembling as she saw Nathan's lifeless body slumped on the floor. His face was grotesquely swollen, his eyes sealed shut under inflamed lids, and his tongue protruding from his open mouth. After a futile attempt to find a pulse, Faith knew, Nathan was dead.

With a trembling hand, Faith reached out for the telephone that sat on the mahogany side table. Her heart pounded in her chest as she dialled the familiar numbers of the local police station. Her voice wavered as she relayed the situation.

'I... I need help, there's a body.'

Faith knew the protocols of such situations, she knew enough to know she shouldn't touch anything, lest she tamper with potential evidence. But her legs felt like jelly, and she needed to sit down. She took a cautious look around before deciding on the kitchen.

She pulled out a chair from the wooden table. She sank into it, her mind a whirlwind of fear and worry as she waited for the police to arrive.

CHAPTER 3

Detective Chief Inspector Pennant McBride, or Penn as he was known to his friends, had found himself in the sleepy town of Willowbrooke for a month now, but it felt like an eternity.

The town was a far cry from the bustling, seedy streets of London he'd left behind. The lack of internet was driving him mad, and his attempts to get it fixed felt like a battle with a mythical beast. He strolled through the town centre, observing the quaint scene before him - a frazzled mother soothing her wailing child, a woman fussing over her pampered poodles on the croquet lawn. Life here was slow and it unnerved him.

'Penn, my lad, you're a Giant!' he could almost hear his friends jesting. Standing at 6 foot three, he was a towering figure. It was sometimes a boon, but often a curse. His life had been a series of highs and lows. The loss of his mother at a tender age of 15 had left a wound that never really healed. And now, he was nursing fresh scars.

His new boss had been warm and welcoming, a stark contrast to the others in the force. They were wary of him, of the baggage he carried. 'Police don't tell' he had learnt the hard way. He had been naive, too trusting, and it had cost him dearly. Now, he was about to lunch with his boss, a tradition he wasn't particularly fond of but had no choice but to partake in.

As he waited, his attention was drawn to a woman leaving at shop. She was young, strikingly beautiful, but her beauty was marred by a deep-seated sadness that made her seem cold and distant. She was heading towards The Grinder, the only decent shop he'd found in this town, and his newfound source of caffeine. He was so engrossed in his observation that he didn't notice the mother with the pram until she bumped into him.

'Sorry, I am new here. Are you okay?' He stammered, receiving a polite smile in return. He cursed his clumsiness, checking his phone for a possible escape from the impending lunch. He was early, so he decided to wait under a tree on the dewy lawn, occasionally glancing at his phone with a glimmer of hope.

'Min, slow down, will you?' The plea came from a man, trudging along with a disgruntled expression. His eyes were squinted against the sun, which had too briefly reappeared, a stark contrast to the excited gleam in the eyes of the woman striding ahead. 'Churchill's got short legs, we're not in a marathon.'

Min, the woman, turned to face him, her eyes rolling dramatically. 'That's why I told you to leave the damn thing at home. Why you insist on coddling that creature is beyond me.'

In the distance, Penn sat up straighter, his attention drawn to the peculiar pair. His eyes widened as he noticed the goat trailing behind them. 'What the...' He didn't finish his sentence, too stunned by the sight of the goat trotting along, its head swinging from side to side as if inspecting the passersby.

Suddenly, the goat changed direction, its hooves clattering on the hard concrete. Penn watched in disbelief as it launched itself at a man he recognised as the estate agent who had rented him his flat. The goat seemed to be aiming for the man's bag, but instead collided with his coffee cup. The contents splattered all over his shirt, staining the expensive fabric.

The estate agent, Nathan, cursed loudly, his face turning red with anger. Penn considered stepping in but stopped when he heard a woman's voice. 'Churchill—Stop!' The woman, presumably the goat's owner, was trying to regain control of the situation. Penn watched as Nathan stormed away, leaving his wife standing alone with two drinks in her hands. As the woman returned to her shop, Penn couldn't help but smile. Life here might be more interesting than he'd thought.

Standing outside the Hung, Drawn and Quartered, Penn took in the sight of the eerie statue hanging overhead. 'Dam, they don't mess about with their punishments here,' he muttered to himself, tipping an imaginary hat to the gruesome figure. 'Let's just hope the grub's not as grim as the pub's name, eh?' He stepped inside, his eyes adjusting to the dim light as a waitress gestured him towards the conservatory. The room was a stark contrast to the bar, bathed in natural light and adorned with quaint farming memorabilia. Plastic vines laden with grapes hung from every corner, giving the place a rustic charm.

In the far corner, Superintendent Donald Harrington sat waiting. Spotting Penn, he waved him over. 'Good to see you found us, Penn. Bit of a trek from Cedarby, I know, but it's a good way to meet the locals.' Penn took a seat opposite him, his nerves evident as he buried his nose in the menu. Donald's chuckle interrupted his scrutiny as a large man stormed through a side door, followed by a flustered-looking woman.

'That's Massimo, our resident Italian maestro, and the poor lass chasing him is Judy, the owner,' Donald explained as the pair bickered.

'This is a pub, not a restaurant Massimo!' Judy's voice boomed through the room. 'You can't just change the entire menu whenever you feel like it!' Massimo, however, was having none of it. 'Genius does not recognise such mundane things!' he retorted, disappearing through another door.

Donald invited Judy to join them. 'Judy, sit down before I have to arrest you for disturbing the peace.'

Judy complied, her frustration melting into a smile. 'One of these days I'll take that axe out back to him,' she muttered, accepting the introductions to Penn. 'Welcome to our little corner of the world, Penn. We might seem a bit standoffish at first, but once you get to know us, you'll find we're a civilised bunch.'

Penn flashed a grin, his eyes glinting with amusement. 'Well, I reckon conversation can be a tricky affair in London as well, so I think I'll manage just fine with the remoteness,' he responded, his voice carrying a light, jovial tone.

Donald chuckled, his eyes twinkling with curiosity. 'Have you had the pleasure of meeting any of the locals yet?' he asked. Penn's grin widened as he recalled his earlier encounter.

'I've met Nathan, the estate agent. And I did witness a rather amusing tussle between him and a goat on my way here,' he shared.

Donald's hearty laughter filled the room. 'Ah, you've met Churchill, our resident thief and troublemaker. My wife is quite fond of him, but the rest of us try to stay on his good side,' he explained, his eyes glinting with mirth.

Suddenly, a loud crash came from the kitchen, causing Judy to jump up from her seat. 'I'm terribly sorry, but I think I might be needed, she announced, her eyes wide with alarm. 'Don, if I lose my temper and end up murdering Massimo, do me a favour and call a solicitor,' she added, her tone half-joking, half-serious. With that, she dashed off towards the kitchen, to where the raised voices had got even louder.

Penn glanced around, but the other patrons seemed unperturbed. Donald shrugged, a wry smile playing on his lips. 'Massimo's cooking is nothing short of spectacular. That's why Judy, Chris, and the customers put up with his...eccentricities,' he explained.

After they had ordered their meal and Penn's drink arrived, Donald leaned back in his chair, looking relaxed. 'So, have you settled into your flat?' he asked.

Penn nodded; 'For now, sir. But I'm hoping to find a house. I'd like to have a garden. My mother was an avid gardener, and I seem to have inherited her love for it,' he replied.

Donald's eyes lit up at this. 'You should visit the garden centre near here. It's owned by my sister-in-law and my niece and nephew, and they have quite the green thumbs. I'm sure they'd be more than happy to help you get started,' he suggested.

Just then, their waitress arrived with their food, and Penn's eyes widened in appreciation. It was clear why Massimo was allowed his eccentricities – his culinary skills were nothing short of extraordinary.

The scent of the Pacific Ocean black cod fillet wafted through the air, making his mouth water. The menu had promised a honey and Japanese tamari glaze that would give a mellower taste than soy, and it didn't disappoint. It was nestled atop a bed of pearl barley risotto, with courgette shaped like beignets and a drizzle of teriyaki sauce. He couldn't help but let out a sigh of satisfaction.

His companion chuckled, a twinkle in his eye. 'See what I mean lad, for this a man could easily sell his soul.'

As they continued their meal, the conversation flowed easily. Penn found himself surprised at how easy it was to talk to his boss, Don. There was an air of camaraderie that he hadn't expected. 'We are all on the same force and I see us as a team,' Don said, a sentiment that Penn appreciated.

Don was a middle-aged man, still handsome despite the deep laughter lines etched into his face. His hair had yet to turn grey and he had a fit, well-kept appearance that spoke of self-care. His easy-going personality put Penn at ease. 'No airs and graces in my house, the wife would stone me,' he joked, a fond smile on his face. 'She's an extraordinarily strong woman, and when you meet her, which I'm sure you will, you'll see why I'm as happy as I am.'

Their conversation didn't touch on Penn's time in London, a topic he was grateful to avoid. Instead, they discussed the changes in the force, the impact of budget cuts on their work in the countryside. Don shared about the types of crimes they usually dealt with and how they took a more hands-on approach in getting to know the people on their beat. It was all about building relationships, he explained, a philosophy that Penn found himself agreeing with.

Penn, declining a sweet, watched Don savour every bite of a decadent chocolate fudge cake. Once finished, Don leaned back, closing his eyes with a satisfied sigh. 'If my missus finds out I've eaten this, I'm a goner. But I see it as my duty to keep these pubs open with my unwavering loyalty and financial contributions,' he said, his voice filled with mock solemnity.

Penn chuckled, his thoughts drifting to his own family. 'My mother was the same, always fighting to stop dad from devouring the entire cake shop. She wanted him to stay healthy, but it didn't work. Ironically, she was the first to go.' He was surprised at how easily he had opened up, and Don noticed his momentary embarrassment.

'It's in your notes that you lost your mum early,' Don said gently, 'And anything you say to me will stay between us. I want you to feel you can talk to me if you have any problems. It's better not to let things fester.' Penn nodded, appreciating the sentiment.

Once they were done, Don paid the bill and they both stepped outside. Don took a deep breath, 'You won't get this in London,' he said, shaking Penn's hand. 'I'll see you either this afternoon at the station or tomorrow. Have a good day, Penn.'

No sooner had Don disappeared towards the car park, Penn's mobile rang. He fished it out of his pocket and saw it was the station.

'Hello, this is Pennant McBride,' he answered. A voice from the station call centre came through, 'I'm going to send you an address, it's near where you are. There has been a report of a murder and SCU request your attendance.' Penn began heading to his car, 'Murder? So much for a quiet life,' he muttered.

CHAPTER 4

The shrill wail of the police siren sliced through the thick silence of the day, followed by an ominous creaking sound at the kitchen door. Faith's heart pounded in her chest as a man stepped into the dimly lit room, casting a long shadow on the wet tiled floor. He a police officer, but not one from the local station that she recognised. 'Pennant McBride,' he introduced himself, his voice a low baritone in the silent room. 'I understand there's been a report of a deceased individual?'

'Yes, in the living room,' Faith replied. Her gaze followed the flurry of activity as more people trickled in, some in the familiar blue uniforms, others in what seemed like protective suits. McBride took charge, directing them towards the living room where Nathan's lifeless body lay.

'Don't worry, we'll sort everything out,' McBride assured her, his eyes meeting hers. As he sat down across from her, Faith had a chance to observe him more closely. His hair was a chestnut brown, a wild mass of curls that he had obviously attempted to tame by keeping them short. His face was rugged, with a strong jawline that was softened by his captivating hazel eyes. His tall frame was lean yet muscular.

'So, Mrs Crawford,' McBride began, but Faith quickly corrected him. 'It's Faith. Nathan wasn't my husband.' A flicker of surprise crossed McBride's face, but he quickly composed himself. 'May I ask you some questions, Faith?' he requested. With a nod from Faith, he continued, 'Can you tell me when and where you found him?'

'I walked in about 20 minutes ago and found him on the living room floor,' Faith explained, her voice steady. McBride scribbled down her words in his notebook before asking, 'Was there anyone else here when you arrived?' Faith shook her head, her gaze never leaving his. 'I wouldn't know. But he was already dead when I found him.'

'Do you have anyone who can vouch for your whereabouts before you arrived here?' The detective asked, his gaze never leaving the notepad in front of him.

'Why?' She retorted, her brows furrowing in confusion.

'Could you just answer the question, please?' He replied, his tone was firm, yet patient. 'Yes, I suppose so. But I don't understand why this is necessary. Shouldn't you be looking for whoever murdered him?' Penn looked up, a flicker of interest in his eyes. 'What do you mean?' He asked, his pen poised over the notebook.

'Nathan had anaphylaxis. He always carried an EpiPen with him. In fact, he had several, just to be safe. But there's no EpiPen here. I've checked. Also, the back door was left open, and so was the garage.' She explained, her words rushed as she tried to make him understand.

'So? That's not unusual. He was probably in a hurry.' Penn countered, his tone dismissive.

'But why would he stop to have his brownie and coffee then? And wouldn't he have shut the back door to keep out the rain?' She argued, her voice rising in frustration.

'It still doesn't mean it's a murder, Faith. Are there any items missing?' Penn asked, his voice calm and measured.

'I'm not sure, but Krista would never have given him the wrong brownie. And Nathan wouldn't have left his car out in the rain. There must be another explanation.' She insisted, her gaze never leaving the detective's face.

'Faith, could you kindly walk me through the events of the day?' The words hung heavy in the air, a stark reminder of the grim reality. Nathan was gone, and Mirry was nowhere to be found. As Faith recounted her actions that day, the weight of the situation began to sink in.

'Faith, I must ask,' the officer began, his tone taking on a more serious note. 'Were there any...romantic ties between you and Nathan?'

Faith looked taken aback. 'Excuse me?' she retorted, her eyebrows knitting together in a frown.

The DCI held up his hands in a placating gesture. 'This is a standard line of questioning in investigations like this. So, I need to know, were you and Nathan more than just friends?'

Faith shook her head vigorously. 'Absolutely not. I'm not sure why you'd assume such a thing.'

The DCI leaned back in his chair, studying Faith. 'Well, you're here, in his house, and his wife isn't. You mentioned the door was open, but you could have a key, couldn't you?'

Faith's face turned a shade paler. 'So, you're suggesting I sneaked in and killed him by...what, stuffing nuts down his throat?'

Penn sighed, rubbing his temples. 'We're still unsure of the cause of death, Faith. But we have to consider all possibilities.'

'Well, let me shed some light for you,' Faith retorted, her voice laced with a bitter sarcasm she couldn't suppress. 'Nathan had a nut allergy, a serious one. He always had his special nut-free brownies made at The Grinder, that coffee shop down the main street.'

Penn's eyebrows furrowed in thought, 'So, you're suggesting he could've been served the wrong brownies?'

Faith let out a hollow laugh, 'No, not at all. Krista, the owner, is meticulous about such things. She wouldn't make a mistake like that.'

'Regardless, we'll need to verify everything once we're done here,' Penn replied.

Faith's sarcastic retort, 'How very thorough of you,' hung in the air as the kitchen door swung open.

The figure that entered was a welcome sight. Chief Superintendent Donald Harrington strode into the kitchen. His tall frame was clad in his crime scene suit, his eyes scanning the room until they landed on his daughter.

With a sense of urgency, Faith stood up, her heart pounding in her chest. She threw herself into the protective embrace of the burly police officer. Despite her years, she was still daddy's little girl, and in moments like this, she needed him more than ever. His strong arms wrapped around her. Gradually, her trembling subsided. He gently guided her back to the chair, his eyes never leaving hers. Turning his attention to Penn, he asked, 'Penn, what have we got so far?'

Penn's gaze flitted between the two of them, a flicker of confusion crossing his features. 'My apologies, Penn,' her father said, 'This is my daughter, Faith.'

'Oh, I see.' Penn turned to Faith, his expression aloof, almost dismissive. Instantly, a wave of antipathy washed over her. She disliked this man. His arrogance was palpable, his condescension, unbearable.

'As a matter of fact,' she said, her voice laced with sarcasm, 'the detective here was just asking me if I was having an affair with

Nathan. He even suggested that I might have sneaked in and killed him with a bag of nuts.'

Her father's gaze shifted from her to the detective whose face was now a shade of crimson. The room fell silent, tension hanging in the air.

'Believe me, Penn,' he said, 'Faith wasn't involved with Nathan. His wife, she's one of Faith's dearest friends. And Mirry...well, Mirry is like a second daughter to me.' The poor lad was bearing the brunt of Faith's wrath, a position he knew all too well to be a perilous one.

'But you're right, Penn,' he continued, his words laced with a hint of amusement, 'this was the only way forward. And Faith, you're aware of the protocol. Go easy on the boy, won't you?' He gestured towards the inner door leading back to the living room, a chuckle rumbling deep in his chest. 'He's new, be kind. Come along, Penn. Let's leave Faith in the hands of one of the constables. They can escort her to her mother's shop.'

Faith, however, had no intention of heading to her mother's. She could already imagine the fuss her mother would make and, truth be told, she craved solitude more than anything. But before she could voice her protest, the door was flung open with a force that made her jump. Mirry burst into the room, her entrance as dramatic as her personality.

'Faith, what on earth is going on? Why are there police swarming outside our house? And what's with the tape?' Mirry's voice was a mix of confusion and panic. Faith rose swiftly from her seat, rushing to her side. Her arms wrapped around Mirry in a comforting embrace.

'You'll need to calm down,' Faith urged gently, her voice steady despite the turmoil around them. 'Please, sit.'

Mirry shook her head vehemently, her eyes wide with terror. 'I don't want to sit! What's happened?' She darted towards the inner door, Faith hot on her heels. They were met in the hallway by her father, deep in conversation with Penn, who was scribbling furiously in his notebook.

Penn looked up, his gaze falling on Mirry. 'Please, wait,' he said, stepping forward to block her path. 'You can't go in there yet. The team needs to finish their work; you could compromise the scene.'

'But where's Nathan?' Mirry's voice cracked, her eyes welling up with tears. 'Is it his allergies?... he has an EpiPen. It was full this morning, and we have spares in the drawer. What do you mean by 'compromise the scene'?'

'Dad,' Faith interjected, her voice trembling slightly. 'The drawer was open, and there were no EpiPens or any other medication.' Her father exchanged a grave look with Penn before disappearing down the hallway. He returned a few moments later, his expression grim.

'The drawer's empty,' he confirmed, his voice heavy.

'That can't be right!' Mirry's voice was hollow, her eyes wide with disbelief. 'I saw them with my own eyes this morning. I personally picked them up from the chemist just yesterday. Nathan had a full Penn and spares in the drawer. I made sure of it myself!' Her voice trailed off, her gaze darting around the room, seeking answers.

Donald, a seasoned detective, took a step towards her, his face etched with a mix of sympathy and determination. 'Mirry,' he began, his voice firm yet gentle, 'I promise to answer all your questions, but first, we need to talk.' He guided her back into the kitchen, his hand gently gripping her arm. Faith busied herself making a cup of tea. The familiar sound of the kettle whistling filled the air, a stark contrast to the tense atmosphere.

'When was the last time you saw Nathan?' Donald's question hung in the air. Mirry, now seated, looked up at him. 'This morning,' she replied. 'I was going shopping, then meeting Faith for a meal.' Donald continued with his line of questioning, his tone steady. 'Was Nathan acting strangely this morning? Did he seem out of sorts?'

Faith, handing Mirry a cup of tea, took a seat next to her. She could feel the tremors running through Mirry's body. Her face was streaked with mascara, a testament to her fear and confusion. 'He was happy,' Mirry said, her voice breaking. 'He said things were looking up, that he had a big sale lined up for this afternoon.'

In that instant, the door swung open, and a police officer emerged, followed by a towering man carrying a body bag. Don, without missing a beat, quickly directed them into the living room.

'This way.'

Mirry's eyes flashed with an intense fury as she watched the men. She sprang from her chair, her heart pounding in her chest as she stormed through the hall and into the living room. There, she was met with the sight that would forever be etched into her memory - the lifeless body of her beloved husband.

'No!' she cried out, 'This can't be happening!'

But it was too late. Her knees buckled beneath her, and she crumpled onto the floor, her screams piercing through the deafening silence.

An hour had passed, and the house was still swarming with police. Officers were meticulously dusting for fingerprints. Faith stood on the periphery; her gaze fixated on the remnants of the brownies that had been carefully sealed in a plastic bag by the DCI. He had concluded, rather hastily in her opinion, that Nathan had succumbed to his allergies after consuming one of those seemingly innocent treats.

'Bag those up and get them off to the lab,' she heard him instruct one of the officers, his voice cold and detached. 'And make sure the body gets to the coroners.'

Faith couldn't help but feel a pang of irritation at the sergeant's thoroughness. She had overheard hushed conversations among the other officers; he was a recent transfer from the hustle and bustle of London, probably bored out of his mind in the quiet countryside.

She found herself more annoyed by the fact that he hadn't acknowledged her presence since her father had introduced her. She was not just a bystander; she was the daughter of his boss. Yet, he seemed to regard her as a mere obstacle in his path to glory.

The hour was late when Faith finally arrived home, Mirry in tow. The house was silent, the ticking of the clock the only sound in the stillness. Mirry had spent the entire journey attempting to contact her father, her fingers dancing anxiously across her phone screen. Each unanswered call only served to heighten her worry. Faith found herself glancing at a small bottle of sleeping tablets nestled in a hidden compartment of Mirry's overnight bag. She wondered when had Mirry resorted to these and for what reason?

'Mirry, change into these pyjamas,' Faith offered, gently pressing a pair of soft, cotton pyjamas into her hands. Mirry nodded, her gaze distant. Instead of retreating to the comfort of her bed, she opted to sit on the worn-out sofa in the kitchen, her fingers wrapped around a warm mug of cocoa that Faith had prepared.

'Mirry, you really should eat something,' Faith urged, placing a plate laden with sandwiches and biscuits on the table. Her own stomach gave a protesting growl, reminding her of her own hunger. When was the last time she had eaten? She couldn't remember.

Mirry glanced at the food, her face pale. 'I can't believe this is happening, Faith. Who would want to hurt Nathan?' she murmured.

'We all knew about Nathan's peanut allergy.' Faith replied, her mind spinning with unanswered questions. She picked up a sandwich, forcing herself to eat despite the knot of anxiety in her stomach. Something wasn't right, she could feel it.

A sudden knock at the door had them both jolted. 'Please, don't let anyone in. I'm not ready to face anyone yet,' Mirry pleaded. Faith nodded, her heart pounding as she crossed the room to answer the persistent knock. As she swung the door open, Simon Montague, Mirry's father, barrelled past her. 'Where's my girl?' His voice was thick with worry.

Simon was a striking figure, even in his fifties. He towered over most with his height, his physique robust and muscular. His features were sharp and aristocratic. He was the kind of man who commanded attention effortlessly, his casual attire doing little to diminish his imposing presence. His daughter was a spitting image of him, her dark hair soft and lush, her eyes a warm chocolate brown.

'Dad, I left you a message. You didn't have to come,' Mirry said. Simon, however, was not to be deterred. 'Mirry, you're my daughter. Of course, I had to come. Tiffany is beside herself with worry.' Tiffany, Simon's second wife, was barely five years older than Mirry. She was a flight attendant on the private planes Simon often used for work, and her relationship with Mirry had been strained from the start.

'Would you mind if I stayed with Faith? I don't fancy the idea of moving around again. Plus, it's a lot more peaceful here,' Mirry implored, casting her father a heart-melting smile she knew he could hardly resist.

'Darling child,' his voice brimming with paternal warmth. 'Of course, if this is what you want. But promise me one thing - you'll keep me posted if you need anything, all right?'

After spending another half an hour in the comforting presence of his daughter, Simon decided it was time to leave. He turned to Faith, who had been a silent spectator all this while. 'Faith, would you mind walking me to the door?' he asked.

'Thank you, Faith. I trust you'll take good care of my Mirry,' he said, rubbing his face in a tired gesture. 'This is going to be a tough time for the family. I'd appreciate it if your father could keep me updated on anything concerning this accident.'

'I'm sure dad will keep you in the loop, Simon. And Mirry can stay as long as she needs to,' Faith assured him, her voice steady and comforting.

When Faith returned to the kitchen, she found Mirry quietly munching on a sandwich. The room was filled with an uneasy silence broken only by the rhythmic pattering of the rain against the window. It was a soothing sound, one that promised to wash away the day's worries and fears.

'I find it rather odd that Tiffany didn't accompany your father,' Faith remarked.

Mirry's shoulders shrugged in a nonchalant way, her eyes never leaving the worn-out kitchen tiles. 'Doesn't surprise me in the slightest,' she retorted, her voice laced with an icy sarcasm. 'She probably couldn't unearth an outfit suitable enough for such an occasion. I bet she'll be out on a shopping spree tomorrow, hunting for the perfect black ensemble. She'll burn such a hole in dad's credit card, it'll be smoking.'

Faith tried to soften the blow, her voice gentle. 'Mirry, she isn't all bad, just a little…' she trailed off, searching for the right word.

'Dopey? Ditsy?' Mirry interjected, her words biting. 'Or perhaps a money-grabber?' For the first time that night, a slight smile touched Mirry's lips.

'Enough now,' Faith said, her voice firm yet kind. 'I think it's time for you to try and get some sleep. You go up, and I will bring you some water and you can take some tablets, ok?' Mirry nodded, leaving Faith alone in the kitchen. Walking to the sink she filled a glass with water then followed Mirry upstairs.

After a night tormented by nightmares and unrest, Faith found herself greeting the dawn much earlier than usual. The only remedy for such a night, she decided, was a strong, black coffee. As she sat at the table, cradling the warm mug, a knock sounded through the quiet kitchen. Still swathed in her dressing gown, she peered curiously through the window. A smile tugged at the corners of her lips as she recognised the figure outside - Krista, with her ever-present delivery basket.

'Krista, love, you're a lifesaver,' Faith exclaimed, gratefully accepting the basket, and placing it on the table. 'I was just pondering what on earth we were going to eat.' As she began to unpack the tubs of food, Krista passed them over, her face etched with concern.

'Faith, how's Mirry doing?' Krista asked, her voice heavy with worry. Faith noted the redness of her eyes, a telltale sign of distress.

'I convinced her to take some sleeping pills and left her in bed. She's calm for now, but that could change.'

Krista swallowed hard, her eyes glazing over. 'I can't believe this is happening, Faith. The police came to the café this morning. They were asking all sorts of questions.' Her voice wavered, the reality of the situation sinking in.

'Did they explain about Nathan's death?' the question hung in the air.

'A bit, why?' came the hesitant response. The room was filled with tension, the words hanging heavy. The silence was broken by the chilling accusation.

'He died because of your brownies. Those 'nut-free' ones. You killed my husband, you did.' Faith's heart pounded as she turned to see Mirry, her face a mask of accusation and pain, standing ominously in the doorway.

'Mirry, the police are waiting for the post-mortem results,' Faith tried to reason, her voice shaking. But Mirry was like a woman possessed, her grief morphing into a terrifying anger.

'I don't need a post-mortem to tell me how Nathan died. You saw his body, Faith. It was clear as day.' She moved closer to Krista, who had turned a ghostly white, her body trembling.

'The police, they didn't say anything,' Krista stammered. 'Mirry, I promise you, Nathan's brownies, they didn't have nuts. I baked them myself; I have a strict process for allergy-friendly food.'

But Mirry was not to be placated. 'Something went wrong. I saw the brownie, there on the floor. I saw the bag it came from. Your café's bag.' Her voice was cold, her eyes filled with an icy resolve. 'Once I'm done, your little café will be shut for good. And I'll make sure you and your husband pay for this.'

Tears welled up in Mirry's eyes, spilling down her cheeks in a torrent of emotion. Faith, in a swift movement, ushered her into the empty chair nearby. Meanwhile, Krista, her own eyes brimming with tears, hastily grabbed her basket. The back door slammed open and shut in quick succession as she made her hasty exit, leaving behind only the haunting sound of Mirry's sobs.

'Mirry,' Faith began, 'don't you think that was a bit over the top? We don't know the circumstances of Nathan's death, and Krista...Krista is your friend. Do you genuinely believe she's capable of something this heinous?' She paused, studying Mirry's face. 'She's always been so meticulous, hasn't she?'

Mirry's response was a venomous glare. 'She was your friend, Faith. And it was clear as day that she still carried a torch for Nathan. Everyone saw it, everyone but you.' Her voice was bitter, filled with accusation. 'She couldn't stand the fact that he chose me.'

Faith sighed, realising that arguing was futile. Now was not the time for a heated debate. She needed to diffuse the situation, to direct Mirry's focus away from the hostility she harboured for Krista and Liam. But Mirry had other plans. She refused to engage in any further discussion, her lips pressed together in a tight line.

Left in an uncomfortable silence, Faith watched as Mirry slowly rose from the table and reached for her phone. She listened to the quiet, polite request for her father to come and collect her. Alone once more, she reached for her own phone, dialling the number of the only person she believed could help.

'Mum, it's me, Faith,' she said, her voice trembling slightly over the line. There was a pause on the other end before her mother's worried voice filtered through, 'Is everything all right, darling? Is Mirry with you?'

'No, Mum. She left after a row with Krista,' Faith declared. She could almost hear her mother's sigh of concern on the other end. 'Come over, Faith. Your sister Hope will be here. You need to be around family right now, it'll help distract you from everything that's been going on.'

Faith knew better than to argue with her mother when she was in this state. She reluctantly agreed, promising to be there later. For the rest of the day, she found solace in her photography, retreating to the cellar to finish developing a series of wedding photos she'd taken the previous weekend. The couple in the photos radiated happiness, a stark contrast to Mirry and Nathan's current situation.

Mirry had been so full of venom that morning, it had left Faith feeling hollow and exhausted. How had things spiralled so out of control in such a short span of time?

CHAPTER 5

It had been a gruelling afternoon for Penn. The paramedics on the scene had quickly concluded that the death appeared to be allergy related. The body had been whisked away for a post-mortem and the crime scene had been meticulously combed through. On the surface, it seemed like a straightforward case. But something had caught Penn's eye - Faith's insistent cries of murder and the conspicuous absence of the victim's medication.

'Could you check Nathan's office?' Penn had asked his team, hoping to find a clue. 'Maybe he used the EpiPen earlier, or he might've taken his medication with him.' He had to admit, something felt off, but he couldn't quite put his finger on it.

Faith, he mused, could just be a woman who had tried and failed to join the police force, now playing at being a detective. Or perhaps her imagination was simply running wild. It wouldn't be the first time he'd seen it - children of police officers, raised in an unusual world, often felt they knew the job as well as their crime-solving parents.

Penn felt the tension in the air, a prickling hostility radiating from Faith. He was baffled, they had barely met and already she was forming judgements about him. He remembered her connections, the pleasant dinner with his boss, and the potential consequences of falling out with her.

Back at the station, his first port of call was the computer. He delved into the lives of Nathan and Mirry. Mirry had landed a position in a prestigious fashion house, a connection from her father's circle, he discovered. Nathan, however, struggled to adapt to the cutthroat work environment of London, managing only to secure a position in a small, obscure estate agency.

Penn found himself drawn into their story, piecing together their separate lives until they intersected again. A reunion, a marriage, and then a return to their roots. Nathan, the working-class lad, had married Mirry, the heir. Penn couldn't shake off the idea that this might have played a part in Nathan's rise, the social climber who had managed to establish his own estate agency at a surprisingly young age, most likely aided by Mirry's wealth and her father's influence.

Pacing the room, he found himself preoccupied with thoughts of Faith. 'What's her role in all this?' he muttered to himself. Of course, it was clear as day that she and Mirry were close - but what about Nathan?

'Could there be more to their relationship?' he asked the silence.

'Would she be interested in a man like Nathan?' he wondered aloud. Somehow, he couldn't quite picture it. Faith didn't seem the type to fall for a man like him.

'But why would she question the initial verdict?' he pondered; his brow furrowed in deep thought. An accidental allergy seemed a much safer explanation - why would she risk drawing attention to herself by suggesting murder?

He paused, his gaze falling on the pile of case files on his desk. Another question was gnawing at the edges of his mind - why was he so interested in this case? After all, it was just a random accident.

There would be an inquest, the body would be released, and that would be the end of it. Or would it?

Once the police had cleared the scene and the night had descended, he made his way back to his flat, a stone's throw away from Willowbrooke.

His dwelling was a refurbished house's top portion, reached by a steep climb up metallic stairs at the rear. The interior was modestly adorned, except for his bed, which was a luxury he allowed himself. Essential appliances were already in place, and all he'd added were some basic kitchen items. His living room, furnished with Ikea's best, still lacked the warmth of a home.

The one thing Penn took great pride in was his culinary prowess. Awaiting him in the kitchen was a slow-cooked chicken in a creamy white wine sauce, a recipe he had mastered over time. He had also managed to pick up a bottle of wine and a crusty loaf on his way back. With his dinner neatly arranged on a tray and the wine bottle uncorked, he began to eat, his thoughts drifting back to Faith.

Her walking stick intrigued him. He could tell she'd suffered an accident in the past. He would've loved to probe further but he knew his colleagues would be tight-lipped about the boss's family matters.

To divert his thoughts, he washed up, settled on the sofa with the remaining wine, and flicked on the TV. But he found himself channel-hopping, unable to concentrate on any of the programmes. His mind was elsewhere. After a futile half-hour, he decided to call it a night, hoping that the next day would bring some clarity.

Penn was out of bed with the lark, the decision to go for a run coming to him naturally. The morning was crisp, the air tinged with the promise of a fresh day. He found himself in a quaint park. The sheer abundance of flowers, the chorus of bird songs, it was a stark contrast to the bustling metropolis he had left behind. London had its share of green spaces, but they were mere pockets of nature, dwarfed by the towering concrete structures. Here, the countryside stretched as far as the eye could see, and Penn found himself growing fond of these invigorating morning runs.

Cedarby was a world away from London, smaller, quieter, and the police station reflected this difference. It was modest, lacking the amenities to which he was accustomed. A surprising discovery was the resident pathologist and coroner, based on the lower floor. In London, these facilities were shared and often located at a distance. Here, despite serving neighbouring police stations as well, they were conveniently close.

Later, arriving at his desk, Penn sifted through the tasks for the day, checking for any pending phone messages. Then a trip to the coroner.

There was a clinical scent to this place that always set him on edge. As he walked in, he noticed two desks situated by the door that led to the morgue and autopsy room. Seated at one of the desks was a tall African man. This had to be Ignatius Scott, better known as Iggy. At first glance, Iggy didn't strike him as a pathologist. His nose had been broken at some point and hadn't set right, and his ebony corkscrew curls were tied up in a man bun. He wore a designer black shirt and jeans, looking more like a model than a scientist.

'Welcome to the pits,' Iggy greeted, gesturing around the room. 'I suppose you're here for the Nathan Crawford case. You're in luck. It's been quiet around here lately, so we managed to get quite a bit done yesterday.' He picked up his tablet and motioned for Penn to sit. 'Fancy a coffee? I can't function properly without my daily dose.'

Penn nodded, and a minute later, Iggy handed him a mug. It had 'I can't fix stupid, but I'm a fairly decent CSI' printed on it.

Iggy laughed, showing off his own mug that read, 'CSI because freakin' awesome is not an actual job title.' 'A friend of mine gave these to me,' he explained. 'Watches too many crime shows, if you ask me.'

Penn, sighed heavily as he leaned against the doorframe, his gaze fixated on the bustling activity of the office. 'You know, sometimes I think television has done us a disservice,' he began, his voice barely audible over the hum of the background chatter. 'They make it seem like we can solve cases in the blink of an eye.'

Iggy, glanced up from his tablet. 'You're preaching to the choir, mate,' he replied, a wry smile playing on his lips.

As if on cue, the office door swung open to reveal a petite Asian woman. Her almond eyes sparkled with intelligence, and the lavender streaks in her short black bob added a touch of vibrancy to her otherwise stern appearance. 'Meet Li,' Iggy introduced, a hint of warmth seeping into his voice. 'My wife, my soul mate, and our top-notch pathologist.'

Li offered Penn a small smile as she took a seat behind her desk. 'I've heard quite a bit about you, Penn,' she said, her having a soft lilt 'But rest assured, I prefer to form my own opinions.'

With a cup of coffee in her hand and her computer already booting up, Li was ready to dive into work. Iggy, meanwhile, flipped through the case files on his tablet. 'Seems pretty straightforward,' he said, his tone matter of fact. 'Nathan had a severe peanut allergy. The brownie he ate was loaded with peanuts. His EpiPen was empty, and there were no refills. Poor bloke didn't stand a chance.

'Right, we'll be conducting a post-mortem, my wife and I, that is. We need to rule out any other potential causes of death, though I suspect we won't find anything else,' the coroner said.

'Appreciated. If anything, unusual turns up, make sure to let me know,' Penn replied, his gaze fixed on the cold form on the table.

Iggy, flipped through his notes, his brow furrowing. 'Something odd I noticed, though. There was only one paper bag from The Grinder.'

Penn looked up, puzzled. 'And? What's strange about that?'

'Well, we found crumbs from a brownie, but no traces of nuts. However, the leftover brownie on the floor was full of them. Could be nothing, could be something. Might be worth looking into,' Iggy suggested.

Returning to his desk. His thoughts drifted to Faith and the possibility of her murder theory being debunked. Instead of relief, he felt an odd sense of disappointment. But the mystery of the single bag and the nut-free brownie crumbs suggested that this case was far from closed.

Penn dialled Nathan's wife, the call answered by her father, Simon Montague. After hearing the grim news, Simon questioned when the body would be released. Penn responded,

'We still need to perform an autopsy, just to check, but I will get back to you as soon as possible and keep you informed of the proceedings.' Simon thanked him tersely and hung up. Penn sighed, it was the same everywhere, money and position always made people feel entitled.

Penn had once thought that being a police officer in the rurales was a quiet job, but he was far from the truth. He had assumed his life now would be full of lost cars, burglaries, and shoplifting. But a friend who had moved from London to County Durham had told him the theft of livestock and farm equipment was a large problem. It was baffling how no one noticed a tractor being towed away or the disappearance of a hundred sheep, yet theft was theft and had to be dealt with accordingly.

In this rural setting, Penn found himself interacting more with the public. Unlike London, where the sheer number of people made it easy to forget who had been mugged, or which nightclub had been raided, here communication and empathy were critical. 'Damn, I will be buying a farm next and a sheepdog,' he mused, realising that he was smiling more these days.

The door swung open and a woman with fiery red hair entered like a whirlwind. Despite her middle age, she commanded attention. Penn recognised her from the shop Faith had visited. As the woman turned, her eyes locked onto Penn and a broad smile spread across her face. She strode towards his desk, 'You must be Penn; I have heard so much about you from my husband and my daughter.'

Penn gave her a blank stare. 'I'm sorry, but I don't believe we've had the pleasure,' he said, his tone formal yet smooth.

Rowan laughed, a delightful sound that seemed to fill the room. 'Oh, what a charming accent! So formal. I'm Rowan, my husband Don is the big man around here. And of course, you've already met Faith.'

Penn took a moment to take in this woman. She was nothing like he'd expected the boss's wife to be. She wore a long blouse adorned with what appeared to be rune prints, and over it, a pair of well-worn dungarees. Her hair was partially held back by a large silver clip shaped like stars, adding to her aura of mystery.

Rowan seemed to sense his surprise and laughed again. 'I know, Don and I are quite the unique pair. I've always been attracted to intelligent men, and Don... well, he likes his women strong. We're a good match on the inside, and as for the outside... we've learned to accept our differences.'

Penn cleared his throat, a touch of embarrassment colouring his cheeks. 'I apologise if I seemed rude. It's clear to see what your husband sees in you. You're an exceptionally beautiful woman, Rowan.'

'Are you trying to woo my wife, detective?' Penn swivelled around to find Donald wrapping his wife in a warm embrace, planting a kiss on her cheek. 'You're early.' Replied Don.

'I am indeed, but I thought I'd extend an invitation to the detective here to join us for dinner tonight. Must be tough, moving to a new town, starting a new job, not knowing a soul, eh?' Rowan's gaze, along with her husband's, settled on Penn.

'I wouldn't want to impose, sir,' Penn responded, feeling slightly cornered. Donald leaned in closer, a knowing smile on his face.

'I learned long ago that there's no use trying to dissuade my wife once she's set her mind to something. I think it would be easier for all involved if you just said yes.' The couple's eyes were trained on him, and Penn knew there was no excuse he could make that would satisfy this formidable woman.

'Thank you, I'd be delighted to join you,' he conceded. Rowan beamed at him, triumphant.

'See, that wasn't so difficult, was it?' she chimed, her voice filled with satisfaction. As the couple turned to leave, a sense of foreboding washed over Penn. He had a sneaking suspicion that the evening was going to be more challenging than any of them could possibly anticipate.

On his way home, Penn mulled over the idea of procuring a bottle of wine and some chocolates, hoping these were the right choices.

The high street was unusually quiet as he made his way home, passing by the library to reach his flat. As he was walking, he noticed a familiar figure emerging from a side gate - it was the man he'd seen on the day of the murder. And trailing behind him was the goat.

The man tipped his hat in Penn's direction, greeting him warmly, 'Hello, great night, isn't it? Going to be a sunny day tomorrow.' Penn couldn't help but feel taken aback as the goat, named Churchill according to his boss, bypassed his master and headed straight towards him.

Churchill stared up at Penn, and then, to his surprise, gently butted him. The man chuckled, 'You seem to have caught Churchill's eye, he's not usually this friendly with strangers but seems to like you right enough.'

Penn cautiously extended his hand towards the goat. Churchill responded by lifting his shaggy head to meet Penn's outstretched hand. A soft bleat escaped him when Penn scratched behind his ear, a sound that seemed to convey contentment.

'You've certainly made a friend there, sir,' the man said, ambling over with an outstretched hand. 'I'm Arthur. My sister Min and I run the Comfy Bottoms Cottages. And this,' he pointed to the goat, a wide grin spreading across his face, 'is Churchill. You'll likely be hearing a lot about him.'

'Pleased to meet you, Arthur. I'm Penn.' He scratched behind the goat's ears, eliciting another pleased bleat. From his pocket, he produced a granola bar. 'May I?' he asked, gesturing to the goat.

Arthur's laughter rang out. 'Go right ahead. You've probably just made a friend for life. I don't know where he puts it all. He keeps disappearing, usually near the hall. When I find him, he's always looking quite pleased with himself.' He affectionately patted Churchill's head. 'You look well-fed, but you'd best be careful. If you keep wandering onto Mr. Montague's land, he might decide you're his next meal.'

With that, Arthur attached a lead to Churchill's collar. The goat stamped a hoof and attempted to pull away. 'Sorry, lad. Min says you need to stop wandering. We don't want to upset Min, do we?' The goat seemed to consider this, then ceased its struggle, casting a last, pleading look at Penn.

'Wishing you a good evening, Penn,' Arthur said, leading the resigned goat towards the village centre and the croquet lawn.

Penn chuckled to himself. 'Well, it seems I've made a new friend,' he mused.

CHAPTER 6

The rain was still coming down, but she was resolute in her decision not to take the moped. Gripping her walking stick, a piece of equipment she had grown to despise, Faith pulled on her waterproof jacket. She donned her walking shoes, opened her umbrella, and set off towards her mother's place.

The Harrington's house was perched atop Gypsy Lane, a walk she had always found invigorating. Yet, with her persistent limp and the dreaded stick, the journey had become increasingly challenging.

The town had managed to retain most of its wild beauty, much to the delight of its inhabitants a vision Faith supported wholeheartedly. Cars were aplenty on the roads, most likely tourists trying to escape the relentless rain. Their haste, however, did little to shield Faith from the splashes as they sped past.

The sight of her family's house, Stoney Lea, brought a sense of relief. 'Mum, Dad,' she called out as she entered, shaking off the rainwater. The house had been a derelict structure when her parents had first bought it. With limited funds, they had put in the work themselves to transform it into a home.

Approaching the back garden, Faith saw her mother's familiar figure framed by the kitchen window. She raised her hand in a wave, her heart warmed by the quaint sights and sounds of home – the babbling brook at the garden's end, the distant bleats of sheep in the neighbouring field.

'Faith, darling, you're soaked through!' Her mother's voice floated out to her. 'When did you last sleep? You look like you're about to drop. Don, look at her! Faith, why don't you get some rest before dinner? We've got plenty of time.'

Her father appeared in the doorway; a towel draped over his arm. He shot her a sympathetic smile. 'Your mother's right, Faith. Best do as she says, or we'll never hear the end of it.'

'Really, I'm fine,' Faith protested, stepping into the inviting warmth of the kitchen. She shrugged off her wet clothes and sank into a chair at the table, snatching a freshly baked biscuit from a nearby plate.

'Easy there, we've got a guest coming tonight. I need some of those biscuits left,' her mother chided gently. At Faith's questioning look, she added, 'That new detective from your father's station. Met him this afternoon. The poor lad needs a good meal.'

Faith's heart sank. 'Not Penn McBride? He's insufferable. Just when I thought things couldn't get any worse.' She pushed back her chair and stood. 'Actually, mum, I think I will take that nap.' She'd need all the rest she could get if she was to endure an evening with McBride.

'Of course, darling. I've left some fresh sheets on your old bed.' Her mother watched her leave, a puzzled look on her face. Alone in her old room, Faith couldn't help but wonder why the mere mention of the detective had stirred such strong annoyance in her.

She awoke in her dark room, her mind foggy and disoriented. The distant hum of voices and laughter drifted up from the kitchen below. She quickly freshened up in the bathroom, using one of her mum's spare toothbrushes, always kept in reserve for forgetful guests. Her hair was a lost cause, so she scraped it back with a band.

Entering the kitchen, her sister Hope was the first person she saw. Hope was the family intellectual, a librarian who lived for her books. She was plain and unadorned, leaving the pursuit of romance to others. 'Hiya, sleepyhead,' she greeted her, placing a steaming drink on the table. 'Thought you were going to hibernate forever. This'll perk you up.'

Faith took a seat and sipped the hot drink. 'Don't worry, the new detective is in the snug with dad. So, spill it. Mum said you two didn't exactly hit it off.'

'That's putting it mildly. He's the most conceited man I've ever met.'

'Come on, Faith. You're just going through your 'man-hating' phase. It's understandable.'

'This has nothing to do with Ben. He practically accused me of having an affair with Nathan.'

'Seriously?' Hope chuckled, and Faith tossed a placemat at her. 'He also accused me of killing him.'

Her Mum entered the kitchen, catching the conversation.

'Faith, you know how the police work. It's just procedure. Life would be dull without a little intrigue.'

'I know, mum. But he just gets under my skin, okay?'

Her mum replaced the mat and advised, 'Just try to be civil tonight, for your father's sake.'

As if on cue, her father and Penn entered the room. The detective asked, 'Is Mrs Crawford not with you?'

'No. Mirry has gone to stay with her father.'

'As long as she stays in the village, I can't see a problem.'

'I've informed my father. As long as he knows where she is, it won't cause any trouble, detective.'

The air in the room seemed to chill, but her mother's call for dinner broke the tension.

Seated across from Penn, Faith did her best to avoid his gaze. He seemed perfectly comfortable, chatting away with her parents.

'I expect all of this is a bit mundane for you, especially compared to London.'

'Mrs Harrington...'

'You still can call me Rowan.'

'Rowan,' Penn began, his voice steady yet respectful, 'In London, we're a bit more prepared, you see. We have a wealth of resources at our disposal.' He paused, glancing at his superior with an earnest expression.

Don simply chuckled, leaning back in his chair. 'Our station may be small, Penn, but we're not lacking in resources either,' he retorted with a hint of pride. 'We've got our own set of tools and tricks up our sleeves.'

Penn nodded, understanding the underlying message. 'I wasn't implying that we're better, sir. Just different. In London, the criminals are more organised, more violent,' he explained, trying to bridge the gap between their perspectives.

'Well, Penn, brace yourself for a bit of tranquillity,' Hope jested. 'The only thrill you'll find here is buried within the pages of my library books.'

They somehow managed to navigate through the meal, with Rowan acting as a peacekeeper. The conversation was kept light and neutral, a task that proved to be quite challenging. She was well aware of Faith's stubbornness and strong-will, and it was clear to her that the young detective and Faith had gotten off on the wrong foot.

When they moved to the conservatory after the meal, the tension seemed to dissipate, replaced by the soothing scent of lavender and the soft murmur of conversation.

'Welcome to my bit of paradise, son,' Don announced, gesturing grandly at the well-kept garden. 'Nothing better for forgetting your problems than a spot of gardening. My wife's sister owns the garden centre, and she's helped me make the most of it.' He led Penn to the seats next to a large tub of lavender, the fragrant scent filling the air. As they settled down, everyone helped themselves to the wine Hope had placed on the table while Donald continued to regale Penn with tales of his gardening exploits.

'Faith, did Mirry give any reason for not showing up at the pub yesterday?' Her mother asked, a worried crease forming on her forehead.

Penn quickly turned to Faith, his eyes searching her face for answers. 'You mentioned you were supposed to meet Mirry, didn't you?'

Faith sighed and placed her glass on the table, her fingers tapping a rhythm against the cool surface. 'Yes, DCI McBride, I was supposed to meet her. But I never said she actually showed up.' Her voice held a defensive edge. 'I trust Mirry. She must've had a good reason.'

Penn frowned, his brow furrowing in thought. 'But Faith, don't you see how this could be important to the investigation? You know the basic procedure. Any information can be crucial.'

Faith's eyes flashed, her gaze holding Penn's. 'I had just discovered my best friend's husband dead in his own home. Do you think I was in the right state of mind to remember every detail?' She retorted;

her voice laced with bitterness. 'Or do people in London not have emotions?'

Donald, watching the exchange, decided to intervene. 'Look, Faith, Penn has a point. You should've mentioned this as soon as you remembered.' He turned to Penn, his voice soothing. 'But there's nothing we can do about it now. You can visit the hall tomorrow and give another statement. We can sort this out then. For now, let's try to talk about something else.'

'Has anyone considered where Nathan's medication disappeared to or why his EpiPens were out of juice? It all seems a bit strange to me,' Faith questioned, her eyes darting between her father and Penn. The room fell silent, the only response was an exchange of uneasy glances between the two men.

'Faith, darling, there's no need for you to worry,' her father reassured her, reaching across the table to take her hand. 'Everything is under control. You don't need to get involved, especially not in your current state.'

Faith pulled her hand away, frustration etching lines into her forehead. 'But Dad, Nathan wouldn't have been this careless. He would've had two full EpiPens. He knew better.'

'Everyone makes mistakes, sweetheart,' her mother chimed in, attempting to diffuse the tension.

'Not Nathan, not with something this important. And Mirry said she had just refilled his prescription. It was right there in the drawer,' Faith argued back, her voice rising in pitch. Penn interjected, promising to look further into the matter, but Faith could feel her anger bubbling up. She was being dismissed, as always.

'I hope for Nathan's sake that you don't just brush this aside. If you do, someone's going to get away with murder,' Faith retorted.

Her mother was quick to change the subject, steering the conversation towards books. Faith was relieved when the evening finally came to an end. As she retreated home, her mind was a whirlwind of thoughts, the most pressing of which was why Mirry had stood her up for their lunch date. She decided to wait until the police had spoken to Mirry before confronting her herself.

CHAPTER 7

'I've got your coffee here, sir. I do hope it's, OK?' said DC Sam Clemence, handing over the steaming cup to Penn. Penn admired the young man. Newly promoted and eager to prove himself, Sam was a refreshing presence in the precinct. His colleagues often ribbed him, but Sam's unflappable nature and dedication to his work made him a valuable asset to the team.

'Spot on, Sam,' Penn said, taking a sip as he moved towards his desk. Sam trailed behind him, a satisfied smile playing on his lips. Penn appreciated the younger man's keen eye for detail and his non-judgmental approach towards people. Despite their age difference, the two had struck up an unlikely camaraderie, even in such a short time.

Penn recalled a recent evening when he'd joined Sam and his fiancée, Magda, for dinner. Magda was a stunning Polish woman who clearly meant the world to Sam. The couple's easy rapport and infectious laughter had drawn Penn into their world, if only for a few hours. It was a refreshing change from the grim realities of their day-to-day work.

Sam's dedication to his job was admirable, but Penn was even more impressed by the young man's ability to maintain a healthy balance between his personal and professional life. It was a quality Penn himself had struggled with over the years. As he settled into his chair, Penn couldn't help but feel a sense of gratitude for Sam's presence. His youthful energy and optimism were a welcome contrast to the cynicism that often pervaded their line of work.

'Sir, there's something I've been meaning to ask you,' Sam began, his hand gripping his pen before setting it back down on the table. Sam was a tall, wiry chap, his head adorned with a crop of ginger hair that made him the butt of many a joke. He wasn't conventionally handsome, but his piercing gaze had a way of seeing right through you, and Penn knew that Sam was far more perceptive than most gave him credit for.

'You know, Magda and I are getting hitched. I was wondering if you'd come to the wedding and the reception afterwards. I realise it's a bit last minute, but it would mean the world to us,' Sam said, his voice steady and sincere.

Penn looked at Sam, his expression softening. 'You don't need to feel obliged to invite me, Sam. I would understand.'

Sam held Penn's gaze, searching for the right words. 'Since you arrived, you have treated me like I belong here, always been supportive. I'm making this sound strange now, aren't I?' Sam chuckled nervously, shifting uncomfortably in his chair.

'Sam, I'd be delighted to attend your wedding. Do pass on my thanks to Magda,' Penn said, his mind elsewhere. The conversation from last night at the Boss's house was still ringing in his ears, making him restless. He'd decided to pay a visit to Mirry Crawford, not necessarily because he suspected her of foul play, but because he felt compelled to explore every facet of this case. It was a gnawing feeling that wouldn't subside until he'd left no stone unturned.

As he prepared to leave, he recalled his first encounter with Mirry and her father. They had an air of entitlement that made him uncomfortable, reminding him of his father's disdain for the upper class. Penn knew it was unfair to tar everyone with the same brush. After all, he had friends who were born into wealth. But he couldn't help but feel a sense of resentment.

'I've always thought the French had the right idea with their revolution,' he'd once argued with his father. His father had retorted, 'You mean the guillotine?' Penn had quickly dismissed that, 'No, not the guillotine. But a stint in the Bastille might do them some good. It would give them a taste of how the other half lives.'

As he picked up his bag, he shook his head at his own thoughts. Was he becoming just as rigid and judgmental as his father? He hoped not. He was a detective, after all, and he needed to keep an open mind.

'Need some company, sir?' Sam was up like a shot. Penn was about to decline, but then he thought about Sam's knack for making people feel comfortable. 'Alright, your help with the locals could be useful. I'm still a new here, and you're a more familiar face.'

'I'll fetch us some coffee for the drive, and I heard a rumour that there were leftover doughnuts from an officer's birthday yesterday,' Sam chuckled. 'All that talk about coppers and doughnuts must be true. Was it the same in London?'

'London's a bit more varied, lots of street food,' Penn replied. 'There was always someone on a diet craze, trying to convert everyone else. I love the simplicity here, but I'm not sure my waistline agrees.'

They reached the car and set off, soon finding themselves on the quiet country lanes of Willowbrooke. Penn rolled down the window and took a deep breath of the cool, clean air. He'd quickly become used to this, and it wasn't until he'd been here for a couple of weeks that he realised how much he'd missed it in the smoggy city.

Acclimatising to the peculiarities of rural life, the errant behaviour of the local livestock on the roads was a constant source of amusement and frustration. The cows, in particular, seemed to have a knack for wandering into the lanes from the fields, causing a sudden and unexpected roadblock. 'Hold on, boss,' Sam would warn, as a particularly large bovine would halt mid-way, seemingly glaring at their car before resuming its journey towards the milking shed.

Then, there were the pheasants and chickens, whose suicidal dashes across the road provided regular tests for the brakes. Sam found humour in their antics, but for Penn, it was a source of stress and a significant timewaster. 'You've got to understand, boss,' Sam said, his voice tinged with humour, 'Out here, natures in charge. We're just along for the ride.'

Penn turned to look at Sam, his eyebrows raised in surprise. 'I remember my first driving lesson,' Sam continued, a faraway look in his eyes, 'I was eager, a bit reckless. Took a corner too fast, ended up hitting a chicken.' He paused, his gaze far away. 'It was lying there, at the edge of the road, and I... I cried.'

Penn watched as Sam's jovial expression turned sombre, a hint of vulnerability peeking through. He found himself wondering about the circumstances that led this man to choose a career in law enforcement. 'It's not the most macho story, I know,' Sam admitted, 'But that chicken...it made me realise that laws exist for a reason, and someone has to enforce them. Can you imagine telling my kids that it was a chicken that made me decide to join the police force?'

Eglantine Hall, as grandiose as the brochures depicted it, was a testament to the opulence of the rich. He detested the class system and the uneven wealth distribution in the country, yet he couldn't ignore the allure of such architectural masterpieces that drew tourists from across the globe. His disdain, however, lay in the exploitation and hardship endured by the working class to erect such monuments.

As he parked his car at the rear of the building, he took a moment to observe a group of workers emerging from a barn. Armed with an array of gardening tools, they were heading towards the sprawling lawn and flower borders that were beginning to stir to life around the main house. A young man and woman, spotting Sam, waved and shouted a cheerful greeting, to which Sam responded in kind.

A commotion drew Penn's attention to two large chocolate Labradors bounding out of the kitchen, followed by a woman clad in jeans and a brown jacket. The dogs, upon noticing Penn and Sam, swarmed them, their tails wagging in a frenzy of excitement.

'Galaxy, Twix, heel,' the woman commanded. The dogs, though reluctant, obeyed instantly, retreating to the woman's side. They sat at her feet, their eyes fixed on her with an adoring gaze, as if to apologise for their momentary lapse in obedience.

'Sorry about that, Sam, they know who sneaks them treats.' The words were accompanied by a warm, radiant smile. Sam chuckled, his eyes twinkling with mischief as he bent to give Galaxy a gentle pat on the head. 'Guilty as charged, Mrs Montague.'

'Sam, don't you think it's time to call me Tiffany? I've never been one for formality.' Her gaze then shifted to the newcomer, a soft, welcoming smile on her face. 'You must be the new DCI. I'm afraid I don't recall your name, but welcome to Eglantine Hall, nonetheless. How can I assist you both this afternoon?'

'DCI McBride,' he introduced himself, his tone professional yet courteous. 'I hope we're not intruding, but we're here to see Mrs Crawford.'

'My stepdaughter is inside. She's still quite distressed, as I'm sure you can understand. She's currently with my husband.' With those words, she disappeared back into the house, only to reappear moments later with a tall man trailing behind her. 'Antony, our butler, will guide you upstairs. I believe they're in the main room. Please ensure they're offered drinks and some of Magda's splendid cakes. Sam, you're marrying an exceptional cook. We'd be lost without her.'

'Thank you, Mrs... I mean, Tiffany. We both appreciate the opportunity you've given her to work here.' Sam's gratitude was genuine, his words sincere.

'Now, boys, it's time for your walk.' She turned her attention back to the dogs, who were eagerly awaiting their daily adventure. 'I hope to see you both again soon. Have a pleasant day.' And with that, she was off, following the dogs as they excitedly bounded towards the expansive woods.

'Follow me, please,' Antony beckoned, guiding them through a labyrinth of staircases and corridors in the Montague's grand home. Penn found himself grateful for their guide; doors seemed to appear at every turn, each leading to a different part of the estate. The Montagues, their staff, and the myriad of rooms they used for conferences, parties, and weddings were all housed here. As he walked, Penn recalled Sam's words about Magda's parents hiring the grounds for a massive marquee, a temporary home for the multitude of guests expected to arrive for the upcoming wedding.

'Wait here for a moment, if you would,' Antony requested before disappearing behind a door. When he returned, he gestured for them to follow him into a surprisingly plain room, its neutral colours and minimal furnishing a stark contrast to the rest of the mansion.

Penn's eyes were drawn to Mirry's Father, Simon Montague as he sat on the sofa next to Mirry. She was the picture of elegance, her flawless appearance and impeccable attire blending seamlessly into the country mansion backdrop. In contrast, her father was clad in casual jeans and a blue shirt, a far cry from the typical country lord.

'Please, have a seat,' Simon invited, gesturing towards the chairs opposite them. His voice was weary as he added, 'My daughter is still in shock. I would appreciate it if you could be succinct and straightforward in your questioning.'

'Of course, Mr Montague,' Penn replied, understanding in his tone. 'We're here to gather the facts, so we can progress with our inquiry.'

Mirry was visibly uncomfortable, her body shifting restlessly. Her father, a comforting presence beside her, gently squeezed her arm. 'Darling, it's all right,' he reassured her. 'Just answer the police's questions as best you can. Then, we can start to move forward.'

'I can't move forward, Father,' Mirry protested, her voice choked with emotion. 'I've just lost the love of my life.' She raised her hands as if to shield her eyes, her body wracked with sobs. Yet, strangely, her mascara remained unchanged.

Penn flipped open his notebook and jotted down the date. He had a habit of keeping a hard copy of his notes. It gave him something to mull over later when he was alone with his thoughts.

'I noticed you didn't mention missing your meeting with Faith Harrington on the morning your husband died,' he said, his gaze steady on Mirry.

For a moment, Mirry's grief seemed to give way to anger. But it was fleeting, swiftly replaced by a composed smile. 'I think it's obvious,' she replied, her voice steady. 'I had just found my husband's body on our living room floor.'

Penn gently asked another question, 'Mrs Crawford, could you enlighten us on why you weren't present at the event?'

Mirry's eyes welled up with tears, 'I... I'm undergoing fertility treatments, my husband and I...' Her voice trailed off into a sob.

Simon, her father, interjected, a glint of frustration in his eyes, 'Is this really necessary, McBride? Nathan's death was a mere accident. How is our personal information relevant to your investigation?' He reached out to comfort Mirry, but she subtly withdrew her hand.

'No,' Mirry interjected, her voice shaky but determined, 'I want to answer his questions. DCI McBride, I got a call from the clinic just as I was leaving the house. They wanted to see me urgently. We've been trying for a baby for so long.'

McBride nodded, his face a mask of empathy, 'I'm sorry to hear about your struggles, Mrs Crawford. But why didn't you inform Miss Harrington about your sudden departure?'

Mirry sighed, her gaze distant, 'In the heat of the moment, I completely forgot. By the time I remembered, my mobile was out of charge. I thought I'd go and apologise to Faith in person afterwards.'

Penn raised an eyebrow, 'It's surprising that your husband didn't accompany you to the clinic, Mrs Crawford.'

'He had an important meeting.' Mirry replied

He leaned back in his chair, eyes narrowing as he studied Mirry's face. 'Interesting... You'd think news of potential children would take precedence. Was the desire for a family more on your side, perhaps?'

Mirry's eyes flashed, a spark of indignation igniting within them. 'I assure you; my husband was just as eager for children as I was,' she retorted, her voice firm.

Penn nodded, taking note of Mirry's defensive tone. 'The day before his death...you picked up his medication, correct?' he asked, eyeing her carefully.

Mirry nodded, a hint of impatience in her gaze. 'Yes, I've told you this already. I would bring it home, fill two pens for him, and store the rest in the drawer.'

'And did he take any to work?' Penn probed, leaning forward in his chair. Mirry paused, her eyes welling up with tears again. He waited patiently for her to gather herself.

'He was supposed to take them to work the day he died,' Mirry finally choked out, tears streaming down her face. 'But he never made it. And the drawer...it was empty. Do you think...do you think he was murdered? Faith seems to think so.'

Penn held her gaze, his expression serious. 'I can't say for sure yet.' he said. 'I need to find out if he took the medication to work, or if someone else did it for him 'Is there anything else you can think of that might help?'

'This is all down to Krista and Liam. You should have a look at their coffee shop. They shouldn't be allowed to serve food that isn't up to standard.' Mirry's voice was firm, her eyes reflecting the same determination.

'We'll certainly be looking into that. Is there anything else you'd like to add?' The detective prodded, his gaze never leaving Mirry's face.

'No. My husband was a well-respected man, liked by everyone.' Mirry chimed in, her voice trembling slightly. Something about this whole situation felt off to the detective. However, he knew an imperfect marriage didn't equate to foul play

'Thank you for your time and patience.' He stood up, extending his hand towards Mr Montague. 'We'll be in touch once we receive the pathologists report.' As they exited the door, the butler reappeared, guiding them out.

Once they were back in the car, the detective turned to his companion, Sam. 'So, what do you make of all this?'

'What, me?' Sam looked taken aback by the question.

'You're familiar with the family, so yes.'

Sam hesitated for a moment before responding, 'I know Tiffany better, she's incredible. But Mr Montague...he's always been a bit intimidating, and I've never really had a proper conversation with Mirry or Nathan. To be honest, they can be quite difficult at times. It's not the nicest thing to say, but both she and her husband were quite snobbish.'

'Well, it seems we have some digging to do. I need to find out what happened to that medication. If he had an allergic reaction and his epi-pen was tampered with and his medication removed, then we need to find out who did it and why.'

CHAPTER 8

The sound of rain tapping against the window filled the room. Faith blinked, disoriented. She was standing in Mirry and Nathan's kitchen, dressed in the same clothes she'd worn when she'd discovered Nathan's lifeless body. A gust of cold wind from the open back door swept across the wet floor, sending a shiver up her spine.

'Hello, is anyone there?' Faith called out. A sense of dread washed over her. Something was wrong. The room appeared off-colour, and a sickening feeling began to gnaw at her stomach. A noise from the adjoining room, where she'd found Nathan, made her heart skip a beat.

Faith tried to turn and run, but her legs seemed to have a mind of their own. They were drawing her towards the room. She found herself standing in the living room, staring down at Nathan's body. His eyes, previously shut tight, were now wide open, staring directly at her. She instinctively lifted her hands to shield her eyes.

Suddenly, a familiar laugh broke the silence. It was Mirry's laugh. She lowered her hands and gasped. Mirry was standing over Nathan's body, holding the brownie bag.

'Mirry, what are you doing here?' Faith stammered.

Mirry stopped laughing and looked up. 'Faith isn't it obvious?' she replied, her eyes glinting with mischief. She tossed the brownie bag on the floor and laughed again. 'Poor Faith, you didn't see this coming, did you?' Her laughter echoed in the room, and everything started spinning. Faith tried to run, but her legs wouldn't move.

Faith jolted awake, her heart pounding. The laughter from her dream still replaying in her ears, morphing into the harsh cawing of magpies outside her window. She glanced at her clock - 6:30 a.m. Too early for anyone to be awake, yet sleep eluded her.

'Damn dreams,' she muttered, swinging her legs out of bed. She padded down to the kitchen, the house silent except for the ticking of the clock. Pulling the blinds open, she was greeted by the starting of dawn. 'Just the birds and me then,' she sighed, putting the kettle on for a comforting cup of chamomile tea.

As she sipped her tea, she tried to shake off the remnants of her dream. 'Mirry killing Nathan? Impossible.' She shook her head, trying to dispel the image. Nathan and Mirry had been the picture of a happy couple. Sure, Nathan was a flirt, but it was always harmless.

'Need to keep busy, Faith. Can't let your imagination run wild,' she told herself, finishing her tea. She decided on a shower, hoping the warm water would wash away her unease. She indulged in her mother's luxurious body wash and scrub, the scent of bergamot and ylang-ylang filling the bathroom.

Feeling somewhat calmer, she dried off and dressed. She glanced at herself in the mirror, the faintest hint of a smile playing on her lips. 'Not quite a Twilight Goddess, but it'll do.' She had a busy day ahead, delivering photographs she had taken for Cedarby's smallest school. As she drove through the main street, she saw her mother in her shop, laughing with a customer. Despite the overcast sky, the sight warmed her heart.

As Faith drove into Cedarby, she mused aloud, 'This place is an artisan's haven, isn't it?' The town was teeming with local craftspeople, their creations sold in quaint shops and even in nearby villages. The city centre was a hive of activity, but it was the school that held her heart. It was nestled in its own grounds, an oasis of learning. 'Ah, the school,' she sighed, 'where it all began.'

She parked her car and stepped out, and entering the school, immediately recognised the unique scent. 'Wood, wax, and...is that aniseed?' she murmured, taking a deep breath. The scent was a constant, a comforting reminder of her past.

She was greeted by Ms Summers. 'Morning, Faith. Brought us the school photos, have you?' the older woman asked.

Faith smiled, 'Morning, Ms Summers. Yes, I have the photos. They're just too adorable, you'll see.' Ms Summers was a fixture at the school. She was still the same spirited, yet stern teacher Faith remembered from her childhood, albeit with a few more grey hairs.

'Faith, dear, you should call me Edith,' Ms Summers suggested, 'You've been out of school for quite a while, haven't you?'

Faith chuckled, 'I know, but it's a habit. You'll always be my teacher.' She then followed Ms Summers to the staff room, ready to share her recent experiences over a cup of coffee and a pink-frosted cupcake.

'Such a terrible thing, isn't it? Nathan was always so careful, and Krista, she's usually so precise with her baking. Why him alone? Wouldn't others have been affected too?'

Faith shrugged; her eyes filled with uncertainty. 'I don't know. Krista keeps track of all the allergies, doesn't she? She must've told the police about it.'

The woman sighed, rubbing her temples. 'Anyway, let's not dwell on the gloomy stuff. Show me those lovely student photos. I love this time of year. Feels like just yesterday I was admiring your and your sister's pictures. Time really does fly, doesn't it?'

Faith's mind was a whirlwind as she left the school. Could Krista have forgotten to mention if anyone else had bought the brownies? She had forgotten to tell the police that Mirry didn't meet her at the pub. The thought unsettled her. Was she defending a potential murderer? It was time she had a word with Mirry.

Eglantine Hall was a sight to behold. It was part of a larger estate that once belonged to Minerva's father.

Their family had built it, and it blended with the surroundings perfectly, not too ostentatious. The walls were made of local stone, and the windows were large and strategically placed. An Eglantine rose bush draped itself at the front wall.

As she stepped into the kitchen through the side door, the aroma of freshly baked bread and chicken made her mouth water. Mrs. Kirby, the previous cook, who had retired, but sometimes helped out when Magda was off, noticed her and broke into a smile. 'Miss Mirry is in the library. Poor thing, she's been so down. Your visit will cheer her up.'

Faith returned the smile, grabbed a biscuit from the table as she walked past, and chuckled as she heard Mrs. Kirby's affectionate admonishment, 'Cheeky girl.'

Faith made her way out of the kitchen. The decor was a mishmash of old and new, antique pieces left behind by previous owners mingling with more modern additions.

The library was her destination. Pushing open the heavy wooden door, she found Mirry huddled on an oversized leather sofa, her petite figure almost swallowed by its vastness. Her eyes, red and blotchy from crying, were framed by dark circles. She was clad in a dressing gown, the fabric falling around her in generous folds, cinched at her waist by a broad sash.

'Mirry,' Faith greeted her, her voice softening at the sight of her friend. 'How are you holding up?'

Mirry's response was immediate and intense. She sprang from the sofa, flinging herself into Faith's arms. 'I'm so sorry, Faith. I've been horrid. The things I said to you, to Krista... Can she ever forgive me?'

Faith guided her back to the sofa, holding her as she sobbed. 'Of course, she will, Mirry. And I was never upset with you. Have the police been?'

Mirry nodded, her voice shaky as she replied. 'Yes, the DCI was here. He was very understanding. After I explained why I didn't meet you at the pub, he went to speak with my father. He reassured me that I had nothing to worry about… that everything would be sorted out.'

'Mirry,' Faith began, her voice soft, yet laced with a hint of concern, 'Why didn't you join me for our meal? We had it planned for weeks.'

Mirry's eyes flickered with a mix of regret and desperation, 'Faith, it was the fertility clinic. They called me in unexpectedly. You know how much I want to have a child. And then, my phone died. I couldn't even call you.'

Faith nodded, understanding her friend's predicament. Yet, there was a question burning at the back of her mind, a question she wasn't sure whether to voice.

'Mirry, do you have any idea who might have wanted to hurt your Nathan?' She asked. Mirry just shook her head, her eyes welling up with tears. Faith sighed, deciding not to push her friend any further. Maybe it was time for her to dig deeper into this herself.

She watched as Mirry tried to blink away the tears, her heart aching for her friend. All the suspicions and doubts she had about Mirry seemed to fade away. She moved closer, wrapping her arms around Mirry in a comforting hug. 'I'm here for you, Mirry,' she replied, 'We'll get through this together.'

The door creaked open, drawing Faith and Mirry's attention. Tiffany, balancing a tray laden with tea and biscuits, stepped inside. 'Sorry to intrude,' she began, her voice soft and unassuming. 'I noticed Faith come in earlier. Thought you two might fancy a cuppa.'

Mirry's expression soured at the sight of her. Faith watched the interaction, feeling a pang of sympathy for Tiffany. The younger woman was forever trying to find her place in this complex family dynamic, perpetually vying for Simon's attention. Despite her efforts, Mirry always kept her at arm's length.

Tiffany cleared her throat, her gaze darting between the two women. 'Shall I set the tray down here?' she asked. 'It'd be good if you both had something to eat and drink.'

Faith gave her an appreciative nod. She found Tiffany likable, she owed her a lot and the two had become incredibly good friends. She just wished Mirry would at least try to be civil. Tiffany was a hard-working woman, striving to be the perfect wife while tactfully refraining from mothering Mirry. She understood it would only exacerbate the already tense situation.

Mirry, however, either pretended Tiffany was non-existent or treated her as an unwelcome servant. 'You can put the tray here,' she said curtly, her eyes cold. 'And we'd appreciate some privacy.'

Tiffany offered a tight smile, nervously running her fingers through her long blonde hair. 'Faith,' she began, her voice strained. 'I hope you can convince Mirry to take better care of herself. Simon's really worried.'

Mirry scoffed, her lips curling into a bitter smile. 'Tiffany, save your pity,' she retorted, lifting her teacup for a sip. 'I know exactly how my father feels. And it'd be best if you didn't use him to pretend you care. Don't worry, step-mummy. Your money is safe with me.' Tiffany turned on her heel and made her exit.

'Was that really necessary, Mirry?' Faith finally broke the silence, her voice laced with a tinge of annoyance. 'She was only trying to help, you know.'

Mirry scoffed, rolling her eyes as she paced around the room. 'Help? Faith, the only thing that woman would like to help herself to is all of Dad's money. I mean, seriously, what on earth was Dad thinking when he married that...that...bimbo?' She spat out the last word with such venom that Faith couldn't help but flinch. 'I know you two are friends, but don't expect me to be included in that.'

Mirry continued her tirade, her voice growing louder with each sentence. 'And that god-awful coconut lotion she uses! It's enough to make anyone sick. Honestly, I don't know how Dad's friends can stand her. She has absolutely no class, no breeding. It's embarrassing!'

Seeing that Mirry was getting more agitated by the minute, Faith decided to steer the conversation in a different direction. 'Mirry, let's not get ourselves worked up over this. You have more important things to focus on right now. Like the funeral arrangements, for instance. Do you need any help with that?'

Mirry sighed, her anger dissipating as quickly as it had come. 'No, Faith. Dad's taken care of everything. We're just waiting for the autopsy results, and then we can set a date. The service will be at Saint Francis, with Reverend Dalton officiating. We're planning to set up a marquee in the garden for the wake. That way, we won't have the entire village traipsing through the house. Nathan was well-liked around here, after all.'

Faith took a sip from her glass, setting it down gently on the wooden table. She looked at Mirry, her eyes filled with understanding but a hint of disbelief. 'Mirry, why didn't Nathan accompany you to the fertility clinic?' she asked, her voice steady yet filled with curiosity.

Mirry, caught off guard by the sudden question, fumbled with her cup of tea, spilling some on her dressing gown. 'Oh dear, look at me,' she exclaimed, quickly dabbing at the stain with a napkin. She set the cup down on the table, her hands shaking slightly.

'In the beginning, Nathan did come with me. He wasn't exactly enthusiastic about it, but he could see how much I wanted it. He always insisted he was fit, even had his own doctor in London that he visited regularly. So, I went through all the tests. The doctors couldn't find anything significantly wrong, they just kept telling me to relax and let nature do its thing.'

Faith reached across the table, placing her hand over Mirry's. 'I can't imagine how hard that must have been for you,' she said, her voice soft and empathetic. 'But I'm sure things would have worked out eventually.'

Mirry shook her head, her eyes welling up with tears. 'It doesn't matter now, does it? I've loved Nathan my entire life. He was the only man for me.'

Faith squeezed Mirry's hand gently. 'Do you really think Nathan would have wanted you to be alone? Give yourself some time, Mirry. But don't ever give up on the possibility of love and happiness.'

'Faith, it's challenging,' Mirry began, her voice filled with a mix of concern and frustration. 'Look at your situation with Ben. Even with him out of the picture, you're still solitary. And don't think I haven't noticed the local men trying their luck with you.'

'True enough,' Faith conceded, her voice carrying a hint of melancholy. She paused for a moment, her gaze dropping to the floor before she lifted her leg, revealing the scar that had forever altered the course of her life. 'But remember, Mirry, it was Ben who left me after the accident. I didn't fit into his picture-perfect world anymore, especially not with this.'

She paused again, letting the silence hang in the air before she continued. 'I need time to heal, physically and emotionally. Right now, men aren't part of that plan. But someday, who knows?'

Mirry studied her friend, her expression dubious. 'Keep telling yourself that, Faith,' she retorted, her tone a mixture of scepticism and worry. 'But we both know there's more to it than just needing time to heal.'

Mirry sighed, her thoughts drifting back to Nathan. 'Nathan and I, we were in sync. We wanted the same things, shared the same dreams. We had no secrets, and he would never have done anything to hurt me.' Her voice wavered, a clear sign of the pain she was trying to hide. 'Oh, Faith, what am I going to do without him? I can't see a future that doesn't include him.'

'Mirry, love, it feels like the world's ended, doesn't it?' Faith asked, her voice soft and understanding. She knew the pain her friend was going through, the feeling of having your dreams snatched away from you. 'Feels like everything you've ever dreamed of has just been yanked out from under you.'

Mirry's eyes, red and swollen from crying, met Faith's. 'I just... I don't know how to go on without him, Faith. Nathan was... he was everything.' Her voice broke on the last word, the pain raw and fresh.

Faith took hold of her hand. 'I know, love, I know. But you will heal, Mirry. You're stronger than you think. And you have to go on. For him. For Nathan.' She squeezed Mirry's hand, offering what little comfort she could.

Mirry's response was low, barely audible. 'I wish it was that simple, Faith. I really do. But without Nathan... I don't know if I'll ever be the same.'

Faith could only nod, understanding all too well the depth of her friend's grief. As she left the hall, heading back home, she found herself reflecting on her own words. Moving forward wasn't easy, was it? And was she, herself, following the advice she'd given Mirry?

CHAPTER 9

Faith had lots to do that week. A doctor's appointment was first on her list, and she found herself sitting in a waiting room, anxiety gnawing at her insides. She'd been neglecting her physiotherapy sessions, the slow pace of her recovery grating on her nerves. Her leg still caused her to limp, her mobility not what it used to be. The medical professionals had warned her this might be a permanent situation, but she was still holding out for a miracle.

'Miss Harrington?' A receptionist called out. Faith glanced up, meeting her gaze. 'Room 4, Dr Josan will see you now.'

With a nod, Faith pushed herself up and limped towards the room. As she stepped inside, the doctor looked up from his desk, a warm smile on his face. Dr Ajit Josan was a tall man, always adorned with a turban that he seemed to match with his outfit. Today, it was a navy colour, blending seamlessly with his suit.

'Good morning, Faith,' he greeted, his voice as warm as his smile. He'd been a fixture in Willowbrooke almost as long as she had, their families bonding over their shared status as outsiders.

'Faith, dear, do take a seat,' he gestured to the chair opposite him.

His eyes held a warm glint as he asked, 'How's the family doing? Your mother, she's well?'

'Yeah, Mum's good. She sends her regards. And, oh, she's got your order ready,' Faith replied. She knew her mother's products were well-loved, and it brought her immense joy.

He chuckled, a hearty sound that filled the room. 'Your mum, she's a gem. I ordered one of her body cream sets for my wife, Gulab. We've got a wedding to attend, and you know how she adores her scents.'

'Yes, Mum mentioned that. She's made something special this time. She believes Gulab will love it.'

His laughter subsided, replaced with a more serious expression. 'That's wonderful to hear. Now, Faith, how have you been? I understand that an injury can take quite a toll, not just on the body, but the mind as well.' His tone was filled with genuine concern.

Faith nodded, forcing a smile. 'I'm feeling much better. I think I've regained more mobility.' The words slipped out so easily, it was almost as if she believed them herself.

'Why did you stop your physiotherapy sessions, Faith?' His question hung in the air, a gentle reminder of the path she had chosen to abandon.

'Look, I've been managing better on my own, alright?' Faith's words hung in the air, a feeble defence against the concern etched on her friend's face. She knew it was a weak response, but she wasn't ready to admit the real reason behind her hesitation.

The Dr, however, was not so easily deterred. 'Faith is being alone really what's best for you?' he asked, his tone gentle yet firm. He pulled out a piece of paper from his pocket, unfolding it with a sigh. 'I've got a letter here from your physiotherapist. He says you're doing well. Really well.'

Faith looked away, her grip tightening on the armrest of her chair. She could hear the rustle of the letter being folded back up, the silence in the room becoming almost unbearable.

'But you need to get used to this stick, Faith,' the doctor continued, breaking the silence. 'It doesn't make you any less of a person to admit you need help. We all do, at some point or another.'

Faith remained silent; her heart heavy with a truth she didn't want to admit. She knew she wasn't strong enough to walk without the stick. But admitting that, accepting it... that was another battle altogether.

'Faith,' the doctor started, leaning back in his chair, 'I've noticed you try not to use your walking stick.' Faith stiffened; her gaze fixated on the worn-out leather of the stick. 'Sometimes,' she admits, a lie hanging in the air between them. She wasn't ready to delve into the real reasons, the ones that kept her awake at night.

The doctor, sensing her discomfort, shifted the conversation. 'Faith,' he began again, his voice gentle yet firm, 'The real question we need to examine is, why do you see the stick, and us, as enemies?' He paused, letting the question hang in the air. 'I want you to think about it. And Faith,' he added, 'why not give the physio another chance? We're here to help you. If you stand still for too long, you won't move forward.'

Faith remained silent, her mind a whirlwind of thoughts. The doctor, undeterred by her silence, continued. 'I was wondering, Faith, have you considered talking to a counsellor?' His question was met with a swift shake of Faith's head.

'I can't see how it would help. What's done is done. Dwelling on the past won't change anything.'

'Faith,' the doctor's voice was soft. 'Your family is worried about you. You lost a child, and you've never spoken about it.' He paused, the weight of his words heavy in the room. 'Think about it, Faith. Will you promise me that?' Faith nodded, her heart heavy. But deep down, she knew her answer would ultimately be no.

Faith left the doctors, her heart heavy with a sense of dread. The doctor and her physiotherapist, Chloe, just didn't seem to comprehend. 'You'll need to work on your strength, Faith,' Chloe had said not long ago. 'Remember, the mind is a powerful tool. Don't let your past hinder your recovery.'

The past. That was a realm Faith didn't want to delve into. The accident, the pain, and above all, Ben. When she had first been confined to the hospital bed, he had been a constant presence. His face, etched with worry, was the first thing she saw every morning and the last thing she saw before sleep claimed her. But as the reality of her injuries sank in, as it became clear that she might never walk the same way again, Ben's visits became less frequent.

One day, all she got was a text. A long, impersonal text that felt like a slap in the face. 'Faith, I can't do this anymore. I can't face you, knowing I was the one behind the wheel. I'm sorry. We're not suited for each other anymore.' The words were etched into her mind, the pain of them still raw. She hadn't deleted the message. She couldn't.

As she trudged down Front Street, the familiar throb in her leg was intensifying. 'Damn,' she muttered under her breath, the bitter taste of frustration and anger mingling with the cold air. She stopped, leaning against a lamp post, her breath fogging up in front of her. She wasn't old, for heaven's sake. She was too young to be hobbling about like this.

'Damn it all,' she hissed. She could still hear the smug voices of her family, urging her to apply for the dreaded blue badge. The symbol of helplessness. The sign that she was, in their eyes, utterly useless.

She had caved in, of course, and the badge had arrived a few days ago. It sat on her kitchen table now, a stark reminder of her new reality. It was as if it was taunting her, its silent message clear. 'You're dependent now. You'll never run, never play tennis, never feel the exhilaration of riding a horse.'

'Shut up,' she growled at the imaginary voice, pushing herself off the lamp post. 'I'm not useless. I'm not.' But the empty street offered no comfort, her defiance sounding hollow in the silence.

Faith struggled into The Grinder, her eyes instantly drawn to Krista who was busily clearing tables. 'Krista how are you holding up?' she asked, her voice laced with concern. Krista paused.

Faith followed her, choosing a table nearby. 'Why don't you take a breather, love? You look absolutely shattered,' she suggested, her gaze steady on the weary woman. Krista sighed, 'A quick one, maybe. It's been mad today. I reckon people are more interested in gawking at the place where a bloke died than our grub. Food's been slow, but the drink? It's flying off the shelves.'

With that, she placed her tray on the counter and turned to one of the waitresses. 'Tell Liam I'm on a break, will you?' The waitress looked taken aback but nodded, disappearing into the kitchen.

Krista then grabbed two mugs of coffee and returned to Faith, sinking into the chair across from her. She took a long, slow sip of her coffee, the dark circles under her eyes a stark testament to her exhaustion.

'Krista, you look as white as a sheet. Have you eaten anything today?' Faith asked.

Krista rolled her eyes, 'I'm fine, Faith. Just a bit of a stomach bug, nothing more.' She paused, her gaze dropping to the floor. 'Liam's just been...overbearing. We've been arguing.'

Faith sighed, folding her arms across her chest. 'About Nathan, I assume?'

Krista nodded, her face flushing a deep red. 'Yes, about Nathan. He's gone, Faith. He's dead. But Liam...he just can't let it go.'

. . .

Faith moved to sit beside her friend, placing a comforting hand on Krista's shoulder. 'Liam loves you, Krista. You know that. Nathan...Nathan just had a way of getting under his skin. He loved to cause friction between you two. He enjoyed it.'

Krista looked up at Faith, her eyes brimming with tears. 'But I chose Liam, Faith. Look.' She held up her hand, showing off the wedding ring that adorned her finger. 'I married him. I love him. That should be enough, shouldn't it?'

Faith nodded, giving Krista's hand a gentle squeeze. 'Of course, it should.'

Krista took a deep breath, her gaze drifting off into the distance. 'There's something else, Faith. Something I haven't even told Liam.' She swallowed hard. 'Nathan wrote to me from London. He...he asked me to go live with him there.'

'Wait, when did this happen?' Faith's eyebrows knitted together in surprise, a hint of betrayal in her voice. 'I never knew about this. There were always secrets, sure, but this... this is something else.'

Krista shrugged, her cheeks flushing a deep crimson. 'It was just when he and Mirry started dating, after she moved to London. I didn't think it was worth mentioning, you know?'

Faith blinked, trying to process the information. 'So, he wanted you back, even when he was with Mirry?'

Krista nodded, her gaze hardening. 'I told him straight up, 'I'm with Liam, and he's twice the man you are. You're dating Mirry and yet you're making promises to me. That's just not right.' That was the moment I realised any lingering feelings I had for him were completely gone.'

Just then, Liam walked past them, carrying a tray laden with cups and cakes. Krista's eyes softened as she watched him, a tender smile playing on her lips. 'I love Liam way more than I ever loved Nathan. We're right for each other.' She sighed, her smile fading slightly. 'I just wish Liam could understood that.'

Faith reached out, placing a comforting hand on Krista's arm. 'Give him time, Krista. Things have changed now. It'll all settle down eventually.' She paused, shaking her head in disbelief. 'Can you believe I'm saying that Nathan's death will make things better?'

Krista was silent for a moment, her gaze distant. 'Maybe, maybe not. Nathan may be dead, but I have a feeling this isn't over yet.'

The dawn had barely broken when Faith found herself meticulously packing her photography gear. Her day was mapped out with precision; a wedding shoot first at the historic St Francis, followed by a stint as the principal photographer and guest at Eglantine Hall. She finished loading her equipment into her mum's car, took a final sip of her lukewarm coffee, and set off for her busy day. First, she headed to Magda's family home and took photos of her getting ready and leaving slowly in the car. Then she hurried off to the church.

'Morning, Faith!' a familiar voice greeted her as she arrived at St Francis. It was Sam Clemence, one of her father's trusted police officers. He was the groom for the day, marrying Magda Kaminski, the hardworking and ever-smiling daughter of Daniel and Nadiya Kaminski.

'Sam, you clean up well,' Faith teased, admiring his smart suit. 'Ready for some photos?' After they were done, she heard a car arrive outside the church.

Faith headed outside and found the bride having her dress arranged by her family and bridesmaids.

Faith turned her lens towards Magda, capturing her glowing smile. Just then, a flash of pink caught her eye. It was Emilia, Magda's sister, parading around in a floaty pink dress. Her hair, dyed a vibrant pink, was styled in ringlets that bobbed as she moved. Faith couldn't help but chuckle as she noticed Nadiya's scowl. The mother seemed less than pleased with her younger daughter's flamboyant style.

'Emilia's certainly making a statement,' Faith commented, sharing a laugh with one of the bridesmaids. As she continued to click away, capturing the candid moments of joy and celebration, she couldn't help but feel a sense of contentment. This was her passion, her calling, and she wouldn't have it any other way.

'Alright everyone, gather round for the photos!' Faith called out. She turned to her mother, who was standing nearby, and asked, 'Could you give me a hand with these steps, Mum?' Her mother, always ready to lend a hand, stepped forward to assist her.

The entire family had taken over the small village a few days prior, their arrival heralding the start of the wedding festivities. 'I tell you,' Faith's Uncle Peter said with a hearty laugh, 'The Hung, Drawn and Quartered hasn't seen business like this in years!' The general mood was infectious, everyone caught up in the joyous occasion.

Once the wedding was finished, the crowd began to move towards Eglantine Hall. 'Look at that marquee,' Faith's cousin Poppy, who had arrived for the evening said, pointing towards the grand structure set up on the grounds. 'It's simply beautiful!' The sun was shining, the flowers were in full bloom, and everything seemed to be falling into place perfectly.

As they entered the marquee, Faith couldn't help but marvel at the scene before her. 'I've been told this part of the wedding is important,' she said to herself, readying her camera once more. 'I better not mess this up.'

As the guests took their seats, the marquee filled with chatter and laughter. Faith moved around, capturing candid moments and shared laughs. The day was turning out to be as beautiful as the setting, and she was there to document it all.

The bride's father took centre stage at the reception, holding aloft a loaf of bread and a pinch of salt. He cleared his throat. 'These gifts,' he began, 'are symbols. The bread is to ensure that you, my dear children, never experience the gnawing pain of hunger. The salt, on the other hand, is a reminder of life's inevitable trials and tribulations and the importance of persevering through them.'

As he finished his speech, Daniel, a family friend, approached the newlyweds with a tray. Upon it sat two glasses, one filled with clear vodka and the other with water. He offered them to the bride first. Faith, a guest from England who was unfamiliar with Polish traditions, watched with curiosity.

One of the local guests leaned over to Faith, explaining in hushed tones. 'It's a tradition,' she said. 'Whichever glass the bride picks are said to determine who'll wear the trousers in the marriage.'

Sam, the groom, lifted his glass to his lips, his eyes crinkling with mirth. As he swallowed the vodka, a ripple of laughter swept through the room. The dominance was decided, and everyone seemed to accept it with good humour.

The couple then flung their glasses onto the floor, the sound of shattering glass cutting through the laughter. The room erupted into cheers, marking the official start of the party. The bride's father looked on, a satisfied smile on his face. The rituals were done, the blessings given. Now, it was time for merriment.

Across the polished white wooden table, Faith found herself sandwiched between Hope and her parents, a situation she would've preferred to avoid. She was idly twirling her fork in her pasta when she noticed Penn, a familiar figure, striding towards them. She stiffened, her eyes widening slightly, but he merely nodded at her, a glint of amusement in his eyes. He then slid into the vacant chair next to her father, a polite smile plastered on his face.

'Good evening, Don, Rowan,' he greeted, his voice smooth and cultured. He then turned to Hope, his smile widening a fraction.

The meal was nothing short of exquisite, the result of Massimo's culinary prowess. The chef, who had been borrowed for the day from the local pub, was basking in the glory of his successful meal. He made his way around the room, graciously accepting the compliments thrown his way.

'Thank you, thank you,' he would say, his Italian accent thick, his hands gesturing wildly. 'But I must give credit where it's due. My staff, they are the real heroes. They work tirelessly behind the scenes.'

Indeed, his staff were still holed up in the kitchen, scrubbing pots and pans, their faces flushed from the heat and exertion. Massimo, however, seemed to think such tasks were beneath him. He was the star of the show, after all. He was the one who had created the masterpiece, and he was determined to enjoy every bit of the praise and adulation that came his way.

'Massimo, you've outdone yourself,' Hope complimented, her eyes gleaming with admiration. Massimo, a man of few words but many flavours, simply nodded, a hint of a smile playing on his lips. 'It's not me you should be thanking,' he responded, 'It's the generations of Neapolitan tradition that my father's family passed down to me.'

Across the table, Faith was silently picking at her food, her gaze flickering occasionally towards Penn. He was engrossed in his meal, seemingly oblivious to Faith's icy stares.

Hope leaned in towards her sister. 'Faith,' she began, 'Do you have to be so openly hostile towards Penn?' Faith looked up, her eyebrows furrowed in confusion. 'I don't know what you mean,' she responded, her voice laced with a touch of defiance.

Hope sighed, a reminiscent look crossing her face. 'Remember when we were kids?' she asked, 'There was that boy in our class, I think we were about 12. You treated him just like this, and we later found out you had a crush on him.' Faith snorted, rolling her eyes at the memory. 'This is nothing like that, Hope. Penn just... rubs me the wrong way.'

Hope shook her head, her lips curling into a small smile. 'Well, try to be less you, okay?' she suggested, her tone teasing. Faith laughed, her eyes sparkling with mischief. 'Okay, Miss Bookworm,' she retorted, a playful smirk on her face.

The reception was in full swing, the evening sky was a pleasing shade of pink, and the smell of fresh blooms was in the air. The marquee lights turned on as the newlyweds glided onto the dance floor for their first dance. Faith was busy capturing moments, first of the couple, then of the guests who lined up to attach envelopes filled with money onto the bride's gown, another Polish tradition.

Faith, clutching a small envelope of her own, made her way towards the couple when her leg gave way. She reached out for a chair, but it was too late, she was already falling.

'Watch your step.'

Suddenly, a pair of hands grabbed her waist, pulling her back. She found herself leaning against a firm chest. Turning around to express her gratitude, she found herself staring into Penn's face. Her smile vanished as quickly as it had appeared. Penn's grin faded too.

'You should slow down,' he suggested, his hands still on her waist.

Faith jerked away, a mix of anger and embarrassment colouring her cheeks. 'I am fine thank you, I don't need your help,' she retorted, her voice sharper than she intended.

Penn raised an eyebrow, 'If I hadn't caught you, you would have been face down on the floor.' His tone was calm, but his eyes held a hint of concern.

Penn was on the verge of uttering something when the distinct sound of a heated argument from the rear of the marquee caught their attention. Faith, recognising the voice, immediately pulled away and navigated through the crowd towards the source.

Upon emerging outside, Penn and Faith saw Krista, standing defiantly with her hands akimbo and a finger jabbed in Liam's direction. She was seething, her voice laced with frustration.

'When will you end this absurd obsession about Nathan? How many times must I repeat that I wasn't having an affair?'

Liam, in return, shot back, 'Then explain the secrets? All those supposed shopping trips, but you never once returned with anything?'

Krista's energy seemed to falter at his words, her face taking on a sickly green hue. She looked exhausted, worn out by the confrontation. 'I didn't want to bring it up,' she said. 'Not until I was certain.'

'Certain of what?' Liam retorted; his voice laced with bitterness. 'That you were planning to abandon me for Nathan? He got what he deserved if you ask me, he can't hurt anyone now.

Mirry, who'd been a quiet guest till now, stepped forward. 'Have you told him you're pregnant, Krista?'

All eyes swivelled towards Mirry, her dark dress a stark contrast against the dimly lit evening. The crimson of her nails was stark against the clear glass filled with wine she held delicately.

Krista's gaze shifted from Mirry back to Liam, her husband. Her shoulders drooped, a physical manifestation of her emotional turmoil. She tried to explain, her words tumbling out in a rush,

'Liam, I wanted to tell you. But then the whole mess with Nathan happened and I feared we'd lose the Grinder. I was worried you'd jump to conclusions, think that the child was Nathan's and do something reckless.'

Liam scoffed, his disappointment evident, 'How much faith you have in me, Krista. It's a wonder you'd want the child to be mine. Is it even mine?' His words hung heavily in the air, a question that Krista didn't seem ready to answer.

Krista's resolve seemed to crumble, and she turned away, brushing past Liam. Her voice was hollow as she said, 'Seems like we've both been mistaken about each other. I'm going home.' Liam watched as his wife walked away, her figure receding into the distance towards the car park.

Suddenly, he turned and stormed past Mirry, stopping abruptly to throw over his shoulder, 'No wonder Nathan was after my wife. Who would want to be stuck with a heartless witch like you?' Mirry smiled and turned and headed back to the Marque

'Lots of pent-up anger in this town,' Penn remarked.

'What are you thinking; that maybe Liam is a suspect?' Her eyebrows raised in question. 'And Mirry too?' she added, a hint of disbelief in her tone.

'And what about Nathan? Do you think he was murdered?' Her eyes, reflecting the faint glow of the solar light, were fixed on Penn.

Penn sighed, running a hand through his hair. 'I didn't believe it at first,' he confessed, his gaze dropping to the floor. 'Murder seemed too... drastic. But now...' He paused, lifting his eyes to meet Faith's. 'Now, I'm willing to consider the possibility.'

Faith spent the rest of the night engrossed in her camera. The images it held, the stories they told, it was all a puzzle she was trying to solve. But the more she delved into it, the more questions arose. The pieces just didn't fit together, and the events of the night only added to her confusion.

For once, she found herself agreeing with Penn. There were many who held a grudge against Nathan, many who might have wanted him dead. But who among them had the motive and the means to commit murder? That was the question they needed to answer.

CHAPTER 10

With a groggy hand, Faith reached for her mobile, which lay just beyond the comfort of her warm duvet. She dragged it under the covers, squinting at the bright screen through sleep-heavy eyes. 'This had better be earth-shattering,' she muttered, thumbing the answer button. 'Hello?'

'Faith, it's Simon,' came the voice on the other end, sounding as if it had been dragged through a thicket of thorns. 'I was wondering if you could spare some time later this morning. I need some advice about Mirry.'

Faith's sleep-addled brain kicked into gear, and she sat up, pushing the covers away from her face. 'I've got a slot around one-ish, but I'm not sure how I can help, Simon,' she said, her voice thick with sleep and confusion.

The line went silent for a few agonising moments before Simon let out a sigh heavy.

'I don't know who else to talk to, Faith. I feel like I'm losing my little girl. She's changed so much since she married Nathan, I hardly recognise the woman living under my roof. Now she's accusing everyone of despising her and Nathan. A couple of days ago, she even suggested that Nathan didn't want to be with her anymore, but she won't say why. Faith, she's never been this secretive.'

Faith held the phone to her ear as she rose from the bed, padding softly to the top of the stairs. She looked down into the quiet house, her mind racing. 'How about I meet you at the pub and we can talk this through over a drink?' she suggested, her voice stronger now.

'Thanks, Faith,' Simon's voice sounded relieved. 'That would be helpful. Thank you.'

She hoped this was the right thing to do, but before she tackled that issue, she needed to pay a visit to Krista. She had not spoken to her since the wedding, deliberately giving her some space, hoping her and Liam would reconcile their differences.

The main road was teeming with life once more, the hustle and bustle adding to the rhythm of the small town. Faith watched from a distance as Hope, her sister, made her way towards the local garden centre. She knew Hope was probably off to meet their aunt and three cousins for their usual coffee catch-up. Their family was remarkably close-knit, a trait that had been both a blessing and a curse in recent times.

After the accident and the subsequent break up with her husband, Ben, the family had rallied around her. The smothering love they showered her with was not as controlling as Ben's had been, but it was beginning to encroach upon the independence she was trying to reclaim.

Lately, though, she had been feeling a strange pull towards her family. She knew they were patiently waiting for her to make the first move, to signal that she was ready to fully immerse herself in their shared lives once more. Nathan's death had been a sobering reminder that life was fleeting, and it was high time she started cherishing the family she was blessed with.

As usual, the Grinder was bustling with activity. The coffee shop was a hub of the community, a place where life unfolded in all its messy glory. It was a constant, a steady presence in the ebb and flow of her life. And today, it seemed more alive than ever.

'Hello, Faith. How's the camera treating you these days?' said Judy. It was a rare sight to see her outside of her usual working hours.

'Can't complain, really. But what brings you out here? Isn't the pub missing its landlady?' Faith asked, her eyes twinkling with curiosity.

'Oh, Chris practically shoved me out the door. Massimo's on one of his tirades again, wants to scrap the pie and peas night. Thinks it's beneath his stature as a 'high-class chef',' Judy replied, rolling her eyes dramatically. She took a sip of her coffee, her face softening a bit. 'I mean, if he's such a culinary genius, what's he doing in our small town? Surely, there are hordes of people in London who'd kill to have him in their restaurants.'

Faith laughed, a light, airy sound that seemed to lift Judy's spirits. 'Well, it'd be a real loss if he left. His food is top-notch, Judy.'

Judy sighed, nodding in agreement. 'That's what Chris said. He practically banished me to cool off before I start a town-wide riot over Massimo's changes.' She paused for a moment, a thoughtful expression on her face. 'Maybe we could find a middle ground? Let him fancy up the name but keep the dish the same. A win-win, right?'

Faith gave a nod of approval, her eyes sparkling with amusement. 'Sounds like a plan. Massimo can be a handful, but you and Chris make a formidable team. I'm sure you'll figure it out.'

'Thanks, I wish the same could be said for Krista and Liam,' she said, her eyes scanning the room for any sign of them. 'I've been meaning to have a word with Krista, but she's been conspicuously absent these past few days.'

Judy sighed 'Haven't you heard the news? She's gone off to visit her sister. Meanwhile, Liam's been causing quite a ruckus for the past half-hour. The poor staff are walking on eggshells around him.'

A sigh escaped her lips. 'Perhaps I should have a chat with Liam, see if I can get to the bottom of this.'

'Good luck with that. If you're not out by one, I'll send in the cavalry,' Judy replied, a glint of amusement in their eyes.

'Appreciate it, though I hope it doesn't come to that.' With that, she made her way towards the counter, the sound of Liam's voice growing louder as she approached the kitchen.

'Is it really that hard to make a cheese toasty? The customer's been waiting for ages!'

'Liam,' Jane, the new cook, retorted, her voice steady despite the tension in the room. 'There's no toasty ordered for table five, just a teacake.' She walked over to the counter, order book in hand, and thrust it towards Liam as he followed her. 'Look, two teacakes and two lattes. The toasty was for table three, and it's already been served.'

Liam looked at the order book, his face pale and drawn. 'Sorry, Jane,' he said after a moment, managing a weak smile. 'My mistake.'

'Time for a break, Liam,' Faith said, signalling Jane to bring two coffees to table seven. As she led Liam away from the bustling kitchen, she couldn't help but feel a sense of foreboding. Whatever was going on, she had a feeling it was just the tip of the iceberg.

Liam methodically cleaned his hands before he ambled to the secluded table at the rear of the shop where Faith was waiting. Her eyes were filled with concern. 'Heard about Krista leaving have you?' he asked, his voice hollow.

Faith nodded, her fingers tracing the rim of her coffee cup. 'Word gets around, Liam,' she said gently. 'I might not have been friends with you as long as Krista and I have been, but I do care about both of you. Maybe there's something I can do to help?'

Liam heaved a sigh, running a hand through his hair. 'I've messed up, Faith. I've messed up big time and now I'm terrified I've lost her. And Mirry...she's got a lot to answer for.'

Faith's expression hardened. 'Mirry's got her own issues, true. But I agree, she crossed a line.'

Liam's gaze drifted to the window, watching as people bustled by. 'Ever since she and Nathan moved from London, she's been different. I didn't know them as well as you did, but Krista told me Mirry wasn't always like this. She never flaunted her family's wealth, she was never a snob. Nathan, on the other hand, always thought he was above us. I'll never understand what Mirry saw in him.'

Just then, Jane arrived with two lattes, setting them down on the table with a soft clink. 'Mirry's always had a thing for Nathan,' she said, joining their conversation. 'The more we told her to stay away from him, the more she seemed drawn to him. I hadn't seen them in such a long time, I didn't realise how much Mirry had changed.'

Liam's knuckles whitened around his coffee cup. 'I've never liked Nathan. He was always flirting with Krista, rubbing it in my face that he was her first boyfriend. Krista said it was a long time ago, but she never understood how it made me feel...like I wasn't good enough for her.'

Faith reached over, placing her hand on his. 'Krista loves you, Liam. But you need to let go of this anger. Do you really believe she was having an affair? That the baby might be his?'

Liam looked down, his face pale. 'No. As soon as I accused her, I wanted to take it back. Things just spiralled out of control and when we got home, the arguing didn't stop. She told me that Mirry must have guessed about the baby because they have the same doctor. When she went for her results, Mirry overheard the nurse congratulating her on her pregnancy.'

'Is everything else alright with you two?' The question hung in the air, heavy with unspoken concerns.

'Work is hard,' Liam finally replied, his voice rough with exhaustion. 'Money is tight,' he added, a bitter laugh escaping his lips. 'Krista likes to use the best ingredients for her cooking, but sometimes, you have to make do with what you have.'

There was a pause, Liam's gaze distant as he was lost in his thoughts. 'You know, when I was young, I got into a lot of trouble.' The words were spoken softly, the regret in his voice evident. 'Nathan, he never let me forget it. Found out about my past from a work colleague who happened to go to the same school as me in Birchwood.'

He let out a sigh, his eyes darkening as he remembered the past. 'I won't lie, when Nathan died, I felt a sense of relief,' he confessed. 'If you ask me, he got what was coming to him.'

'Why would you say that?' Faith asked, her brows furrowing in a look of concern, 'Surely, no one deserves to meet such a grim end.'

Liam shrugged nonchalantly, his eyes darting around the room, avoiding Faith's gaze. 'It's nothing really,' he replied, 'Let's just say Nathan had a knack for making enemies.'

Faith leaned back in her chair. 'I wasn't insinuating that you're in the wrong, Liam,' she said, her tone soft yet firm, 'It's just... there are too many inconsistencies surrounding Nathan's death. It doesn't add up.' She paused, studying Liam's reaction. He was fidgeting in his chair now, a clear sign of discomfort.

'Isn't it being considered an accident by the police?' Liam asked.

Faith nodded, her gaze never leaving Liam. 'DCI McBride mentioned that they're investigating, but they've got no solid leads,' she replied,

'They've been asking some peculiar questions though. They suspect it's got something to do with the brownies Krista bakes, don't they?' he snapped 'Even in death, Nathan can't seem to leave us alone. Do you reckon they'll be inspecting all our ingredients and the stock in the shop? They'd need a warrant for that, right. And it's not like they can penalise you for using cheaper stock as long as the organic stuff complies with the regulations.'

'Why, is something wrong?' Faith inquired, her brows furrowing in concern. Liam shifted uncomfortably, his voice raising an octave as he replied a bit too hastily, 'Nothing at all.' Faith found herself studying him closely. There was a certain tension in his posture, a tightness around his eyes that suggested he was holding something back.

'I'm sorry,' Liam sighed, running a hand through his dishevelled hair. His gaze drifted off, a distant look clouding his eyes as he added, 'I'm exhausted, and I miss Krista. She manages this place far more efficiently than I ever could.' His words hung in the air, heavy with unspoken thoughts and regrets.

Faith nodded, offering him a sympathetic smile. 'I'm certain once Krista has cooled down, she'll return.' Yet, a nagging doubt lingered in the back of her mind. She couldn't shake off the feeling that there was more to their argument than what Liam was letting on. And she couldn't help but worry if it was somehow connected to Nathan's death.

Soon, the shop was bustling with the lunchtime crowd. Liam excused himself, disappearing behind the counter to attend to the influx of customers. Left to her own devices, Faith found herself wandering aimlessly along the main street. She decided it would be more sensible to stay in town rather than return home, only to have to come back to meet Simon later.

Willowbrooke, a town steeped in history and charm, had always been a scenic tableau of artisanal craftsmanship. The town's quaint allure was further enhanced by its rich literary heritage, a legacy that was largely attributed to the annual literary festival, a brain-child of the former librarian.

The festival had been a roaring success in its inaugural year, garnering rave reviews from both the townsfolk and visiting literary enthusiasts. However, the subsequent editions had to be cancelled due to the outbreak of Covid. The head librarian, the driving force behind the festival, had since retired, passing the torch to Hope.

With the responsibility of reviving the festival she was determined to make the upcoming editions a resounding success, a testament to her predecessor's vision and the town's literary heritage.

Faith was passing by the old book shop, a landmark in the town's landscape. She noticed Marlowe Allard, the shop's owner, standing at the entrance. His gaze was fixed on Hope, who was in the process of lifting a large box from her car. The sight piqued Faith's curiosity, causing her to pause in her tracks and observe the scene unfolding before her.

'Someone's busy I see?' Faith quipped, her eyes scanning papers and flyers.

Hope, who was hunched over a stack of posters, looked up at her sister and flashed a weary smile.

'Oh, these are just the promotional materials for the festival,' she explained, her fingers absentmindedly tracing the bold letters on the topmost poster. 'It's only three months away, and there's still a mountain of work to be done.' She paused, her gaze meeting Faith's. 'You're still on board for the photography, right?'

Faith chuckled, her eyes twinkling with anticipation. 'Wouldn't miss it for the world. You and Marlowe have put in so much effort; it's going to be a fantastic event for the town.'

At the mention of his name, Marlowe, who had been quietly observing the exchange, stepped forward and lifted the box from Hope. He shot Hope a grin, his eyes full of admiration. 'Faith, your sister is a gem. When she took the reins of this year's festival, the whole village rallied behind her. It's breathed new life into the shop.'

Faith nodded, a sense of pride swelling within her. 'Once Hope puts her mind to something, there's no stopping her. And it's a good thing too; our town needed this boost.'

Marlowe sighed, his smile fading slightly. 'I just wish my grandson would share your enthusiasm. He's constantly telling me to slow down, keeps throwing around the word 'old'.'

Hope's eyes narrowed at this, her protective instincts kicking in. 'Wait till I get a word with him. What does he know? He's all about computers. I bet he even reads books on his iPad!'

Marlowe smiled. 'You know, if Hope had her way, my grandson would be tarred and feathered in the middle of the town square,' The corners of his mouth twitched upwards, as if he found the mental image amusing. He turned his gaze towards Faith, his eyes softening slightly. 'You seem a bit preoccupied. Fancy a drink to take the edge off?'

Faith's lips pressed into a thin line, her brow furrowing as she considered his offer. 'I appreciate the gesture, Marlowe, but not now. I have a meeting with Simon. Some business that needs sorting,' she replied, her tone brisk and business-like.

'Mirry, eh, she's another one who could do with a right good tarring and feathering, if you ask me.'

'Hope, you've got to remember, she's just lost her husband. We've got to give her some time.'

Hope snorted, her tone dripping with scorn. 'Faith, you haven't been here, you don't know how she's changed,' she retorted, grabbing another box and balancing it precariously in her hands. 'And as for Nathan... well, let's just say I don't think he'll be sorely missed.'

Hope paused for a moment.

'He's bamboozled a lot of people around here, and when the Grinder fell into difficulties, he was hovering around Krista like a vulture, hoping to snatch up the sale.' The words hung heavy in the air, a dark testament to the man they were discussing.

'I didn't know that.'

'He and Liam have nearly come to blows a lot, and Dad had to lock Liam in the cell overnight when he was caught putting a brick through Nathans' office window.'

'It seems I have missed a lot.'

'Well, you're back now, but don't overdo it, you can't save everyone, Sis.'

'Poor Krista,' Faith murmured to herself, her mind conjuring the image of her friend, pregnant and alone, left to fend for herself and the Grinder if Liam ended up in jail. She found herself wishing she'd made more of an effort to visit them, to get to know Liam better. Maybe then, she wouldn't be plagued by these doubts about his involvement.

Faith arrived at the pub slightly late, her thoughts still consumed by her friend's predicament. Simon was already there, his smile broad and welcoming.

'Sorry I'm late,' Faith began, taking the seat Simon had offered. 'I stopped by to see Krista, and then I ran into Hope.'

Simon waved her apology off, his smile unwavering. 'No need to apologise, Faith. You're a good friend,' he said, his tone sincere. 'I heard about what happened at the wedding. I've been meaning to call and apologise to Krista and Liam myself.' His words hung in the air, a silent promise of support.

The cacophony of voices from the kitchen was a familiar symphony to Faith. Massimo, their temperamental chef, was once again in the throes of a culinary tantrum. His voice, a booming baritone, floated through the restaurant, each syllable punctuated with the clatter of pots and pans. Faith's eyes flickered towards the kitchen door just as Chris emerged, a look of weary resignation etched on his face.

'Apologies for the wait. What can I fetch for you today?'

'No harm done; I understand the pressure you're under. Massimo may be a handful, but his culinary skills are unmatched. I've often thought how wonderful it would be to have him at the Hall, but I know his passion lies here.'

Chris chuckled, nodding in agreement. 'You're right about that. I just wish his vocal chords were as passionate about silence as they are about cooking. I'm afraid we're losing staff at an alarming rate due to his...enthusiasm.'

They both ordered, and Chris headed back to the bar.

'Faith, how are you?' The question was gentle, almost tentative.

Faith smiled, a small, sad smile that didn't quite reach her eyes. 'It's been tough,' she admitted.

Simon nodded, understanding etched on his face. He knew all too well the struggles Faith had faced. He'd been there, a silent spectator, watching her wrestle with her demons.

'My friends, they've all moved on,' Faith continued, her voice gaining strength. 'And I'm just... trying to catch up. But it's hard, you know?' She paused, taking a deep breath. 'If it wasn't for my photography, I don't think I would have made it.'

Her eyes lit up as she spoke about her photography. It was her passion, her solace. It was the one thing that had kept her sane in the midst of all the chaos. 'I've put so much of myself into it,' she said, her voice filled with pride. 'And now, I'm finally ready to turn it into a business. To make a living out of what I love.'

Simon leaned back in his chair, a warm smile playing on his lips. 'I must say, I'm quite excited about you taking up the photography at the Folly, once it's all spruced up.

He paused, his gaze drifting off into the distance as he lost himself in memories. 'The Folly... it was a remarkable place in its heyday. I remember how it used to be when you all were kids. It was a real shame to see it fall into disrepair over the years. But, Tiffany and Nathan, bless them, they were doing a splendid job of restoring it.'

'Wait, did you say 'were'? Is Tiffany not continuing with the project?' Simon's eyebrows furrowed in concern. 'My mother was telling me about how well she's been doing. She seemed like a perfect fit for the job. The website she created is top-notch, and the whole village is in full support of her.'

'Nathan confided in me, you know,' Simon began, his words measured and deliberate. 'He said Tiffany was missing a lot of meetings, that her mind seemed to be elsewhere. She was struggling, he said.' He paused, his gaze drifting to a point somewhere beyond the room. 'Tiffany was a stewardess at heart. I thought bringing her into the business would give her a new lease on life. But now, I fear I may have pushed her too far.'

'I've been considering bringing Mirry on board,' Simon began, his gaze flicking to Faith. The pub was bustling with the midday rush, but their conversation remained private amidst the noise. 'She mentioned to me the other day that we're falling behind schedule. Offered to lend a hand. What's your take on that, Faith?'

Faith raised an eyebrow, her lips quirking into a thoughtful smile. She glanced out of the pub window, watching as the village outside moved in its usual pace. 'Mirry could use a distraction, no doubt about that,' she conceded, her gaze returning to Simon. 'But I'd be wary about throwing her into this. It's stressful. I think you should give Tiffany another chance.'

A soft chuckle escaped Simon. He adjusted his tie, a habit he had when he was mulling over something. 'I can't help but wonder if this has anything to do with the... let's say, dynamic relationship between my wife and my daughter,' he remarked, lifting his wine glass and taking a long sip. 'Tiffany does occasionally get a little jealous, but now Mirry must be my priority.'

Faith sighed, leaning back in her chair. This was the crux of the issue - Simon's blind spot when it came to his daughter. And as always, it was Tiffany who was expected to adapt and adjust.

The chatter and clinking of glasses were abruptly interrupted by a commotion at the entrance of the main bar. Faith and Simon, mid-conversation, instinctively swivelled around to see what was causing the disturbance. Their eyes fell on Mirry, who was attempting to barge past one of the young barmaids.

'Do you not recognise me?' Mirry's voice slurred, her words thick with alcohol. 'I've been coming here for years.'

'I know who you are, Miss Mirry,' the barmaid responded, her tone laced with concern. 'I'm just worried that you might fall. You've had a fair bit to drink already.'

Mirry's face flushed a mottled red, a telltale sign of her escalating inebriation and rising embarrassment. But within moments, her embarrassment morphed into indignation. She shoved the barmaid aside, her voice rising in pitch. 'Out of my way! My father and best friend are over there. This is no way to treat a regular!'

With that, she snatched up her half-full wine glass and staggered towards them. 'Daddy, did you see how they treated me?' she whined, her words slurring together. But before anyone could respond, she lurched forward. The remaining wine sloshed out of her glass, drenching Faith in its path.

Mirry paused, her bleary eyes taking in the sight of Faith's wine-soaked dress. And then she started to giggle, attracting attention throughout the now silent bar.

CHAPTER 11

Nestled amidst the thrum of Cedarby's main shopping thoroughfare, Crawford Estate Agents was an unassuming presence. Penn had first ventured into its confines in search of a flat, or as Nathan, the overly enthusiastic agent, had insisted on referring to it, a 'stylishly renovated apartment'. The interior had struck Penn as surprisingly sterile, a stark contrast to the vibrant hustle and bustle of the world outside.

The office window, like any other estate agency, showcased an array of properties available for purchase or rent. A white Venetian blind shielded the inner workings of the office from the casual passer-by. On stepping inside, one would find a cosy sofa, a coffee table littered with magazines, a receptionist's desk, and three additional desks, each occupied by a busy employee hunched over a computer.

The walls were adorned with aerial photographs of grand, stately properties from the surrounding area, creating a visual testament to the agency's success. Penn found himself yet again perched on that familiar sofa, Sam by his side. They each cradled a coffee cup, the bold red logo of Crawford Estate Agency emblazoned across the front. Penn couldn't help but think it was all a bit over the top, bordering on tacky. But then again, subtlety had never been Nathan's strong suit.

Penn's gaze lingered on the secretary, a woman who seemed more suited to the glitz of a fashion show than the humdrum of an office. Her eyes, however, were ensnared by the glossy pages of a celebrity magazine, her fingers intermittently darting to the screen of her mobile phone.

'DCI McBride,' the secretary's voice sliced through his thoughts, 'Mrs Alessi will see you now, she's in the main office.'

Penn exchanged a glance with Sam, his eyebrows arching slightly. 'Seems like someone was quick to fill Nathan's shoes,' he mused.

'Sir,' Sam replied, his voice steady, 'I don't think Mirry would let the work stop. Her father invested a lot in this place. She'll do whatever it takes to keep up appearances.'

'Let's see what Mrs Alessi has to say about her boss then,' Penn said, his curiosity piqued. But before he could knock, the door was swung open by an elegant woman.

'DCI McBride do come in,' she said. 'I've been expecting you.' Penn stepped into the office, a room that seemed to be the only one with a touch of flamboyance in the entire building. They were guided to two brown leather chairs, while Mrs Alessi settled herself on the other side of a large, ornate wooden desk. The last time Penn had been here, the desk had been almost bare, devoid of any personal touch. Now, it was adorned with family photos, lending the room a certain warmth and relaxed feel.

Sarah, cut straight to the chase. 'What can I do to assist you, DCI McBride?' she asked, her face a mask of neutrality. Penn appreciated her direct approach; it saved them both the time and effort of dancing around the subject. 'Mrs. Alessi—' he began, only to be interrupted by her polite insistence. 'Please, call me Sarah. Nathan preferred a more informal approach. He believed that the workplace operated more smoothly when we were friends as well as colleagues.'

Penn couldn't help but smirk at the thought. 'I bet he did.' He mentally noted. Complying with her request, he moved on to the reason for his visit. 'Sarah, I was wondering if Nathan had encountered any difficulties prior to his death. Any unpleasantness from clients or colleagues, perhaps?' he asked, his gaze steady and probing.

'Disagreements with clients are part and parcel of our job,' Sarah responded, her tone matter of fact. 'The world of property buying and selling can be quite tricky, and it's inevitable that someone always ends up feeling short-changed. Nathan ran a professional and reliable business, DCI McBride.'

Penn nodded, acknowledging her point. 'That may be true,' he conceded, 'but we're looking for anything that might be considered more serious than a minor disagreement.' Sarah's face remained impassive as she recounted an incident from the previous year. 'We did have a brick thrown through our office window. No one was injured, but it was Liam Hunter. He held quite a grudge against Nathan.'

Penn's interest was piqued. 'Nathan chose not to press charges, do you know why?' he asked, curious. Sarah shrugged, 'Nathan didn't want to antagonize the locals and tarnish his reputation. He also didn't want to upset Krista, a close friend, according to him.' Penn raised an eyebrow at this information, 'But wouldn't it be in the best interest to have the lawbreaker punished if the law was indeed broken?' he queried. The room fell silent.

'Sarah, do you reckon there was a reason behind all this?' Penn asked, his gaze steady on the woman seated across from him. He leaned back in his chair, arms folded across his chest, a picture of casual curiosity. The soft hum of the office air conditioning the only sound filling the silence as he waited for her response.

'If there was, I wouldn't be privy to it,' Sarah replied, her voice steady. She sat up straight in her chair, her hands folded neatly on her lap. Her gaze, however, was distant. 'And seeing as Nathan isn't here anymore, I don't think we'll ever know the answer.'

Penn nodded, his expression thoughtful. 'Was Nathan a good boss?' he asked.

Sarah's professional demeanour faltered, her gaze snapping back to meet Penn's. She seemed momentarily lost for words. 'People have said in the past he could be difficult to work for,' she finally managed to say.

Penn had decided to see if this shook Sarah's composure.

'We've been receiving rave reviews, and the business keeps pouring in. If there's any dissatisfaction in the village, I'd be the first to want to know. I'd want to correct it immediately. After all, I want this business to not only survive but thrive,' Sarah stated.

'I don't doubt the success of the business side. What I'm interested in is the work environment. Did you enjoy working here?' Penn asked, his gaze steady on Sarah, his notebook ready in his hand.

Sarah laughed. 'Does anyone truly enjoy their work? You just have to make the best of the situation you find yourself in. It's a tough profession, but it can also be rewarding,' she replied, idly spinning her pen on the desk.

'And what situation was that, Sarah?' Penn questioned; his voice gentle yet probing. Sarah straightened in her chair, her smile vanishing as she met Penn's gaze. 'Ah, now I understand why you wanted to see me. Am I under suspicion, DCI McBride? Should I be calling my lawyer?' Her words were sharp, her tone icy.

Penn tilted his head, his expression remaining calm. 'Do you feel you need one? I'm just trying to understand if Nathan had any enemies. I'm not pointing fingers at you, and I apologise if it seemed that way. You must understand, I have to question everyone who knew and worked with Nathan. We're beginning to believe that his death wasn't an accident, and a thorough investigation is required. I'm simply trying to piece together the events of Nathan's last day and see if anything out of the ordinary occurred.'

Sarah's smile returned, albeit a bit forced. 'You're right, and I want to help in any way I can. Nathan's death was a shock, and we're all still trying to adjust. I'm afraid I don't have the information you need. I am sorry I was not in the office the day before Nathan died. If I find any anomalies, you'll be the first to know.'

Penn's brow furrowed in surprise as he leaned back in the plush office chair, studying Sarah with a keen eye, and noticing the wooden name plate that said she was now in charge. You're head of the office now? I thought that was Kyle's spot. He was Nathan's right-hand man, wasn't he?'

Sarah's lips twitched into a smile as she met Penn's gaze, her fingers absently tracing the edge of the mahogany desk that now belonged to her. 'You're correct, Penn. Kyle was indeed Nathan's second,' she confirmed, her tone steady and confident. 'But, you see, Simon - Mirry's father - has been handling the transition. He decided that since I've been around the longest and know the ins and outs of this place, I'd be the best fit for the job.'

There was a pause, a silence that hung heavy in the room as Sarah's words sank in. Penn could see the pride in her eyes, the excitement of the new role mingling with the determination to prove herself. 'I consider it a privilege to take over,' she continued, her voice soft but firm. 'I've got plenty of ideas that I believe could boost our sales.'

As she rose from her chair, her movements signalling the end of their conversation, Penn couldn't shake off a sense of unease. It was odd how quickly she had shut down their discussion, how eager she seemed to usher them out of her office. He exchanged a glance with Sam, both rising from their seats to follow Sarah. It wasn't lost on them how she ensured they left the building without speaking to anyone else. It was as if she had something to hide.

Just as he was about to step out into the brisk air, Penn swivelled on his heel, a question burning on his tongue. 'So, Sarah,' he began, his voice steady but probing, 'What if Nathan had been alive? Would you have ever seen the promotion you so rightfully deserved?' His words heavy with implication.

Sarah, her back as straight as a yardstick, simply stared at him. Her dark eyes, usually so expressive, were unreadable. For a moment, it seemed as though she might respond, her lips parting ever so slightly. But then, her mouth snapped shut, her lips pressing into a thin, hard line. Without uttering a single word, she turned and strode back to her office, her heels clicking against the polished hardwood floor. She closed the door with a touch more force than necessary.

Outside, Penn and Sam began making their way to the car, their breaths visible in the chilly air. 'So, Sam,' Penn began, his gaze fixed on the horizon, 'What do you make of her responses?'

Sam was silent for a moment, his brows furrowed in thought. 'I think she's hiding something,' he finally replied. 'If I had been passed over for promotion, I wouldn't be thrilled. And she's certainly wasted no time in making her mark. Nathan is not even buried yet and she's already changing things. Her persona is well established, but it all feels a bit rehearsed. And your last question... it unsettled her. There's something going on in that office.'

Penn nodded, his mind whirring with possibilities. 'I agree. We need to dig deeper. Maybe get some of the other staff alone, see what they have to say. And I'd like to see a list of the sales from the last six months. You never know, we might stumble upon something. A disgruntled seller, perhaps. It might seem trivial, but sometimes, it's the smallest things that can push a person over the edge.' As they climbed into the car, Penn's stomach rumbled, a reminder of the long morning they'd had.

'Shall we head back for a bite at The Grinder? I'm curious to see how Liam treats his staff' suggested Penn, a playful glint in his eyes.

'Sounds like a plan,' responded Sam, matching his enthusiasm.

The day had been an eventful one for Faith. She had been running around all morning, clicking away on her camera for her Aunt Hazel's new catalogue. Hazel was the proud owner of Blooming Ek, a local florist shop that boasted an array of exquisite flowers. Her creative touch was evident in every corner of Willowbrooke, from the vases in local homes to the wedding bouquets that were the talk of the town.

Rowan's children, unlike their mother, had chosen different paths and hadn't joined her in the business of creams and scents. However, Hazel's offspring, Poppy and Valerian, had decided to stay close to their roots. They had, with the help of their mother, purchased the large building next to their mother's florist and had opened a garden centre named KaBloom.

Their venture had flourished over time, and they had even expanded their services to garden design and maintenance under their new venture, Lawn and Order. The clever name was the brain-child of Faith's younger sister, Charity, who served as a covert observation post, or rural Crop officer in Leeds, dealing with fly tipping and rural theft.

Faith had spent the day visiting and photographing the gardens that her cousins had designed, in addition to stopping off at their shop and her aunts to capture images of the vibrant bouquets and bedding plants. As much as she loved nature, the day's work had left her drained. A cup of coffee and a snack, or maybe two, were definitely in order.

It was Sam who first spotted Faith, a hint of recognition lighting up his eyes. Both he and Penn had just settled into the cosy corner of the café, with a steaming cup of coffee and a sandwich in front of each of them.

'Faith,' Sam called out, his voice carrying a note of friendly familiar-ity. 'You appear to be rather caught up. Why not come and sit with us? It's boring sitting alone.' His gaze was steady on her, a soft challenge hanging in the air.

Penn, seated across from Sam, watched the exchange with interest. He saw the moment of hesitation that flickered across Faith's face before she finally nodded. 'I'd like that,' she said, her voice surprisingly soft. 'Thank you, Sam. Let me just grab something from the counter, and I'll be right over.' Penn couldn't help but notice how she lingered at the counter, her gaze scanning the menu with an indecisive look. Was it just indecision or something more he wondered.

When Liam, the café owner, emerged from the back, Faith greeted him with a warm hug. Penn couldn't help but notice the sympathy in her eyes, a silent consolation for the man. It seemed that Krista, Liam's wife, was still missing.

Sam, meanwhile, was a treasure trove of information - and at times, village gossip. He was quick to fill Penn in on the latest happenings around the village. Penn wasn't usually one for gossip, but he felt the need to keep up with the lives of people connected to his case. So, he let Sam's chatter wash over him, storing away the bits of information that might prove useful later.

Faith, having made her choice at the counter, finally joined them. She took the seat next to Sam, her cane resting against the table. Penn couldn't help but notice her slight limp. He found himself wondering about the story behind it.

'So, Faith, what gems did your lens capture this morning?' Sam's question was filled with genuine curiosity, and Penn could see a subtle easing of tension in Faith's posture.

'Well, I've been working on a new catalogue for Kaboom and Lawn and Order. Aunt Hazel requested a fresh one for her shop. They've been swamped with work and are contemplating a website revamp as well.' As Faith spoke, a waitress set down a sandwich and a large, frothy coffee before her. She took a sip of the coffee and let out a soft sigh of contentment.

Penn looked at Faith with an understanding smile. 'I know exactly what you mean. I've developed quite the addiction to the coffee and food here myself. I believe it's the combination of fresh ingredients and the invigorating country air.'

Faith took another sip of her coffee before responding, 'I'm surprised to hear that this place can compete with London.'

Penn's smile broadened, 'I'm beginning to realise that there's much here that not just competes, but triumphs over London. The acceptance and kindness of everyone here is truly refreshing.' He noticed Faith's cheeks tinge with a blush and knew he had struck a chord.

'You've worked in London, Faith. How was the transition when you returned home? It must've been difficult to settle back in.' Penn silently thanked Sam for his tactful intervention.

'You see, for me, it's a different ball game altogether; I was cradled and nurtured by this land. I'm as native as they come,' Faith said, a note of pride resonating in her voice.

Sam, a kind man with a heart as big as his build, flashed a broad grin. His eyes twinkled with mirth as he said, 'Well then, you could certainly provide our dear friend Penn with some pearls of wisdom on how to adapt to our ways.' His tone was light.

Faith laughed. 'The secret to survival here, Penn, is simple. Be yourself, but don't go around proclaiming that London is superior.'

Penn threw his head back and laughed, the sound rich and hearty. 'Duly noted,' he said, raising his mug in a mock salute. The tension in the room eased.

Faith's eyes flickered with a hint of uncertainty as she asked, 'Have there been any developments regarding Nathan's death?' Her voice trembled slightly, betraying her attempt at nonchalance.

'We're delving deeper into the case, Faith. There are several elements that just don't seem to add up. We're out in the field, trying to uncover anyone who might have held a grudge against Nathan, anyone who might have wanted to harm him. But it's also still possible that it was just a tragic accident, as we initially suspected. Investigations like these can be time-consuming, I assure you we're doing our best.'

Faith smiled, her voice steadied as she declared, 'I'm convinced he was murdered.'

Penn, taken aback by her conviction, responded solemnly, 'If that's the case, Faith, I promise you, I'll leave no stone unturned to get to the bottom of it.'

Out of the corner of his eye, Penn noticed Sam, silently observing their exchange while casually munching on his sandwich. Turning his attention back to Faith, Penn probed, 'Faith, do you know anyone who worked for Nathan?'

Faith nodded, her brows furrowing slightly, 'Yes, Sarah. She's been with Nathan since the beginning. Hope once mentioned that Nathan had a hard time retaining staff, he had somewhat chauvinistic views.'

Penn's interest piqued at this revelation. 'Now, that's interesting indeed,' he mused.

Faith's curiosity was now aroused, 'Why do you say that?'

Penn's eyes narrowed slightly, 'I've just seen Sarah at work, and she didn't breathe a word of this.'

'Hope, you know, she's got this uncanny knack for lending an ear to anyone in distress. It's a bit of a curse for her, but she's always been the empathetic one in our family,' Faith shared, her voice laced with a hint of admiration for her sister. 'I reckon she might have some insights into this whole mess.'

'That would be incredibly helpful, Faith. I appreciate your help,' Penn replied, his gratitude evident in his tone. The conversation then shifted gears, meandering through the various happenings in the village, and inevitably, Sam's newfound marital bliss.

'Life's been a dream, Faith. Magda, she's everything I could have wished for and more,' Sam confessed, a contented sigh escaping his lips. 'I can't help but feel incredibly lucky.'

A soft chuckle escaped Faith's lips as she responded, 'Her family seems to think the world of you, Sam. I must admit, we were all a bit worried at first, what with your line of work and their history as refugees. But you've done an amazing job at helping them feel part of the village.'

Faith's heart swelled with pride for her village. It was a melting pot of cultures, a place where everyone, regardless of their nationality, found their place. 'I love how diverse our village is, Sam. It's like everyone just naturally finds their niche here.'

'I feel the same, Faith,' Sam agreed, his voice soft with sentiment. 'Being an only child, I've always craved a big family. And now, with Magda, I have just that. Her siblings feel like my own. It's a beautiful feeling.'

AS their lunch progressed, Faith, from her vantage point, observed the budding camaraderie between Sam and the new DCI. The speed at which their friendship had developed was quite remarkable. Sam had always been a discerning judge of character, and his immediate fondness for the new DCI was a testament to this. Perhaps she should follow suit and extend her own olive branch.

'I must be off, gentlemen,' she announced, interrupting their conversation. She had a myriad of photographs waiting for her at home. Plus, she was beginning to feel a tinge of embarrassment creeping in. Her initial interaction with Penn had been less than cordial, and now that she was starting to see him in a different light, she felt the need to distance herself.

'I'll have another chat with Hope and let you know if she remembers anything,' she added, hoping to make a graceful exit.

'Much appreciated, Faith. Do convey my regards to your family,' Penn responded, his tone cordial.

Faith rewarded him with a small smile before making her way out onto the bustling streets. As she turned to leave, she caught Penn's gaze fixed on her. A flush of warmth spread across her cheeks and she quickly averted her eyes, focusing on the path that led her home.

CHAPTER 12

'Hello, Dad. Yes, I'm quite alright, thank you. Eating well, making new acquaintances,' Penn responded. His father's weekly calls were a constant reminder of the concern he held for his son. Penn appreciated the sentiment but couldn't help longing for his father to acknowledge his adulthood and independence.

'Son, it's a feeling you'll comprehend when you have children of your own,' his father's voice a mix of wisdom and nostalgia. 'A parent's worry for their child never ceases. It's an unwritten rule in the handbook of fatherhood.'

Penn sighed, pinching the bridge of his nose. 'I understand, Dad. It's just...this week has been particularly taxing. I had this notion that life in the countryside would be serene, but instead, I find myself swamped with cases.'

His father chuckled on the other end of the line, 'What are you dealing with? Cow rustlers?' The jest brought a small smile to Penn's face as he moved towards his desk, cluttered with case notes.

'I wish it were that simple, Dad. It's astonishing how challenging life can be for these farmers. Livestock disappear, equipment vanishes. How does one make off with a massive tractor without anyone noticing?' Penn questioned, his tone laced with frustration and confusion.

His father's laughed, 'I haven't the foggiest idea, son. But I'm confident you'll figure it out. Us McBride's, we don't stop until we've caught our culprit, be it man or woman. We wouldn't want to come across as sexist, now, would we?'

'So, Dad, have you seen Pam lately?' Penn asked,. His father, a man of few words, always had a certain joy in his voice when he spoke of Pamela Rose. They had met at the golf course, a place that held a special place in their hearts. Penn's parents were avid golfers. His dad, a local champion, had given up the game when his mother passed away. Penn had to coax him back into it, and that's when he met Pam, a fellow golfer and a widow herself.

'Dad, I remember how you used to talk about mum, about the games you played and the tournaments you won. When she passed, I saw you retreat into a shell. But then you met Pam, and I saw a glimmer of the old you,' Penn said, his voice soft. His father had been hesitant at first, perhaps feeling like he was betraying his late wife. But Pam was patient, gently weaving herself into his life, offering support without ever pushing.

'We're thinking of going up to St Andrew's for a holiday,' his father said, breaking the silence. 'Play some golf, see the sights.' 'That sounds like a great idea, Dad,' he replied.

'Dad,' Penn began, 'I like Pam. I wouldn't mind at all if you wanted to take your relationship with her further. Mum wouldn't have wanted you to stay alone.. 'Thanks, son,' he said, his voice choked with emotion. 'Pam means a lot to me. After your mother, I didn't think I'd find someone else. But Pam... she understands. She's become important to me.'

'Then it's settled,' Penn said. 'You and Pam must come visit. We have a couple of fantastic golf courses here. Plus, I'd like to get to know Pam better. And thank her, for bringing my dad's smile back.'

'Sounds like a plan, have a good week and stay out of trouble,' his dad chuckled.

'Will do, Dad.' Penn replied. He ended the call, placing the phone down on the table. He stared at his notes, the words blurring together as his mind swirled with thoughts. He stood up, moving towards the kitchen and pulling open the fridge door. His hand reached for a bottle of wine, pulling it out and setting it on the counter. He found a glass in the cupboard, pouring himself a generous amount before making his way to the front room.

He was glad his dad was moving on; even more so that it was with Pamela. He took a sip of his wine, the rich taste filling his mouth. Penn was a man of principles, a man who had joined the force with a burning passion for justice. But now, everything seemed tainted. Had his views changed? He contemplated as he took another sip. No, they hadn't changed, but they had evolved. He had realised that not everything was black and white, and just because one wore a badge didn't mean they were beyond reproach.

He knew now, that for some, it was merely a job. But for him, it was a calling, a responsibility. He pondered on his initial goal, the one he had set out with when he first put on the uniform. Could he still achieve it? He thought of his mother's words, 'One step at a time, Penn. Eventually, what you do can make a change.'

He wondered if his geographical location made any difference. Did the lives in London matter more than the ones here? Based on his experiences so far, the answer was a resounding no.

Faith was taken aback by the sudden invitation from Mirry. The town of Cedarby was often bustling with noise, but the prospect of meeting was too enticing to pass up.

'Why not?' she mused to herself, as she hopped onto her newly acquired Vespa Primavera 50cc, its Verde relax paint job gleaming in the sunlight. She ran her hands over the plush brown leather seat, the sense of freedom it offered was intoxicating. In London, she was used to being chauffeured around by Ben in his imposing BMW. Now, back in her hometown, she was eager to rediscover the countryside that she once knew so well.

As Faith parked her Vespa, she retrieved her walking stick from the back. With a sense of nostalgia washing over her, she proceeded to traverse the familiar high street towards 'Garden of Eat'n', a local eatery renowned for its exquisite salads. It was a perfect choice for Mirry, who was perpetually on a diet. Upon entering, Faith spotted Mirry seated by the side window.

'Faith, darling, I'm so thrilled you could make it,' Mirry gushed, her voice filled with genuine relief. 'I've been unbearably bored and lonely.' Faith accepted Mirry's quick embrace and took a seat opposite her, choosing to face away from the window. 'So, how have you been, Mirry?' she enquired, her voice laced with concern. 'I've been trying to reach you.'

Mirry patiently awaited the young waitress to jot down their orders before leaning back, a frown etching itself onto her face. 'I know I've been beastly to everyone lately,' she confessed. 'But Faith, it's impossible for you to comprehend the overwhelming desolation that comes with losing your husband.'

Faith couldn't help but silently disagree. The sensation was likely akin to the loss of a man you were destined to spend the rest of your life with only to have him shatter your heart and leave you physically broken. Yet, she offered a sympathetic smile, her gaze softening. 'The loss must be unbearable,' she admitted, her tone gentle and understanding. 'But you should allow your friends to provide support.'

Mirry's frown deepened, her eyes clouding over with a storm of emotions. 'You've been through a divorce and Hope has never been married. Neither of you could possibly understand. Dad's been pushing me to assist with the Folly's refurbishment, the project that Nathan was overseeing. I've been thrown into meetings with builders, trying to untangle the mess left by Tiffany.'

Faith's eyebrows arched in surprise. 'When I last talked to Hope, she mentioned that Tiffany had implemented some incredible alterations and that the Folly was on track to be a success,' she pointed out, her voice laced with curiosity. Their conversation was interrupted by the return of the waitress, who began to lay out their food in silence. Faith took a sip of her sparkling water, her gaze never leaving Mirry as she awaited her response.

'Nathan never documented any solid plans,' Mirry finally admitted, her voice strained. 'It seems Tiffany overstepped her abilities while Nathan was preoccupied.' Faith was well aware this wasn't entirely accurate. 'So, you've been devoting all your time to this?' Faith asked, her tone one of concern.

Mirry nodded, her expression pained. 'It's consumed every waking moment. I haven't even seen what the Folly looks like yet. I just can't bring myself to go there, not with the memories of Nathan still so raw.

'Faith, have you heard anything from Krista?' The question was thrown casually into the room. Faith sighed, her fingers tracing the rim of her coffee cup. 'Liam asked me to give her a call. I told him I'd try over the weekend. Krista...she needs some time to think.'

'I've got to be honest, Faith, I'm not sure Liam is the right fit for Krista,' Mirry declared, her tone laced with a hint of jealousy that Faith had come to expect.

'What makes you say that Mirry?' Faith queried. She could sense the undercurrent of bitterness in Mirry's voice, but she chose to ignore it. 'You've always had your reservations about Krista, even when we were younger. You thought she was...how did you put it? Lacking ambition?'

Mirry shrugged, a wry smile curling her lips. 'Well, you know how Nathan was back in the day. He had a thing for the girls who didn't seem to have any drive or motivation. Marrying me changed that.' Faith frowned at this, her mind drifting back to their school days. Nathan was a product of a council estate, his paternity a mystery thanks to his mother's series of disastrous relationships.

'But Krista has proven us all wrong, hasn't she?' Mirry continued, her tone begrudgingly admiring. 'She's done wonders with The Grinder. It's not a huge enterprise, but it's just the right fit for our little village and the people who live here.'

'So, Mirry, what's the plan for the Folly?' Faith asked idly. The quaint little café they were sat in was buzzing with afternoon chatter, the scent of freshly baked pastries wafting in the air. Mirry smiled.

'Well, Faith, as I mentioned earlier, Tiffany seems to have thrown a spanner in the works regarding Nathan's plans,' Mirry began, her tone light and airy. 'It appears we're back to square one, a complete makeover from scratch. If it were up to me, I'd tear it down and erect something a bit more modern.' She said, her hand gesturing an imaginary demolition.

Faith gasped, her eyes wide, 'Oh, Mirry, you can't be serious! The Folly is a piece of village history. I remember going there with my first boyfriend. It would be a tragedy to see it go.' She said, nostalgia filling her voice.

Mirry chuckled, 'I remember him, Christopher, wasn't it? The goth boy your mum adored, and your dad threatened to arrest if he ever introduced you to drugs.' Faith let out a hearty laugh, shaking her head at the memory. 'What they didn't know was that it was all an act. Chris didn't have a rebellious bone in his body. Last I heard, he left town and became a lawyer.'

Mirry sighed, her gaze distant, 'He came back for a visit once, you know. I barely recognised him, what with the suit and normal haircut.' She took a sip of her coffee, her gaze landing back on Faith. 'Maybe you're right, Faith. I'll consider preserving some of what the Folly used to be. Or perhaps I could just have a goth makeover.' She said, her eyes twinkling with mirth. 'I could definitely get on board with that.'

Faith sat there, her mind buzzing with questions. The taste of the olive salad on her tongue was forgotten as she looked across the table at Mirry. 'Mirry,' she began. 'Did you hear anything about...about Nathan's cause of death?' She bit her lip, regretting the words as soon as they left her mouth. She didn't want to upset Mirry, but the question had been eating at her.

Mirry paused, her fork halfway to her mouth. She set it down, her eyes meeting Faith's with an unreadable expression. 'No, Faith,' she said quietly, 'I haven't heard anything yet.' The rest of the meal passed in relative silence; the earlier chit-chat replaced by a heavy tension.

As soon as the last bite of dessert was finished, Mirry stood up abruptly. 'I'm late,' she announced, her voice brisk. 'I have an appointment with a friend. She's just opened a spa, not far from Cedarby.' She reached for her purse, pulling out her wallet.

Faith started to protest, but Mirry held up a hand. 'No, Faith. I insist,' she said firmly. She knew Faith was still finding her feet in her new business. 'Daddy's started giving me an allowance until all the financial matters are sorted out. I can afford it.' With that, she paid the bill and left.

Faith found herself lost in thought, wandering the main street of the town she was so familiar with. A newly opened boutique caught her attention, its window display a stark contrast to the quaint, old-fashioned shops she remembered. She paused, taking a moment to examine her reflection in the glass. When had she last bought something new? She thought of the wardrobe back in her London flat, filled with business suits and glamorous dresses from a life she no longer led.

'Maybe it's time for a change,' she mused aloud. She thought about Hope and her mother, who were always inviting her to join them on their shopping trips. Maybe she should take them up on their offer. Maybe she should step into these boutiques, try on clothes she wouldn't usually wear, experiment with new styles. Just because she was back in the village, didn't mean she had to give up on fashion.

That's when she spotted Sarah Alessi, laden down with shopping bags and struggling to pick up a fallen one. An idea formed in her mind. She remembered what Sam and Penn had mentioned about Nathan's office. Perhaps she could do a little detective work of her own. After all, she reasoned, what harm could it do?

With a newfound sense of purpose, she strode towards Sarah, ready to offer her assistance and, hopefully, gain some insight into the recent happenings at work. After all, she thought, a woman's touch could make all the diff

CHAPTER 13

'Sorry, Faith, you've caught me in a right pickle. I had everything stacked just so, and then this lad, face buried in his mobile and those earbuds in, decided I was in his way. Pushed right past me, he did. Didn't even offer to help me pick up the mess, just carried on like I wasn't even there.'

Faith grimaced in sympathy. 'It's maddening, isn't it? Sometimes I feel like I've woken up in a world I don't recognise.'

Sarah chuckled, shaking her head. 'I'd like to say it was better in our day, but that'd be a fib.'

'I know what you mean. I swear, I'm turning into my mum, and the thought scares the life out of me.'

'Oh, your mum's a force of nature, Faith. I'd count myself lucky to have even a smidge of her spirit. She's a remarkable woman, your mum.'

Rowan Harrington, Faith's mother, was well-loved by most who knew her. But it was a different story when you were the one who had to live with her. Faith loved her parents dearly, but her mother's larger-than-life personality could be overwhelming. She was more like her father, calm and steady, while her mother was a whirlwind of energy and determination.

'I know people love Mum,' Faith admitted. 'But living with her was a different story. She still treats me like a child sometimes, and it drives me mad. But I wouldn't have her any other way. Now, how about a drink? I think we could both use one.'

'Actually, Faith, I could do with a drink. There's a rather decent coffee shop just across the road. It's no Grinder, mind you, but then again, what can compete with the perfection of our local haunt? This one, I'd say, comes in at a close second, or third if you count the heavenly concoctions Massimo whips up.' Sarah's eyes twinkled with a hint of mischief as she spoke.

'True,' Faith agreed, her voice laced with a hint of nostalgia, 'We're rather spoilt for choice back home. It's a tough act to follow but I'm game for trying something new, so lead on.' She gave a small nod, her eyes reflecting the excitement of a new adventure.

Upon entering the café, they made a beeline for the window seats. 'I've always been a bit of a people watcher,' Sarah confessed with a chuckle, her gaze scanning the bustling street outside. 'Ah, me too.' Faith admitted, her eyes following Sarah's. They ordered their lattes, and as the rich aroma of coffee filled the air, Sarah seemed to visibly relax.

Once settled, they dove into a conversation about their quaint village, Sarah's son and daughter, and their respective accomplishments. It was a comfortable chatter. But as Sarah's shoulders began to loosen, Faith decided to steer the conversation in a different direction.

'So, how's work been? Must be tough after Nathan's passing. Has everything settled down? And by the way, congrats on your promotion. Even if Nathan hadn't... well, you know... I'm confident that you would've earned it anyway.' Faith's voice was gentle, her words carefully chosen.

Sarah paused, her coffee cup halfway to her lips. 'I know I should say it's been tough, and don't get me wrong, I miss Nathan but work, work has been incredible. I feel like I'm finally able to reach my full potential. We were worried it would affect sales, but we're busier than ever.' Her voice held a note of surprise, as if she herself couldn't quite believe it.

'Nathan was a handful, wasn't he? I remember him from school. My friend...' Faith's voice trailed off. She hadn't said best friend. Had their relationship changed? 'Well, she did end up marrying him, didn't she?' she finished, a faraway look in her eyes.

'The police came around, their faces stern and probing, asking questions that made my skin crawl,' She confessed, stirring her coffee nervously. 'It was almost as if they thought I wanted the job so much, I'd have murdered him for it.' She let out a bitter chuckle, her gaze dropping to the swirling brown liquid in her cup. 'I was less than forthcoming, I admit. Too defensive, perhaps. There was more I could have told them, more that might have helped.'

Faith leaned forward, her eyes sharp. 'What else could you have told them?' she asked, her voice soft.

Sarah hesitated, her grip on the coffee cup tightening. 'Let's just say, he wasn't averse to a little blackmail. He used it to climb the corporate ladder, to manipulate people in his personal life. We lost a lot of good staff because he couldn't keep his hands to himself.'

'Blackmail? How on earth did you come to know about this, Sarah? Did any of the women dare to lodge a complaint against him?' Faith inquired, her eyebrows knitted together in a frown, her eyes reflecting the shock she felt.

Sarah shook her head, her lips pursed in a grim line. 'No one had the courage to do so. We all needed our jobs, Faith. And Nathan... he could turn your life into a living hell if you didn't dance to his tunes,' she explained. 'That's why he always had a bevy of beauties around him. I detested the way he treated us all.'

Sarah's voice trailed off as she recalled the past. 'Nathan had a knack for gathering information, a lot of it. With the new recruits, he would play the good boss, lulling them into a false sense of security. And once they let their guard down, he would extract all the information he could. Working there was like being in a ruthless competition. One had to fight tooth and nail for any position, and Nathan... he wasn't averse to people offering him juicy titbits about others to climb up the ladder. He had dirt on everyone and there was no escaping from his clutches.'

Faith asked the question that was on her mind. 'Did he try to blackmail you, Sarah?'

For a split second, it seemed like Sarah was going to talk, to confide in Faith. But then, she straightened up in her chair, her expression hardening. Faith could see it, the moment Sarah's walls came up, her eyes turning cold and distant.

'Look, it doesn't really matter now, does it? Nathan's in the grave, so to speak. What harm can he possibly do from there?' Sarah's voice was firm, her words punctuated with a sense of finality that resonated in the small, dimly lit café. Her fingers tightly gripped the handle of her leather bag, her knuckles turning a shade paler. 'Secrets have a way of staying buried, just like the dead. No one's life needs to get ruined over it.' She paused, her gaze meeting Faith's. 'But here's a little piece of advice, my dear. Be careful who you put your trust in. Snakes don't make good friends. Their bites can be deadly.'

With a sigh, she began to stand, her chair scraping against the worn-out wooden floor. 'But it seems this time, Nathan bit off more than he could chew.' She threw a meaningful glance at Faith, her lips curling into a wry smile. Her eyes, however, remained cold, devoid of any mirth.

'I really must be going now, my eldest is coming over for dinner.' Faith, who had been listening intently, rose from her chair as well.

She followed Sarah to the counter, her mind racing with the revelations of the afternoon.

After they had paid their bills, they headed for the door. The air was chilly, carrying with it the promise of a colder evening. Sarah started to walk away, her heels clicking against the cobblestone pavement. But then, she paused and turned around.

'I'm just relieved that my workers are safe now. We all can finally put this unfortunate incident behind us.' As she said those words, her eyes were downcast.

'Sarah,' Faith began, 'the police... they're saying it could be murder.'

'How can they possibly prove it?' she demanded, her voice shaking slightly. 'Nathan... Nathan had an allergy, and he hadn't got his meds.'

Faith studied Sarah, her mind racing. Was that fear she saw in this woman's eyes? Or was it something more sinister? She opened her mouth to speak, to question Sarah further, but she was cut off as Sarah abruptly turned.

'I'm sorry,' she muttered, avoiding Faith's gaze. 'I... I have to go.'

Faith was left alone, her mind spinning. How had Sarah known that Nathan hadn't taken his medication? And why had she looked so scared? Or was it guilt that had flashed in her eyes? The questions swirled in her mind, each one more troubling than the last.

With the picturesque scenery unfolding around her, Faith navigated the winding roads leading back home. She was deep in thought but no matter how hard she tried, she couldn't seem to fill in the blanks. 'Sarah seemed content with her life?' she mused aloud. Sarah's life was picture perfect: a loving husband who was a firefighter in Cedarby, two successful children, each carving their niche in the world.

Her son, living in France, was the proud owner of a bed and breakfast that had garnered rave reviews from Faith's parents a few years ago. Her daughter, on the other hand, was making waves with her newly established vineyard, the first in the area.

Faith's fingers tightened on the handlebars as she thought about Sarah's recent promotion. She had stepped into Nathan's shoes, taking over the reins of the office. It was a job Sarah had always wanted, but was it enough to drive her to murder? Could Sarah really kill for a promotion? Faith pondered. She remembered the guarded look in Sarah's eyes, the way she had hesitated. There was definitely something Sarah was hiding, something crucial.

Nathan, despite his flirtatious nature, had always been surrounded by willing partners. He was charming, charismatic, and had a way with women. But could he have been the type to force himself on a woman? Faith shook her head, dismissing the thought almost immediately. 'No... Nathan... he wouldn't...' she murmured, her voice trailing off. Nathan might have been a lot of things, but a physical abuser? That was something Faith was certain he was incapable of. Yet, the doubt lingered, a nagging thought at the back of her mind, refusing to be silenced.

As the familiar sights of home came into view, the figures of Arthur and Minerva emerged, standing rigidly on the pavement as if they had been carved from the very stone beneath their feet. Faith pulled over to see how they were.

'How did the encounter with our French guests pan out?' Faith asked, her voice laced with a hint of amusement. Minerva, a formidable figure with a face that seemed permanently etched into a scowl, let out a disgruntled grunt.

'Those French think they've checked into some fancy five-star establishment,' she grumbled, her voice as rough as gravel. 'They've been demanding the most ridiculous things. Hypoallergenic pillows, can you believe it? If their allergies are as severe as they claim, they should've stayed in the city instead of venturing into the countryside. And the lot of them are vegetarians. I was half-tempted to serve them a plate of fresh grass, which would've given them a good shock.'

Arthur, chimed in then. 'Now, Min, it's the trend these days, isn't it? Eating healthily and all that.' His voice was a soothing balm to Minerva's harsh tones.

Minerva whirled around to face him, her eyebrows shooting up towards her hairline. 'They looked like walking skeletons to me, all skin and bones. And why were they as pale as ghosts? They're from France, aren't they supposed to be sun-kissed and glowing?'

Arthur shrugged, a small smile playing on his lips. 'Perhaps they're worried about skin cancer, Min,' he suggested, earning a sceptical look from his sister.

'And how do you suddenly become an expert on all this?' Minerva demanded, her gaze narrowing suspiciously.

Arthur simply shrugged again, his smile widening. 'I've been spending some time at the library. Miss Hope has been teaching me how to use the computer. It's quite fascinating, all the things you can learn from it. And there are videos too.' His eyes sparkled with the excitement of newfound knowledge, effectively diffusing the tension in the air.

Faith felt the unexpected chill of a cold nose nudging her hand, breaking her out of her thoughts. She turned to find Churchill, looking up at her with innocent eyes. 'Oh, there you are, boy,' she greeted, her voice softening at the sight of him. 'What kind of trouble have you been stirring up today?' She added, a playful twinkle in her eyes.

'Mischief as usual,' Minerva, interjected. Her tone was stern, a stark contrast to Faith's. 'Reverend Dalton, the vicar from St Michael's, rang us up. It seems that this animal had wandered into the church and decided to feast on the flowers by the font.' Churchill, sensing the disapproval in Minerva's voice, instinctively sought refuge behind Faith, his large eyes peeking out from behind her.

'But he wasn't causing any harm,' Arthur defended, his hand instinctively reaching down to stroke Churchill's head. 'The flowers weren't even fresh. Mrs. Dixon, the vicar's wife, found it rather amusing. She said Churchill was merely trying to recycle the flowers in his own unique way, and she had planned to replace them later today anyway.'

Minerva's face hardened at the mention of Mrs. Dixon. 'Cozzie Dixon is a frivolous woman who should show more respect for the church. And beads in her hair? It's unseemly. What is the world coming to?' she huffed, her disapproval clear.

Faith shrugged. 'I've only met Mrs. Dixon once, but mum says she's like a breath of fresh air, not at all stuffy like Reverend Moxon's wife.' She paused, her gaze falling on Churchill who was now comfortably nestled by her side.

Arthur, a man of few words, leaned against the old wooden fence, his eyes squinting against the waning sun. 'Now, Reverend Moxon, he was a character, wasn't he? Never one to sugarcoat things. Always talking about the end times and damnation. No sun and flowers with him.'

He chuckled, making a low rumble. 'Scared everyone half to death, he did. Especially poor Churchill here.' He gestured towards the goat who had momentarily paused his explorations to look at Arthur.

'Churchill seems to be making lots of new friends. I saw that new police officer running one morning, up at the crack of dawn. Churchill likes him too.'

'Too many new people in this village, it will all turn bad, you wait.' Replied Min turning to Faith. 'Not including you, your parents raised all three of you girls well, good woman your mum.' With that, she marched off over a stile and began to trudge down the field. Faith turned to Arthur, who had pulled a biscuit out of his pocket sharing it with his funny companion.

'Min, is set in her ways, she doesn't mean anything bad by it, it's just how she is.'

Faith laughed. 'At least I am in her good books, and I intend to stay there.' Turning to Churchill she said.

'Churchill, a bit of advice, there are flowers everywhere, leave the church alone, Ok?'

The goat gave a little murmur then jumped up over the style and turned while his beloved companion Arthur joined him. 'Take care Faith, and it's nice having you home again.'

Before going home Faith decided to go see her mum. Her parents had decided to go for a weekend break and Faith said she would take care of the shop on Saturday, which was usually a busy day. Her mum had kept her for over an hour, showing where the stock was and explaining how to use the cantankerous cash machine she had recently bought.

'Your mother has bought a new computerized till, it's easier for receipts and everything.' Faith's father had laughed at his wife telling her it was about time she came out of the dark ages. Her mother had taken a leap into the future. It had all started well, until her mother and the till had a falling out and now it was public enemy number one.

'If you get stuck, ask Pink, young ones are so much better with all this new technology.' Faith had to smile when she thought of mum's assistant. Pink Brannick didn't have pink hair, nor was she a singer. She was a quiet girl and not at all like her family. Pink was small and delicate, with mousy hair and green eyes like her father, Callum.

Her family were from a long line of hairdressers, starting with Marilyn who was the first to start up the business back in the 50s. Then her daughter Madonna had taken over and renamed the shop Dyes and Dolls. They were all hoping that Pink would join in the business, but she did not accept that mantle and much preferred to work with Rowan and study archaeology at the university.

'So, what's been happening in your world today?' her mother queried, her voice carrying a note of habitual curiosity. Faith hesitated, her gaze drifting to the window as she considered her response.

'I had a meeting with Mirry today, and with Sarah,' she began, her voice hesitant. Her mother's eyebrows arched in surprise, but she remained silent, waiting for Faith to continue. 'Mirry... she's changed, Mum. She's not the girl we used to know.'

Her mother's hands stilled on the creams she was passing to Faith for the shelf. A look of concern crossed her features.

Her mother sighed, her gaze distant. 'She was such a sweet child. Her mother's death hit her hard, and then her father... he started spoiling her. Too much, I think. It changed her.' Her voice was heavy with regret, and Faith felt a pang of sympathy. They had all lost something when Mirry changed.

'Raising a child all by yourself after losing your wife, it's tough,' her mum said, her eyes softening with empathy. Her hands were busy with a box of new inventory, but her attention was fully on the conversation.

'There's no guidebook for that, is there?' replied Faith.

'No, there isn't Faith,' her mother replied. 'I had hoped that her friendship with you and your sisters would bring about some change, some semblance of the girl she used to be. But her heart, it was always with Nathan. And when she returned, she was no longer the Mirry we knew.'

The small bell above the door jingled, announcing the arrival of a customer. Both women paused their conversation as a middle-aged woman with a kind smile entered the shop. She made her purchase, exchanging pleasantries with Faith's mother, and left as quietly as she had come. The bell jingled again.

After the customer had left, her mother heaved a sigh. 'I thought things would get better when Simon remarried,' she confessed, her gaze fixed on a point in the distance, lost in a sea of memories. 'Mirry had left for university, then moved to London. Things seemed to have calmed down, at least for a while.'

Faith, meanwhile, had been busy unpacking a new shipment. She paused, a delicate glass of essential oils in her hand. The question had been nagging at her for a while now. 'But why do you think Mirry hates Tiffany?' she asked. The glass seemed to weigh heavily in her hand, mirroring the gravity of her question.

'She was an only child and a spoilt little thing, always had been. It was just her and her dad after her mother died. Just the two of them against the world.' She looked around the room, her gaze distant. 'Mirry, she was so embarrassed by the age difference between her father and Tiffany. And, oh, how she worshipped her mother, Lucinda. She expected her dad to do the same, to keep her on this pedestal, untouched and untarnished.'

'But mum,' she interjected, her voice a soft plea for understanding. 'He couldn't stay single forever. That's just... it's just cruel to expect that of him.'

Her mother nodded; her lips pursed in thought. 'Mirry saw it as an act of betrayal. She saw Tiffany as this seductress, this home wrecker who had lured her father away from the memory of her beloved Mother.' She paused, her gaze flickering towards the window. 'The thing was, Lucinda had had numerous affairs. I knew about them, so did Hazel. But Mirry... Mirry was kept in the dark. Maybe if she knew, maybe things would have turned out differently for Tiffany.'

Faith's eyes widened in surprise, her heart pounding in her chest. 'Mum, I... I never knew that.'

Her mother held up a hand, her expression serious. 'And you must never tell her. She needs her father now more than ever. This... this would just complicate things further.'

'I won't,' she promised, her voice shaking slightly. 'I promise, mum.'

Faith's mind was a whirlwind as she stepped over the threshold of her home, her mother's revelations were astounding. She remembered Mirry's mother, Lucinda, a woman who seemed to have stepped out of a Pre-Raphaelite painting. Lucinda had always struck Faith as a somewhat clingy woman, lacking in any discernible skills or abilities, yet she was treated like a priceless gem, adored, and pampered by all around her.

Faith's mother had painted a vivid picture of the grand soirees that had once filled their home. Lucinda, the belle of the ball, would flit from guest to guest, her laughter ringing out above the hum of conversation. She was the sun around which the rest of the party orbited, soaking in the adoration and flattery with a grace that was almost regal.

But now, as Faith sank into the plush sofa in her living room, she couldn't help but feel a pang of pity for Lucinda. To be so loved, yet so dependent on the validation of others, and Mirry had inherited these traits too.

But what if Nathan was a player? A thought that sent a shiver down her spine, a cold realisation that made her stomach churn.

'Could Mirry have found out?' she muttered to herself. She could almost picture it, the shock and betrayal in Mirry's eyes. But was it enough to push her to murder? Had Mirry changed so drastically, transformed into someone capable of such a heinous act?

Or was it Sarah, sweet and innocent Sarah, with her soft smiles and gentle words. Could she harbour such darkness within her? Or Liam, the ever-loyal Liam, always at Krista's side. Could he have been driven to such an extreme?

The more she thought, the more the situation seemed to spiral out of control. One thing was becoming painfully clear to her - a murder had been committed. The question was, by whom?

CHAPTER 14

Saturday dawned cool, yet bright, the kind that subtly suggested one might need the comforting embrace of a warm sweater. Being attuned to these undertones, Faith slipped into her most cherished knitted jumper while getting ready to unlock her mother's busy shop.

However, as the morning wore on, and the small store began to swell with customers, she found herself regretting her choice of attire. The shop was a hive of activity, filled to the brim with towns-folk seeking skincare solutions. 'Has everyone's skin suddenly rebelled?' she wondered aloud, mopping her brow with the back of her hand. 'Or has the whole town run out of shower cream at the same time?'

'Excuse me,' a customer interrupted her thoughts, holding up a jar of face cream with a questioning look. 'Is this vegan?' Faith blinked at the woman, momentarily nonplussed. Why on earth would that matter? It's not like she was going to eat it.

Just as Faith was about to voice her confusion, Pink, swooped in to save the day. 'Absolutely,' Pink assured the customer, her voice filled with confidence. 'All our products are vegan. They're made with a variety of herbs and extracts, each specifically chosen for their beneficial properties.'

Faith watched in awe as Pink continued to wax lyrical about the virtues of their products. She had no idea Pink possessed such a wealth of knowledge. As the customer left, satisfied with her purchase, Faith made a mental note to ask Pink for a crash course on their product range. After all, who knew when she would need to know whether their products were vegan or not?

'Pink, your memory is astounding! I can't fathom how you recall every small detail. I'm grateful, nonetheless. Losing mum a sale would have been dreadful,' said Faith, her eyes reflecting gratitude. The shop was filled with the soft hum of the overhead fan, and the rustling of papers as Pink continued to sort through the invoices.

'Oh, it's nothing really. You get the hang of it after a while. Plus, your mum is an excellent mentor. She makes learning all of this a breeze,' replied Pink, a warm smile playing on her lips. She paused for a moment, her gaze drifting towards the window. 'By the way, how's Mirry holding up? It must be tough.' The concern in her voice was palpable.

Faith sighed, her shoulders slumping slightly. 'She's struggling, Pink. It's going to take some time for her to come to terms with everything.

Suddenly, Pink broke the silence, her voice filled with disdain. 'I know it's not right to speak ill of the dead, but that Nathan, he was a vile man, a real octopus.' Faith turned in shock, her eyes wide at Pink's unexpected outburst.

'Pink, why would you say that? Did something happen between you two?' Faith asked.

Pink hesitated, her hands paused over the stack of papers. 'He...he used to try and touch me when I worked at mum's shop.' The revelation hung in the air, heavy and stifling.

'Pink, you left when you went to college. You must have been only sixteen. Why didn't you say anything?' Faith asked.

'Mirry was a good customer and Nathan was known for holding a grudge. I was due to leave soon, so I just kept out of his way,' Pink responded, her voice steady but her eyes betraying the fear she had felt back then.

'Was he okay with you here? Her eyes, full of worry, searched Pink's face for any hint of discomfort.

Pink offered a reassuring smile. 'Faith, even Nathan wouldn't have dared make a move here, not with a boss like your mum around.' Her voice was steady, her words calculated, as she tried to alleviate Faith's concerns. 'I reckon Nathan was a bit scared of her, and your mum, well, she did nothing to dispel that fear. To say he wasn't one of your mum's favourite people would be an understatement. He wouldn't even make her top 100 list.' Pink laughed.

'I'm really sorry, Pink,' Faith said finally. 'It's not good to feel unsafe at work.'

'Don't worry, Faith, I love working here. It's like a sanctuary to me, a place where I can balance my passion for archaeology and my need to make a living. Your mum, she's a gem of a boss. Working around my archaeological digs, she never made it feel like a chore.' She paused, her eyes reflecting the sincerity of her words. 'Can we not mention this. Raking up the past would only complicate things.'

Faith nodded, her lips curving into a thin smile. 'I won't breathe a word about it,' she assured, her gaze steady. 'And like you said, it's better to avoid unnecessary complications.'

The shop was quiet now, the only sound the distant hum of the refrigerator in the backroom. Faith made herself a sandwich and sat down at the small wooden table, her mind racing with the day's revelations. The sandwich tasted like cardboard in her mouth, her appetite lost to her swirling thoughts. It was then, amidst the quiet hum of the refrigerator and the lingering scent of lavender and rosemary, that she made the decision to call Penn.

Her fingers trembled slightly as she dialled his number, her heart pounding in her chest. Their relationship was... precarious, to say the least, but she felt he deserved honesty.

The phone rang once, twice, three times. With each ring, Faith's resolve wavered. He hadn't taken her seriously when she had first voiced her concerns about Nathan's death.

The phone rang a fourth time, and Faith's heart sank. She was just about to hang up when she heard the click of the line connecting. 'Penn?' she asked, her voice trembling. She took a deep breath, steeling herself for the conversation to come.

'DCI Pennant McBride.' Faith Harrington's tone was apologetic as she added, 'Hiya, sorry to be calling you at work.' She winced at her own words, feeling a bit foolish for disturbing him during his work hours.

Penn's voice, however, was laced with genuine concern. 'Miss Harrington, Faith is that you? Is everything okay?' he asked, his tone steady and soothing.

Faith hesitated for a moment before she replied, 'I was in town today meeting Mirry and I bumped into Sarah Alessi.' The line went silent for a moment, the pause hanging heavily between them. Then Penn replied, a single word hanging in the air, 'And?'

'We had coffee together and I asked how work was going,' Faith explained, her words tumbling out quickly. She could almost hear Penn's sharp intake of breath. 'Faith, you didn't tell her we had talked, did you? It could put me in a lot of trouble.'

'I am not that stupid,' Faith retorted, her voice defensive. 'This is a bad idea, just forget I called.' She could hear the rustle of papers on Penn's end, and his deep, calming breath. 'I am sorry for being so abrupt. What did she say?' Penn's voice was softer now, more understanding.

Faith quickly described all that had happened, her words painting a vivid picture for Penn. When she finished, he said, 'You know her, it was obvious she was going to talk to you. You were right to pursue it as you did, and I am grateful you told me this. Maybe I need to dig a little deeper.'

Faith sighed, her voice heavy with emotion. 'Sarah is a great person, not the type to kill Nathan.'

Penn's voice was grave as he replied, 'Most of the time Faith, it's not the ones you see as being a killer. It's the circumstances. People are not born killers, but everyone is capable if they are put in a corner with no other way out.'

Faith's voice wavered as she replied, 'I feel as if I have come home to another village, things have stayed the same and changed at the same time.'

'You did the right thing Faith, that's all we can do. Thank you again,' Penn assured her, his voice steady and comforting. 'You're welcome. If I hear of anything else I will contact you,' Faith promised, her voice filled with determination.

Penn's final words were a warning. 'Be careful, if this is a murder, you don't want to attract attention.' Faith's reply was quick and sharp. 'Is that because I am a weak female?' Penn laughed, 'No, I can see you are not, but I would say the same thing to a man or a woman, even a fellow police officer.'

Faith's voice softened as she ended the call. 'I will be careful, take care DCI McBride.' Penn's laughter was a comforting sound in the midst of their grim conversation. 'You too Miss Harrington.'

'Faith, everything alright?' Pink said breaking the silence that had settled in after the morning rush. The shop had quietened down, and Pink had taken over the reins, allowing Faith a moment of respite.

'Yeah, just a phone call' Faith called back, her voice bouncing off the walls of the quaint little shop. She took a moment to admire the organised chaos that was her mother's legacy before deciding to head home, craving the solace of her garden.

Her garden, a sanctuary that her Aunt Penny had lovingly crafted into a paradise, was a balm to her unusual day. The smooth wooden decking was adorned with a plush rattan sofa and chairs, inviting her to sit down and lose herself in the tranquil ambience. An old water feature, carved into the shape of a waterwheel, stood in one corner, its gentle trickle forming a soothing melody that eased her stress.

The garden was a riot of colours, a vibrant homage to the arrival of spring. Daffodils and tulips jostled for space, their bright hues painting a cheerful tableau. A neat border near the back door was dotted with pristine white snowdrops, their delicate blooms nodding in the breeze. Faith had recently added her own touch to the garden, under the guidance of Valerian, her cousin. They had spent hours discussing the best plants for the garden, considering the soil, lighting, and overall aesthetic. She was eager to leave her mark, to carry on where Aunt Penny had left off.

Her latest addition, a bird station, had already started attracting feathered visitors. At first, they had been wary, keeping their distance from this new human presence. But over time, they had come to realise that Faith meant no harm. Now, they happily flitted about, feeding and singing, adding their own melodies to the symphony of sounds in her garden oasis.

The flat she had shared with Ben was a stark, soulless space. Ben had a penchant for minimalism, a stark contrast to Faith's love for warmth and vibrancy. 'I like it clean and clear, Faith,' he'd often say. And Faith, ever the compliant partner, had simply acquiesced, burying her own preferences beneath his.

The thought of the impending summer filled her with excitement. She could already picture the warm nights, the garden bathed in the soft glow of fairy lights. She could hear the laughter of her family and friends, the clinking of glasses, the soft strumming of a guitar. 'This is going to be a summer to remember,' she declared, a soft smile playing on her lips.

In her youth, she was consumed with an insatiable desire to escape the confines of her quaint village, to venture into the unknown and explore. The allure of London, with its pulsating heartbeat and glimmering lights, had been irresistible. She reminisced about her life with Ben, a whirlwind of glamour and excitement, nestled amidst a city that never slept. They had been theatre enthusiasts, soaking up the atmosphere of the West End hits, their laughter and applause loud in the grand auditoriums.

But were the people she had known in London truly her friends? Unlike the steadfast companions she had here in the village, who had remained by her side, the city folks had proven to be fleeting. After her accident, not a single soul from her London life had reached out. She remembered the hospital, the sterile smell of disinfectant, the cold, hard bed. Initially, they had flocked to her, their faces a blur of faux concern, their words dripping with insincere coos and aahs. But when Ben had ended their relationship, they had all vanished, like rats abandoning a sinking ship. 'Fair-weather friends,' she spat out bitterly.

Now, she had come to realise that she was better off without them. Her photography, once a passion that had been pushed to the back of her mind, had begun to flourish again. Sure, she did a lot of wedding photography, but it was a necessary evil to keep her afloat. She found herself appreciating the scenic beauty of her village, the resurgence of crafts in the area. 'Maybe I'll pay a visit to the new craft scene,' she mused aloud, imagining herself capturing the artists at work, their hands deftly bringing to life forgotten crafts.

She felt a sense of purpose, a desire to preserve this way of life through her lens. She wanted people to see the charm of small villages, to understand why they needed to be protected. She yearned to immortalise the people who were reviving lost arts, their faces etched with concentration and determination. 'This is what real life is,' she thought, her heart filled with a newfound appreciation for her roots.

This was the moment for Faith to regain control, to carve a new trajectory in the rocky landscape of her life. She was far from content with the limitations her disability had imposed on her, the aspects of her existence that had been cruelly snatched away. Yet, she had to endure, to validate her strength not only to herself but perhaps to the people who once filled her world with laughter and camaraderie, and maybe, just maybe, to Ben. It was starting to get cooler, so she retreated into the house.

Having indulged in a bubble bath that filled the air with a soothing fragrance, Faith found herself in the sanctuary of the living room. She was wrapped in a bathrobe, so soft and fluffy. Pouring herself a generous glass of rich red wine – a reward she decided she had earned – she nestled into the couch, ready to immerse herself in an action film her dad had suggested.

She used to find solace in romantic films and books, losing herself in the whirlwind of emotions they stirred within her. But now, they seemed to have lost their charm.

With a shake of her head and a chuckle, she recalled her sister's words, 'I don't know why people buy into this rubbish. It isn't real.' It was a sentiment that Faith found herself agreeing with more and more.

Hope had always been an unpretentious child, her beauty lying in her stark simplicity and intelligence. 'Why bother with the frivolities of makeup and fancy clothes?' she would often question, her voice laced with genuine curiosity. She found no purpose in them, her heart yearning for the thrill of learning instead. She was the type of girl who would rather spend hours buried in books than waste a minute on trivialities.

'Hope, you're such a strange one,' Faith would often tease, her eyes sparkling with affection for her sister. She admired Hope's way of seeing things, her relentless thirst for knowledge, and her innate kindness towards others. Hope's dating life, or rather the lack of it, was a constant source of amusement in their household. 'Why waste time on something as fleeting as a relationship?' Hope would chuckle, brushing off her sister's concerns with a wave of her hand.

However, despite her outwardly cheerful demeanour, Faith often caught glimpses of a hidden sadness in Hope's eyes. It was fleeting, like a shadow passing over a sunny day, but it was there, nonetheless. 'Hope, are you okay?' Faith would ask, her voice tinged with worry. But Hope was a master of disguise, a chameleon who hid her true emotions behind a radiant smile and an endless supply of goodwill.

When Faith had first returned home, weak and vulnerable, it had been Hope who had been her rock. 'You need to get up, Faith. You need to start anew,' Both Hope and Tiffany would insist, they nagged and cajoled, pushing Faith to start a photography business. Relentless, always coming up with new ways to help Faith tap into her innate talent for photography.

'Have you ever thought about teaching, Faith?' Hope had suggested one day, her eyes gleaming with excitement. It was just like her to think of something so out of the box, something that could potentially change Faith's life forever.

The village hall had always been a cornerstone of their community, a place where Faith's memories were as tangible as the worn stones that built it. She could still picture her Aunt Penny, her hands stained with paint, teaching art to a motley crew of enthusiastic locals. It was a place where her mother, with her calm aura and flexible limbs, held yoga classes that brought peace and tranquillity to their busy lives.

Hope, always the literary enthusiast, had even managed to coax local authors into their humble village hall to share their writing journey. But Faith? She had always shied away from taking centre stage. The thought of standing up before a crowd, the possibility of stumbling over her words, or worse, tripping on her own two feet, filled her with a cold dread that made her stomach churn.

Hope, ever the optimist, had told her to stop wallowing in self-pity. She had a talent, a voice that needed to be heard. Faith had merely nodded, promising to think about it. But that was when the idea had struck her. A small exhibition. She could combine her passion for photography with promoting the village and its residents. They would be the stars, the focus of attention, and Faith could remain comfortably in the background, her presence felt but not seen.

She decided to do some organising, so she went to the kitchen and seated herself at the worn, oak, kitchen table. Faith meticulously sorted through the myriad of photographs she had captured for her family's budding entrepreneurial endeavours. Her fingertips traced the glossy surfaces, a small smile playing on her lips as she admired her work.

'Brilliant, if I do say so myself,' she murmured to the empty room, her voice bouncing off the faded, yellowed wallpaper. She noted the next task on her agenda – creating larger posters to place around the village and other nearby ones and of course in Cederby itself. Posters for the upcoming literary event her sister, Hope, was orchestrating.

Hope's venture had been a labour of love, years in the making. Faith could still remember the spark in her sister's eyes when she first spoke of it; that spark now a roaring flame as everything was finally falling into place. 'She's worked so hard,' Faith murmured, a note of admiration in her voice.

The event was set to be a boon for their quaint village, a much-needed injection of culture and commerce. Local businesses were abuzz with anticipation, and even the prestigious Eglantine Hall had thrown open its grand doors in support. Faith could already envision the lively talks and bustling activities taking place in its opulent grounds.

'Hope's passion is contagious,' Faith mused, her fingers already sketching out designs for the posters. She could hardly wait to see her sister's face when she presented them. The thought warmed her heart, fuelling her creativity as she delved back into her work, the quiet hum of the house her only companion.

It was a hopeful thought, that the impending literary festival could serve as a balm to the wounds of Mirry and her father, a tragedy that had shaken their lives to the core. The Folly, a symbol of resilience, was nearing its completion, and Faith couldn't help but imagine it in all its glory - a perfect setting for the author's pictures and book launches.

'Imagine the authors, their faces lit up with excitement as they launch their books, the flashes of my camera capturing their moments of triumph,' she mused, a sense of anticipation filling her. This festival wouldn't just be good for her, it would be a milestone. The photographs she would take, the moments she would capture - it would all add to her portfolio, a stepping stone towards bigger opportunities beyond the confines of her current sphere.

Before retiring to bed, she made it a point to check the doors. Her eyes inadvertently drifted across the road to Mirry and Nathan's house. The darkness seemed to have swallowed it whole, the lights were all out, and an eerie quiet hung about it.

She stood there for a moment, lost in her thoughts. The silence of the night was broken only by the occasional rustling of leaves, a stark contrast to the turmoil that the house across had witnessed. The darkness seemed to add to the sorrow that had befallen its inhabitants, its stillness a grim reminder of the tragedy that had struck.

The four houses in the vicinity of her home looked more like silhouettes than actual homes in the deepening twilight. A shiver of unease snaked its way down Faith's spine at the thought of her isolation. The two holiday homes nearby were deserted, their owners wouldn't visit until the weather turned warmer. She glanced at Mirry's house shrouded in the darkness of the night. For the first time in her life, Faith felt a tinge of fear creeping into her heart. The stark reality hit her - Nathan had been murdered. The tranquillity of her idyllic village had been shattered, replaced by the chilling shadow of death. 'Time to beef up security around here,' she muttered to herself, making a mental note to install lights at the front entrance.

With a sigh, she decided it was time to retire for the night. In the cosy confines of her kitchen, she prepared herself a cup of hot chocolate, the rich aroma filling the room, cradling the warm mug in her hands. Ascending the stairs to her bedroom, she could feel the day's stress slowly ebbing away. She changed into her fluffy pink cat pyjamas, a quirky gift from Poppy, and snuggled into her bed. The softness of the pillow against her cheek and the warmth of the sheets embracing her brought a sense of security.

The rustling of the wind through the trees next to her house created a soothing melody, a lullaby of nature. 'Just the wind and the trees,' she told herself, finding comfort in the familiar sounds. The tension gradually left her body, replaced by a sense of calm. With the song of nature serenading her, Faith finally succumbed to the realm of sleep.

Faith was rudely yanked from her slumber by the insistent shrilling of her phone. She groaned, her fingers fumbling over the smooth surface of her phone as she squinted against the harsh light of the screen. 'Hello, darling,' her mother's voice chirped from the other end, brimming with an energy that Faith found borderline offensive at this hour. 'Thank you so much for helping at the shop.'

Faith could practically see her mother's beaming smile through the phone. Faith found herself wondering how anyone could be so perpetually bright and breezy.

'Did you both have a nice weekend?' Faith asked, sitting up in bed. She switched the phone to speaker mode, freeing her hands to reach for a scrunchie on her bedside table. She gathered her unruly hair into a messy bun, her fingers working on autopilot as she focused on her mother's response.

'Faith, you absolutely must try this place,' her mother gushed, her voice full of excitement. 'It was divine. Your father and I had a great time. It was like a second honeymoon if you know what I mean.' Faith grimaced. Like any child, she didn't want to imagine her parents being all lovey-dovey and romantic. That was a mental image no one should have to endure.

'Mum, I'm really glad you and dad enjoyed it,' Faith said, trying to keep the discomfort out of her voice. She glanced around her small, cluttered room, her gaze landing on the stack of paperwork waiting for her on her desk. 'Maybe when things quiet down a little bit and my job gets better, I may go for a visit. I could do with a holiday.'

'That sounds like a brilliant idea, love. It might just divert your attention from this newfound detective obsession of yours,' her mother commented with a hint of concern lacing her words. Faith chuckled lightly, shaking her head as she retorted, 'Mum, you make me sound like I'm turning into Miss Marple. I'm merely seeking the truth, that's all.'

Her mother sighed. 'I know, love. But remember, I'm your mum and worrying about you is part of my job. Alright?' Faith knew there was no point in arguing. 'I promise to be careful.'

'Ah, there I go again, playing the overbearing mum. Yes, let's leave it for now. Have a good day, whatever you're up to.'

Once her mother had ended the call, Faith quickly dressed and found herself at the kitchen table, her mind started to churn, thoughts racing about how she could uncover any clues about Nathan's unfortunate demise. Mirry had been avoiding any conversation related to death, busy as she was, working on the Folly.

Faith found herself questioning her friendship with Mirry. They had nothing in common anymore, and Mirry's behaviour was increasingly becoming intolerable. Everyone had warned her that Mirry had changed dramatically, but it took Nathan's death for her to see the real Mirry. So, why was she so invested in proving the circumstances of Nathan's death?

With a sigh, she decided it was time to get to work. It would stimulate her mind and perhaps even spur her detective instincts. Grabbing her helmet, she hopped onto her moped and headed towards her job - a photography gig for Marlowe's bookstore. The weather was gradually warming up, and Faith found herself hoping for an early summer. She was looking forward to adding the finishing touches to her garden and maybe even hosting a few gatherings. The question of whether or not to invite Penn was a tricky one. Their relationship had started off on the wrong foot, but things seemed to be improving. Perhaps inviting Sam and Magda could act as a buffer. Yet, she couldn't help but wonder why the mere thought of inviting Penn stirred up such a flurry of emotions within her.

Indeed, he was a handsome man, the kind that could effortlessly turn heads in a crowded room. His eyes, a captivating shade of blue, held a certain charm that was hard to ignore. She barely knew him, and he was far from her usual type. 'Enough of this foolishness,' she scolded herself, 'There's absolutely no room for romantic notions where DCI McBride is concerned.'

Her afternoon was unexpectedly free, and Faith decided to pay a visit to The Grinder. She wanted to see how Liam was holding up and if there were any updates on Krista However, Liam was nowhere to be seen. Perhaps he was in the back, dealing with a delivery or inventory.

Making her way through the crowd, she decided to check the alley adjacent to the shop. The narrow alley was dimly lit, with the afternoon sun barely making its way through the tall buildings on either side. As she walked, the noise from the coffee shop gradually faded.

Suddenly, she stopped in her tracks. There was a voice raised through in the alley, the tone unmistakable. It was raised in anger, a stark contrast to the peaceful afternoon.

'Listen, Donovan, I think we need to be a little more cautious with our dealings. The deliveries, they're too conspicuous. People may start putting two and two together, and I don't need any more trouble.' The voice was unmistakably Liam's. His tone was laced with a mix of desperation and fear that Faith had never heard before.

She edged a fraction closer, her feet moving almost involuntarily. 'It may be best if we meet at the picnic area in the car park near the river. It's secluded, hidden from prying eyes. No one can see us there.' Liam's voice sounded strained, as if he was trying to convince himself as much as he was trying to convince Donovan.

A sense of dread washed over Faith. What was Liam involved in? Krista had mentioned her worries about Liam when Penn had first suggested that the brownie that had killed Nathan may have been contaminated. She had dismissed it at the time, but now, could Liam have been that reckless? Could he really have been involved in something so dangerous?

'I will meet you on Friday at 9.30, and don't tell anyone.' Liam's voice was stern now, his words hanging in the air long after he had finished speaking. Faith felt a chill run down her spine. Whatever Liam was involved in, it was serious, and she couldn't shake off the feeling that things were about to take a turn for the worst

CHAPTER 15

Faith was on edge for the remainder of the week, her nerves frayed. The mundane tasks of her day-to-day life became arduous, her concentration slipping. Even the hum of the cameras, which she had installed for security purposes, seemed to mock her heightened state of alert. She was grateful, at least, that they were digital and not the old film type. The cost of film cartridges would have been a financial burden she could ill afford, given her current state of distraction.

Her mind was constantly drawn to Liam. She was planning to go to the very place where he was meeting this mysterious Donovan. She felt a shiver as she contemplated the idea of playing the spy. Would she discover that he was the culprit behind the brownie's incident? The mere thought of it made her heart pound in her chest.

What if she found out he was to blame for the brownies, could she tell the police, and what consequences would it have for Krista and Liam's relationship? Not to mention the child that would soon be born.

Would it be for the best just to forget the whole thing? Nathan had not been well-liked; he had by the sounds of it made both Krista and Liam's life unbearable. They could both now heal, and things would be better. Mirry was young, she could still find love and have the children she had so desperately wanted. No, she couldn't let it go, maybe this was for her too. Why, she did not know, it came from deep within and it pushed her on to pursue the truth.

When had she become this focussed, this driven? Looking at the walking stick and then at the marks on her legs. No one should get away with ruining a life. It would have been better if Ben had paid for his drunk driving, which shows what a good solicitor could do. The truth be told she should not have got in the car with him, he had been way over the limit, so maybe she too was responsible for the state of her life.

Turning to look at her clock in the hallway, it was 8 o'clock, better to be early and get in position. Picking up her bag with her camera in it she grabbed her coat and made her way out of the front door and outside to the garden in front of her house.

The birds were singing, and Faith saw a squirrel shooting up the small tree by the side of her cottage. From the top, he leapt to the larger tree to its side and turning glanced at Faith for a minute then continued up higher, until completely hidden by the branches

The honk of a horn made her jump and as she looked up, she saw her Mum in her flashy metallic blue Nissan Juke driving past, a huge smile on her face. Her mum was heading to work, and she waved happily back.

What would her parents think of the foolhardy expedition she was headed on? She could imagine her father, he would say she was being inexcusably selfish, these things should be left to the police, what if she got hurt, or worse. He had nearly lost her once, think of the consequences on your family.

Her Mother on the other hand would try to reason with her, her weapon of choice would be mental, she would tell her how upset everyone would be, how what she did could affect the lives of her friends and family.

Faith stopped, where did she come into this. Yes, she knew her parents loved her; they would do anything for her. When had she gone from giving her independence to Ben to now giving it to her parents?

'Stop putting yourself down, dam you, just do something for once.' She looked up to see the squirrel staring at her from the high up branch.

'What do you think, am I a lost cause? The squirrel jumped to a lower branch and stared at her. Faith's breath caught in her mouth and for a few seconds, they shared a small connection. Then it turned and with a mighty leap landed on a branch on the next tree, a feat that left Faith astonished.

'So, what you are saying is if someone as small as you can jump such a distance, I should stop being a wuss. Fine I will do as you recommend.'

She was sure she heard the squirrel make a chattering noise at her. It was agreeing with her assumption. Well, that was good enough and gave her the confidence to carry on with her plan. She quickly moved on just in case the creature changed its mind.

Her Vespa was ready and waiting. Making sure her helmet was secure she set off towards the stream at the side of the picnic grounds. She had decided the night before not to head straight to the car park, not wanting to arouse any suspicion. Her plan of action was to park at the side of the river, cross in the shallow bit where it was easiest to cross and spy on Liam from the bush at the other side that surrounded the picnic car park.

Penn was driving in his car, his favourite band blasting from the speakers, singing happily. He had gained his taste in music from his father, much to the ribbing from his friends. Ok maybe the Bee Gees was an acquired taste, and yes, he was not in the right generation to be liking ELO, but who wants to be totally normal, the music reminded him of wonderful days out with his parents, everyone happily singing from their beaten-up old camper van, and at the moment he needed those memories and that stability to calm all the chaos that had recently entered his life.

He was on his way to look at a small cottage that he hoped would be just what he was looking for to proceed with his next step of settling down to country life. The cottage would not have been his first choice, but it had been the best of a tired bunch. And it did have a garden. He wasn't sure if this would be the place to settle down, but it was a start. He was still mulling over what to do next with his current case. Faith had phoned him, and he was deciding what his best course of action was.

He knew he was going to ask some of Nathan's work colleagues about Nathan and even check out some of his friends from London. He would have to check with Don his boss and get Sam to get in touch with the Met in London for some help in interviewing the said friends.

Was he a coward for not making the call to his old station in London, would they even help him? He knew what he had done was right, but to his friends and colleagues to have another policeman arrested was disloyalty to the force.

He opened his car window, turning down the music. Finding to his relief that nature was a great mood enhancer. Inhaling the scent of the daffodil's and fresh grass, he felt himself relax. Today was not going to be a day to stress, it was going to be easy going with no complications.

Faith reached the shallowest part of the river, a part that had numerous flat stones that a person could hop on and traverse easily. As children, she and her siblings spent hours jumping from stone to stone and with their cousins had hunted for the aquatic creatures that lived their lives beneath the waters. Looking at the stones now, Faith forgot all the practice she had gained in her youth. It was so strange that the things you found so easy as a child, terrified you as an adult.

Why hadn't she dressed better, she looked down at her soft pumps and three-quarter trousers. And at the beautiful gold silk scarf she had gotten in Naples on a holiday and sighed. What had she been thinking? Yes, Poirot and Miss Marple's always looked so well turned out in the books, yet she never remembered them really getting into a position where there was a chance, they could get their clothes damaged. Next time she needed to rethink her wardrobe for times like these. Though, to be truthful, Faith hoped these kind of daily activities were going to be just the once.

With trepidation, she took one step, her walking stick becoming nothing more than a hindrance to her balance. Reaching the first stone she wobbled for a second then stabilised herself, first trying to place her stick on the stone, then deciding it was best to place it in the water at her side. One down ten to go. With slow precision, Faith stepped from one stone to another until she reached the centre rock. Halfway there she thought, she would manage this, without any mishaps.

Were Penn's eyes deceiving him, or was that Faith stood on a rock in the middle of the river, her bag in one hand and her walking stick in the other. Did this woman have no boundaries? Well, bang goes his easy day. He parked up and got out of the car. Walking down to the edge of the river he called.

'Not a particularly good day for fishing Faith. And I don't think the weather, or your attire is appropriate for swimming.'

This was a mistake he later came to regret as Faith turned and looked at him indignantly, then she began to wobble. Penn beginning to see this was not going to end well, leapt across the road and down the bank until he was almost close enough to catch her when, splash! Faith fell back, her bottom hitting the gravel.

Faith dropped her walking stick and desperately trying to lift the bag above her head. 'Quick grab this, it has my camera equipment in. Penn complied, then started to smile.

Faith glared at him, 'Pray do tell me what you find so amusing about this situation?'

Penn wiped his eyes. 'I was just thinking instead of a comfy bottom, you have ended up with a soggy one.'

That's when Penn felt like a total prat. Faith was trying to grab her walking stick and grimacing as she desperately tried to lift herself up on her good leg.

As Penn tried to reach down for Faith, she pushed his hands away, tears of pain and frustration welling up in her eyes. The heat on her face told her she was blushing, and she wanted nothing more than to creep under one of the stones like the fish she remembered finding as a child.

Penn tried again to lift Faith up and at that moment her scarf fell from her neck and before he or Faith could reach it had drifted down the river to who knows where.

'No, not my best scarf.'

With Penn's unwanted help she got to her feet, glancing at the river she saw the scarf drift out of sight, she was not going to get it back and her anger seethed.

'So, is there a reason why you are here in the middle of a river?'

Faith grabbed the bag back off Penn and tried to reach the next stone, again she started to wobble, and she felt Penn's arms grab her waist.

'Will you stop manhandling me.' Faith yelled.

Penn took in a breath, refusing to be baited into saying something that would inevitably make this situation worse, if that was even possible.

'I will stop manhandling you when I get you on the other side of this river unscathed, then I would like an explanation as to why you are doing something so stupid.'

Faith was about to give a scathing reply, then she realised she would need help in getting to her destination. Tightening her lips, she directed Penn to where she wanted to be. They both stumbled to the other side and Faith looked down to see that Penn's trouser legs were drenched, totally ruining his usual pristine appearance.

Penn looked up when he heard Faith's snicker. 'You have changed your tune. One minute you want to kill me, now I am the object of great amusement. You are a total enigma.'

'It's the first time I have seen you ruffled DCI McBride; I want to just bask at the moment.' She began to laugh again and began to open her bag. 'I expect people would pay to see a picture of you at this moment. Dad says his team have a WhatsApp page where they put the most embarrassing pictures of one another. Maybe I should just take a quick picture and get Sam to share it.'

Penn looked down at his dripping trousers and joined in with Faith's obvious merriment. 'If it stops you from being angry with me, go ahead.' He glanced back at the river. 'I am sorry for startling you, and for grabbing you, I was worried.' He ran his hands through his hair and sighed when Faith felt her neck. 'I am also sorry for making you lose your scarf. I never make a good impression with you, do I?'

Faith put her bag over her shoulder and smiled. 'Let's say we both seem to bring out the worst in each other and better the scarf floating down the river, than me. Thank you for coming to my aid.'

'You're welcome. I like to save a least one fair damsel in distress a day.' Penn glanced up the bank to the bushes. 'Strange place to be taking photos. Though I wouldn't say I am very knowledgeable about the best photography locations.'

Noting Faith's face turn scarlet, he decided to pry more. 'Is there another reason why you are here?' Faith stared at the floor. 'You can tell me, I could help.'

She had been truly caught and decided to do something she never thought she would do again, let someone in. Looking up she took a deep breath and told Penn what she had heard Liam say and what she intended to do, then she waited for the repercussion.

What she didn't expect was the silence, looking up she found Penn not angry but pensive.

'As much as I dislike people trying to do our jobs, I have to admit that you have come up with a few good leads. Maybe at first, I didn't agree with your assumption of murder.' Faith snorted and Penn tightened his lips. 'I now have to admit you may be right. Too many things don't add up, especially the loss of his much-needed medication. I need now to check and make sure a crime does not go unpunished.'

Faith gathered her belongings, opening her bag to check the contents. Her treasured photography equipment was safe. 'That must have smarted. You don't seem the kind of person to admit when they are wrong but thank you, it means a lot you believe me.'

'Let's say I am open to the idea of there being another explanation for Nathan's death.'

'Then I will accept that.'

'Under the condition, you let me accompany you and if I think it is in the best interests of the case, take action.'

Penn watched the indecision on Faith's face, turning she nodded.

'Well then lead the way and let's see if we can shed any light on this unusual situation.'

With Penn's help, they both made their way up the steep bank and found a good position behind some bushes that gave them a great view of the entire car park.

'So now what?' This wasn't what Penn usually did on a case and felt a little embarrassed being this close to Faith, though he had to admit the musky scent of her perfume only added to Faith's allure. She was an unusual female, fiercely loyal to her friends, close to her family, with a dry sense of humour. What saddened him was her lack of belief in herself and the way she often let her friends and family smother her.

'Penn. Look over there, a van has arrived and behind it, that's Liam's work van.' Faith pointed to a place near to where they were crouched and sure enough, as they watched, Liam exited his van and walked over to the other vehicle, where a tall broad set man greeted him.

'Faith is that the man you saw Liam talking to?'

'Yes, that's Dominic, he's a local thug, into lots of unsavoury things. He's not the sort of person Liam would associate with, not since being with Krista. Wherever Domonic is there is usually trouble not far behind. My cousin Poppy says he has been good recently, this may all be innocent, I just don't get why the need for a secret meeting'.

'So, the question is, what is he doing with him now? You said he was going to pick something up, let's see what transpires and then we can decide what to do next.'

'If I take my camera out and take photos, we can check over them later, just in case we miss something.'

'Good idea Faith, just try to be inconspicuous, ok?'

Faith gently retrieved her camera from her bag and taking off the lens protector, began to snap photos. She saw both men go to the rear of Dominic's van and open the doors.

'Liam, I am sorry to have to tell you, but next time the prices will have to go up. It's getting harder to find the products you need, and I have to make a profit too.'

Liam turned and frowned at Dom, 'Then this looks like your last sale with me. Remember I have been doing you a favour too. This is off the books. I wasn't born yesterday, Dom, I know all the tricks'

Faith noticed Dominic's lips tighten for a second, then he smiled. 'That's up to you mate, but what do you think your wife would say if she knew you were buying cheaper products for The Grinder.'

Liam's face blazed with anger, 'Dom, you should know better than to try that kind of tactic with me, we go back a long way, and I was good to you when you first moved to town. I gave you work and helped you get back in with the locals. They can be an unforgiving lot. What do you think will happen if they find out you mean harm to my pregnant wife? You too have a lot to lose.' Liam turned to fully face Dom, then moved closer. 'You know that could change and you wouldn't want to get on the wrong side of me, would you?'

Dom looked visibly shaken. He had tried his luck and realised it had failed. 'Of course not Liam, I'm only joking, I will keep mate rates for you.'

Penn leaned in closer to Faith, 'I need to know whether there is anything in the contents being sold that could have caused Nathan's death. I am sorry Faith, but I have to call this in, it's a solid lead and the best we have had so far.'

Faith couldn't disagree but knew the consequences would be far-reaching and she hated to think what this would do to Krista's relationship with Liam. Faith was now realising the implications of all this and how quickly everything had gotten out of hand, typical Faith, running in, all guns blaring.

Liam moved back down the bank and Faith heard him talking on the phone. A few minutes later he climbed back up beside her and they both waited.

Soon they heard the sirens and two police cars pulled up next to Liam and Dom, who had tried to jump in his car and make a quick exit.

The two men were placed in separate cars and policemen started to take an inventory of what was inside the vehicles.

'Faith, will you be ok getting home if I help you back across the river?'

'Yes, I think I need to phone Krista and tell her what has happened.'

'Rather you than me.' Said Penn.

Faith gave a weak smile. She wasn't looking forward to this at all. It seems that since getting back she was getting on the wrong side of everyone, and her friends were something she could not afford to lose.

CHAPTER 16

Krista answered on the second ring. 'Hiya Faith, how did you guess I was home.' This was going to be harder than she thought, it would have been better for Krista if she had been with her parents.

'Krista, are you sat down?' Not the best way to start a conversation, but what else could she do.

'Why are you asking that, please don't you start the fussing routine. My parents have been driving me nuts. I told them women have been getting pregnant for years and it's not as though I am an older parent. I am trained in nutrition and still, my parents have been trying to coach me on what to eat.'

Better to rip the plaster off fast, thought Faith. 'Krista, Liam has been arrested.'

Total silence, then Faith heard sobs. 'Krista, do you want me to come over, it might be better if I explain in person what's happened.' It may have been better to have not said anything at all and waited till she knew what would happen where Liam was concerned.

'Yes please.' That was all Krista said and it was enough for Faith to quickly get her coat and bag and drive her moped to Krista's small cottage near Eglantine Hall.

She found her friend slumped on the sofa, tissues in hand, sobbing uncontrollably. Quickly sitting beside her Faith enveloped her friend in a hug and waited until the sobs subsided. How could she tell her she had played a part in her husband's arrest? Had she been so hell-bent on proving her point she had inadvertently caused all this distress to her friend? What had she been thinking? Of course, this would be the outcome and she felt like a traitor.

'Krista, please calm down, I know you don't want the fuss, but this can't be doing the baby any good.'

Krista sniffed and sat up straighter. 'You're right, do you know what happened?'

Faith couldn't look Krista in the eyes as she told her. If Krista threw her out, she would have deserved it.

'The flaming idiot, wait till I get my hands on him. If he is to blame in any way for Nathan's death, they won't need to punish him, I will do it myself. I have worked so hard to build up The Grinder's reputation. He told me he didn't have any contact with his old friends. I begged him not to help Dom, he has always been trouble.' Faith could only nod in agreement, this wasn't the outcome she had been expecting.

'Krista, are you mad at me too?' Faith waited for Krista to advance on her with her wrath, but there was none. 'I can't say I am happy with your snooping, but I am glad it has come out. As much as I am angry with Liam, he is my husband and I know in my heart that as much as he hated Nathan, he would not have intentionally killed him. I just hope if he has done anything that contributed, the court will be lenient.'

Krista walked over to the window and opened it; she leaned forward and took a deep breath. Faith rose and joined her, both watching the birds on Krista's bird feeder. 'I am glad he didn't forget to feed the birds; I love sitting in the garden and hearing them sing. Liam had his problems and I know this looks serious.' Sighing she turned to face Faith. 'I know I am not acting rationally, but I think it's time I went to the station and see what the damage is. I don't suppose you could come with me?'

'Wild horses wouldn't stop me.'

Krista was quiet on the way to the police station, and this gave Faith some time to think. Her friend's response had not been what she had expected. Anger yes, but not this total calm. Her friend was in shock, or maybe Krista knew more than she was letting on. *Oh, Faith for goodness sake, stop seeing villainous intent in everyone, your paranoia is unwelcome.*

On arriving at the station Faith decided to ask for Penn in person, he wouldn't be happy, but as he was dealing with the case and Krista was Liam's wife, this course of action would be the best. The woman at the desk smiled at Faith, partly because everyone knew she was the boss's daughter. Taking Krista's details, she asked them to take a seat, telling them she would notify DCI McBride of their arrival.

Penn had quickly driven back to the station, shouting Sam over to explain the situation. Liam had been booked in and was quickly ushered into interview room three, which was the most comfortable. Hopefully, this would help in making him a little bit more loose tongued and cooperative.

When he and Sam entered the room, Liam jumped, then banged his hand on the table.

'Would anyone care to explain to me why I am here, I know the procedure and I know I have done nothing wrong?'

'If you will be patient Mr Hunter, I will get to the reason why you're here.' Both officers took a seat opposite Liam. Penn turned the recorder on and started the interview, stating the time date and their rank and credentials, then Liam's name. Turning to Liam, he sat for a minute and stared. This worked as he expected, and he soon noticed Liam visibly becoming uncomfortable.

'Today you were witnessed meeting at Brushwood picnic grounds. There you were seen completing a transaction with Dominic Sharp of 36 Bramble Lane Cedarby. You were observed handing money over to Dominic Sharp in exchange for goods. When we searched your van, we found products used in cooking. Flour, sugar, and mixed fruit. There was also, coffee, and other beverages.' Penn read the list in front of him, making Liam think he was checking that list. 'Were these things stolen?'

Liam tightened his hands into fists, then released them. 'All the essentials I buy for The Grinder are from legitimate places, nothing is stolen. I do not receive or sell products made from stolen ingredients.'

Penn looked at his notes again. 'So why the secrecy?'

Liam turned to Sam, hoping his friendship with the young man could lead to some understanding. 'Dom likes to do business that way and I didn't want people to see I was buying cheaper stuff for the Grinder. Reputation is everything.'

'When you mean cheaper, does that include say, cheaper products that may not be strict on the inclusion of peanuts?'

Liam was about to say something, then forced himself to calm down, taking in a deep breath and exhaling slowly. 'I can see exactly where this is going, and the answer is no. I always buy those kinds of ingredients from a specialist place that can prove their flours etc are free from any kind of allergen, like nuts.'

'So, there isn't a chance the good flour could get mistaken for the cheaper flour?' Penn waited as Liam sighed again.

'Krista is the one who always gets the supplies for things like allergies, she goes to a very reputable place, and you can see all the invoices and check the numbers against all the bags, which are kept in a different storage place.'

Penn decided to change his approach. 'People have mentioned you didn't have a good relationship with Mr Crawford?' Again, he saw Liam's hands tighten, this seemed to Penn to be a visible tell where Liam was concerned, showing that Liam had a quick temper. But enough to kill?

'Cut the crap out, you want to know did I hate Nathan enough to kill him?'

'You did throw a brick through his window. That could be construed as disliking him and wanting to hurt him.' Turning to Sam he nodded and allowed his younger colleague a chance of questioning the suspect.

'You have no idea what Nathan was like. Yes, I disliked him and for good reason.'

Sam smiled and leaned in closer making eye contact with Liam. 'We all know Nathan could be difficult but take it from our point of view. First, you have an altercation with the deceased, this is witnessed by a great many people. You then are taken into police custody for destroying property.' Sam paused, 'You have to admit with what you were found doing now, this puts you up as a suspect.'

'Look, I know I am hot-tempered, and I know you have in those files all the stuff about when I was younger, but it's not that simple.' Liam said.

'Then make it simple and cooperate, give us something that proves your innocence.' Sam sat back, lifting his pen.

Liam looked at both men, then placed his hands on the table taking a deep breath. 'We were having money trouble at the Grinder and Nathan found out. He tried to talk Krista around telling her I would ruin the place and that it would be better if she sold it to him.' Said Liam. He stopped as if trying to find the right words. 'Nathan was always flirting with my wife, always goading me saying he was a much better man and she had chosen someone lesser.

Sam began to write it down and when Liam stopped, he said, 'go on Liam continue, contrary to what you think we are here to help you.'

'Ok. I found out what was happening. I knew this was so Nathan would get the shop for a cheaper price and sell it for more. He didn't want to help us, just himself.'

'Is this why you threw the brick in the office window?' said Penn.

'Krista and I had argued, and I am sorry to say I had too much to drink. Do you realise how hard we have worked to make the Grinder what it is? So, I decided to cut some costs and when Dom, an old acquaintance said he could get me some supplies for a cheaper price…' Liam ran his hands over his face, beginning to look tired.

'Nathan had some underhand ways of doing business, what he wanted, he got, by good means or bad.' Liam finished.

Penn interjected, 'What do you mean by underhand?' and waited for Liam to reply. He could see the internal struggle in Liam's face and waited a little longer for the reply hoping to get to what had caused the anger Liam had towards the deceased.

Liam finally looked up, 'I found out he was blackmailing Krista. I was furious and I suppose I let it get to me. I had a bit to drink and when I found out Nathan was working overtime I went to his business and told him to leave us alone and that I would sooner burn the Grinder down than sell to him.'

'What happened next?' Said Penn.

'Nathan came out of the shop and began to berate me. He told me I was the second choice and that Krista and he would always have an extra special relationship and for all I knew, we could be having an affair, and I would be too stupid to notice.' Said Liam.

Penn frowned, 'And I expect that made you angry, didn't it?'

'Wouldn't it you?' replied Liam.

Penn had to agree, there was only so much a man could take and he was beginning to get a better picture of Nathan. 'Did you hit him?' he asked.

'I wanted to so bad,' growled Nathan. 'But that would have hurt my wife, and she means the world to me. Can you understand that?' he pleaded.

Penn could but pushed on. 'Liam did you hit him. The statement Nathan gave said you did.'

'I did not hit him. Nathan laughed at me, called me a coward, and walked back inside the office. I turned to walk away, saw the rock at the side of the plant display. Before I knew it, I picked it up and threw it through the window.' Liam sighed, 'No one was going to take my word against Nathans, and I was arrested. Later he dropped the charges. I think he did that to show how much more powerful he was than me, but I did not hurt him.'

'So, going back to the stuff in the van, to your knowledge were these supplies legal, and could there have been a chance that a mistake was made with Nathan's brownie?' said Penn.

'Not a chance, we have been doing better lately and we now can go back to buying from our normal suppliers. Why would I give Nathan a poison brownie that would easily lead you back to us? You can ask all the staff, Krista makes the brownies, she would have noticed if those ingredients were different. One of the other staff makes the normal cakes and sandwiches. Krista makes the ones that are say gluten-free, lactose and such. She would not make those kinds of mistakes.'

'And you have no contact with the area she uses?'

'No, you have to wear a special uniform, Krista was meticulous with hygiene. She was the one to bring them out and put them in a special drawer away from other products. Even the sandwiches were made only by Krista.'

Penn could see the logic in what Liam said. Why would Liam fight to keep his and his wife's livelihood afloat, then purposely sabotage it by killing Nathan with the brownie from his shop. What had seemed clear cut this morning, now seemed flawed and unlikely. Krista would also have to have had something to do with this, and his gut told him she wasn't involved.

'I want you to give us a statement of what has happened so far, and how long you have been purchasing the ingredients. Then I am going to have a word with your friend Dom and see if he can collaborate your story on the ingredients you purchased from him.' He saw Liam relax. 'I suggest you stop with all the cloak and dagger meeting, and you come clean to your wife. You will be released when I have Dom's statement. This does not mean you are off the hook. I will be investigating this further and if I find out you have at any time lied to me, you will feel the full force of the law. Am I understood?'

Liam nodded and the interview was ended.

As Penn left the room, he was stopped by one of the sergeants, and he was surprised to hear both Krista and Faith were waiting for him. Had Faith told Krista what had happened that morning, and if so, why was Faith accompanying Liam's wife?

Krista rushed over to Penn as he entered the waiting room. One of the officers had kindly brought them both a hot cup of tea, and this had to some degree kept her pregnant friend calm. This changed however when she briskly walked over to Penn and raising a finger poked him extremely hard in the chest.

'I demand you tell me why you and your cohorts have arrested my husband. We told you all we knew, and if you need to talk to anyone about the ingredients and the way my food is made.' She prodded him again a little harder. 'I suggest you talk to me, with my lawyer. This kind of thuggish treatment is unacceptable. You have obviously got away with this behaviour in London, but it will not be tolerated here.'

Penn tried not to smile. Here was someone who watched way too many crime programmes, but he had to admire her strength and resolve. 'Mrs Hunter, I can assure you we had a solid reason to interview your husband, he didn't want anyone else present, and he has not been charged. He has been extremely helpful and answered all our questions.'

Krista did not seem convinced and still glaring at the DCI she folded her arms. 'That may be the case, but what I would like to know is, what now, is my husband free to go?'

'At the moment yes.' Said Penn.

'And what does at the moment mean? You cannot possibly feel my husband has anything to do with this?' Said Krista, then she wobbled slightly. Penn leaned forward, catching her in his arms. 'Please Mrs Hunter, take a seat, are you ok, when was the last time you ate?' He manoeuvred Krista to a seat and told Sam who had just walked into the reception to go get Krista a sandwich from the canteen. He had just got her to sit down when Liam came through the door Sam had just disappeared through.

'Krista, your back.' He walked toward her, then noticed her visible pallor. Rushing and kneeling at her feet, he took her hands in his and began to rub them. 'What's wrong, it's not the baby, please say it's not the baby.' When Krista shook her head and started to cry, he sat at her side and took her into his arms, soothingly talking to her.

Penn felt like an intruder and walked over to where Faith stood by the main window, her face crestfallen. It must have been hard for her to watch her friend in such a state and to know you were partly to blame for her being here and in this situation.

'It's not all adventure and fun being a policeman, sometimes it means getting to the truth even when it may concern family or a good friend.' Faith just nodded and turned back to stare out of the window. Penn was going to say more but he heard her sniff and he turned and walked over to the main desk.

CHAPTER 17

Faith was hunched over the table, her eyes fixated on the letter in front of her. She had combed through the words four times over, and their meaning hadn't changed. The paper felt cold and impersonal, just like the message it carried.

'Dear Miss Harrington,' she read out loud to the empty room. *'I have considered the options stated in our last conversation. I have decided to pay you for your share of the apartment, situated in East Finchley. Please contact my solicitor, Mr Harold Appleby at his number above and make an appointment for all parties to sign. Kind Regards Ben Laughton.'*

She paused, her fingers tracing the typed words. The letter also contained the details of what Ben was willing to pay. It was a sum less than what she had hoped for, but she knew she would have to make do. This was the final thread tying her to her ex-husband, and severing it was worth the financial hit.

She sighed, feeling a strange mix of relief and sadness. She had truly wanted that life with Ben, but now all she was left with was the hurt and the pain. But this was also a chance for her to move on, to start anew.

Her thoughts drifted to her struggling business. The money, though less than ideal, would provide a much-needed boost. She could finally breathe a little easier, knowing she wouldn't have to shoulder the burden alone anymore.

The letter had arrived five days prior, and she'd promptly taken it to her parents to seek their counsel. They had both been supportive, with her father making the necessary arrangements on her behalf and insisting on accompanying her. 'Ben will toe the line if he sees me,' he'd assured her, 'he knows full well that I could make his life a living hell. I've got mates down at the Met and I'm not afraid to use them.' Her mother had been in full agreement. 'Better your father than me. If I laid eyes on that man, I'd slice him up and feed him to the pigeons in Trafalgar Square, the repugnant little weasel.'

This had elicited a laugh from Faith, and despite her initial reluctance to have her father accompany her, she had to concede that it was probably for the best. Now, as she sat at the kitchen table, she found herself questioning why she was so averse to confronting Ben alone. Things were different now, she was different. She needed to heed her sister Hope's advice and show some backbone.

Hope had whisked her off to a dinner at a rather splendid pub, nestled just outside the charming town of Briarthorne Edge. Having only opened its doors the previous year, Hope had been singing its praises ever since her library colleagues had their year-end celebration there.

On arrival, Faith was taken aback by the modernity of the building, quite unlike the antiquated establishments Hope usually had a penchant for. 'I know what you're thinking, Sis. No gothic mystery or romantic intrigue here. And yes, it's a building that's less than a century old,' Hope had teased. Faith merely shrugged in response. 'Didn't think this would be your first choice, you're usually all about the old, the mysterious, the quaint.'

'Well, sister dear, prepare to have your mind utterly blown,' Hope had giggled, leading Faith by the arm towards the entrance. Faith couldn't help but stare at her. 'Alright, alien, what have you done with my sister? I must warn you, her family won't take this lightly and you will be annihilated.' Hope merely laughed it off, her arm still looped in Faith's as she led them inside. 'That's the sister I've missed. Come on, I'm absolutely famished. I haven't eaten in at least three hours! My brain needs constant fuel to maintain its high intellect. This body didn't build itself; you know.'

Faith frowned slightly at Hope's self-deprecating humour. She had always hated when Hope joked about her weight. After a childhood filled with teasing and countless attempts at conforming to societal standards of beauty, Hope had finally begun to embrace her own body. However, Faith often wondered if the old scars still lingered beneath the surface of her newfound confidence.

Inside, Faith paused, her gaze sweeping across the room. It was a bibliophile's dream. It was as though they'd stepped into a library; books of all sorts filled the shelves, and the walls were adorned with images of book covers in varying sizes.

'Look, Faith. The Lion, the Witch, and the Wardrobe,' Hope pointed out, her eyes gleaming with affection. She guided them both to a seat beside a tall, wooden bookshelf, sighing contentedly. 'I could settle down here and never leave. If it wasn't for my love of my job, I'd take on waitressing here just to be surrounded by these walls every day.'

'I'll hold my judgment until after I've eaten,' Faith retorted, her tone light. The food turned out to be excellent, and for a while, they managed to avoid discussing Ben, work, or the haunting spectre of Nathan's death. Instead, Hope chattered excitedly about the upcoming festival, her enthusiasm contagious. 'You won't believe the authors who've agreed to come and give talks. Marlowe is over the moon; he's been calling all his literary friends. It's going to be massive.'

'How's Krista? It's great news she's expecting.' She halted when she saw Faith's expression. 'Too much, you know I can be a bit over the top at times.' Faith leaned over and clutched her sister's hand, disliking the look of melancholy that had crept onto her face. 'It's alright to bring it up. Yes, I can't have children, it's not the end of the world. And no reason why I shouldn't find joy in my best mate's pregnancy.'

'Nature will find a way sis. Sometimes we don't know why things happen, I just know it will all come good.'

'Hope, are you quoting Jurassic Park at me?'

'Perhaps, it is a cracking film.'

'Well, I hope your life pans out well, like those soppy romance novels you read.'

'I haven't the foggiest what you're on about.' A coy look settled on her face, which made both women burst into hearty laughter.

Faith couldn't help but smile at her sister's happiness. Hope knew what she wanted and loved her role as an educator. She preferred to stay in the background, letting others take the limelight. Hope was at her happiest when others saw what she saw in the books she cherished and found solace in.

On getting home, Faith felt lighter than she had in a long time. Hope had a way of making everything ok. Tomorrow she would go and see Krista, her friend also needed some support and Faith felt she should be the one to do it.

She found Krista sitting in the main room eating a large dish of chocolate ice cream. For someone pregnant, Krista lacked the glow associated with this joyous occasion. Her face was pale and there were dark lines under her eyes. On seeing her friend's arrival Krista smiled weakly.

'Hiya Faith caught me in the act.' She beckoned her friend over, patting the seat by her side. When she saw Faith staring at the huge tub in her hands she laughed weakly. 'Bet you never thought you would see me wolfing my way through ice cream.'

That was true, as Krista hated the stuff, not really been keen of sweet things in general. Even more strange was when Krista told them all she was going to college to learn to cook and make those confections.

'Seems the little one here is going to have their father's sweet tooth, and for once I can see what you all saw in this stuff.' Krista popped another spoonful of the delicious delight into her mouth, licking the excess off her spoon.

'Mum craved grapes with me. I think she would have preferred them fermented in a bottle but had to make do. She drove dad crazy, waking him up in the night and begging him to get her some, and if they ran out, he had to go to my aunt's house for extra provisions.' Faith smiled. 'Everybody had to keep extra stocks in, as mums' appetite was voracious.'

When Krista put the empty carton down Faith helped her adjust the cushions. 'I cannot stop crying. I am not sure if this is natural, or whether it's the situation we are in. My head is spinning, and sleep has been impossible.' And on cue, she began to cry again, accepting the tissue Faith offered her.

'Krista darling please, this isn't good for you or the baby.' Faith turned to see Liam enter from the kitchen and kneel at his crying wife's feet, taking her hand in his, and rubbing them gently as he tried to soothe her tears. Krista stared down at her husband. 'What if they blame you, I will lose you and the baby wouldn't see its father. What about the Grinder, we were doing so well, now we could lose everything?'

Faith turned to Liam, 'This is all my fault. Me and my stupid idea of turning detective. I should have come to you and just asked.' Liam put his hand up. 'Faith, maybe you were a little too quick to see the worst in me, but maybe I deserved it. I let Nathan get to me and I didn't check on where Domonic got his stuff from. If I hadn't acted like a thief, then you wouldn't have suspected me. Let's agree to be equally guilty and move on.'

'I think you are a better person than me, Liam, I was out of order.' Faith felt the tears well up in her own eyes and Krista handed her a tissue.

'Faith, it's all out in the open and maybe it's for the best. I want everyone to know we were not responsible for Nathan's death and that The Grinder is always a safe place to eat.' said Liam

'Darling, I wish it were that simple.' Said Krista. 'They still see you as a suspect, what if they don't believe we had nothing to do with it?'

Faith stopped her. 'Penn will find out what's going on, I am sure. He doesn't seem the type to hastily jump to conclusions without evidence.'

'Look, let me make us a drink and let's see if we can find a way to exonerate you both.' Said Faith, standing and heading to the kitchen.

She arrived back moments later with a tray with hot drinks and some biscuits and deposited them on the table, before seating herself opposite Liam and Krista.

Liam sat close to Krista, reaching over, and taking one of the cups, then passing it to his wife. She in turn looked at Liam and smiled.

For a moment Faith felt envy. These two had been through so much in a short time, yet the love remained. When Faith had arrived home, she had been numb, wanting to retreat and hide, hating the world and most of the people in it. Her life had appeared colourless, and she was drowning with no way of escaping. The accident involving her and Ben had left not only visible scars but the added trauma of being told she would not be able to have children; this was one scar that would never heal.

But these people in front of her, and her family and others had refused to let her go, they had begged and cajoled her, pulling her from the depths of despair and bringing her back into the light.

What had possessed her to want to hurt them? Had she become the person she had hated the most; Ben?

Liam as if reading her thoughts, threw a pillow at her. 'Sorry Faith not allowed. It was my stupid stubbornness that has got us here. You made me come clean and for that I am glad.' Krista joined in. 'Nathan manipulated a lot of people, yes, I am sorry he is dead. Still, you have to admit, he reaped what he sowed in a way.' Krista's parents were avid churchgoers, but Krista herself had not followed suit. But sometimes bits of her parents showed through, and it always made Faith smile.

'I agree Nathan seems to have made many enemies, and I know I shouldn't be bothered, but Mirry is still my friend, and she is hurting.' She turned to see Krista frowning. Krista turned to Liam and took his hand. 'But your right Faith, if possible, we should all help to find his murderer. Though I don't think I will be able to help much, not now as my priority is helping my husband.' She tapped her belly. 'Also running after villains and the like maybe a little impossible as this bean gets bigger.'

'And I would not expect anything different Krista. I will do anything to help sort the mess I contributed to.' She turned to Liam. 'No arguments.'

Liam lifted his hands in mock surrender. 'As if I would dare try anything with you two ladies present. Then Faith there is your mum, your dad and I would do nothing to agitate Hope, she knows hundreds of ways to destroy a person.' He laughed when Krista playfully punched his arm and then began to act seriously wounded.

Faith had to admit she did feel better, but she still needed to do something. Liam laughed again and straightened up. 'I think order is needed dear friends; I can see Faith looking serious again. Fun over for the time being, now serious work is needed.' Two sets of eyes fixed on Faith, and she was at first lost for words. Then she decided on a plan. Reaching into her bag, she retrieved a pen and notepad.

'Let's see if we can come up with some suspects for Nathan's death, it's what they do on Tv and in most books.'

'Can I be top of the list? I mean, I was the first person you thought had killed him, and I am still on the police's main suspect list.' Krista rolled her eyes. 'You were taken to the station and interviewed, and you want to be put on the top of the list?'

'Why not, I like the idea of being a notorious criminal mastermind, I just need a white cat.' Faith lifted her pen, 'Okay, you are number one.' Said Faith as Liam fist-pumped the air. 'We have to put Mirry on the list too,' added Liam, and Faith was transported back to the dream where she had seen Mirry standing over Nathan's body, and she shivered. Looking up she saw both Krista and Liam staring at her.

'I suppose it could be possible,' said Faith

'I know it wasn't poisoning but it was close,' said Liam. 'Poisoning is usually the murder tool of the female of the species.'

Krista laughed. 'My husband now thinks he's Sherlock Holmes.' Liam placed his hand on his heart. 'Wife, you wound me, you know I love crime novels and it is usually the woman who poisons her victims. Just saying.'

'We must have a motive, Liam. Mirry was deeply in love with Nathan, we all knew that,' said Faith.

Krista put her hand up, then down when her two friends began to smile. 'Sorry had a flashback to school. Can you remember when I told you I had seen Mirry and Nathan arguing?' Faith thought for a moment. 'Actually, I do, I don't remember them ever arguing, so I did find it strange when you told me.'

'Lots have changed since you left. I think Mirry was getting bored of just being arm candy for Nathan. At one time she did have a great job in London, but it all changed when they returned home. Nathan just wanted her to organise parties for his partners and clients.'

'I had noticed that too. I feel as though I abandoned you all.' Admitted Faith. Krista threw a pillow at her, and she peered up.

'If you are guilty of anything Faith, it's letting that scumbag of an ex-husband steal your identity, just like Nathan did with Mirry.'

Faith looked at Krista. 'Did anybody like Ben?'

'To be truthful we only tolerated him because you seemed so happy at first, then when he started mentally abusing you, we didn't want to rock the boat and make things worse for you. Later, we hoped you would see sense and leave him. I feel we abandoned you too. We were so scared when we heard about the accident and so glad when you came home. Can you forgive us?' Krista said starting to cry again.

'Wow, this is really deep, do we need to hug?' Liam said lifting his arms and handing his wife a box of tissues.

'Maybe later husband, for now, we are supposed to be finding a murderer.'

'Heard loud and clear darling,' Liam replied. 'So where were we?'

Faith lifted her pen and began to write. 'Putting Mirry on the list. I also think we should put his work colleagues on, especially Sarah Alessi, the new boss at Nathans office.' Krista seemed surprised. 'Why Sarah?'

Faith explained about her meeting, leaving Penn's involvement out of it. 'Let's say she was never promoted even though she did most of the work. It's a sound motive to want to get rid of the boss, then have his job.'

'But kill him to get that job, isn't that a little harsh. She could have left and got a promotion elsewhere,' said Liam.

'I feel something else is involved and there could be another reason too.' Faith said adding her name to the list.

'Will any of this get Liam off the hook though?' said Krista.

Faith sat up and stared at her friends when she remembered what her teacher had said the day she took the pictures. 'Faith you are an idiot!'

'I wouldn't say an idiot, maybe a little ...' Krista put her hand on Liam's arm. 'Shush. What do you mean Faith?'

'Krista, on the day Nathan died, did anyone else have any nut-free brownies?'

Krista thought for a minute then smiled. 'I had forgotten. How could I have forgotten? Mrs Craven always takes her grandson out after school, then buys him some brownies as a treat. She came in that morning, it was strange as she had him with her, I remember as it was a school day.'

'So, all we need to do is ask if he was ok and that will show the brownies were not affected.'

Liam jumped up, grabbed Faith, and hugged her, then he hugged his wife and began to dance. Krista stared at Faith, shaking her head. 'Liam, you are crazy.' Liam kissed her hard. 'And that my sweet is why you love me.'

'That and much more.' Said Krista smiling. Faith nodded and for the first time in days felt a little relief.

CHAPTER 18

Faith woke up early, brimming with a newfound positivity. She was under no illusion that she was equipped to solve the enigma of Nathan's murder; perhaps this was her way of injecting some positivity into her own tumultuous life. Her role, she decided, would be to help absolve Liam of the accusations against him and then attempt to piece her life back together.

And so, there she was, sauntering towards the Grinder, ready to meet her two allies who had managed to coax Ms Craven to join them for a discussion. Liam had been eager to interrogate the woman over the phone immediately, but Faith had suggested they meet at the venue where the infamous brownie was purchased, hoping that the familiar surroundings might spur Ms Craven's memory.

Liam had responded with a playful, 'Alright, our leading lady detective, I am at your service'. Both women had exhaled a sigh and rolled their eyes at his comment, but that was Liam for you – incorrigible and charming in equal measures. And it was clear to Faith why Krista was so smitten with him.

Just as Faith was about to step into the Grinder, her path was abruptly blocked by a flustered Tiffany, her face flushed a deep shade of red. Tiffany clutched a coffee cup in one hand and a bag in the other, looking every bit the picture of disarray.

'Sorry!' Tiffany blurted out, her eyes darting up to meet Faith's. Recognition flashed across her face. 'Oh, it's you, Faith. How have you been?' She paused, her brows furrowing as she recalled something. 'I haven't forgotten about your invitation for a meal at your cottage.'

Tiffany paused, her chest rising and falling with a deep, steadying breath. She seemed to be grappling with her thoughts, her words tumbling out in a rush. 'You must understand, with everything that's been going on...' She trailed off, taking another deep breath as if trying to gather her wits.

'This is all so new to me,' she admitted, a hint of vulnerability creeping into her voice. 'Simon has never let me be involved with the running of the hall before. And now, everything's falling apart, and I can't help but feel responsible.' She sighed heavily, her shoulders sagging under the weight of her words. 'I'm sure you don't want to hear all this. I must sound like such a mess.'

Faith extended her hand, gently clasping Tiffany's arm. 'I remember the pressure from all those deadlines at work,' she confessed, her voice a soft murmur. 'It was like walls closing in, always second-guessing yourself. But Mum thinks you're doing a remarkable job, and the Folly... it's practically reborn under your guidance. I'm glad you persuaded Simon to breathe life back into it. The villagers, they've got a soft spot for it, you know.'

Tiffany's face creased into a frown, her gaze dropping to the floor. 'It's good for the hall, no doubt,' she admitted. 'But it's not all roses for me.'

Faith's brows knitted together in concern. 'I'm sorry to hear that,' she said, her voice laced with worry. But Tiffany just stiffened, a smile quickly replacing her frown. 'It's nothing, really. Just... all the hard work. And then there's Nathan's death... it was so sudden. We're all still reeling from it. And then, there's...'

Tiffany's voice trailed off; her cheeks flushed a deep shade of crimson. Faith filled in the blanks, her tone understanding. 'I know Simon's given Mirry the green light to help out. I also know she can be a bit... challenging.'

Tiffany was quick to defend her. 'No, Mirry's okay. She's just... grieving, you know? She's been a great help, really. And she's so clever.' Faith could tell that Tiffany was exaggerating, probably to convince herself more than anyone else. She could imagine how Tiffany felt, sandwiched between her assertive husband and equally forceful stepdaughter.

'Mirry's probably also struggling with the infertility issues,' Faith added, her voice softening. 'But Tiffany, don't worry. It will all work out.'

Tiffany nodded, her fingers nervously twisting the hem of her dress. 'Yes, and Nathan... he didn't want children, not like Mirry did. That's why he went to a different doctor.

Faith's eyes widened in surprise, her lips parting to form a question that Tiffany pre-empted. 'I'm sorry, Faith,' Tiffany blurted out, her own eyes reflecting a similar shock to what she'd just revealed. She turned slightly, her hands wringing together in discomfort. 'I shouldn't have said that. It's not my place to meddle.'

Before Faith could utter a word, Tiffany was already in motion, her words tumbling out in a rush. 'I really need to get going. This morning is just...it's madness. Simon is on my case about finishing the Folly by month's end.' She offered a weak smile, her eyes darting away from Faith's. 'Take care, Faith.' And just like that, Tiffany was hurrying down the road, leaving a perplexed Faith in her wake.

Faith was still processing the unexpected conversation when she noticed Krista waving enthusiastically from inside the building.

Shaking off her confusion, she pushed open the door and stepped inside. Krista was already moving towards her, her face beaming with excitement.

'Faith, over here!' Krista called out, pointing towards a table tucked away in the corner. A woman with dark hair and warm, brown skin sat there, her smile inviting. Beside her, a young boy was engrossed in the dual task of drinking a milkshake and devouring one of Krista's famous brownies.

'So, you're the Faith Harrington everyone's talking about,' the woman extended her hand, a warm smile lighting up her face. Faith took the offered seat next to her, a polite smile gracing her lips. 'I wouldn't exactly say I'm famous, just an ordinary girl doing an ordinary job.'

The woman let out a soft chuckle. 'Well, if your mother says you're extraordinary, then who am I to disagree? All children are miracles to their parents. I should know, I have five of my own, three boys and two girls.'

A small boy, his face smeared with chocolate, looked up from his seat. 'Me too, Grandy,' he piped up, his voice filled with childlike innocence. His grandmother's smile widened. 'Of course, you're extra special because you're my grandbaby.' The child seemed satisfied with the answer and went back to his chocolate treat, his small hands moving with a concentration that was nothing short of adorable.

Liam approached, a smooth latte in his hands, and placed it in front of Faith. The rich aroma wafted up to her and she couldn't help but let out a soft moan as she took her first sip. Liam let out a hearty laugh, his eyes twinkling with amusement. 'I seem to have that effect on women,' he joked, earning a playful shove from Krista. He bowed in mock surrender and retreated to the counter, leaving the three women alone.

Faith turned her attention back to the woman next to her. 'So, Mrs Craven...' she started, but was quickly interrupted. The woman raised a hand, a stern looks on her face. 'Faith, call me Marcia. Mrs Craven was my mother-in-law.' Faith nodded, her mind already racing with questions. 'Alright, Marcia, we were wondering if you remember the day Nathan died?'

Marcia's brow furrowed, her eyes narrowing in thought. 'It was a rotten day, that one,' she began, her voice gravelly with age. 'The lad, Nathan, he was a bit too cocky for my taste. But I wouldn't wish what happened to him on anyone. It was a ghastly way to go.' She paused, her gaze distant. 'I had my grandson with me that day. He's got the same blasted nut allergy as Nathan.'

Faith leaned forward, intrigued. 'Did you bring him to The Grinder?' she asked.

Marcia nodded, her lips pursing. 'Yes, I did. The poor mite had been sick, off school for days. But when he finally got his appetite back, I thought a treat was in order.'

A warm smile spread across Faith's face. 'Do you remember what you two had?'

Marcia's eyes flickered to the counter, then back to Faith. 'Let's see,' she mused, her gaze thoughtful. 'Ah yes, I remember. I had one of those delightful paninis the lovely lady here whips up. My grandson had soup, a special kind that's safe for him. And then, those heavenly chocolate brownies. He can't have much, mind you, but he does love a bit of sweetness when he can get it.'

Faith's eyes narrowed. 'Are you completely sure that's what you had?' she challenged.

Marcia's hand shot up, her fingers tapping her forehead. 'Absolutely certain,' she declared. Then, her eyes widened. 'Hold on...' She bent over, rummaging through her bag before pulling out a purse. She fumbled with it, producing a bunch of receipts. 'I really should clear this out more often,' she mumbled, more to herself than to Faith.

Her fingers sifted through the receipts until she found what she was looking for. 'Here,' she said, handing one to Faith. 'This is the bill from that day.'

Faith studied the receipt in her hands, her eyes scanning over the details - date, time, even the specific order of a no nut chocolate brownie. Her gaze lifted as the sound of footsteps approached, and she saw Liam and Krista moving towards their table. 'Look at this,' she said, passing the receipt to Krista as she and Liam took a seat.

Krista's eyes widened in shock as she read the receipt, the implications of it slowly sinking in. She turned to Liam, her hands trembling slightly as she passed the receipt to him. 'This... this means everything to us,' she choked out, her eyes glistening with tears.

Liam's reaction was immediate and jubilant. He leapt to his feet, wrapping Marcia in a bear hug and planting a kiss on her cheek. 'Marcia, you've just become my favourite customer,' he declared, his voice filled with gratitude.

Marcia laughed, a soft, warm sound. 'All this fuss over a receipt,' she said, her eyes twinkling with amusement.

Liam shook his head, his smile never fading. 'This is more than just a receipt, Marcia,' he said, his voice serious. As he went to fetch fresh drinks, Faith filled Marcia in on the details. Upon his return, Liam added that he had spoken with Sam, who had told him to bring the receipt and Marcia to the station.

Marcia nodded; her face determined. 'Well, if this is what it takes to clear your names, then let's do it,' she declared, her voice filled with resolve. 'This is quite the adventure.'

'Krista, clad in her usual apron, surveyed the bustling scene at the Grinder. The clattering of dishes and the hum of the espresso machine filled the air. She knew the cafe couldn't function properly without her, especially on such a busy day. Her gaze fell on little Abe, playing with a spoon on one of the tables. The thought of taking him to a police station made her stomach churn. It was no place for a child.

Faith, amid a mountain of pending tasks, felt a pang of anxiety. Yet, she found herself nodding, swayed by the genuine happiness that seemed to radiate from her friends. 'Don't you worry, Krista,' she assured, 'I've got your backs.'

As they stepped outside, the world seemed to mirror their optimism. The sun hung high in the sky, a radiant beacon of hope. Fluffy clouds meandered across the azure expanse, their unhurried pace a stark contrast to the turmoil in their lives. Faith inhaled deeply, the crisp, fresh air filling her lungs. She waited with Marcia, the anticipation of their journey building up.

They both got in the car and watched as Liam started the car and set off for the police station. She sat back watching the scenery pass, people milling about and getting on with their lives.

Faith was jolted back to reality when the car stopped, and she realized they were in the police station car park. Liam rushed out and came and opened the door for Marcia. He offered her his arm and with Faith following behind as he led them inside the police station.

Sam was waiting inside and when he saw Marcia he grinned. 'Hello Marcia, how is the family?'

'All well, and how is your beautiful new wife?'

Sam laughed, 'Not happy I am working late this week, but she will keep herself busy with decorating our house.'

'Going to cost you a lot of money Sam, I remember when Krista and I married. Ouch, my wallet burned.' Said Liam.

Sam stopped grinning, lost in thought, then Liam slapped him on the back. 'Don't worry, I can give you some shifts at the Grinder, or you could ask the boss for a raise.'

Sam extended a hand towards the door of the interview room, his fingers lightly brushing against the cool metal. 'After you,' he said, inviting them in with a courteous gesture. Marcia, her eyes softening, reached out to take Sam's arm.

'Sam,' she began, her voice carrying a tone of familiarity, 'I know your wife, Magda. She's a good woman, you know.' She then swivelled towards Liam, her eyes narrowing slightly as she wagged a finger at him. 'And you,' she added, 'don't you dare disrespect him.'

Liam, in a playful defiance, mimed zipping his mouth shut. 'Whatever the lady says,' he responded, a smirk playing on his lips.

Meanwhile, Faith found herself seated in the reception area, alone with her thoughts. She remembered how Liam had wanted her to accompany them, and a part of her wished she had. Yet, she didn't want to appear as though she was prying, always lurking around the corners.

Her mind was a battlefield, torn between the need to find Nathan's killer and the voice in her head that screamed at her to stop. The question that haunted her, the one she couldn't find an answer to, was why finding the truth was so important. The reception area, with its sterile lights and hushed tones, offered no answers.

Penn's hand froze mid-air, holding his third coffee of the day, as his phone began to ring. He sighed, placing the cup down and answering the call. 'Sam, everything alright?' His voice was laced with a hint of urgency, the anticipation of a potential lead on Nathan's case making his heart race.

Sam's voice came through the other end, a tinge of excitement in his tone. 'Liam Hunter's here. I tried to call you earlier, but you were tied up. He's brought a Mrs Marcia Craven with him.' Penn could almost hear the grin in Sam's voice. 'She claims to have evidence that the brownies sold on the day Nathan Crawford died were not contaminated.'

Penn's heart sank a little. This was not the outcome he had been hoping for. He had wanted to pin the case on Liam, but deep down, there was a part of him that hoped Liam was innocent. The man was about to become a father and despite his eccentricities, Penn had grown fond of him during their interviews.

'Alright,' Penn said, his voice steady. 'Take them to an interview room. I'll be right down.' He hung up, leaving his coffee untouched. This was going to be a long day.

As he meandered past the reception, his eyes were drawn to Faith, slumped in a chair, a magazine lying forgotten in her lap. Her gaze was lost in the ether, an absent stare that spoke volumes of exhaustion. He nudged the officer beside him, a hushed sound escaping his lips, 'Fetch Faith a coffee, and some food.'

Stepping into the interview room, he was greeted by the sight of Sam and Liam, engaged in conversation with an elderly lady. So this was Marcia Craven, a woman whose warmth radiated off her in waves. Her voice was a symphony of rich, Caribbean notes, a testament to her Trinidadian roots.

'I fell in love with an Englishman,' she shared, a nostalgic twinkle in her eyes, 'and that love brought me here, to this slightly cooler island.' Her laughter was infectious, filling the room with an unexpected joy. 'No regrets though. My husband and I, we had five children and spent fifty glorious years together. I could've gone home, but my heart, it's here now. With my babies, and their babies.'

With a playful twinkle in his eyes, Liam leaned towards Marcia, his voice dropping. 'This place seems brighter, more alive, with a kind and beautiful woman like you around, Marcia.' Her laughter filled the room again, a sound so youthful and vibrant, it was as if time had reversed itself.

'You're quite the charmer, young man. If you weren't already married, I'd snatch you up myself,' she retorted with a teasing wink.

Liam placed a hand over his heart, feigning a dramatic sigh. 'Ah, but I am taken. Otherwise, it would have been an honour.'

Just as the laughter began to fade, Sam cleared his throat, drawing the attention back to Penn. 'Mind telling me why you're both here?' he asked, his tone serious. Liam's eyebrows shot up in surprise. 'Didn't Sam fill you in?'

Liam reached into his pocket, pulling out a few crumpled notes and spreading them out on the table. 'He did, but I need to hear it from both of you. I need to take your statements for the record,' Penn explained.

As the room fell into silence, Liam and Marcia took turns narrating their story. Penn listened with rapt attention, scribbling down notes. Once they had finished, he had Sam escort Marcia out to join Faith for a drink.

Left alone in the room, Liam shifted uncomfortably in his seat, a desperate look in his eyes. Penn glanced down at his notes, then back up at Liam, taking in his anxious expression.

'The forensics on the bag the brownie came in found no trace of nuts,' Penn said. He leaned back in his chair, studying Liam's face. 'This leads me to think the brownie came from somewhere else, or it was swapped with a contaminated one to harm Mr Crawford.'

Liam exhaled, his shoulders sagging with relief. 'So, you believe me?' he answered.

Penn held his gaze for a moment before responding. 'I follow the evidence, Liam. Today, it seems to be on your side.' He paused, his stern expression softening slightly. 'But what you did was foolish. Your wife is pregnant, Liam. I hope you'll be more careful in the future. This time no one was hurt, next time you may not be so lucky.'

Liam sighed, extending his hand to Penn. After a moment's hesitation, Penn reached out and shook it. 'Thank you, DCI McBride,'

Liam said, his voice filled with gratitude. 'My wife and unborn child are my world. I won't do anything to risk losing them.'

Penn nodded, rising from his chair. Together, they exited the room, finding Faith and Marcia waiting for them in the dimly lit hallway.

Faith's cheeks warmed with a blush as Penn's gaze found her. She dipped her head, a frown etching itself onto her face. Liam, oblivious to the tension between them, thanked Marcia for her efforts and proceeded to lead her towards the car parked outside.

Penn, however, had other plans. He laid a gentle hand on Faith's arm, stopping her in her tracks. 'Give us a moment, Liam,' she called out, her eyes never leaving Penn's. As Liam and Marcia disappeared outside, Penn broke the silence. 'You did well, Faith. I'm grateful.'

Faith shook her head modestly. 'It was a group effort, Penn. I only remembered something my old teacher once said.' On seeing his puzzled expression, she shared the wisdom of her former mentor. Penn, in turn, lifted her bag from the seat and handed it over. 'You look worn out,' he commented, his voice laced with concern.

Faith nodded, her shoulders sagging slightly under the weight of her bag. 'Just a few things left to sort out,' she admitted. When Penn remained silent, she rose and headed for the door. 'I need a drink, some relaxation time, and then I'll be packing for London this weekend.'

Penn followed her with his gaze, curiosity piqued. 'A job?' He inquired, his tone casual. Faith paused at the door, her back to him. 'No, just tying up some loose ends,' she replied cryptically. As she stepped out of the station, Penn's gaze lingered on her retreating figure. Even as Liam's car pulled away, he remained rooted to the spot, watching.

'Faith, won't you stay for a meal?' Liam asked, his eyes pleading. Krista stood at his side, nodding encouragingly.

Faith felt the gnawing hunger in her stomach. She hadn't eaten properly in days, but she shook her head. 'I can't, I've a case to pack.' Her voice was laced with uncertainty. She had been procrastinating, uncertain of what to pack. The London fashion she was used to now felt out of place.

She glanced at her open suitcase, filled with comfortable yet stylish clothes. 'I think this is the new Faith,' she said aloud, her fingers tracing the texture of a soft cashmere sweater. Or perhaps, she thought, it was the old Faith, the one she had buried deep within herself during her time with Ben. She sighed, closing the case with a firm click.

That night, sleep was elusive. The unfamiliar sounds of the countryside - the hooting of owls, the gentle gurgle of the water feature in her back garden - were a stark contrast to the constant city noise she was accustomed to. But slowly, the soothing rhythm of nature lulled her into a restless sleep.

CHAPTER 19

Don Harrington made his way to his daughter's house earlier than planned. The day was just beginning to lose its morning chill and the quiet neighbourhood was still bathed in the soft, diffused light of dawn. He found her in the kitchen, the heart of the house, where she seemed to have taken permanent residence since her return from London.

She was sat there, at the old oak table, with her packed case. Her face, usually so vibrant and full of life, was etched with exhaustion. Her eyes, once sparkling with youthful energy, were now dull and distant. It was a sight that made his heart clench painfully in his chest.

'Dad,' she greeted him. The smile she attempted to put on was more of a grimace.

'Hey, sweetheart,' Don replied, forcing a cheerfulness he didn't feel into his voice.

He moved closer, taking in the sight of his little girl looking so defeated. The urge to hunt down the man who had done this to her was almost overpowering.

He remembered his wife's words from the night before. Her pleas for him to keep his anger in check, to remember that their daughter needed him now more than ever. He had promised her he would but seeing his daughter like this made it a promise that would be hard to keep.

She poured a steaming mug of coffee, and pushed it across the table towards him, her fingers brushing against his in the process. 'Give me a minute to wake up properly, this is my extra fuel.' She lifted her own cup in a mock toast before taking a generous sip.

'You look like you haven't slept a wink,' her father observed, his eyes full of concern as he mirrored her actions, taking a sip of his own drink. 'I heard about the incident with Liam. Quick thinking on your part.'

Faith looked up at him, her eyes narrowed slightly in suspicion. 'Why do I get the feeling there's a 'but' coming?'

Her father chuckled, a soft, warm sound that filled the small kitchen. 'You know me too well, my girl. It's just...you're spreading yourself thin. You've got your new business to focus on, and then there's everything with Ben. And I know you don't like talking about the accident...'

Faith's laughter cut him off. 'So now I'm losing my mind, am I? Cheers to that, Dad.' She raised her cup in a salute again before taking another sip.

Her father sighed, running a hand through his thinning hair. 'That's not what I meant, Faith. Your mum and I, we're just worried about you. And now you're getting involved with Nathan's case...'

'Murder,' Faith corrected him, her voice cold. 'Nathan's murder. And yes, I'm involved. But ask yourself this, Dad - would you have looked deeper if I hadn't? Or would Nathan's death have been just another accident?

'Dad, you've got to concede,' Faith implored, her eyes sparkling with a mix of mischief and determination. 'I was spot-on, wasn't I?' She paused; her hands clasped together as if she was pleading. 'I assure you, I'll tread carefully. I know how much both of you worry.'

Her words hung in the air, a silent plea for understanding. Then, as if a switch had been flipped, her face lit up with a radiant smile. 'I love you both, even though everything's a bit bonkers at the moment,' she admitted, her voice softer now. 'Let's just deal with this situation, and then I swear,' she made a cross over her heart, her eyes earnest, 'I'll try not to bite off more than I can chew. But let's be fair, you two did raise me. What did you really expect?'

Don rose from the table, his movements slow and deliberate. He cast a glance at his daughter, a mix of exasperation and affection in his eyes. He reached for Faith's suitcase, his hands wrapping around the handle. 'You'd think being surrounded by three women, I'd have learned by now to follow orders,' he grumbled, his tone teasing.

He motioned towards the door, his gaze now settled on Faith. 'Grab your stuff, love,' he instructed, his voice firm yet gentle. 'Let's go sort out that ex-husband of yours.' His words were simple, but they carried a promise - a promise of support, of protection, and of a father's unwavering love for his daughter.

They had decided not to drive down to London as the traffic was hectic, so they parked up at the train station, boarded first-class, a treat her dad had told her and much more comfortable. The trip down was relaxing and they both chatted about the weather, Hope's upcoming literary festival and Charity her younger sister's recent promotion.

Faith could see Dad was proud, partly because one of his daughters had followed him into the police force, also there was the fact that Charity had been a very wild child and in her early life her experience with the police had not been the best. She had been the rebellious one and when she had reached her late teens and announced to her family, she wanted to join the force, it had been met with a first astonishment, then jubilation.

They ate and her father fell asleep leaving Faith to her thoughts. Looking out as the landscape changed as it passed, she wondered how she would react when she saw Ben after so long. Over the last few weeks, her feeling for her ex had altered greatly and she was surprised to find herself wondering what she had ever seen in him.

The trip was over before she knew it and waking her dad up, they disembarked, caught a taxi, and soon arrived at the hotel. Which was quite impressive. 'Dad, you didn't have to book something so pricy.'

Her dad shrugged. 'You deserve it, and I haven't been on holiday with my daughter for ages, so let me spoil you.'

'I wouldn't say this is exactly a vacation dad.'

'Maybe not in the typical sense. Let's just say we are celebrating the end of one thing and the start of something new and exciting.'

When Faith arrived at her room, she flung herself on the bed and squealed like a child. 'This room is the best; I could get used to this lifestyle. She unpacked and took a long relaxing soak in the deep tub, lifting foam onto her hands and blowing it, watching bubbles lift into the air.

'Well done girl, you have scrubbed up nicely. Now to dinner with a handsome man.' That handsome man was sitting waiting for her downstairs in the reception. 'Good evening sweet lady. May I escort you to your meal?'

Faith took her father's hand. 'Thank you, kind sir, lead on.' The restaurant was as luxurious as the bedrooms and the menu was to die for. Faith and her father took their time ordering and when the drinks came, a rich and fruity red her father had recommended, she took a deep sip and moaned. 'Wow, I could get used to this, even Ben never took me anywhere as nice as this.'

As the meal was served, Don looked at Faith and raised his eyebrows. 'Salmon, your favourite,' he said, his voice filled with warmth. The fish, glazed with a soft and peppery sauce, sat alongside a colourful array of slightly crunchy vegetables. Faith nodded, her mouth watering at the sight.

After they had polished off the main course, Don beckoned the waiter over. 'The white chocolate and strawberry cheesecake, please,' he ordered, a twinkle in his eye. As the dessert was served, covered with fresh cream, Faith let out a soft gasp. 'This looks amazing,' she said, her eyes wide with delight. They savoured the cheesecake, their conversation flowing easily, careful to avoid the topic of the following day.

As Faith stifled a yawn, Don glanced at his watch and cleared his throat. 'Time for bed, I think,' he said, his tone gentle. 'It's been a long day and we've got an early start tomorrow.' He walked Faith back to her room, his hand resting lightly on her shoulder.

At her door, Don leaned down and kissed her gently on the forehead. 'Goodnight, baby girl. Sleep tight,' he said, his voice soft. Faith smiled up at him. 'You too, Dad. And thanks... just for being here,' she replied. She slipped into her room, leaving Don standing in the hallway. He watched her go, then turned and opened the door to the room next to hers.

Once inside her room, Faith quickly undressed and slipped into bed, the satin-soft sheets cool against her skin. As she closed her eyes, sleep claimed her instantly.

Faith studied her reflection in the mirror, her fingers tracing the healthy glow of her skin - a stark contrast to the acne-ridden pallor London had left her with. 'You've come a long way, haven't you?' she murmured to herself, her eyes sparkling with contentment.

Her chosen attire for the day was a calf-length floral dress featuring a soft blue backdrop, the colours complimenting her newly radiant complexion. She had woven her hair into a braid, letting it cascade down her back, a silver necklace and earrings adding a touch of elegance. A pair of sensible blue sandals and a matching shoulder bag completed the look. With a final approving nod at her reflection, she spritzed on some perfume, grabbed her bag, and made her way downstairs.

Her father was waiting for her, his gaze softening as he took in her appearance. 'Wow, Faith, you look amazing,' he said, crossing the room to plant a kiss on her forehead.

'Thanks, dad,' she replied, her cheeks flushing slightly. 'Just make sure I don't overeat at breakfast. I don't want to ruin this dress.'

His laughter filled the room. 'Just like your mother,' he said, his eyes twinkling with mirth. 'Don't worry, I'll make you a bib out of some napkins. I'm an expert at this sort of thing.'

The air of London was thick with tension, the city's hustle and bustle closing in around Faith as the taxi wove its way through the streets. It was a relief when the office building came into view.

Upon entering the solicitor's office, a surprise awaited her. Ben and his solicitor were not alone. Eloise, a woman of ample size and clearly in the late stages of pregnancy, stood by one of the chairs. A wave of shock washed over Faith.

'Faith, I'd like you to meet Eloise,' Ben said, his voice carrying an undertone of pride. The room seemed to close in around her.

Eloise was taller than him, a statuesque figure swathed in designer attire that clung to her generous curves. Her skin had the unnatural sheen of a tanning salon regular, stretched taut in a way that made Faith suspect a little help from Botox. Her hair, a waterfall of meticulously coiffed blonde curls, cascaded down her back. Faith found herself gaping at the vertiginous heels that made Eloise loom even taller over Ben.

'Faith, you look stunning,' Ben said, flashing a smile as he stepped forward.

'I think we'd all prefer to get this over with as soon as possible,' Faith's father said, his voice as frosty as his demeanour.

The office they were led into was awash with harsh, sterile light, a stark contrast to the warm hues of the hallway. A man of short stature, his scalp gleaming under the fluorescent lights, sat at a large table. His face was flushed, an uncomfortable grimace etched into his features as he fidgeted in his seat.

He finally looked up, his gaze steady and business-like. 'I've got a copy of my client's proposal here,' he began, his tone matter of fact, 'to compensate you for your stake in the flat you both resided in.' He distributed copies of the document to everyone present, allowing them a moment to digest the information.

Faith's brows knitted together in a frown. She broke the silence, her voice laced with disbelief. 'I had the flat independently valued,' she began, her gaze flickering between the solicitor and Ben, 'and this figure... it's not what I was told.' Ben's grin faded, his eyes dropping to the paper in front of him.

The solicitor's previously impassive face mirrored Faith's frown. 'My client felt it was fair that he doesn't pay the full half,' he explained, 'given his claim that he contributed more to the property's purchase.' Her father, silent until now, hoisted his briefcase onto the table. He retrieved a stack of notes, extending them towards the solicitor.

'See this?' Donald held up a piece of paper, his eyes never leaving the solicitor's. 'This shows that my wife and I paid the deposit and the first three months of the mortgage on the flat.' A frown creased the solicitor's forehead as he took the paper, glancing over at Ben, who was sat uncomfortably in his chair.

'Also,' Donald continued, passing over another set of papers, 'These are my daughter's bank statements. After the first few months, she was the one paying the lion's share of the bills and the mortgage.' Ben cleared his throat, shifting in his seat. 'We had an agreement,' he exclaimed. 'Until I got my first promotion, Faith would pay more. She wanted to. We were a couple, we shared everything.'

Faith couldn't hold back any longer. 'We're not a couple anymore, Ben,' she said, her voice steady. 'And I don't live in the flat anymore. I think it's only fair I get my share back.' She put extra emphasis on the word 'share', giving Ben a tight smile.

Ben turned to Eloise, who was watching Faith with wide eyes. 'I understand you're upset,' she said, her voice trembling. 'Upset that I'm with Ben now.'

Faith's mouth felt open. 'And why do you think that is, Eloise?' she snapped. 'I invested a lot of money into that flat.' She took a deep breath, steadying herself. She wouldn't let Ben see her lose her cool. Not after she'd come so far.

'Ben, our past together doesn't change the fact of the matter now,' Faith said, her voice steady and calm. She paused, taking a deep breath before continuing. 'I'm glad you've moved on, really. I'm happy for you both and the baby on the way. But what I want, what I need, is to move forward with my own life. And that starts by settling this apartment issue.'

Ben's face tightened, his eyes darting towards the solicitor. The solicitor shook his head solemnly. 'Given the information provided by Mr. Harrington,' he began, his voice carrying an air of finality, 'it's clear that Miss Harrington is entitled to half of the apartment's purchase price.'

His gaze shifted to Ben, whose face was now flushing a deep shade of red. Faith watched him, recognizing the telltale sign of his simmering anger.

'Ben,' the solicitor continued, 'I suggest you consider Miss Harrington's offer. If she chose to pursue this further, she might end up with more than just half. It's in your best interest to settle this now and pay her what she's asking.'

The room fell into a tense silence, broken only by the harsh slap of Ben's hand against the polished mahogany table. Faith and Eloise jerked in their seats, eyes wide with shock. 'I refuse to accept this!' Ben's voice was a venomous hiss, his eyes boring into Faith. 'I was the making of you, Faith. You were a nobody before me, and without me, you're nothing.'

He leaned across the table, his sneer a grotesque caricature of his usual suave charm. 'Look at yourself, Faith. You're a shadow of the woman I once wanted. You've let yourself go, and in your jealousy, you're trying to take what's rightfully mine.' His voice dropped to a low growl, 'All while my fiancée is carrying our child.'

Faith's attention was diverted by the grating sound of a chair moving. Her father had risen to his feet, his face hardened with anger. 'Jealousy, Ben?' His voice was laced with disbelief. 'What exactly is my daughter supposed to be jealous of?'

Ben didn't flinch, his arrogance unyielding. It was as if he truly believed that their relationship had somehow elevated Faith, lifted her from the ranks of the ordinary. 'Your daughter, sir, is hardly a prize. She should consider herself lucky that I even deigned to date her.'

Faith's father's knuckles whitened as his hands balled into tight fists. He was a man of few words and even fewer expressions, but his anger was palpable in the tension that filled the room. Faith, sensing his anger, gently reached over and squeezed his hand, a silent plea for calm. Her father, however, merely flashed her a reassuring smile before he straightened up, his hand disappearing into his bag.

'My dear Eloise,' he began, his voice as smooth as silk despite the tension in the room. He pulled out an envelope and slid it across the table towards Eloise. 'I believe my daughter deserves better than a man who seeks to elevate himself through marriage.'

Eloise, her cheeks flushed with embarrassment, picked up the envelope and opened it. Her eyes widened as she pulled out a photograph and turned to Ben. 'Who is this woman you're kissing?' she demanded, her voice trembling.

Ben froze, his eyes darted to the photograph. It showed him locked in a passionate embrace with a young girl, scantily clad and visibly intoxicated. His heart pounded in his chest as he took the picture from Eloise.

Her father, a stern figure with greying hair, leaned forward, his eyes piercing through Ben. 'I've had you investigated,' he said, his voice as cold as ice. He pointed a gnarled finger at Ben, 'You're drowning in debt. You thought you could leech off this woman's family, didn't you?' He then turned to Eloise, his gaze softening. 'My dear, do you really want to be with a man who's only interested in your money?'

Eloise, her face pale, stiffened at Faith's father's words. She took a moment to collect herself before she rose from her seat, her movements graceful and deliberate. She removed the ring from her finger, her hand trembling slightly, and placed it on the table in front of Ben. She then turned to Faith, her lips curling into a small, sad smile, before she exited the room, her heels clicking against the polished wooden floor.

Ben was left gaping, his face a mask of shock. He quickly recovered, his shock morphing into anger. He spun around, his eyes blazing. 'This isn't over,' he spat, 'I'll drag you to court. I have connections.'

Her father sat back down and leaned back in his chair, a smug smile playing on his lips. 'The detective also informed me that you've lost your job,' he said, his voice dripping with satisfaction. 'I'll make sure everyone knows about your debts and your other...endeavours. You won't be welcomed anywhere in London. You thought you got away with hurting my daughter, but don't think for a moment that you'll get another chance.'

He turned around to face the solicitor, who was perched in his chair with an expression of revulsion etched onto his features, a direct result of Ben's tantrum. 'I look forward to our little dance in court,' he sneered, 'though I suspect your client will be preoccupied with other matters.'

Then he directed his gaze towards Ben, his eyes hard and unyielding. 'I'll be expecting payment from you, for my daughter's share. And once that's settled, I want you to vanish from Faith's life. Permanently.'

His voice dropped to a dangerous tone, his words a lethal promise. 'Let's hope they never let you near your child. You're nothing but a pathetic excuse for a man.'

Faith, who had been silent throughout the heated exchange, rose from her chair. She followed her father out of the room, down the stairs and into the bustling street, leaving the tension and bitter words behind.

'Faith, what's the matter?' Her father looked concerned as he saw his daughter doubled over outside the building. Faith was shaking, her hands clutching her stomach, but the sound that filled the air was not of pain but laughter.

'I'm alright, Dad,' Faith managed to gasp out between bouts of laughter, waving him off. 'Just give me a moment.' Don stood there, a look of bemusement etched on his face, as he watched his daughter try to regain her composure.

Finally, Faith straightened up, wiping tears of mirth from her eyes. 'Oh, Dad,' she said, still chuckling. 'You should've seen Ben's face when Eloise walked out. And a private detective, really?' She raised her eyebrows at him, her grin wide.

Don shrugged, a mischievous glint in his eyes. 'Well, darling, did you really think I'd go into that meeting without some backup?' He asked, his voice filled with satisfaction. 'I've been waiting for a chance to show that man what he really is.' His words hung in the air, a statement of victory.

Faith walked over to him, wrapping her arms around him in a tight hug. 'Thank you, Dad,' she said her voice filled with gratitude. As they pulled apart, Don gestured towards a waiting taxi. 'Come on, Faith,' he said, opening the door for her. 'It's time to celebrate.

CHAPTER 20

The rhythmic chug of the train as it traced its path back home was the only event of note on Faith's journey. She found herself ensconced in the comforting familiarity of her cottage, the soft embrace of her bed beckoning. The phone rang, jarring her from her tranquil state.

'Hi, mum,' she muttered, stifling a yawn, 'Yes, I'm back safe.'

Her mother's voice was a soothing balm, but her exhaustion was too profound to engage in a lengthy conversation. 'Sorry, mum, I'm just really tired. Can we chat tomorrow?'

By the next day she was depleted. She had to apologise to her mum, cancelling the family meal she was due to attend at her parents' house. Sleep proved elusive, so she decided on a different form of relaxation.

With a glass of wine in hand, she stepped into her garden. The first signs of spring were evident in the budding flowers, and despite the encroaching darkness, the nights were beginning to stretch out longer. She nestled herself on the bench next to her greenhouse, taking a sip of the crisp, fruity wine.

'Good choice, Valerian,' she murmured to herself, making a mental note to thank her cousin for the wine recommendation.

Faith's mobile pinged with a notification. A hefty sum had been deposited into her account. Her brows furrowed in confusion. A call from her father soon followed. He explained, 'Eloise's solicitor contacted me. Ben sold the apartment. The money in your account is your share.'

'Eloise did this?' Faith asked, incredulous.

'Yes,' her father confirmed. 'She froze their joint account, stopped Ben's cards. She's the one who sent you the money.'

Faith felt a pang of sympathy for Eloise. Pregnant, alone, and yet still thoughtful enough to ensure Faith received her due. The next day, a letter arrived. Faith retreated to her conservatory with a glass of wine and the letter, flicking on the light. She took a sip of her wine, unfolded the letter, and began to read.

'Dear Faith,' the letter began. *'I hope you've received your share of the apartment. I regret that I initially listened to my fiancée. I assigned you the role of villain without giving you a chance to explain. Many warned me about Ben, and I didn't listen. I hope you're not angry, but I've spoken to some of your friends. They told me the truth about your relationship. I hope you can forgive me for any discomfort I've caused.'*

Eloise continued, *'There will be no reconciliation between Ben and I, and I doubt he'll want much to do with his child. I'm content to raise this child alone. It's the only joy that's come from this relationship. Take care and grow strong. In another life, I think we could have been friends.'*

Faith folded the letter, a mix of emotions washing over her. She took another sip of her wine, staring out of her conservatory.

'Poor Eloise,' she murmured to the empty room, her heart aching for the woman and her sudden, life-altering circumstances. Yet, amidst the sympathy, a sliver of envy crept in. Eloise was having a child, a joy she would never experience.

Penn was in a rush; he had had a late night at work. The month had been busy with a spate of burglaries, and it had been a hard slog to find the culprit.

It had eventually come to light that a gang of youths from a nearby village had been apprehended when a couple who had arrived home early had seen said boys leaving next door with what looked like a large Tv. Fortunately, the woman had worked as a secretary at the local college and had recognized one of the boys.

Her husband had been a quick thinker and had kept himself and his wife out of sight, so there would be no retribution on his wife. The boy had been easily apprehended and it hadn't taken long for him to identify the rest of the team of thieves. What had been the hardest was the screams and abuse the officers had faced when the boys were picked up.

It was easy to see where these youth had picked up the proclivity to steal as one or more of said parents had frequented the same station on multiple occasions.

There had been nothing the parents could do but watch as their children were placed in the police van and taken away. It had been fortunate that all the culprits had been over 18 and it had not been necessary to have a parent with them, still the whole thing had been a gruelling experience and Sam had said this would cause tension on the housing estate where the boys had lived.

'It's hard to see this happen and a measure of the blame falls equally on parents as well as the kids. Still, there is nothing for them to do, no jobs and no help at all for them to train.' Sam had a kind heart and he felt things like this deeply.

'Sometimes you have to rise above how you are raised.' Replied Penn. 'It's not easy and I agree, something needs to be done for this cycle of offending to stop.'

Penn arrived late at the station and was surprised to find Don sitting at Sam's table, a mug with the words BOSS MAN splashed on it. The two were laughing and when Don saw Penn, he ushered him over. Sam rose and lifting his mug asked. 'I think you need caffeine; I am getting a refill; I'll get you one too.'

Penn pulled his chair up to Sam's table and sunk into it. Don raised his eyebrows, 'Bet you thought it would be quiet in the countryside mmm?' Sam returned with a hot cup of coffee and Penn practically inhaled it. 'It is surprising how the same problems arise everywhere.

'Penn, how's the progress on Nathan's case?' Penn looked up, his eyes weary from hours of poring over case files.

'This is what we know so far. Nathan died from anaphylactic shock. The odd thing is his epi-pen was empty. No trace of his medication.

'His wife, Mrs. Crawford, swore she'd picked up all his medication. Said his epi-pen was full and he even had spares. This has been checked and is true, but we found his medication drawer wide open, all contents gone.' Penn continued.

Don frowned, 'And we've found no trace of the missing medication?'

'No,' Sam chimed in from the doorway, a stack of files in his arms. 'We thought maybe he'd taken it to work but turns out he had a separate stash in his office safe. The ones at home are still missing.'

Don leaned back in his chair, his mind racing. 'So where are we with suspects?' he asked, his voice heavy with the weight of the unsolved case.

'Right, we visited Mrs. Crawford for a chat,' Penn began, leaning back in his creaky office chair. He flicked open a worn notebook, its pages filled with hastily scribbled notes. 'She was supposed to have dinner with your daughter, Faith - sorry, Miss Harrington. But she didn't show.' He paused, glancing up at Don.

'The reason? She'd been called into the fertility clinic last minute,' Penn continued, his gaze steady. 'An unexpected appointment, she said.' He watched as Don nodded his understanding, a silent cue for him to go on.

'Faith, your daughter, she was in the clear too. Solid alibi,' Penn added, his voice flat. He then tapped a finger on the notebook, moving on to the next suspect. 'Then there was Liam Hunter, the man who owns The Grinder coffee shop.'

Penn's face hardened. 'Hunter had been making some dodgy purchases. We thought at first that Nathan might've died from a peanut allergy - contaminated flour from Hunter's shop.' The room fell silent, the gravity of the situation sinking in.

Sam leaned forward, his fingers tapping against the cold metal of the table. 'So, here's the thing,' he began, his voice steady, 'Liam and Domonic Sharpe, they were brought in for questioning. Some stolen food products, you see.' He paused, glancing at Don, who merely nodded, urging him to continue.

'Turns out,' Sam continued, his voice dropping to a murmur, 'the purchases were above board. Legitimate. Even the flour they used in those brownies Crawford ate, no nuts. Nothing suspicious.'

Don's eyebrows shot up in surprise. 'What about that brick? The one chucked through Nathan's office window?' He asked, leaning back in his chair, his legs crossed at the knee.

Sam flicked through his notebook, his eyes scanning the pages. 'Well, it seems our Nathan wasn't exactly a saint,' he said, a grim smile playing on his lips. 'Had a bit of a side job, extortion. He wanted The Grinder. Funny thing is no one is talking, but rumours say he wasn't averse to cheating, lying and conning, to get what he wanted.'

'Have you checked his work colleagues, any suspects there?'

'None, all checked out and had alibis. Friends, and even those he knew from school, and college have also been interviewed. Lots of people disliked him, but we cannot connect anyone to the crime.

Don's expression hardened, his surprise morphing into a grim understanding. 'I never really liked Nathan,' he admitted, 'but it seems he had a side that could seriously make someone mad enough to kill him. Still, the murders seem more like a random act than a calculated move.'

Don rose from his chair, the worn leather creaking under his weight. 'Keep me in the loop,' he said, his voice gruff but not unkind. 'We've got a murder on our hands. Doesn't matter if the victim had it coming or not - there's a crime that's been committed and a perpetrator that needs to be brought to justice. That's our job.'

Across the room, Penn flicked his computer on, the screen lighting up with a soft, blue hue. He swivelled in his chair to face Sam, his eyes serious. 'We've got our work cut out for us, Sam.'

Sam only nodded. 'What gets to me,' he started, his voice quiet, 'is that it could be someone we know. And if they feel cornered... they might not stop at one.' His gaze flicked to the photos scattered across the desk, worry etching lines into his face. 'Makes me worry about everyone else involved. About their safety.'

Penn, the silent observer, remained quiet. His eyes, however, spoke volumes. They met Sam's across the room, the unspoken agreement between them clear.

Faith's mobile buzzed on the coffee table, pulling her out of her thoughts. 'Hello, Faith speaking,' she answered, her voice slightly shaky.

'Faith, it's Mike from Nathan's office,

"I'm calling on behalf of Mrs Alessi. She's keen to arrange a meeting with you at the office about a new brochure we're working on for the business. With the changes we're implementing, we're looking to bring a fresh perspective to our visual marketing material. This includes acquiring new photographs of the area to adorn our office walls and collaborating with a new photographer for the pictures of the properties we have on the market. Are you available for such a project?"

"Certainly, I'd be happy to get involved. Would it be convenient for me to swing by now?"

"That would be excellent, we appreciate your prompt response. Mrs Alessi will be pleased to hear it. See you soon then."

She had decided to walk to town as it would allow her to catch any interesting sites she could capture on her camera; it was times like these you could capture that one picture that would typify the season and could be stored for future use.

With the swift departure of March, April had unfurled itself, draping the world in the sights and scents of spring. 'Look at them bluebells,' she murmured to herself, noting how they had punctured through the forest floor and roadside like a stubborn army of indigo soldiers. Birds were a flurry of activity above, their chirping resonating through the sprouting trees as they hustled for nest materials. She drew in a deep breath, the scent of rain on parched earth filling her lungs with its crisp freshness.

She was nearing the shops on the main road now. 'Finally, some warmth,' she overheard a passerby exclaim. The townsfolk were bidding adieu to the harsh winter that had gripped them for months, embracing the milder weather with open arms. Even the intermittent rainy days hadn't dampened their spirits.

The shops bustled with activity, a harmonious cacophony of chattering locals and out-of-towners. 'Never seen it this busy before,' the shopkeeper, Mr. Jenkins, commented as she entered his store. 'Seems like everyone's been waiting for this weather.' She nodded, stepping aside as a family of tourists bustled past.

Pink was busying herself with a new window display and waved as she passed. Liam smiled at her as he tidied the tables outside and took some orders while making faces at a young girl with curly blonde hair; she was clapping her hands and giggling loudly.

It didn't take her long to reach the estate agents and as soon as she entered, she was greeted by a cheerful young girl at the front counter.

'You must be Miss Harrington the photographer, please come this way.' She was led to another desk where a slightly overweight middle-aged man sat and was asked to take a seat.

'Mrs Alessi couldn't greet you herself as she is in a meeting with a client. I have a list here of all she wants you to do, and I have been advised to give you the brief and leave you to do your work as you will know exactly what is needed from you.'

After reading the brief Faith walked around the outside of the office to get a feel for the job, then entered again took stock of what she felt would be best to shoot to get the effect the client wanted.

What struck Faith was how many new faces had appeared at the office. There was now an equal number of men to women. Some had been kept on and that was probably more due to their work ethic than looks. Another thing that struck her was the change to the shop front and the décor within. It still had a professional air to it, but also a few added comforts that made it feel more welcoming and less sterile.

Faith was in the midst of snapping a few photos of the exterior when she noticed the sign. It was now splashed with vibrant colours, adorned with strategically placed potted plants, and boasted a picturesque layout that advertised both houses for sale and lettings.

Her heart skipped a beat as one particular advertisement caught her eye. The centre image was unmistakably Nathan and Mirry's house. She leaned in closer, her brow furrowing in confusion.

'Nathan and Mirry's place? When did this happen?' She responded, her finger tracing the image. She couldn't recall Mirry mentioning anything about selling the house.

Faith felt a pang of sadness at the thought. Despite Nathan's efforts to strip the house of its charm, she had loved having her friend live so close by. When she had first arrived, wounded and broken from London, Mirry had been a lifeline. She sighed, lowering her camera and staring at the image of the house. She felt a profound sense of loss.

Faith's jaw dropped at the sight of the house's value. The memory of her hospital stay in London after her accident came rushing back. She remembered the visit from Mirry and Nathan, and the conversation they had.

'I know this isn't the time,' Nathan had said, his voice a soothing melody in the sterile hospital room. 'But I'd be willing to sell your aunt's old house. You could use the money to go anywhere you want.'

Faith, now looking back, couldn't help but wonder if Nathan's concern was genuine or if he was more interested in the huge commission, he'd get from selling her aunt's cottage. After all, it was significantly larger than their own house and came with a vast expanse of land.

There was no sign of Mirry moving out. She seemed to have made herself quite at home, renovating the Folly. Had she decided to move back into Eglantine Hall for good? The thought didn't sit well with Faith. Tiffany had just started to find her footing, managing the massive house and earning the trust of the staff.

Mirry, always one to vie for the top spot, would not take kindly to Tiffany's newfound authority. Faith feared that Tiffany would bear the brunt of Mirry's jealousy and her often malicious attitude towards her stepmother.

Simon was always there for his daughter, a fact that never ceased to baffle Faith. She couldn't help but wonder why he had chosen to marry Tiffany. 'Why, Simon? She worships the ground you walk on,' Faith mused aloud, her camera hanging idly by her side. The woman had done everything in her power to fit into his life, his circle of friends.

She stepped back into the building, her professional mask sliding into place. The staff were busy at their workstations, oblivious to her presence. She began snapping pictures, capturing the essence of their dedication and hard work. When she was satisfied, she had the photos she needed, the same woman who had directed her earlier approached her.

'You can use the kitchen,' he said, gesturing towards a small room at the end of the hallway. 'Help yourself to tea and coffee.' She thanked him, grateful for the offer. The aroma of brewing coffee wafted through the air, a comforting scent amidst the chaos of her thoughts.

Stepping through a discreet door nestled in the corner of the office, Faith found herself in the kitchen, just as the estate agent had directed. The ambience here was more inviting, full of recent renovations. The practicalities of the kitchen were neatly arranged; an electric kettle and a petite, barista-style coffee maker sat on the counter, while a full-size fridge stood guard in one corner. Across from it, a table was tucked away, accompanied by six chairs.

What truly caught Faith's eye was the surprising addition of two petite sofas, forming a cosy seating area around a small coffee table. The arrangement was comfortable, bordering on the luxurious, and contrasted the otherwise functional space.

Three people occupied the room. A tall woman with dark hair was busying herself making coffee, while the other two were comfortably ensconced on the sofas, sandwiches resting on the coffee table before them. The dark-haired woman looked up as Faith entered, a warm smile playing on her lips. 'Please, join us,' she invited, her voice as welcoming as the kitchen itself.

'Would you like a drink?' A lean man with sandy blonde hair, thinning a bit at the top, announced as he headed towards the kitchen. His voice causing the two women to look up from their conversation.

'Can that fancy machine of yours whip up a latte?' replied Faith.

The man let out a hearty laugh, his eyes crinkling at the corners, 'That machine, my dear, could fly you to the moon if you asked it nicely.'

As the laughter subsided, the man continued, 'Yes, it does indeed do lattes. Take a seat, I'll fetch you one. And while you're waiting, help yourself to the sandwiches and cake. They're leftovers from yesterday's party.'

'Thanks.' Said Faith 'I was thinking of grabbing something from the Grinder.'

'Don't you worry,' the man replied, a knowing smile playing on his lips, 'All these goodies are courtesy of the Grinder. You won't be missing out on anything.'

Faith, comfortably ensconced on the opposing sofa, reached for a paper plate and began to sample the treats arrayed on the table. The man, placed a latte before Faith, taking a seat beside her. 'Sugar and sweeteners are right there on the table, if you need,' he said, gesturing.

'Allow me to introduce ourselves,' a woman began, 'I'm Tanya, and these are Daniel and Deena.' As introductions were made, the conversation flowed naturally, soon turning to Faith's plans for the new brochure.

The talk shifted to office relationships and gossip. Faith, taken aback by the intimate knowledge everyone had of each other's lives, thought about the difficulty of maintaining privacy in such an environment. Tanya, breaking the silence, said, 'Let's hope all these changes improve the turnover.'

Deena, in response, said, 'It's been good so far. Sarah knows what she's doing. I reckon her ideas should've been heeded long before things got this bad.' Daniel grumbled, 'We all had good ideas, but not all of us slept with the boss to get the top job.'

Tanya, her voice shaking slightly, confessed, 'I walked in on a terrible argument once. Sarah was red in the face, threatening to kill him. I shouldn't be repeating this, but it was really quite shocking.' Faith, taken aback by this revelation, remained silent.

Deena, noticing Faith's silence, said, 'Ignore us, we're just a bunch of nosy gossips. Work's much better now, and Sarah ensures we're recognised for our sales and get a good share of the profits.' Daniel, crumbs from his pork pie littering his tie, added, 'With Nathan dead, you've got to wonder if Sarah carried out her threat.'

Deena nodded in agreement, 'Nathan did have his secrets, didn't he?' After a moment of silence, the conversation drifted back to more mundane office gossip. Faith, having finished her food, thanked Daniel for the coffee and swiftly exited the room. As she approached Sarah's office, she could hear Sarah's raised voice from within, sounding far from pleased.

CHAPTER 21

'Mrs Crawford, I understand your interest in the day-to-day operations of the shop. However, I must remind you that your expertise doesn't encompass instructing me on how to execute my duties,' came the stern voice from the other end of the phone line. The room fell silent, the tension hanging in the air palpable.

'Listen, I believe it's crucial for you to understand that your husband was hardly involved in the hands-on work around this office. I've implemented my own methods, which have proven to be effective in improving our operations. If you find these methods unsatisfactory, I suggest you seek someone else's services. I'll be discussing this matter with my solicitor and Mr Montague, who holds a larger share in the business. I'm sure he'd be interested to know that you're dissatisfied with my work ethic and input.'

With that, the phone was slammed down with a resounding thud. It was then that Faith heard the unmistakable sound of a woman crying; she recognised it as Sarah Alessi's. Despite the thick walls of the office, the sound of her sobs carried through.

The door creaked open, interrupting the silence that had settled in the room. Faith, standing at the threshold, looked at Sarah who was huddled in her chair, tears carving a path through her mascara.

'Sorry for intruding,' Faith began, stepping inside, 'But it seems like you could use a friend right now. And, as luck would have it, I have time on my hands.'

Sarah, reaching for a tissue from her desk, dabbed at her eyes and blew her nose. 'I suppose you heard that previous conversation,' she sniffled.

Faith, taking the seat opposite Sarah, nodded. 'It was rather difficult not to. The argument was loud, heated, and it was quite clear who you were speaking to.'

Sarah sighed, her shoulders slumping. 'Not one of my more professional moments, I admit. I know Mirry is your close friend, but she can be so...interfering. She knows nothing about estate agency, yet she feels the need to constantly phone and meddle in the business.'

Rising from her seat, Faith moved towards the corner cabinet where Sarah's personal coffee maker sat. 'How about I make us a drink? You can vent all you want after a dose of caffeine.'

Sarah nodded, her sobs resurfacing. As she reached for another tissue, Faith returned with two steaming cups of coffee. She handed one to Sarah, waiting for her to take a sip and regain her composure before she spoke again.

'Mirry hasn't been herself since Nathan's death,' Faith began, leaning back in her chair, her hands gesturing as she spoke. 'She was never good with loss, not after what happened to her mum. I don't think she knows where she fits in now, especially after giving up so much for Nathan.'

Sarah leaned back in her chair, her fingers playing with the rim of her teacup. 'You know, Faith,' she began, her voice steady yet filled with a hint of regret. 'Mirry has always been the sort to interfere. '

'Nathan was never really involved in the business, was he?' Faith asked, her tone more of a statement than a question. She remembered how he'd bask in the attention and praise from others, despite his lack of contribution.

Sarah chuckled, a bitter sound in the small room. 'Nathan was a charming man, Faith. He knew how to get what he wanted, and he'd stop at nothing to get it.' She paused, her eyes meeting Faith's. There was a moment of silence, where Sarah seemed to be deciding whether to continue. Then, with a sigh, she did. 'He had a way of making you feel special, while all the while bending you to his will.'

'You know, he was always trying to get our attention, both me and my sister Charity,' Faith began, her voice low. She paused, a small smile playing on her lips as she remembered. 'Until Charity had enough and punched him square in the face at one of the summer balls. After that, he gave us a wide berth, poor lad.'

Sarah chuckled, her eyes sparkling with amusement. 'Oh, I would have paid good money to see that. Your sister sounds like my kind of girl.'

Faith laughed. 'He didn't just take it lying down. He fell backwards, right onto the buffet table. His friends wouldn't let him live it down for weeks. He was the butt of every joke, and he was furious.'

'That sounds just like Nathan,' Sarah mused, her laughter subsiding. 'Always ready to hit back, no matter what.'

Suddenly, Sarah's laughter turned into sobs. Faith looked at her, surprised by the sudden change in mood. 'What's wrong, Sarah?' she asked, concern etching her features. Sarah didn't respond, her body shaking with the force of her sobs. Faith reached out, placing a comforting hand on her shoulder.

Sarah held Faith's gaze for a long, drawn-out moment before she finally broke the silence. 'I've got to get this off my chest, Faith,' she admitted. 'I can't keep looking at my own reflection knowing what I've done. I'm a good person, Faith. I love my husband, my family...' Her voice trailed off.

Faith leaned forward, her hands clasped tightly in her lap. 'No one would ever doubt that, Sarah,' she reassured her. 'My mum always says you've got a wonderful family, a loving husband, and that you adore your kids.'

Sarah's lips twitched into a half-hearted smile. 'Maybe that's true, in a way,' she conceded. She reached for a framed family photo on her desk, her fingers tracing the smiling faces of her husband and children. The backdrop was a restaurant, somewhere foreign by the looks of it. 'But Faith, I... I cheated on my husband. With Nathan.' The words tumbled out of her in a rush, each one a painful admission of guilt.

'And that's not all,' she continued, her voice shaky. 'Nathan started blackmailing me after that. That's why I never got promoted, why I was running this business on my own while he took all the credit...and the lion's share of the profits.'

With her confession out in the open, Sarah slumped back in her chair, looking as though she'd just bared her soul to a priest.

'I can see this is hard for you,' Faith said, her eyes never leaving the woman's face. Sarah, her face pale and drawn, clutched a tissue in her trembling hand. 'It was one of those office parties, wasn't it?' Faith asked, her voice soft, coaxing.

Sarah nodded, her eyes welling up with tears. 'My husband couldn't come. His mum had broken her leg and he had to go out of town to help her. Nathan convinced me to stay overnight. I didn't want to, but he insisted.' She paused, taking a shaky breath. 'I was foolish. I drank too much. I remember dancing with Nathan and then... then…well you can guess.'

Faith leaned back in her chair, her mind racing. 'You must have been livid,' she said. 'I don't know if I could have kept quiet like you did. It would have eaten at me until I exploded.'

Sarah's forehead creased into a frown as she spoke. 'I suppose you reckon I'm the one who killed Nathan. Can't say I blame you, the thought crossed my mind more than once.' She reached for a pen, her hands moving restlessly as she tidied her desk, a futile attempt to impose some semblance of order on the chaos. 'Truth is, I'm a coward. I should've come clean ages ago, stripped Nathan of his power over me.' Her lips trembled as she confessed, 'But I was too afraid of what my family, my children, would think of me.'

Faith listened, her expression solemn, understanding. 'I don't think any less of you, Sarah. I've been there, feeling trapped with no way out. The fear of being a disappointment, a failure, it's crippling.'

Sarah's voice was barely audible as she continued, 'I swear, Faith, I didn't kill him. But I can't say I'm not relieved that he's gone. Nathan caused a lot of pain, and it wasn't just us staff he played around with. He had a string of affairs, with clients, at business parties and shows. He was a menace.'

'In the end, the sins you commit come back to haunt you. People you've wronged, they reach a breaking point... that's when they break,' Faith mused.

Sarah, seated across the desk from her, shifted uncomfortably, her fingers nervously fiddling with a pen. She bit her lip, her eyes darting to meet Faith's. 'I... I know Nathan was involved with someone else, not Mirry, before he...before he died,' she stammered, her words tumbling out in a rush.

Faith's eyebrows shot up in surprise. 'Are you certain?' she queried; her tone sharp.

Sarah nodded vehemently. 'Yes, yes, I'm sure. I overheard him on the phone once. He was...he was being so charming, so sweet. He kept saying how much he enjoyed their meetings and how he was looking forward to the next one. He...he said he couldn't live without her,' she confessed.

Faith slammed her coffee cup down on the table. 'Typical Nathan,' she spat out, her eyes flashing with anger. 'He also mentioned a secret meeting place,' Sarah added, her voice trembling slightly.

Faith's eyes narrowed thoughtfully. 'It must be somewhere nearby. He hasn't been out of town for months. I wonder where it could be,' she mused. Turning to Sarah, her expression softened slightly. 'Sarah, you need to report this to the police. It could be a significant lead in their investigation. Now that we know there was someone else...'

Sarah wrung her hands anxiously, her voice quivering with uncertainty. 'What if my family found out? I must tell my husband first.'

Faith, her eyes filled with determination, shook her head. 'I don't think the police would go spilling your secrets to your family, Sarah. You need to tell them first, then your husband. There's a murderer out there, and we haven't got a moment to waste.'

Sarah hesitated, her eyes darting between Faith and her phone. Finally, she nodded, her fingers trembling as she dialled the police. Her voice was surprisingly steady as she relayed everything she had shared with Faith. 'They're sending someone down immediately to take a statement. Her voice flat.

With a sigh, she crossed the room to the window, the breeze playfully ruffling her hair. She brushed it back from her face, her eyes staring vacantly out at the street below. 'Faith,' she said, turning back to look at her friend. 'Will you stay here with me while the police take my statement?'

Faith nodded, her face softening. 'Of course, Sarah. I'll be here for as long as you need me.'

Penn tucked himself into his motor, his mind racing as fast as his wheels towards Nathan's office. He'd just wrapped up a chat with a bewildered couple whose barn had been burgled. The audacity of the thieves, making off with a massive tractor, left him astounded. 'No witnesses, you say?' He'd asked, his brow furrowed in disbelief. It was a curious, and increasingly common, brand of criminal who could make such a hefty piece of machinery vanish into thin air.

The drive gave him time to mull over the case, but nothing could have prepared him for the surprise waiting for him at the office. As he was ushered into Ms Alessi's room, he found himself face to face with Faith. She was seated, a picture of calm, across the desk.

He quirked an eyebrow at her, a silent question hanging in the air. She responded with a subtle shake of her head, a clear signal to put a pin in his queries for now. He took the hint, turning his attention to the business at hand, the interview with Mrs. Alessi.

'Thank you, Mrs Alessi, for sharing this crucial information,' DCI McBride said, his voice steady and reassuring. 'Rest assured; I'll do my utmost to keep this under wraps until you can settle things with your family.' He watched as a wave of relief washed over Mrs Alessi's face. The tension in her shoulders eased, her eyes softened.

'Thank you, DCI McBride,' she apologised. 'I should've been more open during our initial meeting.'

'Indeed, Mrs Alessi,' Penn replied, rising from his seat. 'But you've been truthful now, and that's what matters.' He was about to depart when Faith rose from her chair, her stick by her side.

'Sarah,' she said, her voice a comforting murmur. 'If you need me, you have my number. Don't fret, everything will work out. Just be honest with your family. They'll understand, they'll forgive. I'm certain of it.'

Once outside, Faith leaned against a lamppost. 'I'm starting to think you've got the detective gene too,' Penn said, a hint of a smile playing on his lips. 'Just like your younger sister and your father.'

Faith's laughter filled the air. 'Too squeamish,' she said.

Before she could make her exit, Penn stopped her. 'Wait, Faith. I have something for you,' he said, quickly moving towards his car. He pulled out a bag from the car and handed it to her, his eyes averting hers. 'I hope you like it,' he said, a hint of nervousness in his voice.

Faith, taken aback, hesitated before opening the bag. Inside, she found a sky-blue scarf adorned with daisies. The sheer material felt soft against her skin, and she held it up to the light, admiring it. 'Penn, this is beautiful. Thank you,' she said, her voice filled with genuine appreciation.

Penn blushed, rubbing the back of his neck. 'After I tossed your other one into the river, I thought you deserved a new one. I saw this and it reminded me of spring... and of you,' he admitted. Faith couldn't help but laugh, touched by his thoughtful gesture. 'Thank you, Penn. You didn't have to, but I love it,' she said, her eyes meeting his.

Their moment was interrupted by Penn's shift in demeanour. His face turned serious as he complimented her work with Mrs Alessi. 'Your work will significantly help the investigation. Well done, Faith,' he said, a proud grin on his face. Faith, struck by his handsomeness, quickly gathered her things. 'I have to go, Penn. These photos won't develop themselves,' she said, pointing to her bag filled with camera equipment. 'Take care, Penn.'

'Mind how you go,' he said, raising his hand in a brisk salute before sliding into the driver's seat of his car. The engine purred to life, and with a final, lingering glance in her direction, he eased the vehicle onto the road and out of sight.

Faith stood there for a moment. She felt a sudden, overwhelming need for the comfort and familiarity of her mother's presence. Pulling out her phone, she dialled her mother's number, asking if she could spare a few minutes for a cup of tea and a chat. The events of the day, particularly Sarah's revelations about her family, had left her feeling raw and unsettled.

As she made her way to her mother's shop, she spotted Arthur strolling down the street, Churchill, covered in an uncharacteristic layer of grime. He tipped his hat in greeting as he approached. 'Good day, Faith. You've been keeping busy, I see,' he remarked, his gaze dropping to the bag she was clutching.

Feeling a blush creep up her cheeks, she quickly lowered the bag to her side. 'Oh, this? It's a... it's a gift,' she stammered, suddenly feeling self-conscious.

Arthur's eyes twinkled with amusement. 'I saw our dashing DCI McBride with a bag like that earlier. How very kind of him,' he said, a teasing note in his voice.

'Wait!' Faith started to protest, but it was too late. The bag containing the scarf was already being yanked from her grasp by a grubby Churchill. The goat's inquisitive eyes examined the contents of the bag, his crooked teeth dangerously close to the fabric.

Arthur swiftly intervened, reclaiming the bag from the mischievous goat. 'Now, now, Churchill,' he admonished, his tone stern yet affectionate. 'You can't just go around nicking things. Remember what Min said.' The goat seemed to understand, flinching at the mention of Min's name. He turned to Faith, his eyes wide and apologetic.

Faith accepted the bag back from Arthur, giving Churchill a gentle pat. 'It's alright,' she assured him, checking the contents of the bag. 'It's just a scarf. And it doesn't look like he's damaged it.'

Arthur nodded, a hint of amusement in his eyes. 'He's got a bit of a thing for scarves and handkerchiefs, that one. Min's always losing hers and has threatened to turn him into a coat more than once.' At the mention of Min's name again, Churchill flinched, and Faith couldn't help but laugh.

'Don't worry, Churchill,' she promised, her tone full of warmth. 'I won't tell Min.' The goat let out a squeaky noise in response before his attention was captured by another bag on the floor. As he scampered off to investigate, Arthur sighed. 'You'd think he'd learnt his lesson, but Churchill will always be Churchill.'

He tipped his hat; a gesture so antiquated it left Faith momentarily disarmed. His voice, a gravelly yet gentle timbre, broke through her thoughts. 'I hope you savour the rest of your day, and your present too,' he said, his eyes twinkling with an unspoken secret.

With a casualness that seemed almost out of place, he turned and began to amble off, his goat trailing behind him obediently.

CHAPTER 22

Faith stood amidst the crowd; her heart heavy with the weight of Nathan's funeral. She was torn between the sorrow for Mirry's loss and the bitter taste of the truth she had recently uncovered about Nathan's dealings. It was a cruel irony, she thought, looking around at the sea of mourners. How many of them had actually cared for the man now reduced to a lifeless body.

The local vicar, Dalton Dixon, stood like a stoic sentinel by the grave. His face was a mask of solemnity, etched with lines of sadness and strength. Beside him, stood Simon, who seemed to be showing no emotion at all. Mirry was wrapped in the comforting embrace of Cozzie. Dalton's flamboyantly eccentric wife. The colourful beads in her hair danced and shimmered as she gently patted Mirry's back, speaking words meant to soothe and console.

The area was filled to the brim, a sea of black-clad figures, all gathered to bid their final adieu to Nathan. Faith's gaze swept across the crowd, her mind teetering on the precipice of a question - how many of these mourners were genuine friends of Nathan's? Or had they merely come to ascertain that the man was indeed dead? Mirry, his wife, had insisted on a proper burial and a memorial angel carved from stone. Faith wondered if it would serve as a place for

Mirry to grieve, to remember the man she had loved since her teenage years.

A faint smile tugged at the corners of Faith's mouth as she noticed Liam and Krista. They were huddled together with Hope and her mother, their voices muted in the sombre quiet of the graveyard. Nathan's mother was being comforted by his older sister, a stranger to Faith. The sister had fled to Sheffield for university and never returned, choosing a nurse's life over familial ties.

Nathan had always kept his family at arm's length, considering them beneath him. He had shed his humble beginnings like an unwanted skin, metamorphosing into the suave businessman Faith had known. A man who indulged in lavish holidays and drove a luxurious car. He had not even visited his mother when she had a severe heart attack three years ago.

Mirry, too, had shown no warmth towards her husband's family. She had even relegated them to the back seats in the church, a cold gesture that had drawn disapproving glances from the locals. Nathan's mother, despite her son's indifference, was now weeping openly. A testament to the undying love of a parent, irrespective of her child's actions.

'Graveyards, they're supposed to be places of sorrow, aren't they?' Faith mused aloud, her gaze sweeping over the meticulously maintained landscape of St Matthias. She felt a strange sense of tranquillity here, a stark contrast to the sadness that was expected. 'But Auntie always found beauty here, didn't she?'

Poppy her cousin nodded. 'She did. Painted it a dozen times over. Said it brought her peace.' Poppy's voice was quiet, filled with the same tranquillity that Faith felt. 'When she passed, she wanted her ashes scattered in the garden of remembrance. Remember the roses there, Faith? The scent was enough to make you think you were in paradise.'

Faith nodded, her eyes misty. 'And the lake. The lilies floating on the surface, dragonflies dancing in the summer. It was her paradise.'

When the rain began to fall, it added to the melancholy of the day and Faith looked up as she saw her sister wave her over.

'Shall we head back to the hall, Faith? Seems like the crowd's thinning.' Hope's voice was soft, her arm linked with Faith's, giving her a gentle squeeze.

Faith leaned heavily on her cane, a grimace pulling at her features as they moved slowly towards her father's car, where her mother was already seated in the front. Hope guiding Faith with a tender hand on her back. As they settled in the back seat, the car's engine hummed to life. It was then that Faith spotted Penn, standing a few feet away with Sam.

Penn was opening the car door for Magda, his movements slow and deliberate. As their car pulled away, he looked up and offered them a tired smile. Faith found herself studying his face, etched with lines of exhaustion.

She remembered snippets of a conversation she'd overheard between her parents. Penn had lost his mother when he was just a child. Faith couldn't begin to imagine the kind of impact it must've had on him, the kind of pain he must've endured.

The hall had an air of melancholy, as if it was privy to the day's sombre proceedings. As she stepped out of the car, Faith was greeted by the scent of freshly mown grass and newly turned earth. The air had a biting chill, prompting her to pull her coat snugly around herself. She made her way inside, where two women were waiting. One she recognised as Magda's sister, both carrying trays laden with what appeared to be sherry.

She didn't typically drink during the day, so she was taken aback when she saw Hope reach out and take two glasses. Hope turned and handed one to her, saying, 'It will stave off the cold and help you relax.' Faith was sceptical until she took a tentative sip. The rich, warming drink slid smoothly down her throat, spreading a comforting warmth through her. She turned to Hope with a grateful smile. 'Right as always,' she conceded.

'Right, then,' Hope affirmed, her gaze sweeping across the grand dining hall. She was taken aback by the sparse number of mourners who had been invited back to the estate. She glimpsed Liam and Krista in a corner, their heads bowed in solemn conversation. She chose to join them, flanked by Chris and Judy Carpenter.

Judy's face was etched in a deep frown, her gaze fixated on a spectacle unfolding across the room. Following her line of sight, Hope's eyes landed on the larger-than-life figure of Massimo. The man was at the buffet, his animated gestures dictating the placement of dishes with theatrical flair.

'No, no, no! Place those dishes here,' Massimo commanded, his voice booming across the room. A young server was at the receiving end of his critique, her face a mask of confusion. 'This will not do. Let me show you how it's done,' he declared, taking over the task with exaggerated precision.

Once satisfied, Massimo darted off to a tall man at the entrance, tasked with offering canapes to the arriving guests. 'Stand upright, man! You're slouching. Our guests must feel your desire to serve, your pleasure in their company,' he instructed, his tone authoritative. The man hastily corrected his posture under Massimo's watchful eye, who then scanned the room for his next 'project'.

The tall man, extended his hand towards Faith, offering her a canape. She received it gratefully, her lips curving into a polite smile. As she turned to look at the small crowd, a feeble touch on her arm halted her. It was Mirry, her eyes a bloodshot red. 'Would you mind sitting with me for a while?' she implored.

'Of course, dear. Let's find somewhere quiet,' Faith responded, her gaze falling on a secluded two-seater sofa in the corner of the room.

She gently guided her friend towards it, taking note of the tremors that were shaking Mirry's hands as she helped her sit down.

Faith raised her hand, signalling to Massimo. The usually boisterous man approached them, his steps unusually soft. He carried a tray bearing a teapot and two cups and saucers. A small jug of milk and a sugar bowl were neatly arranged next to the pot, also on the tray were two sherries, maybe these were needed more than the tea. Without uttering a word, he placed the tray on the table before them and retreated, his usual flamboyant demeanour replaced with a surprising display of sensitivity.

Faith meticulously poured two cups of tea. She added a pinch of sugar to Mirry's drink, noticing her friend's pallid complexion. 'You look like you could use some sweetness in your life, Mirry,' Faith asserted

Mirry, her face drawn and tired, shook her head feebly. 'Faith, I... I can't...' she began, her voice trailing off. Faith, however, was not one to be easily dissuaded. With a determined look in her eyes, she gently pushed the glass of sherry towards Mirry. 'How about a sip, of this? Mirry. For me,' she pleaded.

Mirry looked at Faith, her eyes filled with a sorrow that made Faith's heart clench. After a moment's hesitation, she finally nodded, reaching out to take the glass. She took a tentative sip, her face softening slightly at the taste. 'What am I to do, Faith? I feel so lost without him.'

Faith reached and took Mirry's cold hand in hers. Her touch was warm, comforting, a stark contrast to the chill that seemed to have seeped into Mirry's bones. 'You mourn, Mirry,' Faith said softly, her voice filled with understanding. 'You take all the time you need. And then, you take one step forward. Just one.'

She moved closer, ensuring that she had Mirry's full attention. 'It won't be easy. The pain will never completely disappear. But in time, hopefully, you'll be able to remember the good times, and fight off the bad ones.' As she spoke, Mirry's gaze drifted towards Liam, who was gently coaxing a visibly pregnant Krista to eat something. Despite the sombre atmosphere, there was a glow about the couple that was impossible to ignore.

The first thing that struck Faith was the transformation of Mirry's face. It was a visage of longing, a deep-seated yearning that was quickly overshadowed by a storm of anger, maybe even hatred. Her entire countenance twisted into a grotesque grimace.

'Your new DCI friend leaves a lot to be desired,' Mirry spat out, her voice a venomous hiss. 'How can someone like Krista Hunter get away with murder? It's a mockery of the very essence of policing.' She slammed her glass on the table with force. The clatter caused a momentary pause in the humdrum of the room, drawing the attention of the mourners towards them. Then, as quickly as they had turned, faces averted, retreating into their own worlds, leaving an air of embarrassment hanging in the wake of the outburst.

'And him,' she pointed a trembling finger at Liam, 'how can he even consider himself fit to be a father? When Nathan and I were left bereft and wanting?' The accusation hung in the air, a palpable tension that seemed to suck the air out of the room.

A chair scraped against the floor, cutting through the silence. Faith turned to see Liam rising, his hand gently supporting Krista as he helped her up from her chair. The room watched in collective sadness as he led her towards the door, their exit marked by sympathetic and pitying glances from the onlookers.

Hope, who had been with her parents walked over and placed herself firmly between Mirry and the prying eyes of the crowd, creating a protective barrier. 'Mirry, you must regain your composure,' she pleaded, her voice soft yet firm. 'You're working yourself into a state. You'll fall ill.'

Mirry, her face flushed with anger and grief, ignored Hope and continued her tirade. 'How dare they come to Nathans funeral, flaunting his pregnant wife as if nothing's amiss! Nathan is dead, and where is the justice for him? Where?'

Faith sighed, her patience unwavering. 'The police are doing all they can, Mirry. It's been confirmed that The Grinder wasn't involved in Nathan's death. The brownies he consumed didn't come from there.'

Mirry's rage seemed to only intensify at Faith's words. Her eyes blazed with a hatred so intense it was almost palpable. 'I don't care what they say! I want justice for Nathan!

'Of course, you'd be the one to defend them,' Mirry spat, her eyes flashing with anger. 'You had a soft spot for Nathan. It was clear he fancied me, not one of the flawless Harrington sisters. Watch your step, Faith. One day, your meddling will land you in hot water.'

Hope, unruffled by the outburst, responded calmly, 'Mirry, isn't it more crucial that we let the authorities find the real criminal?'

'Mousy Hope, always rushing to her sister's aid. You'll never have what I had. Go on, run back to your books,' Mirry sneered.

Hope's anger flared. 'Today, Mirry, you've insulted your husband with your behaviour,' she retorted. She grabbed Faith's hand and started to walk towards their parents. Then, she paused and turned back to Mirry, her eyes ablaze with defiance. 'And just so you know, Mirry, Nathan did ask both Faith and Charity out before you. They turned him down.'

The change in Mirry's expression was impossible to miss, a grim acceptance and resignation that washed over her features. She rose from her seat with a quiet dignity, her retreat from the room leaving a trail of murmurs in her wake. The mourners' eyes followed her, then landing on Hope with a newfound respect.

Faith's mother ushered the family out, leading them through the courtyard towards their car. Don was quick to assist, rushing over to help Liam still trying to settle a distraught Krista into their vehicle. Her tears were flowing freely.

Faith felt a shudder run through her, her body trembling as if she were cold. The unexpected touch on her shoulder made her jump. Turning, she found Minerva and her brother standing there. He was holding a paper bag, from which he was feeding Churchill cheese sandwiches.

Minerva leaned in close, her voice conspiratorial as she pointed towards their car. 'It'd be best if you all headed home. That young lady doesn't need your sympathy. She knows what you're saying is true, but it's wounding more than her pride. It's shattering the rose-tinted glasses she's been viewing life through.'

'I know she doesn't mean it,' Faith explained. 'It's just the grief talking.'

Minerva sighed. 'I wish that were true, but we both know she's been allowed to have her own way far too often. It's about time someone took her to task. Your sister did well if you ask me.'

Arthur was now performing a rather peculiar ritual, one that involved feeding Churchill a pink iced bun. The icing was mostly smeared across the goat's long chin whiskers, a sight that would have been comical if it wasn't so absurd. Minerva watched the spectacle unfold, her expression a mixture of resignation and exasperation.

'Really, Arthur,' she said, her voice laced with dry humour, 'if anyone deserves sympathy around here, it's me. I was looking forward to a quiet evening, a nice meal, and some stimulating conversation. But instead...' Her sentence trailed off as she pointed an accusatory finger at Churchill, who had the audacity to look surprised.

'Instead, this beast,' she continued, 'decided to try his luck at sneaking under the food table. I swear, one of these days, Massimo will turn him into a curry.'

Churchill's ears drooped and he quickly retreated, seeking refuge behind Arthur.

The sudden uproar brought everything to a standstill. Mirry was there, at the threshold, her body wracked with sobs. Her father, a pillar of strength, was trying his best to console her.

'Everyone's turned against me,' she cried out, her voice raw with emotion. 'I can't even lay my husband to rest without being judged and tormented.'

Rowan Harrington gave a disapproving click of her tongue. She wrapped an arm around Faith and began to guide the family towards the waiting car. Minerva and Arthur fell into step behind them, with Churchill bringing up the rear. They were halfway to the main gate when another heart-wrenching sob floated through the air. Then she heard Tiffany's voice.

'Mirry, please come inside before you catch a chill,' Tiffany implored, her voice strained with concern. But Mirry wasn't interested in any consolation from her stepmother. With a glare that could freeze blood, she stormed towards Tiffany, her fiery eyes locked onto the woman she so despised. Faith, watching the scene unfold, could only wince in anticipation of the impending confrontation.

Mirry's voice was cold and unyielding. 'And wouldn't that just make your day?' she spat, her words dripping with venom. 'You strut around here like you own the place. But you're nothing more than a glorified trolley dolly who married up. You're not fit to fill my mother's shoes. You never will be. Your charade of a marriage to my father is a farce. He could never love you the way he loved her.

'You're nothing but a fraud, Tiffany. No amount of designer clothes can hide the fact that you're just trash.' Her words hung heavy in the air, a palpable tension that left a bitter taste. With a final sob, Mirry turned on her heel and fled into the house, leaving a shattered Tiffany and a stunned Simon in her wake.

As Tiffany made to move towards Simon, seeking solace in her husband's arms, he gave her a pained look. The silence that followed was deafening, the aftermath of Mirry's harsh words hanging in the air around them.

'You should leave well alone Tiffany; you're not suited to this kind of thing. Now, look what you have done.' Simon turned and followed his daughter threw the door and Tiffany was left alone again. Her two dogs came to her side, and she reached down and caressed each dogs' ears, then she called the dogs and headed off down the field, smiling at Faith and her family as she passed.

'If it wasn't for the fact that young lady's husband had just died, I would have taken her over my knee and given her what she should have had as a child.' Rowan Harrington said. As Don took the helm, the car hummed to life, a subtle vibration beneath them. 'Is everyone settled in?' he asked, glancing over his shoulder. The only response was a chorus of clicks as seat belts were fastened.

The car pulled away from the curb, its tyres crunching on the gravel driveway. Outside, the sky had darkened considerably, and larger drops of rain had begun to fall. They splattered against the windscreen, distorting the view of the rolling countryside beyond.

Finally home, Faith flopped onto the sofa, her body sinking into the soft cushions. She flicked on the stereo, the soft strains of a piano concerto filling the room. It was a soothing balm to her frazzled nerves.

She sat there, lost in thought. Today had been a nightmare. The vindictiveness, the malice - it was all too much. She shook her head, trying to dispel the dark thoughts. She had to focus on the here and now, not on a friendship turned sour.

The sound of shattering glass cracked through the room, followed by the thud of a brick landing first on the sofa at her side, then rolling onto the floor. She froze, caught off guard. Her heart pounding in her chest as she tried to make sense of what had just occurred. The room was a mess, shards of glass scattered everywhere, reflecting the lights in a thousand directions.

She gently lifted herself from the sofa. Careful to avoid the shards, she moved to the far side of the room, her mind racing as she tried to figure out who could have done this. She checked herself and found she had cuts to her arm and legs, not deep, but stinging.

Reaching into her pocket, she pulled out her mobile, her fingers trembling as she dialled her dad's number. 'Dad,' she said, her voice shaking as she spoke. 'Something's happened. Someone's thrown a brick through the window.' She paused, taking a deep breath before adding, 'I'm scared, Dad. I don't know what to do.'

Then she noticed something on the floor, that was wrapped around the brick.

With a cautious grace, she navigated the disarray, her heart still pounding in her chest. Her eyes were locked onto the brick, an alien object in the pristine environment and the paper that wrapped it. Her fingers itched to unravel the mystery it held.

Ignoring the voice of reason in her mind, she bent down and picked it up. The brick was cold, the paper crisp under her touch. Carefully, she unwrapped it, her breath hitching as she read the ominous message scrawled across it.

'Stop interfering, or what happened to Nathan could happen to you.'

CHAPTER 23

Penn had been mired in one of those gruelling days where the workload seemed to multiply exponentially. As he finished one task, it felt as though three more sprouted in its place. His time in this line of work had imparted him with a grim understanding: crime was an omnipresent spectre, haunting every corner of society.

'Another day, another crime,' he muttered to himself, rubbing his temples as he surveyed the mountain of paperwork on his desk. He was a man who thrived on action, not bureaucracy. Yet, here he was, drowning in a sea of reports and case files.

Eventually, he managed to extricate himself from the clutches of his office. He decided to get a meal from The Hung, Drawn and Quartered to take home. As he continued his drive home, his mind began to wander, his thoughts turning to the recent funeral of Nathan. The rumours of what had transpired at the hall afterward had reached his ears, and he found himself grappling with curiosity.

Faith Harrington seemed to share the same busy lifestyle as he did, but this was his job. Faith on the other hand either had it thrust upon her, or she willingly ran into it.

The glare of oncoming headlights momentarily blinded him. As the vehicle sped past, he caught a fleeting glimpse of Mirry in the driver's seat of a car, her face etched with distress. She was another one who seemed to have an uncanny knack for stumbling into trouble. Money, he mused, certainly didn't guarantee happiness - Mirry was living proof of that.

'What on earth is she rushing about for at this hour?' he muttered to himself, his brow furrowed in concern. He had a sinking feeling that whatever mess Mirry had found herself in would inevitably land on his desk, another problem to solve amidst the constant chaos.

All he wanted was to get home, to sink into his comforting armchair and forget about the world for a while. But just as he was visualising the inviting scene, his phone jolted him back to reality. The screen lit up, displaying Sam's name.

'Sam?' he answered, his voice weary. 'What's happened now?'

'Boss,' a voice crackled over the phone, 'We've got a situation. I'm enroute to Faith's place. Looks like someone's chucked a brick through her window.'

'Right,' the response was curt, there was an urgency in the voice. 'I'm on my way.' The call ended abruptly with the line going dead. He hadn't even thought to ask if Faith was alright. A twinge of guilt knotted in his stomach but there was no time for that now.

He pressed his foot down harder on the pedal, the speedometer needle creeping dangerously over the limit. The streets blurred past in a haze as he navigated the familiar route to Faith's cottage. The sight that met him was as he'd expected, yet it still made his heart lurch.

The once charming window of the cottage was now a gaping hole, shards of glass littering the ground, glinting ominously in the faint light. Two uniformed figures stood guard outside, their stern faces doing little to mask their concern.

He nodded curtly at the policemen, his mind already racing with questions and possibilities. Without wasting another moment, he stepped over the threshold and into the chaos.

The first thing Penn registered was the flurry of activity in the living room. The murmurs of voices, the shuffling of feet, the occasional snap of a camera. The crime scene was alive with action. Sam's voice sounding loud from the back of the house. Penn followed the sound, finding Sam and Faith huddled at the kitchen table. Faith was swaddled in an oversized cardigan, cradling a cup of tea in her hands.

Penn's gaze flickered between them, his brow furrowed in confusion. 'Would someone like to tell me what's happened?' he asked. Sam relayed the events, the words tumbling out in a rush. As the story unfolded, Penn felt a surge of anger. 'What kind of coward throws a brick through a window?'

Faith's lips curled into a wry smile. 'Someone with a good aim,' she quipped. As she lifted her cup for a sip, Penn caught sight of the bandages swathing her hands. He moved towards her, reaching out to gently lift one of her hands for closer inspection.

Faith shrugged, a nonchalant gesture that didn't quite mask the pain in her eyes. 'They look worse than they are,' she said, her voice steady. 'They only sting a little.'

Penn's face furrowed into a frown. Without waiting for a response, he moved towards the kettle. 'Anyone mind if I make myself a drink?' he asked, half-turning to look at the others.

Faith's lips curled into a small smile. 'Help yourself,' she said, gesturing towards the plate of cookies on the counter. 'And try one of the biscuits. Baked them last night, they're still fresh.'

As Penn filled the kettle, he glanced back at Sam and Faith, raising an eyebrow in silent question. They both nodded, extending their mugs towards him. He noticed they'd been drinking coffee - black, with a splash of milk. He added the coffee and milk to their mugs, then filled them with hot water. Placing the mugs on a tray, he added a sugar bowl and a spoon, then returned to the other counter to pick up the plate of cookies.

He selected one of the golden-brown biscuits, placing it in his mouth before he returned to the table with the plate. The sweet, spicy flavour of cinnamon exploded on his tongue, causing him to close his eyes in appreciation. 'These are fantastic,' he said, looking at Faith with newfound respect. 'You'll have to give me the recipe.'

Faith's smile warmed the room. 'These are my Aunt Penny's specialty. When we were kids, she'd bake them for us. I was always eager for the day she'd pass on the recipe,' she explained, picking up a biscuit and taking a bite. She closed her eyes and sighed. 'I use her old aga, and the aroma that fills the kitchen… it's like she's still here with us.'

Penn looked around, his gaze lingering on the quaint decor. 'So, this was her house?' he asked. Faith nodded, her smile fading slightly. 'Yes, she left it to me. I love this place, but it's hard to feel the same warmth when someone's just shattered your front window.'

Penn grimaced, offering a sympathetic nod. 'Not exactly the ideal end to a day, especially after a funeral. And if I heard correctly, there was some kind of disagreement at the hall too. Do you reckon there's a connection?'

Faith paused, her brow furrowing in thought. 'I'm not certain. It could be related, but with everything that's been going on lately, it's hard to pinpoint one cause.'

Penn leaned back, his gaze steady on Faith. 'Why don't you walk Sam and me through what happened today? And tell us about when you got back home tonight?'Faith was on the verge of starting her task when an abrupt, loud noise was heard throughout the house. The front door was flung open with a force that made her heart skip a beat. A trio of familiar voices reverberated down the hallway, their boisterous tones bringing a smile to her face. 'Faith, where are you?' Her mother's high-pitched voice cut through the noise, and Sam, upon recognising it, opened the kitchen door to let them in.

In poured her mother, with her father and Hope trailing behind. Hope, ever the composed one, sauntered over to the table with a calmness that contrasted the chaos. She picked up Faith's hand, scrutinising it with a furrowed brow. 'You just cannot be left unattended, dear sister,' she tutted, her frown deepening.

Before Faith could muster a response, her mother swarmed her with a tight hug, only letting go when Faith winced in discomfort. Both women took the remaining seats, and Rowan immediately began to fret. 'I hope the idiot who did this has been caught,' she seethed, her voice laced with venom. 'If he had no hands, he wouldn't be able to do this again. It would be doing society a favour if you ask me.'

Don placed his hands on his wife's shoulders, attempting to calm the storm within her. 'Firstly, there will be no archaic chopping off of hands,' he began, his voice steady and firm. 'And secondly, I am not sure whether we have ascertained it was a man.' He turned to Penn, seeking confirmation.

Penn's frown deepened as he addressed Don 'I haven't had the chance to get the full story from Faith or the team yet.' Sam vacated his seat for Don and set about boiling the kettle again. A small smile tugged at Penn's lips, appreciating his friend's unwavering belief in the healing power of tea.

'Give the police some time, Mum,' Faith interjected, trying to placate her mother's anger. 'I didn't see who it was or hear anything before it happened.' She winced, a sudden pain shooting up her leg. Hope exited the room, returning moments later with a bottle of painkillers from Faith's bathroom.

She had a glass water and handed it to Faith along with the tablets. Settling back into her seat, she placed a soothing hand on her mother's trembling one. Don, sensing the tension in the room, chimed in, 'If Penn doesn't mind, we'd like to stay while Faith talks to you.'

Before Penn could respond, Hope responded, 'I for one am not going anywhere.'

Penn sighed, turned to the family and gave a resigned nod. Faith took a deep breath, her voice steady as she recounted the events - from the moment she got home to the brick smashing through the window. She then pulled out the crumpled piece of paper from her pocket, handing it to Penn.

His eyes scanned the paper quickly, then he looked up at Faith, his expression stern. 'You really should have left this where you found it for evidence. You could have destroyed any fingerprints on it.'

Faith turned to Penn, 'I have a feeling that this person is too clever to leave any, don't you?'

'Maybe,' Penn conceded, 'but we have procedures to follow.'

'Well, fire me,' Faith retorted with frustration. 'Let's just say I wasn't really in my right mind. I'm not used to having bricks thrown through my window.'

Penn observed the smirk on his boss's face, just as his wife's hand connected with his arm. 'Wife, love, you pack a punch,' he grumbled, rubbing his arm with a wince.

Rowan shot him a sharp look, her eyes shimmering with unshed tears. 'This isn't a time for jesting, Don. Our Faith could've been seriously hurt. All that shattered glass... It could've been so much worse. She could've been alone, bleeding out...' Her voice trailed off, choked with emotion.

Don turned to his wife, wrapping a comforting arm around her. 'Hey, hey, Rowan. No need for tears,' he said softly, his usual stern demeanour softened. 'There's no point worrying about what could've happened. The important thing is that Faith is safe. My team's on it now, we'll find whoever did this.'

Penn nodded, his face grim. 'We know Nathan's killer is still out there, possibly even hiding in our village. They're scared, lashing out because Faith is stirring the pot, making the police take a closer look.'

'I assure you, we won't rest until we get this sorted,' Don confirmed, his gaze shifting between Penn and Sam. Both men responded with a curt nod.

'Sir,' Penn began, his voice steady as he addressed Don. He then turned his attention back to Faith. 'You were about to recount the events that transpired after you left the hall. But I believe it might be beneficial if you could start from the beginning of the day. There could be something relevant from the funeral.'

Don agreed, 'Take all the time you need, Faith. If you need to pause or rest, feel free to do so.' Concern was etched on his face as he looked at his daughter. For once, Faith allowed herself to be enveloped by the comforting smiles of her parents.

She began to narrate the day's events, starting from the funeral to the incident at the hall. As she recalled the brick smashing through her window, shards of glass scattering everywhere, she felt herself tremble. Hope, ever the efficient sister, immediately stood up to refill the kettle. She gathered all the empty cups and busied herself with making fresh tea.

'We might find other prints on the paper, it's worth a shot. Sam, could you take it to Iggy?' The detective looked at Faith, his eyes softening a bit. 'Faith, it might be best for you to stay with your parents for the time being.' He raised his hand as he saw her open her mouth to protest. 'Listen, we can only board up the window for tonight, and I can't say for sure when the team will be done here.'

Faith's face was set in a stubborn line, but before she could argue, Hope interjected, her voice filled with sisterly concern. 'Faith, you know I always have your best interests at heart. Sometimes, it's better to step back and clear your head. You might even remember something that could help the police. Besides, this place isn't safe right now, not until we get that window fixed.'

Penn felt a wave of relief wash over him as Faith departed with her parents, but a niggling thought arose in his mind. Why was Mirry in a car this late at night and in such a rush? She had a lot of questions to answer, and Penn was not letting her wangle her way out of answering them.

CHAPTER 24

The harsh glare of the morning light pierced through the thin veil of her eyelids, nudging Faith awake. 'Too bright,' she muttered, pulling the covers over her head in a vain attempt to block out the light. Sleep had been elusive, a fickle companion that left her tossing and turning, haunted by the events of the previous evening. The memory of the window shattering, glass shards scattering like deadly confetti, still lingered, fresh and raw.

As her eyes fluttered open, she found herself not in the familiar confines of her cottage room but in the room of her childhood at her parents' home. The wallpaper, adorned with lavender flowers, the dressing table by the window, the patchwork quilt at the foot of her bed – all of it was a vivid reminder of a simpler time. A time when her life was filled with love and laughter, with family outings and leisurely walks in the woods with her mother. A time when her world was scented with the sweet fragrance of violets and the earthy aroma of nature.

She reached out, her fingers grazing the worn-out quilt that her mum had sewn one summer. The scent of violets filled her nostrils, a comforting memory that tugged at her heartstrings. 'How did life get so complicated?' she wondered aloud. Her life should have been different, she mused, her gaze drifting towards the mirror on the table.

The face in the mirror was not the one she had imagined for herself. It was not the face of the carefree girl who had once roamed the woods with her mother, but the face of a woman who had been shaped by the harsh realities of life. She didn't recognise the woman in the mirror, but she knew she had to live with her.

After a brisk shower and swift change of clothes, Faith found herself being drawn by the sound of laughter coming from the kitchen. As she stepped through the doorway, she was greeted by the sight of her parents lost in a moment of affection by the sink.

Don broke away from the embrace and, with a theatrical flourish, draped a tea towel over his arm. 'Welcome to café Harrington,' he said, guiding Faith to a seat at the table. 'What can I get for the lovely lady this morning?' Settling into her chair, Faith played along. 'Any recommendations?' she asked. Don stroked his chin, pretending to ponder. 'Well, the cinnamon toast is a delight, and the eggs Benedict are not to be missed. Perhaps a glass of fresh juice, followed by a smooth, milky coffee?'

Before Faith could respond, the back door swung open and in walked Hope. She greeted her parents with a kiss before seating herself opposite Faith. 'That sounds delightful, make it two,' she said, catching the tail end of the conversation. Don winked at her, then turned to his wife. 'I'll get started on the eggs Benedict, love. You sort the toast and coffee?' He gave his wife a gentle squeeze. 'We make quite the team, don't we?'

As he busied himself with the breakfast preparations, humming a cheerful tune, Hope leaned across the table towards Faith. 'Dads over the moon when we're both home,' she said. 'If he had his way, we'd never have left.' Faith gave a nod of agreement. 'So, sis,' Hope continued, 'how are you feeling today?'

Faith took a moment before answering. 'I'm aching all over, but my head's clearer. I spent a lot of time thinking last night. I must be on the verge of uncovering something about Nathan's death, otherwise, why would someone have thrown a brick through my window?' Hope shook her head, a smile playing on her lips. 'You're turning into a regular Pearl Nolan, aren't you? I'd tell you to stop, but I know you too well. Once you get your teeth into something.'

Both siblings sat quietly, their eyes fixed on their parents bustling about preparing breakfast. The aroma of freshly brewed coffee filled the air, a comforting scent that brought back memories of simpler times. As their father placed the plates in front of them, laden with hearty fare, they eagerly picked up their cutlery, their stomachs growling in anticipation.

Faith, taking her first mouthful, let out a sigh of satisfaction. 'I'd forgotten how well you cook, dad,' she said, her eyes twinkling with mirth. 'Massimo should be on his toes, you know. You might just steal his job. We should do this more often.'

Don, her father, frowned slightly at her words. 'As much as I'd love to have more of these moments,' he said, his voice tinged with a hint of seriousness, 'I'd prefer it if we could do without the near-death experiences of a child. And as for Massimo, he can keep his job. I save my culinary talents for family only.'

'Dad, it wasn't that bad,' Faith protested, but her words fell on deaf ears. Turning to her family, she noticed the slight fear etched on their faces. The remainder of the meal was spent in light-hearted conversation, discussing work, village gossip, and everything in between.

Around midday, there was a knock at the door, jolting Faith from her thoughts. She opened the door to find Penn and Sam, their faces stern and serious. She led them to her father's office, a cosy room at the back of the cottage. The office was a gift from her mother to her father on one of their anniversaries, a space where he could balance his work and family time.

The office was filled with the muted sounds of serious discussion for a good fifteen minutes before the three men emerged, their faces sombre. Her father sat across from her, his usual cheer replaced by a look of concern. 'They didn't find anything in your cottage or on the brick that could point to who threw it last night,' he began, 'but the investigation is ongoing. I think it would be best if you stayed here for a couple more days, Faith.'

'Dad, I want to go home,' Faith interjected, her voice steady. 'Whoever did this has made their point. I'm sure they know the police are involved now. I promise I'll be careful.' She looked around at her family, their faces etched with worry. She hated causing them distress, but she also couldn't let this incident halt her life.

Penn took a step forward, extending his offer. 'I can give you a lift if you'd like. Sam has his own car.

His offer was met with a teasing smile from Faith. 'See, Dad. I even have a police escort. What could possibly go wrong?' Before her father could utter a word in response, Faith was already edging up the stairs. She reappeared moments later, bag in hand, and after a round of hugs, she led Penn out to his car. As she settled into the passenger seat, she let out a long sigh, the tension visibly leaving her body as she leaned back against the seat.

The drive to Faith's cottage was a quiet one. Penn chose to let the silence linger. He had to admit, she had been reckless at times, but she never shied away from taking responsibility for her actions.

Upon arrival, Penn was quick to get out and open the door for Faith. He was taken aback when she flashed him a genuine smile instead of chastising him for treating her like a damsel in distress. The surprises didn't end there. She not only accepted his offer to help with her bag but also invited him in for a drink.

'Don't look so surprised,' she teased, gripping her walking stick firmly. 'I can be social, on occasions.' With that, she led the way into the house, leaving the door open for Penn to follow. As he walked into the hallway, he noticed the repaired window and the spotless interior. The kindness of the Willowbrooke residents never failed to amaze him.

Penn placed Faith's bag near the staircase, his eyes following her as she moved into the kitchen. The room was warm and inviting, a stark contrast to the cold outside. It melted away the tension in his muscles, reminding him of the kitchen back home, where his mother used to cook. The sudden memory caught him off guard, a pang of nostalgia hitting him hard.

Faith's voice broke through his reverie. 'Tea or coffee?' she asked, her back to him as she busied herself with the kettle.

'Tea,' Penn replied, a little too quickly. He cleared his throat, hoping to cover up his momentary lapse. 'I know it sounds odd, but tea tastes different here. Better, somehow. Maybe it's the water, or the air. I've always been a coffee man, but I find myself craving a good cup of tea these days.' He paused, suddenly self-conscious. He didn't want to come across as rambling.

Faith turned around, a knowing smile on her face. 'I understand. When I worked in London, all I drank was coffee. Maybe it's the fast-paced life there, the constant need to stay alert. But here, you can afford to slow down, to take a moment to breathe. A good cup of tea is perfect for that.' She turned back to the kettle, her words hanging in the air between them.

Once the tea was ready, Faith carefully arranged the cups and a plate of biscuits on a tray. Penn took the initiative to relocate the tray, setting it down in the centre of the table. As Faith took her seat, she poured a touch of milk into each of the cups, followed by the hot tea.

'Help yourself to biscuits,' she invited, reaching out to claim one for herself. She dunked it into her tea, a sheepish smile on her face as she looked up at Penn. 'Sorry, I know it's a bad habit. I've lost many a biscuit this way. I just can't resist the taste when they're dunked.'

Penn laughed, a warm, genuine sound. 'I'm glad you did it first,' he admitted, selecting a biscuit and following her lead. He took a bite, the biscuit soft and warm from the tea. 'I feel vindicated now.'

Faith's smile wavered, her gaze dropping to her cup. 'I'm sorry for all the trouble I've caused with this case,' she confessed quietly. 'I inherited my mum's nosy personality. It's gotten me into a lot of trouble in the past.'

Penn shrugged, a nonchalant gesture. 'I would've preferred a more straightforward case for my first big assignment here,' he agreed. 'But life is seldom easy. A crime was committed and we wouldn't be investigating if you hadn't refused to back down.'

A determined look crossed Faith's face. 'As much as I didn't get on with Nathan, Mirry is my friend,' she said firmly. And that was all the motivation she needed.

In the quiet stillness of the room, Penn scratched his head, a memory surfacing. He turned to Faith, his brow furrowed. 'Faith,' he began, 'Last night, did Mirry drop by, or did she call?'

'No.'

Penn sighed, rubbing his temples. 'I've spoken to many people, Faith. And I hate to say it, especially since Mirry is your friend, but not many people were fond of Nathan or her. He wasn't exactly Mr. Popular around here.'

Faith's lips curled into a wry smile. 'There are people I'm not exactly fond of, some even intensely so. Would I kill them? Absolutely not. Maybe a bit of maiming, some light torture...' she trailed off, wringing her hands in a mock strangling gesture.

Penn laughed, raising his hands in surrender. 'I'll remember not to get on your bad side.'

Faith chuckled, a mischievous glint in her eyes. 'Blame my mum. It's the crazy Scottish genes. I'm always going full Braveheart.'

Penn grinned, shaking his head. 'Actually, I see you more as a Boudicca, all wild hair and swords.'

Faith raised an eyebrow, a smirk playing on her lips. 'Why, thank you, I think?'

Penn's smile faded, his gaze serious once again. 'So, Mirry didn't come over last night?'

Faith looked at him, her expression puzzled. 'Why do you ask?'

'She overtook me. She appeared to be in quite a hurry, and if my memory serves me, she was coming from the direction of your cottage,' Penn said, glancing at Faith. Her face was a mask of shock.

'Look, I know Mirry and I didn't part on the best of terms. She can be a bit unpredictable. And it was a tough day, she could've been out for any number of reasons.' Faith paused, a frown creasing her forehead. 'You know, Penn, I've been away in London for so long, I feel like I hardly know my friends anymore.'

'So, you can't be certain that Mirry wouldn't do something like this?' He asked, leaning back in his chair. Faith shook her head, her expression troubled. 'I can't be sure of anything anymore. Mirry had her share of troubles, and her desperate desire for a child took over her life. And Nathan, well, he didn't help matters.

'Recently, someone mentioned to me that Nathan didn't even want kids. It made me wonder if that's why he had a different doctor, a fertility specialist in London. Could he have been lying to her? And if so, what else was he hiding?' Faith mused, tapping my fingers on the table.

'Well, that's something I plan to investigate. If Nathan was lying, maybe Mirry had enough,' He suggested, watching Faith's reaction.

She looked taken aback. 'You're not suggesting she... killed her husband? She loved him, Penn.'

'Love and hate are often two sides of the same coin. I have a new lead now, and I need to follow it. Remember, on the day Nathan died, Mirry stood you up. Her alibi is only as good as her word.'

Penn stood up, ready to leave. 'I know she's your friend, Faith. But as a detective, I have to remain impartial. I have to verify everything.'

'Her father's going to have a fit, he's so protective of her, particularly since her mum passed.'

'That may be the case, but I'll cross that bridge when I come to it. Right now, I need to get going. If you need anything, give me a ring, and Faith, do be cautious,' he warned, his gaze meeting Faith's. He saw her wince slightly, an involuntary reaction.

'I'm not saying this because I perceive you as weak or incapable. Just bear in mind, Nathan was a lot tougher than you and look where he ended up. Consider it this way, if anything happened to you under my watch, your family wouldn't hesitate to come after me. Spare me the trouble, I implore you.' His plea was met with a soft, pleading smile which broke through Faith's stern facade, making her chuckle.

'Alright, this time I'll try to heed your advice,' she replied, her tone light yet sincere.

'Thanks for the drink, and do try to get some rest,' he suggested, before disappearing out of the door.

The sound of the door closing announced he had left. She picked up the scattered cups and plates, the kitchen slowly returning to its usual order under her meticulous hands. 'You wouldn't believe what happened here, would you?' she muttered to herself, her voice barely audible in the quiet room. Her hands, though steady on the surface, trembled slightly.

Moving from the kitchen, she found herself drawn towards the front room. Her fingers traced the smooth surface of the newly installed glass window, a stark reminder of last night. The room was impeccably neat, the evidence of any disturbance scrupulously erased.

Her gaze drifted outside, scanning the quiet lane. The world outside seemed so normal now. Faith shook her head, trying to dispel the ominous thoughts.

She sank down onto the couch, her heart pounding in her chest. She was alone. The silence of the room felt oppressive. Despite the calm facade, Faith knew she was still in danger, and the thought chilled her to the bone.

CHAPTER 25

Tiffany stood there, in her usual casual getup — jeans, a sky-blue hoodie, and looking like she'd walked off a magazine cover despite her simple attire. 'You should have just walked in, Tiff? Perks of being on my friends list, you know,' Faith playfully chided.

Tiffany looked taken aback, 'I am, am I?' She followed Faith down to the kitchen.

'Absolutely,' Faith confirmed, 'Good friends are hard to come by. And I know one when I see one.'

'That goes both ways, Faith,' Tiffany admitted. There was a pause. She seemed to want to say more, but instead, she placed a bottle of wine on the table, 'And that's why friends always come prepared.'

Faith chuckled, 'Indeed, they should. And I must say, you've got a knack for picking out excellent wines. Top cupboard by the sink's where I stash the glasses.'

As Tiffany reached for the glasses, Faith couldn't help but remark, 'I keep forgetting how tall you are.'

Tiffany laughed, 'It was a nightmare growing up — taller than most boys in my class. Made dating quite a challenge.'

'Oh, I can relate to that,' Faith joined in her laughter, 'Once dated a guy who bought high-heeled shoes to match my height. Looked ridiculous and that was the end of that.'

'Nothing beats a good laugh, huh?' Tiffany handed Faith a filled wine glass and made herself comfortable on a stool by the island. With a flick of her long ponytail and a long sip of wine, she sighed, 'A good wine can make a lot of things better.'

'But not everything?' Faith asked, catching the sudden shift in Tiffany's tone.

'At one time that would have been my response. but things change,' Tiffany confessed, her smile fading.

Faith decided against pushing it further — tonight was about fun and laughter. 'I've got my mum's recipe for broccoli and feta quiche for dinner. Is that okay?'

'Sounds perfect,' Tiffany replied, 'A normal meal's a welcome change after all those formal dinners I have to endure.'

As Faith got the cutlery and salad ready, she asked, 'Fancy dining in the conservatory?'

'Sounds delightful. Could do with a bit of sun,' Tiffany replied.

It had begun cloudy that morning, now the sun was shining, the floor emanating a glow as if covered with crystals and the flowers that were blooming in all their spring glory looked as though they had had an invigorating shower.

The sofas in the conservatory were lush and comfortable. Her Aunt had bought new ones before she died and Faith just adored them.

They both sank into a seat and began to fill their plates. Faith could see the white crocuses and snowdrops in the tub outside. The evening light had not yet diminished and there were tinges of peach and pink, creating a magical backdrop and casting warm sunlight inside the small conservatory.

'How's life been treating you?'

Faith had expected her to talk about Nathans death, oddly she had been very quiet. In fact, she seemed to be slightly subdued tonight and all the smiles and joy she showed seemed a little contrived.

'Tiff, you know you can talk to me, I found you a great help when I first returned. I have relied greatly on your advice.'

Taking another long sip of her wine, she tucked her feet up on the sofa and laughed. It wasn't a happy sound, more dispirited.

'Nobody really asks me my opinion, sometimes I feel invisible. I love Simon but,' Tiffany took another drink, this time for courage. 'I am a disappointment, not talented like his first wife, or Mirry.'

'If Simon had felt like that, he wouldn't have married you. Look at what you have done. The Hall has never looked better and that's all down to you. You have been a breath of fresh air, and don't you dare but yourself down. You are not invisible and if people see you like that, you make them see you.'

'You seem to have had experience with this, Faith. Can I ask? And if I am being too nosy, tell me. I know you and Ben split up; I am still not sure why?'

It was Faith's turn to fidget slightly, she too wanted to draw back into the sofa, easier said than done, as her leg would begin to throb, so she was stuck with both legs on a pouffe. A position where she was exposed to the world, laid out like a useless individual and she hated it; hated not being able to do the simple things in life.

'Mine is a long and sad story. My family know, but no one else has really asked.

'Ben and I met at university, he was taking business and travel, and I was taking art. We met at a running club and hit it off at once. He was funny and romantic, and I just fell in love with him and him me.' She smiled, those days had been so wonderful, everything falling into place.

'We finished Uni and got married. I would have lived together, but Ben insisted, and I said yes. Ben got a great job in London, and I started a small job in a gallery. I had wanted to start painting again and it worked at first.'

Faith paused, the memories flooding back. 'Ben's promotions came thick and fast, and eventually he had his own business, and I fell behind.'

Tiffany nodded. 'Sometimes in a marriage, the woman stands back and lets the man progress. It works for some, and there's nothing wrong with that. I would just want something for myself too, that feeling of accomplishment.'

'Ben knew I had begun taking a photography course and he found that I had a talent for it. He even arranged for me to go with him and do the photos. I didn't realise he had seen an opportunity to make himself look better. But as his success grew, my own dreams and aspirations started to fade into the background. My usefulness was no longer needed, and he stopped taking me. I became the supportive wife, always there to cheer him on, but never feeling fulfilled myself.

'It wasn't just about recognition or being noticed, although that would have been nice. It was about having something that was mine, something that made me feel alive and accomplished. But as Ben's career soared, mine remained stagnant. The more he thrived, the more I felt left behind.

'I can't blame Ben entirely for this. He was driven by his own ambitions and I admired him for that. But somewhere along the way, we lost sight of each other. We became two individuals chasing our own dreams, rather than partners building a life together.'

'So, what went wrong?'

'It was a gradual erosion, a slow unravelling of the love we once had. Maybe it could have been saved.' One solitary tear fell onto her cheek. Was this all it was worth now, just one tear.

'We can stop if you want, I don't want to make you upset.'

Faith wiped the tear away. 'No, this needs to stop, I need to talk.' Sitting upright she gathered her thoughts, 'Ben had an important meal, one that could have led to a big promotion. I was really looking forward to it, we hadn't been out for ages. Ben, of course, got chatting with his boss and friends, I got left with the wife's and girlfriends.'

Tiffany nodded. 'I know that feeling, there to look good, not to fraternise.'

'If it had stopped at that I would have coped. Ben on the other hand had other ideas. The drinks had been flowing all night and the inevitable happened. By the time we were ready to leave, he was more than tipsy. He yelled at me when I offered to drive, said I was trying to ruin his chances when I suggested a taxi.'

She was beginning to remember that cold, wet night. And she shivered.

'I should have left him, got a taxi myself. I should have done a lot of things but I ended up deciding to get in the car with him. We argued on the way home, maybe some of it was my fault. I could feel the swerve of the car, the feeling of being thrown forward. The smell of petrol and the flashing lights. It went quiet then I heard the voices, felt so much pain as I was placed in an ambulance, then nothing.'

Faith waited for the tears, there were none, only a dull ache in her heart.

'When I woke up, my family was there, and they comforted me when I was told about the damage to my leg and that I had lost the child I didn't know I was carrying.'

'I am so sorry Faith.' Tiffany began to cry.

'If that had been all, I would have coped, but they left the best for last. The doctor took my hand and told me I would not be able to ever have children, the damage had been too bad. It was too much; I began screaming for everyone to get out. I could see mum crying and Hope in my dad's arms, still I kept screaming.

'Of course, they had to sedate me, and everything became a blur. My leg was a mess, I couldn't walk.' She could feel her leg beginning to ache and she gently massaged it. 'This,' pointing to her leg, 'Is permanent; a reminder of my folly.'

It was dark now and she stared at the moon, the only illumination other than the lamp. 'I hated myself for a long time, hated everyone else too. But I am gradually becoming stronger and more focused. And I can see my family are proud of what I have accomplished,' said Faith.'

'I wish my husband saw that. I try so hard, and still, I am in the wrong. He is so busy with work; we spend hardly any time together. When I started working on the Folly, I was so excited. Simon talked with me, shared ideas. Now it's all Mirry. Am I being selfish?'

'No, Mirry has always been close to her father, he spoilt her when her mother died, and it never stopped. I don't think her relationship with Nathan was as good as she hoped for or what she portrayed to everyone else.'

Tiffany shook her head. 'There were a lot of lies in their marriage, even I didn't think he deserved her. He has hurt a great many people and the only important person in his life was himself.'

Faith wondered just how much Tiffany knew, but she wasn't going to push things, not now. This evening was for Tiffany, not Mirry.

'We should start an underappreciated wives club. Meet every month and plot ways to punish our Ex's and other halves.'

Tiffany raised her glass, 'I will drink to that. There are a lot of people out there who have constantly hurt those around them.' She shuddered. 'The only problem is that it's everyone else who ends up paying for it.'

Faith was about to say who, then stopped. She was still thinking about this when Tiffany had gone home.

CHAPTER 26

The following morning, Penn clocked in at work and immediately spotted a note from Iggy and Li on his desk. After a quick detour to grab a coffee and some fruit for breakfast, he made a beeline for their office. On the way, he crossed paths with Sam. 'Sam, I need you to bring Mirry in for questioning,' Penn said, his tone leaving no room for argument.

Sam, however, still had questions. 'And if her father refuses?' he asked, raising an eyebrow. Penn responded without missing a beat. 'Tell him I couldn't care less.' Sam's eyebrows shot up even higher at Penn's audacity, but he said nothing more. Instead, he simply picked up his coat and headed out the door.

Penn couldn't understand why everyone seemed to think Simon Montague was untouchable. Sure, the man owned Eglantine Hall and had money to burn, but that didn't exempt him from the law.

Upon entering Iggy and Li's office, Penn found them chuckling over something on Iggy's phone. Li noticed him first and quickly returned to her desk to retrieve her iPad. 'Penn, I was reviewing the notes from the Nathan Crawford case and found something rather interesting,' she began, handing Penn the iPad and pointing to a specific section of the notes.

Penn's gaze flickered between the iPad and Li, a crease forming between his brows. 'I'm not exactly sure what I'm supposed to be seeing here,' he admitted, scratching his head. Li simply tutted in response, rolling her eyes in a playful manner. 'Men,' she muttered under her breath, a teasing smile tugging at the corners of her mouth. She held up the iPad so they could both see the screen, her slender finger jabbing at a particular spot. 'If it weren't for Magda mentioning how distraught Mirry was over their fertility issues, I wouldn't have thought twice about this,' she explained.

Penn squinted at the screen, trying to make sense of the information presented. 'And how is this unusual?' he asked, his tone laced with genuine confusion. Li sighed, setting the iPad down and folding her arms across her chest. 'I have *all* of Nathan's medical records,' she stated, her voice steady and serious. 'When Sam asked about his fertility doctor in London, I decided to double-check. It turns out, Nathan had a vasectomy just before he married Mirry.'

Shock registered on Penn's face. 'That's impossible,' he protested, shaking his head in disbelief. 'He was undergoing fertility treatments just like his wife.' Li simply shrugged, a grim expression on her face. 'It seems his wife was under the impression that she was the one with fertility issues. Now, I'm beginning to wonder if she even had a problem at all.'

'Li, how did you get this information without a warrant?'

Li smiled, 'A friend of a friend, of a friend may have mentioned something and I checked.'

Iggy, who had been silently observing the exchange, finally spoke up. 'Man, Oh what a tangled web we weave,' he quoted, shaking his head solemnly. Penn nodded in agreement, finishing the quote. ''When first we practice to deceive.' The question now is, did Mirry find out about Nathan's deception? And if she did, was she angry enough to kill her own husband?'

Iggy raised an eyebrow, 'Well, detective, this is where you put on your deerstalker and start sniffing out a killer. We deal with the dead, but you, my friend, have to deal with the consequences and bring the living to justice.'

Penn nodded, his expression serious. 'I've asked Sam to bring Mirry in. I have a few more questions for her and this time, I won't be accepting any evasions, regardless of how much her father believes he's above the law.' He turned to Li, offering her a grateful smile. 'Thanks, Li. The information you've provided is invaluable.'

'And don't forget beautiful, clever, and funny,' Iggy chimed in, grabbing his wife's hand and pressing a kiss to it. Li let out a laugh, swatting her husband's shoulder playfully.

'Iggy, we're at work. I don't think Penn wants to hear your flirting.' She said, her cheeks flushing a rosy pink.

Penn chuckled, pushing off from the desk and heading back to his own office. 'Don't worry about me. At this moment, I think Iggy and I are on the same page.' He left Iggy laughing and Li blushing, his mind already turning over the upcoming conversation with Nathan's wife. It promised to be interesting, to say the least.

Penn found himself immersed in his work when Sam's figure appeared in the doorway, breaking his concentration. 'Mrs Crawford and her lawyer are huddled in room one,' Sam informed, his voice laced with a hint of amusement. 'Her father's been banished to the waiting room. He's not pleased, to say the least.'

Penn smirked, 'I think I can live with that. Fancy joining me in the lion's den?'

Sam hesitated for a moment, then nodded. Together, they steeled themselves for the impending confrontation and made their way to the interview room.

The sight that greeted Penn was a composed and business-like Mirry, a stark contrast to the flustered woman he had expected. A tall, stern-looking woman with a briefcase sat next to her, her sharp eyes scanning the room. Penn recognised the type immediately; a lawyer who, for the right price, would strive to absolve even the guiltiest. This was going to be a long, arduous conversation.

As they settled into their seats, Penn flicked open his iPad to review his notes. He noticed a new email from Li containing a copy of Nathan's autopsy and lab results. He glanced up to find Mirry looking slightly pale, but her stern expression and ramrod posture were a clear indication of her disdain for the situation. She shot Penn a glare that seemed to say he was beneath her.

Penn shrugged mentally. He had taken an instant dislike to Mirry when they first met, and his opinion hadn't improved over time. There was an air of entitlement about her that he found off-putting, Simon seemed the same. His wife Tiffany however was a kind-hearted woman whose compassion outweighed her stepdaughter's haughtiness.

'Mrs Crawford,' Sam began, 'we've called you in because there are some additional questions we need to ask.'

Mirry Crawford's eyes shot daggers at him. 'And was it necessary to humiliate me by having me escorted here in a police vehicle?' she spat. Penn watched as Sam's confident facade wavered for a moment.

'My colleague informed me that he'd contacted you about coming in voluntarily, but you declined. I had no other option,' Sam explained, trying to keep his tone steady.

'I had matters to attend to,' Mirry retorted, her voice icy. 'I have far more pressing issues on my mind than participating in a pointless interview with an inept police force.'

Her solicitor, sitting next to her, placed a soothing hand on Mirry's, but she swiftly removed it, turning her face away in a clear sign of defiance. 'Since it seems I'm trapped here for the foreseeable future, let's get this farce over with,' she grumbled.

'Alright, Mrs Crawford,' Penn cut in ignoring her harsh words. 'A couple of nights ago, a brick was thrown through your friend Faith Harrington's window. Were you aware of this incident?' At the mention of her friend, Mirry's face paled further and her hands clenched into tight fists.

'Poor Faith, is she alright? I wasn't informed about this otherwise I would have rushed to her side,' Mirry exclaimed, her voice filled with concern. Penn had to admit, this woman was a master at manipulating her emotions on cue. 'There was a threatening message attached to the brick,' Sam added, watching her reaction closely.

'And what does this have to do with me?' Mirry asked, her voice now appearing sharp.

Penn looked at her, his eyes serious. 'You were spotted leaving the area. Rather hastily, I might add, on the night in question.'

Mirry scoffed, crossing her arms over her chest. 'Then your witness must be mistaken.'

Penn shook his head, a small smile playing on his lips. 'I assure you, my eyesight is in perfect condition. I can describe your car down to the last detail. Even the registration number.'

A flicker of surprise crossed Mirry's face, her composure slipping for a moment. 'Alright, you've got me. I was having a dreadful day. You see, I had just buried my husband and was humiliated by my so-called friends at the Hall afterwards.' She straightened herself, fixing her gaze on Penn.

'I heard about that,' Penn replied, his tone gentle. 'One of those friends was Faith, wasn't it? That must have made you quite angry.'

Mirry let out a bitter laugh. 'Oh, please. Yes, I was angry, so I decided to go for a drive. But I can assure you, I'm not the type of person who would resort to such actions. Have you tried looking into the housing estates? The residents there are far more likely to fall into a life of crime.'

Sam, who had been silently observing the exchange, finally spoke. 'Mirry, wasn't Nathan from one of those estates?'

Mirry nodded, her expression hardening. 'Yes, but his father was from Devon. His mother had to raise him alone, and he had no choice. But he rose above all that, through honest, hard work.'

Penn observed Mirry's reaction carefully. 'It's fascinating, isn't it, how money can make one's past vanish into thin air?' He said, 'From what I've gathered, the phrase 'good, honest, hard work' doesn't quite paint an accurate picture of Nathan. 'Cutthroat' and 'dishonest' seem to fit the bill more accurately, don't you think?'

Mirry's solicitor, a stern-looking woman with a hawkish nose, interrupted before she could respond. 'I fail to see how this is relevant, DCI McBride. You're merely harassing my client in her time of grief. If you don't get to your point soon, we'll have to end this conversation.'

Penn held up his hand, the smile never leaving his face. 'Patience, my friend. I'm getting to my point.' Turning back to Mirry, he continued, 'I find it rather odd that you and Nathan didn't see the same doctor. Nathan had his own, someone he had trusted for years, correct?'

Mirry frowned, her brows furrowing in confusion. 'Yes, that's correct. What's your point, Penn?'

Penn leaned forward, his eyes never leaving Mirry's. 'Well, it's a bit tricky, isn't it? Trying to have children when one has had a vasectomy?' As Mirry's face paled, Penn sat back, the smile on his face widening. She knew. This changed everything.

'From your demeanour, I gather you were aware of this too. I can only imagine the rage that must have stirred within you. All those medical appointments, the constant wondering if you'd ever bear a child of your own,' Penn said, his voice steady.

Mirry's eyes glistened with unshed tears. 'My husband must've had his reasons. Yes, I was livid when I discovered the truth just a week before his untimely demise. But, had he been forthright with me, I would've been understanding.'

Penn nodded, appreciating her honesty. 'You're far more forgiving than most, Mirry. But tell me, why were you so irate with Faith?' His gaze never left hers.

'She was meddling,' Mirry retorted, her voice bitter. 'I was trying to grieve for my husband, and there she was, playing detective. It was downright embarrassing.'

Penn was studying her. 'Mirry, without Faith's interference, we would've dismissed your husband's death as a mere accident. Was that what you wanted us to believe?'

'I'm sorry, DCI McBride,' Mirry's solicitor interjected, her tone icy. 'But are you suggesting that Mirry had a hand in her husband's murder?' She shot Penn a challenging look.

Penn held her gaze. 'Until this case is resolved, every lead is worth exploring. If Mrs Crawford is innocent, she has nothing to fear. However, the fact remains that everyone involved seems to be hiding something, which raises suspicion. Furthermore, after the altercation at the Hall, Miss Harrington's house was vandalised, and she received threats. Interestingly, I saw Mrs Crawford speeding away from the crime scene.' He paused, allowing his words to sink in. 'Would you care to explain that again, Mirry?'

Mirry sighed, her gaze never leaving Penn's. 'On the night in question, I had to rush back to my cottage due to a plumbing issue. I can provide the contact details of the plumber who was waiting for me and stayed until I left. If you saw me driving in a hurry, it was because I was rather upset about the situation.'

'Thank you for sharing that information, Mrs. Crawford. I'll be sure to note down the plumber's contact details,' Penn said, his tone even. He paused, looking at her thoughtfully before he asked, 'I'm curious, though. Why did you visit the fertility clinic on the morning your husband died, especially when you were aware that he was infertile?'

Mirry smiled, a touch of sadness in her eyes. 'Isn't it obvious, Detective? I went to inform my doctor that I no longer required his services. All my tests were clear - I was perfectly capable of having children. The stress, the issue... it all lay with my husband.'

Penn leaned forward, his gaze steady on Mirry. 'Did you tell them about the years you spent under the impression that you were the one who couldn't have children? Did you speak of your husband's deception - his secret vasectomy that he never thought to mention during your marriage?'

The solicitor raised a hand, her eyes flashing a warning at Mirry. 'Don't answer any more questions,' she instructed, her gaze then shifting to Penn. 'Detective, my client has cooperated and answered your questions. I believe there's nothing more to add. You either charge her with a crime, or we're leaving.'

Penn nodded, his expression unreadable. 'No, that will be all. I appreciate your cooperation, Mrs. Crawford.' As they left, he returned to his desk.

'So, what's your take on this?' Penn asked, leaning back in his chair. Sam gave a noncommittal shrug, his gaze fixed on the case file spread out on the desk. 'Well, it's plausible. After the plumber left, Mirry could've doubled back and thrown the brick through the window.' His voice was steady, matter of fact, betraying nothing of the turmoil that the case had stirred within him.

Suddenly, the station's office door was flung open with a bang. Simon Montague, a man of imposing stature and even more imposing wealth, strode in. Without a word, he marched straight up to Penn's desk and slammed his hand down on the polished surface. 'I demand to know why my daughter was subjected to the trauma of reliving her husband's death!' he barked, his face contorted in anger.

Penn rose slowly from his desk, his towering figure casting a long shadow over Simon. His voice was calm, but there was a steeliness in his eyes. 'I assure you, we did not discuss your son-in-law's death with your daughter. We merely questioned her about her whereabouts on the night of the vandalism and the threats made against Miss Faith Harrington.'

Simon recoiled slightly, but his anger didn't waver. 'And you think my daughter could do such a thing to her best friend?' he spat out, his voice dripping with contempt. Penn's response was swift and unyielding. 'The same best friend she threatened at the manor house on the same day?'

Simon's face turned a shade paler. 'That's a lie!' he roared, but Penn was unshakeable. 'We have two key witnesses, and numerous others who overheard the conversation. Your daughter has lied to the police on multiple occasions and obstructed our investigations. I suggest you have a serious talk with her.'

Just then, they heard a new voice in the room. It was Donald Harrington, his tone stern and commanding. 'And Penn has the full backing of his superiors, Simon. I suggest you stop harassing the police, which by the way is an offence, and go home to cool off.'

Simon, looking somewhat chastened, turned on his heel and strode out of the office. As the door closed behind him, Sam let out a sigh of relief. 'Anyone for coffee? Magda's baked brownies. I think we could all use a bit of a pick-me-up.'

'Couldn't agree more,' Penn replied, finally tearing his gaze away from the window and taking a seat. His mind was already forming theories about the strange events unfolding. As he waited for Sam to return, he couldn't help but wonder what his superior would make of all this.

When Sam returned, two plates stacked with brownies in hand, Penn had already started to organise his thoughts. 'Alright, boss, let's get to the bottom of this,' he said, accepting the plate from Sam and taking a bite of the sweet treat. The rich, chocolatey taste was a welcome distraction from the bitter reality they were about to delve into.

CHAPTER 27

Faith was wracked with anxiety as she approached Eglantine Hall that morning. She had received a call from Tiffany, who had requested her to come and photograph the Folly. It was still under renovation, but Tiffany wanted to capture the process. 'People enjoy seeing the evolution of a project,' she had explained, 'It piques their interest. Well, I hope they do, what do you think?'

'Great idea Tiff,'

Faith could see the logic in Tiffany's idea. She was aware that Tiffany regularly updated the village website with pictures, keeping the community informed and prepared for the times when construction could cause traffic jams.

But no matter what Tiffany did, she had no belief in herself, and that was sad.

Faith's mother had once told her. 'Poor Tiffany is always striving, but nothing ever seems to go her way. Sometimes I think her husband neglects her, always favouring Mirry. That's not a healthy dynamic for a marriage.'

'Everyone is drawn to Mirry, she had a difficult childhood,' Faith defended, 'She doesn't mean to do half the things she does, Mum.'

'Faith, you've had your share of hardship, and so have I. Everyone experiences suffering at some point. It can either break us or make us stronger. But it's no excuse to inflict pain on others, that's simply cruel. Tiffany wasn't responsible for Mirry's hardships, and she couldn't expect her father to grieve his wife forever. But that doesn't justify the way they treat Tiffany.'

Faith could hear her mother's words in her mind as she ambled towards the Folly, the walking stick tapping rhythmically against the cobblestones. Her mother had always been partial to Tiffany and always tried to encourage her. The sun was high in the sky, casting shadows that danced playfully around her. The Folly was a hive of activity; the cacophony of machinery and the banter of workmen filled the air.

A burly workman detached himself from the crowd and approached her, his face crinkling into a frown as he took in her walking stick. 'Can I help you?' he asked, his voice gruff.

'I'm Faith Harrington,' she replied, meeting his gaze steadily. 'Mrs Montague has asked me to photograph the Folly for advertising purposes.'

The workman, a grizzled man with a beard that had seen better days, pointed at her stick. 'That's going to be a bit of a hindrance on a worksite,' he remarked.

Unfazed, Faith retorted, 'I assure you; I can handle myself just fine. If you could just show me where it's safe to stand, I'll keep out of your way.' He shrugged noncommittally, turning on his heel and leading her towards the Folly. Faith followed, her resolve unshaken.

The Folly, a magnificent domed structure erected on a fancy by Arthur and Minerva's grandfather for his ailing wife, stood unscathed amidst the sprawling estate. Once upon a time, when taken ill, their mother would be carried here, to bask in the warmth of an open fire and lose herself in the pages of her beloved books.

Simon had paid little mind to the Folly. The dilapidated structure had become a secret haven for courting couples seeking a romantic escape, hidden away from prying eyes. It wasn't until Simon's wife, Tiffany, stumbled upon the forgotten edifice and pleaded for its revival, that the Folly was given a new lease on life.

She envisioned it as an enchanting addition to Simon's budding business venture - hiring out the grand hall for wedding ceremonies. With Tiffany's persuasion and Simon's acquiescence, the Folly and its surrounding landscapes were soon lavished with the care and attention they had been deprived of for so long. The forgotten gem was being brought back to life.

Faith couldn't help but notice the curious glances cast her way by the workmen, but she was quick to dispel any tension. 'Where's the best spot for a good shot without getting in anyone's way?' she asked, her question earning her a few appreciative nods and smiles. The camaraderie within the group was infectious, and Faith soon found herself enjoying the atmosphere.

One of the workmen, a young lad named Jack who had a knack for comedy, struck a pose in front of the Folly, a bunch of weeds clutched dramatically in his hand. 'What do you reckon, Faith? Would this make the cut for the new brochures?'

With a chuckle, Faith raised her camera and captured the moment. 'It might not make the brochure, but it'd certainly liven up the village website,' she teased, her comment earning a round of laughter from the crew. The morning passed in a flurry of activity, punctuated with short breaks during which Faith was invited to join the crew in their makeshift break area by a caravan stationed near some trees.

As Faith settled into a chair, she spotted a familiar figure approaching. 'I hope you've done some work this morning,' Mirry stated, her immaculate dark blue trouser suit and slightly high heels starkly contrasting the dusty work site.

'We're going to finish on time, hence the pause,' Bill said, his tone heavy with the weight of responsibility. 'We're keen to get that well sealed and bricked over, but we've to wait for the inspection before we can proceed.'

Mirry's brows furrowed in displeasure. 'Why wasn't this addressed earlier?' she queried, her voice sharp.

Jack met her gaze steadily, 'Miss Tiffany has arranged for an expert, but securing the right individual has been a challenge.'

Mirry sighed, her gaze drifting across the site until it landed on Faith. She offered her a faint smile, which Faith reciprocated. 'I see why my father insisted on my involvement, or should I say, rescue of this project,' she said, her tone laced with bitterness.

'I need this project wrapped up before my departure to London. I've to offload that tiny, horrid cottage and then I can finally bid farewell to this pitiful place and the unpleasant memories it holds,' Mirry continued, her voice cold.

'Well, if you can expedite the arrival of the inspector, we can get cracking on the well,' Bill replied, his tone firm. He was clearly unimpressed with Mirry's attitude, but he held his ground. 'Until then, we're left to slow down and do what we can.'

'As per usual, it seems I'm left to clean up the mess,' she declared, her voice laced with icy disdain. She spun on her heels, her coat billowing behind her as she stormed off towards her car. 'And I can assure you, my father will be far from pleased with the lack of progress here.' With a final, dismissive wave of her hand, she climbed into her car and sped off down the dirt road.

Jack watched her retreating figure, shaking his head with a low whistle. 'That woman... she's a right piece of work,' he muttered, his hands shoved deep into his pockets. Bill, standing beside him, gave a nod of agreement. 'You'd think I'd tell you to respect her, given her position. But my old man always said respect's something you gotta earn, not something you're just handed.'

Stigg, a lanky man with a shock of dark blonde hair rose from his seat and moved to refill his coffee cup. 'Poor Miss Tiffany,' he sighed, his eyes distant as he stared into the black liquid. 'She's poured her heart and soul into this place. A genuinely kind soul, that one. But her step-daughter and that good-for-nothing husband of hers... they're a pair of stuck-up snobs, wouldn't know the first thing about running a place like this.'

He paused, his gaze turning to the others. 'Do you remember what Nathan said about his boss? That he had some grand plan to show Mr. Montague who was really in charge?' Stigg's words hung in the air, sparking a flicker of interest in Faith. She'd known Nathan had a knack for rubbing people up the wrong way, but this plan of his... that was something new.

'I always thought Nathan and Simon were on good terms?' she questioned, her brows furrowing in confusion. Stigg shrugged, a grim smile on his face. 'He liked the power and the opportunities Simon's position offered him. But other than that, no. He was always boasting about how he was the better man, how he'd one day steal something precious right from under Simon's nose.'

Jack chimed in, pointing towards the Folly. 'And he wasn't just stealing from Simon. He was having an affair, right under his wife's nose. Brought his mistress here, to this very place. We'd find empty wine bottles, a freshly used fireplace, clean blankets on the bed. He told us to keep quiet if we wanted to keep our jobs.'

'And to be honest, his wife kind of had it coming.' Stigg replied.

'Do you have any idea who the other woman might be?' Faith inquired; her tone laced with curiosity. Jack shook his head, his brows furrowed in thought. 'I'm not entirely sure, but I did happen to overhear him on the phone with her once. He was trying to persuade her to accompany him to London. She didn't seem thrilled by the idea, and he made it clear that she had more to lose than he did.' He paused, his frown deepening. 'She didn't seem as smitten with him as he was with her. I got the feeling he'd use anyone to get what he wanted. I'm not even sure the man was capable of genuine emotion.'

Their conversation was interrupted by Bill's sudden interest in the well. 'We need to cover this thing up before we leave today, can you do it Stigg? It's an accident waiting to happen. It might not be deep or filled with water, but someone could still get hurt. I'd hate to think of some poor creature falling in there. There are plenty of animals around here, and that daft goat is always sniffing about for food.'

Stigg chuckled at this, a grin spreading across his face. 'Alright, I will get back to work.' All of the men ambled off towards the Folly, their banter and laughter lingering behind them.

Faith was left standing there, her mind reeling from the conversation. This revelation cast a new light on everything. Was the woman Nathan had been seeing another victim of his manipulative ways? The thought that it could be someone she knew was deeply unsettling. As she returned to the site to gather her belongings, her eye caught something shiny near the Folly door. It was a single unicorn earring; the same one she remembered seeing Tiffany wear at a party Mirry had thrown to celebrate her return, she must have lost it while working on site. She tucked it into her bag, her mind buzzing with questions. She had a lunch meeting with her father later; perhaps he could help her make sense of this new information.

The Hung, Drawn and Quartered, was bustling with activity. The arrival of warmer weather had drawn in visitors from all over, making it a challenge for Faith to spot her father amidst the crowd. Finally, she saw him rise from a corner table and wave her over.

'Hello, little girl' he greeted, pulling out a chair for her. 'Managed to snag us a spot just in time.'

'Dad,' Faith sighed, rolling her eyes, 'I'm not a little girl anymore.'

'Perhaps not,' he conceded, settling himself into his own chair, 'but I'd like to think I still have some gentlemanly manners left in me.'

He handed her a menu just as Judy approached with the specials for the day. They both opted for Massimo's Cheesy Broccoli Soup in a Bread Bowl, followed by white chocolate cheesecake for dessert.

As Judy set down their drinks – two non-alcoholic fruit ciders – and made polite conversation, Faith took a moment to sip hers before turning to her father. 'Dad, I was at the Folly this morning and heard some interesting chatter from the workmen there.'

Her father raised an eyebrow. 'Since when do you listen to gossip, Faith?'

'I don't usually,' she admitted, 'but they were talking about Nathan.'

Her father sighed, clearly not thrilled about the mention of her amateur detective work. 'I thought you were going to give that up, Faith.'

'So, you don't want to hear what I found out?' Faith challenged, lowering her gaze to her drink.

'I didn't say that' he replied, a twinkle in his eye. 'If you think it's important, I'd be a fool not to listen.'

With that, Faith quickly relayed the conversation she'd overheard earlier that day. Her father remained silent for a moment after she finished, just as Judy arrived with their food. 'It's certainly intriguing,' he finally said, unfolding his napkin onto his lap and taking a spoonful of soup. 'Especially the part about the phone call.' He paused to savour the soup. 'Delicious as always. We'd be lost without Massimo's cooking.' He waited for Faith to try hers and nod her agreement before continuing their conversation.

'I'll have a word with Penn and Sam about this,' he said, his voice laced with concern, 'there's something about Nathan's time in London that the police aren't telling us. And the way they're treating Penn… it's getting under my skin.'

His daughter raised an eyebrow, a smirk playing on her lips. 'Penn?

You've got to admit, Dad, he's a stickler for the rules. He's bound to have rubbed a few people up the wrong way.'

He sighed, leaning back in his chair. 'I think you're misunderstanding him, love. Yes, he's a man of principles, a bit rigid at times...'

'Just a bit, Dad?' she interjected, her smirk growing wider.

'They treat him badly,' he continued, ignoring her interruption, 'I shouldn't be telling you this, and I trust you'll keep it to yourself. He had a mate in the force, a good one, who crossed the line. Penn did what he had to do.'

She looked taken aback, her smirk fading. 'Are you serious? Even I know the police don't take kindly to a rat, even if it's justified.'

'That's why he's here, not there. He was pushed out. I won't go into details, but imagine having to leave everything you've built, to move somewhere you see as a step down. Don't be too hard on him, Faith. He's just trying to adjust, same as you.'

Faith knew what that felt like. When she'd first started her job here, it was a far cry from the thrill of London. She was her own boss now, but the weight of responsibility was heavy. She'd never make it as big as she'd hoped in her previous job.

'Thanks for telling me, Dad. I won't breathe a word. And you're right, it's not easy.'

He nodded, a sad smile on his face. 'You have your family and friends here, love. That's a safety net, a comfort. Penn only has his father, and he's not here.'

The cheesecake arrived, breaking the tense atmosphere between Faith and her father. As they indulged in the sweet treat, the conversation shifted to lighter topics, allowing her father some space to digest the heavy truths he'd been served.

Later, as Faith strolled down the main street of her village, her fingers absentmindedly traced the fabric of her scarf, the gift from Penn. A smile danced on her lips as she thought of his unexpected kindness. 'Perhaps there's more to Penn than meets the eye,' she mused.

Meanwhile, Penn was engrossed in his work when his phone rang. It was Don. As he listened to the information being relayed, he scribbled notes on his pad. His brow furrowed in concentration as he replied, 'Was Nathan ever kind to anyone, Don? It's hard not to feel a bit sorry for his wife.'

Don sighed over the line, 'Can't say I know of anyone, Penn. His job demanded people skills, but Nathan... he was more about manipulation. What goes around, comes around, as they say. It's just unfortunate it had to end this way.'

Penn rubbed his temples, 'It feels like we're going in circles. All the obvious suspects are clean. Even Mrs Crawford's house and her room at the hall are clean. I'm drawing a blank here, Don. Maybe I need to revisit the case notes. There might be something we overlooked.' His voice trailed off, deep in thought about the complex web they were trying to untangle. 'This is certainly a tough one, Don.'

'It's not easy,' Don replied. 'When something like this happens, it's like a punch to the gut. You look at people you've known for years, people you've shared pints with at the local, and you start wondering... could they be capable of such a thing? It's bad.'

'I can imagine,' his gaze drifting to the window. 'I guess that's why it's good I'm here. I haven't been around long enough to know the history of everyone, which means I can look at things objectively.'

Don chuckled, a sound that was more of a sigh than a laugh. 'True that. And we could use all the help we can get. We've been hitting dead ends left, right, and centre. Even Faith's still pitching in, though I'd never admit it to her that I'm happy about it.'

'Faiths got quite the knack for this, hasn't she?' Penn said, grinning at the thought of the spirited young woman. 'Ever thought she might follow in your footsteps?'

'No, Faith and Hope have always danced to their own tune. Charity, though, she was a bit of a wild one growing up. Then she up and surprised us all by joining the force. My wife keeps telling me she's a chip off the old block, but that doesn't stop me from worrying about her.'

Both men ended the call laughing and Penn headed off in search of Sam.

Meanwhile, Faith had just stepped through the door of her home, her thoughts still lingering on the day's events. She was halfway to her darkroom when her mobile buzzed, the caller ID flashing 'Ben'. Her heart sank. She had been hoping to end the day on a high note, but it seemed that was not to be.

'Hello Ben,' she greeted, striving to keep her voice neutral. 'What can I do for you?' There was a pause, then Ben's voice filled the line, honeyed and full of regret. 'Hello darling, I am glad I have found you in. I have so missed your voice.' Faith frowned, pulling the phone away from her ear to stare at it. 'Well, you decided to leave, so I have to say that is your fault.'

'Leaving you was the biggest mistake of my life, Faith,' Ben confessed, his voice trembling with sincerity. 'We were the perfect team, you and me. You understood me, Faith. We shared the same goals, the same dreams.'

Faith sank into her chair, her mind a whirlwind of conflicting emotions. She wasn't sure whether to feel elated at his confession or incensed at his audacity.

'Faith,' Ben continued, 'I know a lot has happened. And I know it was all my fault. What I'm trying to say... what I'm asking is... can we try again?' He paused, swallowing hard. 'I've had a lot of time to think, Faith. I'm not the same man I was.'

'Ben, I'm not sure this is a good idea...' Faith's voice trailed off, uncertainty lacing her words.

'Faith, just hear me out,' Ben implored. 'We could make a home here, in London. You could return to your job, and we could...we could start again.'

Faith felt a surge of anger bubbling within her. Once upon a time, she would have relished this attention, this declaration of love from Ben. But now, it was too much, too sudden. Especially after everything that had transpired in London. She couldn't help but question his motives. 'What about Eloise? And your child, Ben?' She stressed the last word, hoping it would jolt some sense into him.

'I made a mistake, Faith,' Ben confessed. 'I was wrong to leave you for Eloise. She may come from a wealthy family, but she uses her money as a means of control. She'll manage just fine raising the child. As for us... you know you can't have children. We could finally live the life we've always dreamed of.'

Faith inhaled deeply, her brows furrowing in thought. 'And where exactly do we plant our roots, Ben? Our flat's been sold off.' She questioned; her tone laced with uncertainty.

'Well,' Ben started, a hint of hesitation in his voice, 'I was thinking, you still have the funds from the sale, don't you? Plus, there's that grand old cottage of yours. It's bound to be worth a fortune.'

'And what would you be contributing financially, Ben?'

'Faith, I've exhausted all my savings. Life down here isn't as affordable as it seems. Once I secure a job, I'll be able to pitch in. You, on the other hand, can easily land a job and keep us afloat until I get back on my feet.' Ben replied, his voice steady and reassuring.

Faith's softened, 'And what does Eloise think of all this?'

'Faith, her opinions are irrelevant. What truly matters is that I love you and I want us to be together again. I thought you'd be ecstatic about this.' Ben said, a touch of disappointment in his voice.

Faith shook her head, even though he couldn't see her. 'I'm not the same woman you remember, Ben. And I can't help but wonder if your sudden interest in me has anything to do with your current situation - homeless, jobless, and clinging onto your reputation. It's unsettling to think that I might be your second choice.'

Ben hardened, 'I'm not pleased with your attitude, Faith. I took the time to call you, to give you a second chance. I assumed you'd be thrilled.'

Faith's eyes narrowed, 'What do you mean by that, Ben?'

'Faith,' Ben sighed, 'You're not in a position to be picky. You're not exactly a beauty queen, and if you don't accept my offer, I can see you leading a solitary life well into your twilight years. Most men desire offspring, something you can't provide. Don't be foolish, Faith. You won't find anyone better than me.'

Faith struggled to mask her disbelief as Ben's true colours unfurled. His callousness was no surprise, her family had warned her, but she had been too obstinate to listen.

'At last, the real Ben emerges,' she said, her voice laced with bitter irony. 'So, I'll give you, my answer. It's a resounding no. You're nothing but an arrogant, self-centred swine. You're only calling because you're homeless, friendless, and your last girlfriend has kicked you out and is squeezing every penny out of you.'

'How did you...' Ben stammered, but Faith cut him off.

'I know about everything, Ben,' she said, her voice cold and unwavering. 'And if you think I'll sacrifice my successful business to gamble on a worthless excuse of a man like you, you're sorely mistaken. So, have a nice life, Ben. I hope you learn to be a better human being.'

Before Ben could muster a response, Faith ended the call with a definitive tap. She rose from her chair, her heart pounding in her chest, and made her way to the kitchen. She poured herself a generous glass of wine, grabbed her coat, and ventured into her garden. The evening had a cool edge to it, and Faith welcomed the chilly bite. She settled onto her wooden swing seat, took a large sip of her wine, and let the silence envelop her.

Her Friendly squirrel had found its way onto the bird feeder, its small paws deftly picking out the nuts Faith had scattered there the day before. She watched it from her chair, the cool air wrapping around her as she sipped her wine. The creature's features struck her as distinctly masculine, though she couldn't be certain. As it noticed her gaze, it paused, its bright eyes meeting hers.

'A word to the wise, Mr. Squirrel,' she spoke, her voice carrying across the quiet garden. 'Should you ever find yourself a Mrs. Squirrel, do treat her kindly.' The squirrel chittered in response, a sound she chose to interpret as agreement. With a final nut clenched in its teeth, it scampered away, up the fence and into the tree that led to the backfield.

Faith's thoughts returned to Ben, her anger bubbling up anew. The audacity of the man, expecting her to drop everything and rush to London. To once again prop him up, to drain her parents' resources for his benefit, only for him to cast her aside once he'd found his footing. *Not this woman*, she thought fiercely.

As her anger subsided, replaced by a sense of calm, she found herself feeling a strange sense of pride. She had finally closed the door on that tumultuous chapter of her life, a part she was sometimes embarrassed to admit she had played.

Now, the future was hers to shape. The thought was exhilarating, yet terrifying. But she knew she was ready to face whatever came next on her own terms.

CHAPTER 28

After a brisk shower, Faith slipped into her clothes, her fingers deftly securing the new scarf that Penn had gifted her. She snagged a piece of fruit from the kitchen, her bag slung over her shoulder as she stepped out into the day, making her way towards the village and her mother's shop. She wanted to express her gratitude for her mother's generosity in lending her the car, the very same car she had used to photograph the Folly at the hall.

Spring was unfurling itself, the days growing warmer, the air thick with the cries of lambs calling for their mothers in the nearby fields. The buds she had spotted weeks ago were now bursting into a riot of green leaves, the scent of blooming flowers filling the air. She paused in her journey, her gaze falling on Mirry and Nathan's house, a 'for sale' sign staked into the front yard. She hoped Mirry would find solace and a fresh start in a new place, and perhaps, in time, they could mend their fractured friendship.

A sudden noise jolted her out of her thoughts and she spun around to find Arthur, peering over one of the walls that bordered a field teeming with sheep. 'Are you alright, Arthur?' she asked, concern lacing her words.

Arthur responded with a worried frown, 'I've been looking for Churchill. He went off on one of his adventures this morning and hasn't returned. I'm starting to think he's got a secret girlfriend.'

Faith chuckled at the thought, 'Wouldn't that be something?'

Arthur didn't look convinced, 'I doubt Min would be thrilled. Listen, if you happen to spot the little escape artist, could you give me a ring?' He rummaged in his pocket, pulling out a card and handing it to her. 'It's got my number. Min insisted I get a mobile phone and these cards. She just wants to keep tabs on me. The phone's got one of those tracking apps on it.'

Faith promised to keep an eye out for Churchill and let her mother know as well.

'See those cows, Faith? All sitting down they are,' Arthur remarked, pointing towards the next field. His voice was filled with a certainty that made Faith glance up at the sky, despite herself. 'Best be heading home early today. It's going to pour down, mark my words.'

Faith squinted at the horizon. The sky was a clear, unblemished blue, not a cloud in sight. 'Are you certain, Arthur?' she asked, her tone laced with doubt. Arthur simply nodded in response, already clambering over the stile to continue his trek up the field towards the top woods.

A chuckle escaped Faith's lips as she watched him go. Between Arthur and his weather prophecies, and Churchill with his bustling social life, the characters in her life were certainly colourful. She couldn't help but feel a twinge of envy - even Arthur's beloved pet seemed to have a more exciting life than her.

The walk to her mother's shop was a welcome distraction, the fresh air invigorating her senses. Despite having to use her stick, she didn't feel the slightest bit tired upon reaching her destination. The shop was a cocoon of warmth, the familiar scents enveloping her as she stepped inside.

Faith's mother, Rowan, was embroiled in her usual battle with the cash register. Threats of mallet-induced demolition reverberating through the small shop as Faith walked in. Upon seeing her daughter, Rowan's stern expression softened and she left the till, leaving it in the capable hands of Pink. She enveloped Faith in a warm hug before leading her to the back of the shop, a labyrinth of stock and uncollected gifts.

'I've got a pile of gifts to sort through,' Rowan began, her fingers already deftly tearing through a box of assorted items. 'Some folks haven't picked theirs up yet. Fancy being mummy's little helper for a while?' Faith, with a small smile, agreed and began to help her mother organise the gifts.

As they worked, Faith broached a subject close to her heart. 'Mum, I wanted to say thanks for letting me borrow the car. If my photography keeps going well, I might need to get my own.' Rowan looked up from her work, her eyes twinkling with pride. 'The artisan trail is getting more popular, and when Hope starts the literary festivals, I think you'll be in high demand. You are in the right place at the right time, love.'

The conversation eventually shifted from Faith's burgeoning business and the possibility of hiring new workers to her phone call from her ex. The mention of Ben brought a sudden tension to the room. 'What did he want?' Rowan asked, her voice tight. Faith, perched on a stool and recounted Ben's pleas; her mother's gaze never leaving her face.

'I can't believe the audacity of that man,' Faith's mother exclaimed. 'After all the heartache he's caused you, he has the nerve to expect you to help him rebuild his life. It's pure arrogance. I hope you didn't give his words any weight. You're worth more than he'll ever comprehend.'

Faith shrugged, her fingers tracing the rim of her coffee mug. 'Ben's never been one for tact. His ego's always been larger than life.' She paused, her eyes narrowing. 'I do feel sorry for the child, though.'

Her mother shook her head. 'Don't waste your sympathy on them, dear. Eloise will manage just fine without Ben. And that child won't lack anything in life.'

Changing the subject, Faith said, 'Before I forget, Mirry's decided to sell the house.'

Her Mum wasn't surprised. 'Country life was never Mirry's cup of tea. She stayed only because Nathan had made a name for himself here. She'll be happier in London. And hopefully, it'll ease the tension between her and Tiffany.'

Faith nodded. 'You're probably right. But I think she'll miss having Nathan. Despite everything, she did love him. And I believe he had some feelings for her too.'

Faith couldn't help but grin at her mother's raised eyebrows, but before she could reply, her mother abruptly rose and retrieved a box from a shelf.

'I found this yesterday,' she said, handing the box to Faith. 'Nathan bought it two days before he died. He was supposed to pick it up, but I didn't want to give it to Mirry then. I had completely forgotten about it. I hope she won't be too upset.'

'This might be just what Mirry needs right now, Mum. Something to cherish.'

'Faith, hand me that paper. This has seen better days, I'll replace it with a fresh sheet,' Rowan requested, her nose scrunching at the scent wafting in the air as she took off the old wrapping and bow. Faith, drawn by the smell, ambled over to her mother, her curiosity piqued.

'Mum, what is it?' she questioned, her eyes fixated on the package. Rowan passed the box to her daughter, a soft smile playing on her lips. 'That's the Bali collection, why do you ask?'

'It smells like coconut. Mirry can't stand it,' Faith interjected, her brows furrowing in confusion. 'Why would Nathan buy his wife something she detests?' Rowan shrugged, her mind already running wild with possibilities. 'I can't say, Faith. I just assumed it was for Mirry. He requested it to be wrapped in heart paper and adorned with a beautiful bow. He even put a letter in with it. Seemed like a romantic gesture.'

Faith bit her lip, her mind whirling. 'Before we hand this over to Mirry, I think we should have a peek at the letter.' Rowan looked taken aback, her eyes wide with surprise. 'That's private, Faith. It's not professional.' But Faith was insistent. 'Mum, imagine if this isn't meant for Mirry and she opens a letter intended for someone else. It would shatter her.'

Something in Faith's tone must have hit home because Rowan hesitated for a moment before passing the envelope to her daughter. Faith carefully opened it, her breath hitching as she read the contents. She glanced at her mum, her heart pounding in her chest, before reading it aloud. "We are meant to be together and remember you have more to lose than me. Do what you have to do, get the money and we will leave this rotten place."

Faith could see the confusion etched on her mother's face. But for Faith, everything clicked into place. This wasn't for Mirry. It was for Tiffany. Nathan must have been blackmailing her too. The poor woman, she had enough on her plate already. 'Mum, I'm sorry, but I have to go. This is urgent,' Faith announced, her mind already racing with her next steps. 'You're not going to get into trouble again, are you?' Rowan asked, her voice laced with worry.

Faith was in the midst of buttoning up her coat when she spoke, her voice a low murmur. 'I think I know who this is for, and I think they need my help. It's not dangerous, just something that needs to be sorted,' she said, her fingers closing around her bag. 'I'll tell you everything later. You have my word.'

With a nod of understanding, she stepped outside, the chill of the air hitting her immediately. She pulled out her phone, her fingers quickly dialling Tiffany's number. The dial tone seeming to go on forever. Tiffany picked up after what seemed an eternity. Faith hesitated, her mouth opening and closing as she searched for the right words. Then, she remembered the earring.

'Tiffany,' she began, her voice steady. 'I hope I'm not interrupting anything. I found an earring, a unicorn one. I think it might be yours. And there's something else...a gift that mum forgot to deliver. I think it's for you, from Nathan.' The line was silent for a moment before Tiffany finally responded, her voice laced with confusion. 'From Nathan? Why would he send me a gift? You must be mistaken.'

Faith shook her head, even though Tiffany couldn't see her. 'No, I'm quite sure it's for you. There's a note and everything. Look, Tiffany, I know what Nathan was doing and I want to help you.'

The silence returned, stretching out for so long that Faith thought Tiffany might hang up. But then, her voice came through the line again, a hint of despair creeping into her words. 'I'm just checking some work at the Folly; you can meet me there. But please, don't tell anyone and come alone. I'm so distraught about the whole thing.'

Faith nodded, her voice firm. 'Your secret is safe with me, Tiffany. I'll come alone. Mum is letting me use her car this morning I'll be there in about 15 minutes.'

The silence on the other end of the line was deafening. Tiffany had hung up, leaving Faith with her swirling thoughts. 'Poor woman,' she muttered under her breath, her mind racing with the implications of their conversation. Nathan had been up to no good, she was certain of that now. Was it possible that Tiffany was another victim in all of this and had been extorted by Nathan? The thought made Faith's blood boil.

Faith sighed, rubbing her temples. This was a mess, a real mess. She knew it was going to hit Mirry hard. The poor woman was already on the edge; this could very well push her over. Yet, there was a chance, a small chance, that this could bring Mirry and Tiffany together. They were both victims of Nathan's manipulations, after all.

But there was also a risk, a big risk, that this could drive a permanent wedge between them. Faith knew she had to tread carefully, for the sake of both women.

Chapter Twenty- Nine

Faith, her fingers wrapped tightly around the steering wheel of the car, navigated the quiet streets to the Folly. She glanced upwards, noting the clear sky. Arthur, with his ever-so-reliable weather predictions, had been wrong this time.

Her mind, however, was far from the weather. The cruel treatment of Tiffany was a heavy weight in her heart. And then there was Nathan. His plot to use Tiffany, to have her steal money for his escape to London, was a betrayal of the worst kind. The scandal that would have followed would have shattered Mirry. How could he have even considered such a heartless act?

Faith shook her head. Mirry must never know, she decided. It would be kinder to let her believe in her husband's love. Despite knowing that Mirry, in all probability, would lay the blame at Tiffany's door.

As she approached the Folly, she noted the deserted surroundings. The workmen had either called it a day or Tiffany had asked them to leave. The caravan, usually bustling with activity, was eerily silent. Perhaps they had taken the day off.

And there stood Tiffany, in front of the Folly, her face a canvas of raw emotion, streaked with tears.

'Tiffany'. She shouted. An overnight bag sat at her feet, hinting at a planned journey. Her attire mirrored her intentions.

Faith approached her, extending a box and a card towards Tiffany. She watched as Tiffany's eyes scanned over the words, her expression unreadable. Breaking the silence, Faith's voice was gentle, filled with regret. 'I am so sorry, Tiffany. Nathan's actions were inexcusable. You didn't deserve to be treated that way.'

Tiffany looked up, her eyes brimming with tears. 'I should've come clean sooner,' she admitted. 'I wanted to blame Nathan, to say he tricked me. But that wouldn't be true. I've been having such a difficult time... Mirry despises me, and Simon... he treats me as though I don't exist.'

Faith shook her head, her gaze softening. 'I'm sure that isn't true, Tiffany. Simon does care.'

Tiffany's shoulders slumped, her gaze dropping to the floor. 'Faith, you've seen how they both treat me. People might think otherwise, but I do love Simon with all my heart. I know I'm not as clever and sophisticated as they are, but I wanted to learn, to make Simon proud of me.' Her voice trailed off, her words hanging in the air as she shifted uncomfortably, uncertain of what else to say.

'Life didn't hand me this lot, you know?' Tiffany said. Faith merely nodded; her eyes soft with understanding. Tiffany continued, her voice a mix of bitterness and longing, 'My father was a philanderer, always leaving my mum to clean up after his mess. He'd disappear, then reappear and she'd just...welcome him back. I never understood it. Didn't she have any self-respect?'

Faith sighed, her gaze distant, 'Love, Tiffany, it has a way of making us do strange things. We know it's wrong, but our hearts, they follow their own compass.'

Tiffany's eyes welled up again, 'But what about me? What about what I wanted? I just wanted to be loved. Mum only had eyes for dad, and I... I was just...there. I just want to matter, to be seen, to be cared for. I can share, I don't need it all. I just want to count.'

She gestured towards the Folly, her voice filled with pride and a hint of defiance, 'This was my dream, my idea. I wanted to renovate this.'

Faith looked at her, her eyes filled with admiration, 'Tiffany, you've done a wonderful job here. The entire village agrees. You're a part of us now. Everyone loves you.'

Tiffany's face fell, 'Then why did he put Nathan in charge first, then Mirry? It's because he thought I'd mess up, embarrass them. I was never good enough. And then, when Nathan started comforting me, it all spiralled out of control.' She paused, her voice choked with regret, 'I had an affair with my stepdaughter's husband. What kind of person does that make me?'

Faith sighed, her voice gentle, 'It makes you human, Tiffany. We all make mistakes. This can be sorted out. You don't need to run away.'

Tiffany's gaze was distant, her mind seemingly lost in a world of its own. 'I never intended for him to die, you know?' she murmured.

Faith felt as though she had been physically struck. The revelation was too much to process. Tiffany, the woman she had known for so long, had killed Nathan. It was an unthinkable reality. She recoiled instinctively, her heart pounding against her ribcage. 'Do you mean you killed him?' she managed to stammer out.

Magda had been trying her hand at replicating Krista's delectable brownies. 'The morning Nathan died, I had decided to confront him,' Tiffany continued, her voice trembling. 'I was going to tell him that I would no longer be his accomplice, stealing from my husband. I wasn't going to leave with him to London.'

Tears welled up, spilling over and trickling down her cheeks. She rubbed them away impatiently, her fingers leaving wet streaks on her skin. 'I took one of the brownies, wrapped it in foil and put it in my bag. I was supposed to be at the Folly, and I thought I could sit there, have my brownie and try to forget about the mess my life had become.'

Faith's mind was spinning, but she needed to understand. She needed to know what had driven Tiffany to such a desperate act. 'But instead, you went to Nathan's. What happened there?' she asked, her voice shaky but determined. She couldn't begin to comprehend the torment Tiffany must have been enduring before she finally snapped.

Tiffany's hands moved animatedly as she spoke, her voice imitating the turmoil of her emotions. 'I walked in on him mid-change, his shirt drenched in coffee. He was livid,' she confessed, her eyes clouded with guilt. 'Churchill had struck again. That was my doing. Whenever Nathan and I would rendezvous at the Folly, Churchill would somehow know and come begging for treats. I could never resist his adorableness.' A small smile on her lips; a brief moment of respite from the heavy conversation.

'Nathan's cruelty wasn't just limited to his fellow humans. He had a dark side that extended to animals too. He had tried multiple times to shoo away Churchill, but he was stubborn.' Tiffany's attention was momentarily diverted as she pulled out her mobile from her pocket, her gaze fixated on the screen before she quickly switched it off.

'Sorry, it's Simon,' she said, a hint of worry tinging her voice. 'He's going to be livid when he finds out. But it won't last long. I think they'll both be relieved to be free of me.'

Faith was quick to shake her head, refusing to accept Tiffany's self-deprecating words. 'That's not true, Tiff. I'm certain it was just an accident,' she said, trying to reassure her friend. But Tiffany just sighed, the frustration in her voice palpable.

'He had the nerve to ask me to fetch his brownie and remaining coffee from the kitchen. Can you believe that? And I did it. That's when I remembered the brownie in my bag. I swapped it, just to give him a fright.'

A gasp of disbelief escaped Faith's lips, her eyes widening with shock. 'You knew he was allergic?'

Tiffany nodded, her hands trembling as she clutched at her top. 'Yes, I knew,' she admitted. 'I thought he could use his EpiPen and that would be enough. I never imagined...I never wanted...I just wanted him to stop, not...not stop breathing.'

'Did you at least try Tiffany?'

Tiffany shook her head.

A sob caught in Faith's throat as she reached out, her fingers brushing against Tiffany's arm. 'Oh, Tiff,' she murmured, her voice thick with unshed tears. 'No one deserves to die like that. Not even him.'

Tiffany's voice wavered as she confessed, her eyes staring blankly at the floor. 'I panicked. I didn't know what to do. I took his EpiPen and made it look like an accident. I left him there, alone. It was...it was monstrous.' She took a deep breath, her shoulders sagging. 'I can't stay here. I need to start over. I'm tired of being seen as the fool, always second best. I can't stand it any longer.'

Faith reached out, her fingers closing around the handle of Tiffany's overnight bag. 'Tiff, you have to tell the truth. People will understand. You're not a fool. Look at what you've done with the Folly. That was all you.' Tiffany looked up, a weak smile playing on her lips. 'I wish I could believe that' she said. 'But thank you, Faith. You've been the only real friend I've had here. I'll miss our girls' nights.'

Tiffany's hand was now clamped around her bag, her knuckles white under the strain. Tiffany suddenly yanked with a violent jerk of movement to snatch the bag from Faith. It happened so fast; scared, Faith stepped backwards. Her fingers, frail and trembling, lost their grip on her walking stick. It clattered to the ground. The grass that had been under her feet gave way to nothingness, and instead of a soft landing, she found herself falling straight down.

It was the well, she realised with a gasp. Partially filled with water, it had cushioned her fall to an extent. Why wasn't it deeper? The workmen must have started to fill it in with concrete. But it was deep enough to stop someone like her getting out. The pain in her legs and arms sent her heart into a frenzy. She had a lump on her head but had not been knocked out. Panic clawed its way up her throat and she called out to Tiffany in desperation. The response she got was nothing but an eerie silence that bounced off the cold stone walls of the well.

Tiffany's face appeared above her, a silhouette against the dimming light of the day. Her voice, when it came, was hollow, slicing through Faith's hope. 'I'm sorry, Faith,' she said. 'I can't help you. I need to vanish, and you... you'll try to stop me. Once I'm far from here, I'll ring the police. Tell them where you are.'

Her words hung in the air, heavy and ominous. 'It's not just about me anymore. There's someone else who needs me more than you do. I do like you, Faith, and I hope... I hope you can forgive me.' And then, she was gone.

Faith was left alone, the darkness of the well pressing in on her from all sides. She stared up at the sky, now a dark abyss. The rain began to fall, each drop a soft sound against the stone.

'Damn it, why did Arthur have to be right today of all days?' Faith muttered under her breath. The rain had started as a gentle patter, each drop a soft note. But it didn't stay that way for long. The delicate patter soon morphed into a relentless onslaught, each raindrop a bullet, mercilessly bombarding the already sodden grass. Faith huddled in the well, her heart pounding in sync with the rain, praying that Tiffany would have a change of heart and return.

As the icy water began to seep down the stone wall of the well, Faith knew she had to act. Her fingers, that were becoming numb from the cold, began to probe the rough surface, desperately searching for a hold. But the wet stones were slippery and treacherous. Each time she managed to hoist herself up a little, she would lose her grip and slide back down, a sharp pain shooting through her injured leg. Her walking stick, her only aid, was nowhere to be found, having slipped from her grasp during her tumble down the well.

'Help!' she cried out. But her pleas were drowned out by the relentless patter of the rain. Despair began to creep into her heart, each beat a reminder of her dire situation.

Suddenly, a shadow loomed overhead. Looking up, she saw Churchill, peering down at her, her favourite scarf dangling from his mouth. 'Churchill, do you reckon you could play the hero and fetch some help?' she asked, hope creeping into her voice. The goat cocked his head to one side, seemingly considering her proposition. 'I promise you a whole cake just for yourself, and I bet Min would be over the moon.'

At the mention of Min, Churchill's ears perked up. He gave Faith one last look before disappearing into the rain. 'Churchill, wait!' Faith cried out, but it was too late. The mention of his rival had spooked Churchill, and he had made a hasty retreat. 'Don't leave me here, Churchill,' she whispered, her voice barely heard over the sound of the rain.

The chill of the stone wall seeped through the thin fabric of Faith's shirt causing her to shiver uncontrollably. Her back was pressed firmly against the rough, cold, surface as she tried to make herself as small as possible. The dank, musty smell of the well filled her nostrils, a constant reminder of the dire situation she found herself in.

'Help!' she cried out again in the dark space. Her throat was raw from her previous screams for help, each one becoming more desperate than the last She could even feel her heart pounding like a drum against her rib cage.

'Is anyone there?' she yelled, her voice breaking on the last word.

She swallowed hard, trying to push down the lump of fear that had lodged itself in her throat. 'Please!'

Opening her eyes, she stared into the darkness, straining to hear any sound that might indicate she was not alone. But all she could hear was the rain. She was in a lot of trouble, and the way out seemed impossible to find.

CHAPTER 29

Penn's fingers were drumming an erratic rhythm on the edge of his desk as he dialled Don's number for the third time. Each call was met with the same monotonous drone of the voicemail. He had been informed by one of the officers, a casual comment thrown over a shoulder, that Don had taken his wife for a lunch date. Penn's mind was a whirlwind of thoughts, his gaze fixed on the cold, unresponsive phone in his hand.

In the midst of his dilemma, Sam had approached him. He relayed the information he had received from their contact in London. Nathan had been offered a lucrative job in the city. The contact had also mentioned, rather hesitantly, about Nathan's scandalous affair with his father-in-law's wife.

Sam had been sceptical, finding the revelation hard to swallow and had sought Penn's opinion. Penn, however, felt it was a lead worth pursuing. He wanted to discuss this further with Don to decide their next course of action.

Penn and Sam peered through the window of the Heaven Scents shop, he caught sight of his boss, heartily chuckling at a quip his wife had thrown his way. Don laughed again, as he helped his wife into her coat. Halting them as they exited the shop, he requested a moment, sharing his burgeoning suspicions about Tiffany's involvement in Nathan's murder.

The retort was swift, not from Don, but from his wife, Rowan, her voice filled with disbelief. 'You can't possibly think Tiffany is involved; she couldn't murder Nathan.' Her voice was laced with incredulity, her eyes wide with shock.

Penn held her gaze, his own eyes steady. 'Maybe, maybe not, but I still would like to ask her some questions. I've tried the hall, no one seems to know her whereabouts. Even Mr Montague has attempted to reach her, to no avail.'

Before he could further his argument, the familiar voice of Pink rang out, causing him to spin around. 'DCI McBride.' Penn swivelled, his gaze landing on Pink. 'She might be with Faith. I overheard Faith calling her outside the shop, she seemed in a hurry. She said she knew what Nathan had done and wanted to help.'

The sudden commotion in the doorway had attracted the attention of the patrons, their curious gazes turning towards the unfolding drama. Among the onlookers was Liam, who had been busily cleaning a table near I Grinder. He hurried over, hastily wiping his hands on his tea towel. 'Is everything okay?' His voice was filled with concern, his eyes darting between the group.

Rowan, her face drained of colour, fumbled for her phone, her fingers trembling as she dialled Faith's number. There was no answer. She tried again. 'Don, something's wrong. Faith isn't answering. What if she realised Tiffany had hurt Nathan and confronted her?' Don placed a comforting hand on her shoulder, his voice steady. 'Let's not jump to conclusions just yet. Faith isn't stupid and can handle herself.'

Another sudden commotion halted everyone in their tracks as Churchill appeared from nowhere with Arthur panting heavily in his pursuit.

The Goat rushed up to Penn, trying to butt him with his head, determined to attract the DCI's attention. 'Churchill! What on earth has got into you?' Penn exclaimed, his eyes wide with disbelief, then he noticed the object clutched in the goat's mouth. He kneeled down, extending a cautious hand to retrieve the item. Churchill, surprisingly, offered no resistance. Penn held the damp, muddy scarf up to the light. 'This is the scarf I gave Faith,' he muttered. There was no blood, a small mercy, but the state of the scarf suggested Faith was in some sort of trouble.

Rowan's tears began to flow freely, her body shaking with sobs. Don quickly wrapped his arms around her, trying to offer some comfort. 'Faith was wearing this scarf this morning, Don,' she cried, pointing at the scarf in Penn's hand. 'Something's happened to her, you have to do something!'

Arthur, still panting from his chase, reached out to grab Churchill, who stubbornly refused to move. 'You shouldn't have taken this, Churchill,' Arthur scolded, a hint of concern creeping into his voice. Liam quickly intervened, stopping Arthur from making another attempt to grab the goat. 'Arthur, if Faith was wearing this, Churchill couldn't have reached it unless it fell I... or unless Faith is lying on the ground somewhere,' he said, his voice grim.

Rowan's cries grew louder at Liam's words. 'Pink, take Rowan back inside,' Don instructed, his voice steady despite the worry etched on his face. Pink nodded, gently guiding a distraught Rowan back into the shop.

Turning back to Arthur, Don asked, 'When did you notice Churchill was missing?' Arthur, now inspecting the mud caked on Churchill's legs and back, replied, 'This morning, Don. He's been wandering off a lot lately, always coming back covered in mud.' He sighed, running a hand through his hair. 'He's got a thing for that Folly. I think the workmen there have been feeding him. And you know Churchill, he'd scale a mountain for a snack.'

Penn, his voice urgent. 'The Folly? At the Hall? Is that where you think he's been?'

Arthur, still preoccupied with examining the goat, nodded absent-mindedly. 'Absolutely. It's a mud pit there. And this rascal,' he gestured towards Churchill, 'has a penchant for rolling in it. Drives Min up the wall, we have...'

Cutting him off, Penn interjected, 'I think I can visualise that, thank you, Arthur. You might have just given us a lead to where Faith might be.' He stooped down to Churchill's level, scratching behind the goat's ear affectionately. 'Well done Churchill.' The goat bleated and he trotted off towards the tables outside The Grinder, eyeing the customers' meals with hopeful eyes.

'Don, it might be best if you stay here with your wife. Call us if Faith gets in touch.' Penn's tone was firm, but Don was quick to retort. 'Not on your life, I'm coming with you. Don't force me to pull rank.' Penn sighed, trying to reason with him. 'What if we encounter a situation? Can you keep your cool? Is that what will help Faith?'

Don's shoulders tensed, his face hardened, and Penn could see he was on the verge of an argument. But after a moment, he relented. 'Don't make a habit of bossing me around, okay?' Don muttered, retreating into the shop.

Penn turned to Sam, his voice steady and authoritative. 'Sam, ring the station. We need an ambulance and additional officers. Direct them to the Hall but steer clear of the Folly. The last thing we need is Tiffany doing something reckless at the sight of the police.' Sam nodded, understanding the gravity of the situation and stepped away to make the call.

'Penn, I reckon we got off on the wrong foot, didn't we?' Liam said, rubbing the back of his neck awkwardly. His gaze was steady, sincere. 'Tiffany and I share a good rapport, same with Krista. If things go south, I believe she'll listen to me.'

Penn raised an eyebrow, his stern face softening a bit. 'You know, Liam, it's not exactly by the book, bringing civilians into a situation like this. But right now, it's Faith's safety that's paramount. I appreciate your help, truly.'

Liam nodded, a glint of determination in his eyes. 'What say we take my car? It's less conspicuous. We can get closer to the Folly without rousing Tiffany's suspicion.'

As if on cue, the torrent from above began, teeming down relentlessly. Penn's heart roared thunderously in his chest, matching the storm above. 'We need to get moving, and pronto. '

'Sam, you handle Tiffany. Liam and I will go after Faith,' Penn ordered, his tone brooking no argument. Liam nodded, a grim expression on his face.

'I've got some rope in the back of my van. Don't give me that look, Penn,' he said, noticing Penn's sceptical glance. 'I use it to secure the stock sometimes.'

As Sam headed off to his car, Penn waited for Liam to fetch his van. The rain was relentless, soaking them through to the bone and making Penn shiver. He muttered a silent prayer, hoping against hope. 'Hang in there, Faith. Just a little longer.'

CHAPTER 30

The well was rapidly filling and Faith found herself submerged in an abyss of icy, muddy water. She could feel it's cold creeping up her body, a chilling reminder of her predicament.

'Damn,' she muttered to herself. Her leg throbbed with an intensity that made her grit her teeth, the numbness creeping up from her toes like an unwelcome intruder. 'A stick...any support would've been a blessing,' she murmured. But what good would it have done? She was trapped, disabled, and helpless. A bitter laugh escaped her lips as she thought about the cruel twist of fate. Maybe it would've been better if she had died in that accident.

Her gaze fell on the bricks jutting out from the well's side, like a stairway to freedom just out of her reach. 'If only I could use my legs,' she cried, her voice choked with despair. She could almost picture herself climbing to safety, each brick a step closer to life. But it was a futile dream. Her tears, hot against the cold rain, flowed freely now, blending with the water around her. She thought of Tiffany, the one who'd left her in this hellhole. Would she have called the police as she'd promised?

Her family, her friends, they'd miss her. A pang of sadness hit her as she thought about Penn. Why did he suddenly cross her mind? Was it the cold getting to her, or was it something else? Penn, who'd faced so much yet remained unjaded. Would he be disappointed?

The water level was rising quickly now and Faith found herself floating, a puppet at the mercy of the elements. Drowning, she'd heard, was a terrible way to die. It wasn't quick, it was agonising. She closed her eyes, trying to block out the relentless drumming of the rain, the biting cold that seemed to seep into her very bones. She was lost in her thoughts, each one a desperate plea for a miracle.

'Faith, are you there?' A voice cutting through the icy silence. It was a voice she knew, Liam's voice. Was it her frozen mind playing tricks on her, conjuring up the sound of his voice in her desperate state?

'Faith!' Another voice joined in, this one unmistakably Penn's. The cold was known to induce hallucinations, but could it be that real? She could hear them, their voices growing louder, more urgent. She knew she had to respond, had to let them know she was here. Despite her body trembling violently from the cold, she gathered the last vestiges of her strength. 'I'm here,' she croaked out, her voice barely audible, the well's stone walls and the relentless rain muffling her desperate plea for help.

A surge of anger coursed through her veins, replacing the numbing cold for a moment. She was a survivor; she had proved it before. A car crash hadn't been her end, and neither would this well. With newfound determination, she braced her good foot against the rough brick wall of the well, seeking a foothold. Taking a deep breath, she hoisted herself up, ignoring the searing pain in her injured foot.

She began her painstaking ascent, her hands seeking out the safest spots to grip, her feet testing each brick before trusting it with her weight. The top of the well grew larger as she climbed higher. With an effort she didn't know she was capable of, she reached out, her fingers grazing the cool mud and the wet grass at the edge of the well.

Her hand slipped, and she barely managed to keep herself from falling back into the icy water. She was running on fumes now, her strength waning. Accepting the inevitable, she prepared herself for the fall. But then, a strong hand grabbed hers. She looked up into Penn's worried eyes. 'Faith, reach up with your other hand!' His voice was urgent, desperate. She tried, but her hand slipped from his grasp. 'Faith, you can do this! Grab my other hand, now!'

Penn's voice rang out, 'Hold on, Faith!' He called out, his tone commanding and powerful. Faith, summoning what strength remained within her, dug her heels into the slick wall of the well. With a desperate lunge, she threw her other arm out, her fingers clawing at the air.

Penn's hand closed around hers, his grip painfully tight as he hauled her upwards. The sensation of being yanked from the pit was a mix of terror and relief. 'Liam!' Penn called out; his voice strained from the effort. Liam appeared at Penn's side, his face a mask of determination. As Faith's body emerged from the well, Liam grabbed the back of her coat, pulling with all his might. The world tilted as Faith was flung from the well, the three of them landing in a heap in the mud.

Faith turned, wincing at the pain and saw Penn, his usually pristine appearance marred by mud and rain. His clothes clung to his frame, the rainwater making them appear darker than usual. His hair, normally so meticulously styled, was a sodden mess. Yet, his eyes sparkled with relief and a hint of amusement.

'Seriously woman, what is it with you and water?' He asked, chuckling despite the situation. The absurdity of it all, the mud, the rain, the near-death experience, it was too much. Faith's laughter bubbled up, a light sound amidst the storm.

Soon, Liam and Penn joined in, their laughter mixing with the sound of the rain. They lay there, a trio of drenched, mud-covered, survivors.

Penn, with a grimace of effort, heaved himself into an upright position. His hand, reached out for Faith. His voice carried an urgency that made her heart pound. 'I can hear the ambulance sirens in the distance, Faith. I need you to get checked over immediately.'

Attempting to rise, Faith's legs wobbled beneath her, causing her to stumble. Penn clicked his tongue in disapproval, a frown etching into his weathered face. Without a second thought, he scooped her up in his arms, his strength a comforting presence. It was only when the harsh white lights of the ambulance bathed her in their glow did Faith think about how close she had been to dying.

Inside the ambulance, the paramedic, a young woman with a stern face, insisted that Faith needed to be taken to the hospital for further observation. But Faith, stubborn as always, refused. She yearned for the familiar comfort of her home. Liam, ever the mediator, phoned her parents, who promised to be there for her upon her return.

Back at home, her parents' fussing over her was a soothing balm to her frazzled nerves. For once, she didn't argue, even when they firmly insisted she must retire to bed and rest. Penn, after a serious conversation with her father, decided to take his leave. Before he could disappear into the night, Faith called out to him.

'Penn,' she shouted. 'I'm grateful you were here.' Soon, Faith found herself ensconced in the comforting warm cocoon of her covers. The day's exhaustion quickly swept over her, pulling her into a deep, dreamless sleep. Her last conscious thought was a profound sense of gratitude for the safety of her family.

CHAPTER 31

The ensuing weeks whirled by in a flurry of activity, with Faith confined to the sidelines, her world reduced to the four walls of her quaint cottage. She had come to terms with her dependence on her walking stick, a newfound strength blossoming within her after the harrowing incident at the well. Her home was now a veritable shrine of well-wishes, brimming with thoughtful gifts and heartfelt cards. Krista, ever the pragmatic friend, had stocked her freezer with ready meals, while both her doting parents and Hope fluttered about her, their concern and attention reminiscent of a brood of mother hens.

Tiffany, once, no still, a friend, was now in custody, her fate hanging in the balance as she awaited trial. When Sam had noticed that Tiffany had not been at the well when they found Faith, he had phoned it in, immediately.

After she had fled, CCTV had spotted her car and a tail was set. Eventually, the police in Rockingham Pike detained her. She admitted everything, keeping her promise as she told them that Faith was in the well at the Folly.

Simon, in a strange twist of fate, had procured the services of a top-notch solicitor for his estranged wife. It was an odd show of support, particularly when it seemed too little, too late. Perhaps it was the aftermath of Nathan's destructive rampage that had moved him.

Faith hadn't seen Penn since the incident, a fact that filled her with a strange sense of anticipation. She had organised a small gathering in her garden that day, a chance to show her gratitude to those who had stood by her. Her mother and Hope had arrived early, their hands busy setting tables and welcoming the early guests. Faith picked up the scarf from her bed, the very one that had played a crucial role in her rescue, happy it had not been ruined and draped it around her neck.

The day seemed to understand the significance of the occasion, with the sun peeking out from behind the clouds, casting a warm glow over the proceedings. The first faces she recognised in the garden were Arthur and Minerva, with Arthur engaged in a playful tug of war with Churchill, who had set his sights on the food table.

Arthur's grip tightened on Churchill's collar, straining to keep the overzealous goat from the buffet. His brow furrowed in concentration, his knuckles turning white.

'Arthur, get a hold of that creature!' Min's voice seeming to rebound throughout the garden, her tone as sharp as a whip. Both Churchill and Arthur froze in their tracks, like statues in the midst of chaos.

'Min,' Arthur protested, his voice a mix of exasperation and amusement, 'this is his party. He's a hero, remember?' Min shot back, her eyes flashing with mischief, 'If he doesn't settle down, he'll find himself the main course.'

Churchill seemed to grasp the gravity of Min's words and scuttled towards Faith, seeking refuge. As he hid behind her, Faith turned to face him, revealing a bright green bandana in her hand. Churchill sniffed it cautiously, then allowed Faith to fasten it around his neck. 'There we are, boy,' Faith cooed, bending down to plant a kiss on his head. Churchill, now adorned in his new attire, strutted around the garden, his chest puffed out in pride.

Faith, her face glowing with laughter, joined her parents. Her heart fluttered when Penn approached, holding two glasses of wine. He handed one to Faith, who accepted it with a gracious nod. 'How is Tiffany?' she asked. Penn sighed, running a hand through his hair. 'She's managing, Faith. Simon not so good, I think she's relieved it's all out in the open now. Oddly enough, the village seems to be on her side. Turns out, Nathan wasn't as popular as he thought. Even after everything, there's no animosity towards her.'

Hope chimed in; her voice laced with bitterness. 'Serves him right. Men always seem to be absent when you need them the most, and wallowing in self-pity when it's too late.' A chuckle escaped her lips as her father wrapped her in a warm embrace.

'My daughter, the man-hater. I hope these men don't include your father?' he teased. Hope shook her head, a smile tugging at her lips. 'Never Daddy, you're the exception to the rule.'

Her mother cut in, a touch of bitterness lacing her tone. 'Nobody's seen hide nor hair of Mirry. She's vanished into thin air. But can you blame her?'

'She wrote to me. Said she'd sold the house and was off to London, just like that.' Said Faith

Rowan snorted. 'I know why,' she declared. 'She's livid because Tiffany's pregnant. She knows it's not Nathan's, so there's no sympathy to be had there. You should've heard her, ranting and raving about how Tiffany was selfish, how she'd ruined her life. Now there's going to be another child and she couldn't bear to see her father fawning over it.'

Liam, leaning against the door frame, replied, 'That's just like Mirry, expecting the world to revolve around her.' Faith, sitting quietly, looked up at him, her eyes soft with sympathy. 'I feel sorry for her, Liam,' she said. 'She's lost her husband and her life here. Now she'll have to share her father with the child of her husband's murderer. I don't think I could've stayed either.'

As the guests fell into silence, Sam sauntered over to sit next to Magda. 'What surprised me was Tiffany swearing she didn't put the brick through Faith's window. I still think Mirry's the culprit, and that could be another reason she ran.'

Faith, cradling her wine glass, sighed. 'It doesn't matter now, Sam. I just want to forget everything that's happened and move on.'

Her father, loosening his tie and draping it over the back of the chair, looked at her with a questioning gaze. 'So, does this mean no more amateur detective work?' She smiled wryly, raising her glass in a toast. 'I'll be sticking to photography and leaving the sleuthing to you guys.'

'Faith, I must admit, your knack for unravelling mysteries has left us all in awe,' Sam chuckled, until he was met with the steely gaze of his superior. His mirth was abruptly cut short as his wife, Magda, jabbed him playfully in the arm. 'Oi, that's not fair, love!' he protested, rubbing his arm theatrically. Magda, her eyes twinkling with mischief, leaned over and offered him a peace offering in the form of a cake from her plate.

Penn, ever the cautious one, interjected, 'I don't mean to cause any panic, but...' His voice trailed off as he gestured towards the dessert table. All eyes followed his gaze, landing on the sight of Churchill, his front hooves propped up on a chair, tongue lapping up the frosting off the cake. The cake that Krista had painstakingly baked for the occasion. The cake Churchill thought should be his as Faith had promised.

A collective gasp was heard. Both Arthur and Minerva jumped out of their chairs in alarm. Churchill, his face now sporting a beard of pink frosting, seemed to realise his transgression and bolted, darting around the table in an attempt to evade capture.

Churchill darted towards Faith with a hopeful glint in his eyes but skidded to a halt when he spotted Don's tie draped over the back of his chair. With a swift movement, he snatched the silk tie. 'You little scoundrel, drop that this instant!' Don the normally composed man was now in a state of distress as he too darted after the goat, his pleas falling on deaf ears.

Rowan, seated comfortably in her chair, watched the spectacle unfold with a broad grin on her face. She took a sip of her wine, her eyes sparkling with amusement as she watched Don's futile attempts to retrieve his tie.

Faith, meanwhile, had been distracted by a movement at the bottom of the garden. She looked up to find her squirrel friend perched on a tree, a new companion by his side. The newcomer was smaller, with a softer look about her – a female, Faith guessed. She couldn't help but smile as the pair stared back at her before scampering up the tree and disappearing from sight. Well, at least someone's finding love, she thought, a touch of warmth spreading through her.

'I noticed a 'Sold' sign on Mirry and Nathan's cottage today,' Faith announced, her voice cutting through the garden as she bit into one of Magda's cakes. 'I wonder who the new owner could be?'

Liam, always one for a bit of mischief, leaned back in his chair with a smirk. 'Maybe it's a tall, handsome, stranger who'll sweep you off your feet Faith,' he teased, earning a round of laughter from the group.

Faith rolled her eyes but couldn't suppress her grin. 'Knowing my luck, he'd probably turn out to be a serial killer,' she retorted, causing Penn to lean forward with a smirk.

'A serial-killing Lothario, now that's an interesting concept,' he mused, his eyes twinkling. 'You never know, Faith. Stranger things have happened in this village recently.'

Laughter was once again heard as their attention was drawn back to Don and Churchill locked in a tug of war on the floor. 'My husband, the gallant policeman,' Rowan sighed, shaking her head in mock exasperation. 'I'd better go help. Magda, could you pass me a cake? Don has no idea how to handle Churchill.'

As the laughter subsided, Faith turned the conversation back to the cottage. 'So, who do you think has bought the place?' she asked, her curiosity piqued. Penn, who hadn't said much until now, cleared his throat. 'Actually, I know,' he announced, causing all eyes to turn towards him. There was a moment of silence as they waited for his answer.

'It's me.'

Printed in Great Britain
by Amazon

45493481R10179